The Queen's Consort
The Story of Mary Queen of Scots and Lord Darnley

STEVEN VEERAPEN

© Steven Veerapen 2018

Steven Veerapen has asserted his rights under the Copyright, Design and Patents Act, 1988, to be identified as the author of this work.

First published in 2018 by Sharpe Books.

ISBN: 9781728720821

CONTENTS

Chapters 1- 28

Author's Note

The Queen's Consort
The Story of Mary Queen of Scots and Lord Darnley

1

Their swords clashed. Drew back. Thrust forward. Parried. A fatal blow was struck and Henry Stewart, Lord Darnley, fell to the ground dead, the soft skin of his cheek pressed against rough wood, his eyes glazed. The victor, his brother, laughed. Charles Stewart was five. He prodded the still form of his older brother with his foot and the body jerked to life, one hand clutching at Charles's skirted leg and pulling him to the rush-littered floor. The two dissolved in laughter, the older boy's arm wrapped around the shoulder of the younger.

Darnley recovered first. 'See, we shall yet make a worthy soldier of you' he said as Charles' high-pitched laughter subsided, 'as soon as you are in breeches!' He stood up and gave a hand to the boy, who was still convulsed by occasional hiccoughing. 'I'll be a worthier soldier than you, Harry. Taller too,' he said as he was pulled to his feet.

'We shall see about that, shrimp.' He smiled down at his red-cheeked brother from his vantage point of nearly six-foot-four. During his recent, extended visit to his French cousins, he had enjoyed a remarkable growth spurt. He had to stoop to avoid hitting his head on all the lintels in Settrington, his parents' Yorkshire home. 'Anyway, enough horseplay. Look, we are begrimed. Your nurse will tan your hide.' He gathered up the wooden swords they had been playing with and dropped them in a chest at the foot of the bed, closing the lid with a hollow bang.

'Henry! Charles! Master Eworth has finished. Attend me!' Their mother's excitable voice drifted into the room.

'Well, shrimp – let us see if Master Eworth has done his subjects justice.' Charles grinned up at him, stretched out his hand, and the two trotted out of the nursery. She was in the house's wood-panelled Long Gallery where Hans Eworth, the Flemish artist, had completed his latest work: a study of the Stewart brothers painted in the gallery itself commissioned by the boys' parents. Though she pleaded poverty often enough, the countess always seemed able to find and expend money on what she considered necessary outlays.

As they entered the Long Gallery Margaret Stewart, Lady Lennox, glided towards them, a whirl of dark blue velvet, her red hair peppered with a patrician grey. She was alone, the servants having come to avoid wherever possible the strictures imposed by a woman for whom exaggerated manners and abject deference had become a comfort in her genteel poverty. She passed the room's own cast of portraits: Henry VIII of England, double-chinned and copper-bearded; his daughter Mary, froglike and suspicious; King Philip of Spain, youthful and fair; even a coy likeness of the countess herself. As she reached her sons her sharp eyes narrowed. 'Why, you are both covered in dust! What have you been doing?'

'Harry was instructing me in how to be a great soldier,' said Charles. 'I killed him'.

'Is that so? A great soldier who has not yet taken to his books, nor learned his manners.' A thin eyebrow was arched. The boys looked at one another. It was best not to bandy words with Lady Lennox.

'Charles, you are excused. Harry, you ought to know better than to roll around on the floor. You are a man. If you are to make a good match – a productive match – you must let the ladies see that you are no longer a boy. I would have hoped that your time in France would have rid you of childishness. I hoped your uncle would take you in hand whilst your father and I suffered.' He fought back a blush. He had not come back from France the innocent who had left England. Further, he found it hard to believe that his mother had entirely disliked her recent status as a prisoner of Queen Elizabeth in the mouldering palace of Sheen. An inveterate old intriguer, the countess had revelled in the drama. Certainly, the story of the Lennoxes' imprisonment was one which lost nothing in his mother's many retellings. Despite having only been back in England and in the company of his parents a few weeks he could already prompt her on it. Attempting to forestall her before she could warm to her theme – and before his cheeks betrayed him – Darnley gathered up his modest reserves of humility. 'Forgive me, mother. I led Charlie – *Charles* – astray,' he said, quickly correcting himself. 'Charlie' was his father's mocking corruption, so he said, of the wild Scots of the western isles' version of the name. His mother disapproved. He hurried on. 'Shall we regard Master Eworth's work?' Her eyebrow descended, and they strode towards the painting.

He had to admit that he was impressed. Eworth had done a job of work, and left it standing on its easel in good light. On the right stood Darnley in his black doublet and hose, a white ruff framing his weak jaw: an imperfection which he found any excuse to hide. The perspective was manipulated to accentuate his height, and the painter had omitted the gallery's own artworks so that nothing drew the eye from its central figures. His own misty grey eyes gazed out from the portrait with brooding menace – had he been giving that look when posing, he wondered – and his hair had been painted in the tousled, glinting gold of a cherub. His arm rested on Charles', who shared the same gilded crown. The little Stewart had one hand on his skirted hip and coupled with the sword that hung forebodingly from Darnley's waist, the pair carried an air of challenging, reckless allure. The inscription proclaimed them the sons of the Earl and Countess of Lennox, aged seventeen and six in the year 1563.

Darnley looked from the new painting to those studiously ignored by Eworth – the collection of ancestors, royals and kinfolk who stared down from their own frames in the Long Gallery. Each was heavy was its sitter's story and the weight of their experiences, as captured in varying degrees of subtlety by artists of differing talents. Was this, he wondered, how he was to be seen by the world?

'It is marvellous.' said Margaret. 'My beautiful boys!' Her tone was light, gasping, full of excitement. She ruffled Charles' hair. He was staring at the painting nonplussed, unimpressed by either his likeness or its beauty. Unnoticed by his mother, he wriggled away and wandered towards the door. The countess did not even appear to notice. 'And Harry, consider the possibilities. Look here – your father and I had Master Eworth paint with tempera on linen – you see, look closely at the paint.' He leant forward, the sour smell wrinkling his nostrils. 'The whole thing can be rolled up and transported easily. This might be in Scotland in a few days.'

So that was her plan. His mother was nothing if not unoriginal. A granddaughter of Henry VII of England through her mother, Margaret Tudor, Lady Lennox had an abiding fascination with thrones, sceptres, and royal blood. It was a fascination that she and her husband had done their best to inculcate in their sons. But the primary goal of her royal ambitions was, and had been for years, to marry off Darnley to Mary Stewart: the Queen of Scots, Dowager Queen of France and, as she styled herself, the rightful Queen of England.

Darnley was lukewarm on the madcap idea. Though he had briefly met Mary, his cousin through their mutual grandmother, on two occasions, she had had little opportunity to make an impression on him. Once she had been a teenage bride notable only for being so strikingly regal in comparison to the puny French husband she likely never unbelted. More recently she had been a distracted widow, hidden by a white veil and uninterested in a young, unknown English relative. He did not know her.

Yet his return to the stultifying atmosphere of rural Yorkshire had left him hungry for something – anything – to do with his life. The glory of a grand marital alliance would provide an escape at least. Nevertheless, it all seemed fanciful; and it was his mother's last attempt at playing the great chess game of politics that had landed her in custody at Sheen, her husband in the forbidding Tower, and made Darnley himself a refugee thrown on the mercy of his family in France. Moving about that chessboard was a risky business.

'Mother, is it not dangerous to play these games?' he said, doubt and weariness in his voice.

'Child, life is always dangerous for people like us.' She took his face in a pasty hand and fixed him with a sad look. 'We are feared because we are important. But we owe it to our blood to recover our fortunes. Would you not rather see me as the mother of a king, and your father restored in Scotland than have us marooned here? It would kill him to know it, but I see how being disliked here and in the north wears on him. He would make amends; he would have our family in favour, give us all friends again. No one visits us – we are adrift.' She paused, letting the guilt – her favourite weapon – do its work.

'And this is not just for me and your father, it is for you. Look at you: you are destined for great things – not to be a country squire, friendless and lonely in this godforsaken armpit of England. You have seen how slovenly things have become here, how low fortune has brought us. Think of it, Harry: a king. Another "Great Harry".'

His mother's wheedling tone betrayed her. Not for the first time he felt himself unable to escape the uncomfortable sense that, like the pedigree hunting dogs that had delighted him as a child, he had been bred for an especial purpose. It was, he supposed, the responsibility of his parents to curb him of his natural instincts and desires and bring him to heel. It was a job at which they had been only partially successful given his adventures in the brothels and taverns of the Parisian suburbs, where sex, wine and vice were welcomed. Redness threatened his cheeks.

Yet the image his mother painted was seductive. When Mary's former husband, the sickly King Francois, had died three years previously his mother had been almost overcome with excitement at the possibilities it offered. Whilst Mary had been bombarded with offers of marriage from Spanish kings, Italian dukes and German princes, the indomitable Margaret had dispatched the pimply-faced Darnley, then fifteen, to the Court of France with the Stewart family's insincere condolences. The visit had been a secret – Elizabeth of England had neither agreed to it nor known of it. Yet despite having been on her throne for only five years, the English queen was already proving herself assiduous in expanding the reach of her tenacious network of spies and informants into every noble household in England. She had somehow discovered his parents' machinations and ordered the whole family's hasty imprisonment; Darnley had escaped only by slipping again to France before the drawstring tightened. To

Darnley, Elizabeth's Janus-like knowledge of her subjects' activities illustrated the awesome power of sovereignty. That was what his parents wanted for him. That is why they cherished this notion of marrying him off to the Scottish queen. But achieving that kind of power, surely, could not be as simple as convincing a widowed lady to open her bedroom door.

His mother took his thoughtful silence – a rare thing – for acquiescence. 'You can see yourself in a crown.' She shucked his chin with her thumb. He smiled. 'And why not. Your grandmother wore the crown of Scotland, and Queen Mary herself is not far from her rightful English throne.' This was dangerous talk, and even the countess seemed to realise it, stumbling over her next sentence. 'At any rate, it can do no harm to remind the Queen of Scots that she has a natural suitor by lineage. Always remember that, Harry: you are descended from great stock, no matter where fortune's wheel might carry us.'

'Yes, mother. Whatever happens, Queen Mary can always be reminded that we are her friends and kin, and worthy of her favour.'

'That's the spirit.'

Favour of some kind was certainly needed. The portrait, standing on its easel, had captured a sense of life at Settrington. The blank, empty walls imagined by the painter were eerily reminiscent of the isolation the family endured. His mother had been right about one thing: neither Darnley nor any of his immediate family had any friends. No one wanted to visit impoverished nobility recently tainted by royal disgrace.

In France he had seen something of the world. His relatives there – his father's kin – were easy in their ways, vital and uninhibited. A young man liberated for the first time, he had grasped that taste of freedom – and grabbed several willing Frenchwomen, who were only too pleased to introduce a tall, inexperienced English nobleman to new vistas. He smiled at the memories. He had not lost his virginity when he had visited his uncle and cousins in France; he had thrown it away with some force when a poor French girl had offered to make a man of him. The smile faded. Back home, he felt himself a captive. Just as his father must have looked out on an uncertain future from the windows of the Tower, he found himself granted only occasional glimpses at wet, scrubby moorland and proud meadows of blooming weeds. Accustomed to immurement, his parents had found solace in indulging in ever more elaborate fantasies of the future. For Darnley there existed only the most nebulous sense that there must be something that would provide access to the world of pleasures and excitements that lay beyond northern England.

As a child he had lived at Court under his mother's friend, Queen Mary Tudor. That brief period of Court life, full of presents, people, and adoration, had taken on the quality of a dreamlike childhood memory, part real and part imagined. Life at a Court, a travelling circus of monarch and nobility would mean friends; comrades; people other than his parents, brother, and servants. All of these were things necessary to a real sense of belonging. And he very much wanted to belong.

At that moment a truculent voice carried into the Long Gallery and Darnley hastily patted down his front, wary of any lingering dust that might remain. 'What news, Madge? This love token had better be worth the money, or I shall have blood.' The Earl of Lennox had returned from his afternoon's ride.

2

Matthew Stewart, the Earl of Lennox, was a chimera, part English country gentleman, part French dandy, part gruff Scot. Darnley's indulgent, comfortable childhood had been filled with colourful, if selective, stories of his parents' adventurous lives, and seasoned with anecdotes about the famous personalities with whom they had rubbed shoulders. Since the family had lost royal favour, the Lennoxes had had only the ghosts of the past to keep them company and remind them of better times, and so the stories increased. Each tale was calculated to allow the earl and countess to relive their glory days and emphasise to their son the enormous weight of his family's influential past. From childhood he had absorbed his parents' memories with avid interest. Gathered before the fire in the evenings, he could almost envision the squeaky-voiced Henry VIII, a fat and fearsome old Bluebeard. He would watch his mother shed tears for old Mary Tudor with her imaginary babies and absent husband – always too busy with his own realm to share his wife's crown – as his father rolled his eyes and clucked his tongue. Both natural storytellers, the Lennoxes were that most curious of couples: a genuinely loving pair whose shared interests in power, gossip and ambition made theirs a marriage of minds as well as bloodlines. As long as they had one another, they had a magnificent ability to form a united front, pushing back against the world and anything that threatened their goals.

Although his stomach had started to protrude, and he covered his thinning hair with jaunty caps, Lennox's face bore the remnants of handsomeness. By his own admission he had been a romantic adventurer, a gentleman of the world. This at least was the image he presented to Darnley, who lived in adoration of his worldly father. The earl's less savoury qualities – his frequent double dealing, switching of sides and willingness to trim his sails to the prevailing winds of politics and religion – he admitted only to stress that he was, above all, a survivor. Deprived of his estates in the west of Scotland, his complaints and demands for their restoration were a familiar refrain in the household. Even survivors, Darnley supposed, grew weary of disapproval and disfavour, especially when old age beckoned.

That his father might have been a traitor was an idea he rejected without thought, for the earl was a handsome, charming gallant. Like his mother a natural eavesdropper, a young Darnley had overheard vague, hushed whispers about Lennox's involvement in the slaughter of child hostages in Scotland. These were also something to which he had closed his ears and shut his mind.

For a man of the earl's force of character and breeding only a rich prize would ever have sufficed. This he had found in Margaret Douglas. Margaret had been a beauty, and she still carried an air of elegance and heightened manners, despite the boxy figure and lined face.

Before she had become Margaret Stewart, the countess gaily told all that would listen, she had been a darling in the Court of her uncle Henry and a friend of the late Queen Mary, his daughter, who had died half-blind and nearly all-mad. Darnley could recall being forced to write fawning letters to the old queen. It was an activity he had never understood, given his father's lack of tolerance for her apparently increasing madness. Still, it had bred in him little reverence. To be a great prince, he mused, was surely not to be the subject of rumour, slanders, rolled eyes and secret talk.

As he strode into his home's Long Gallery that afternoon to

inspect the newest tool in the marriage game, Lennox was buoyant. During his captivity Margaret had, she frequently claimed –brushing her forehead with the back of her hand – feared for his sanity. Had she been serious, her fears would have been misplaced: the earl wasn't a man to be kept down for long. Nor was he a man likely to endure disaster without turning an eye to opportunity.

'A fine portrait,' was Lennox's opinion, after giving the painting a curt glance. 'But we can dispense with your high-flown ideas of golden nuptials for now, madam-'

'*My* high-flown ideas, my lord?'

'Peace – we can dispense with thoughts of grand marriages. After all, our son's not yet quite so polished or ripe for the marital bed as he's soon going to be. Even this pretty picture's not half so fine as the news I bring.'

Margaret's eyes lit up. Without a trace of self-awareness, her tongue even ran over her lips. 'What news?'

'Why, my lady and my lord are welcome back at Court. And what's more, they're to make haste there to pay homage to the Queen of England.' He took a theatrical bow, sweeping off his hat, before looking up into two the astonished faces. Darnley gaped, trying to work out what it all meant. As confusion and delight fought for control of his mother's face, Lennox swept her up in his arms and spun her around in a circle, her skirts billowing behind her and her feet coming off the floorboards. Delight won, and she laughed before smacking at her husband's arms for release.

'Oh, you brute. Such behaviour – where do you think you are?' Her laughter subsided. 'When are we to be lodged?'

'Not "we", my lady. You. And my young lord.' His eyes clouded.

'What? How is this?'

'Soft, woman. The queen wishes to accommodate her blood

relatives without the protection of their master. A crafty stratagem. You know she makes great show of disallowing married couples to bed at Court. Normally she bars wives, but the effect is much the same. I shall accompany you to London, naturally.' His wife's eyes flashed, her mind racing.

'Released from prison, sent back to the wilderness and then recalled to Court by the queen all within a few months? What is the woman's game?' How like his mother to seek ulterior motives in other's actions. She always did assume that everyone thought and acted as she would. Well, perhaps she was right.

'It'll be the wish of her councillors,' said Lennox. 'The whole Court was in confusion worrying that the smallpox would carry her off during the winter. The Council must have convinced Elizabeth that her old aunt Margaret's a better bet than those whey-faced Grey cousins.'

'We can do without the "old", thank you,' sniffed his wife, but the indignance was feigned. 'Anyway, I should imagine it is not her aunt Margaret that she considers worthy of attention, but her dear cousin Harry.' His ears pricked up at his name.

'Aye, and that's the truth.' Lennox's attention had turned to him and he returned an obedient gaze.

'Yes father.' His voice always climbed an octave when addressing his father, no matter how hard he tried to erase all traces of childishness. 'What shall I do? What will the queen want with me?'

'What does the queen want with any handsome young man?'

'Sir, that is quite enough of that,' said Margaret. Lennox chuckled before continuing.

'Maybe so, madam – but we both know Elizabeth likes a pretty face. She still favours that gypsy, Robert Dudley.'

'Hmph!' Margaret's face clouded. 'That heretical murderer? The queen would not sleep soundly sharing his pillow.'

'Now, my dear, you know better than that. That mousy wife of his did *not* die from being pushed down the stairs. No. She died from landing at the bottom.' Lennox barked laughter. His wife rolled her eyes. The joke was stale. Darnley was familiar with the tale of Lady Dudley, who had obliged him in his pursuit of the queen by conveniently snapping her neck. He was tempted to ask his father what the great favourite was really like. Did he look like a killer? Did he storm around threatening women? But Lennox was in mid flow.

'The Queen of England's a young woman yet. Small wonder she keeps that rakehell Dudley by her side: next to him she looks lily white in complexion as well as character. But she also surrounds herself with the best of men, handsome, skilled. As her cousin and nearest kinsman, you're a king-in-waiting. You must shine at Court. Your mother and I have taught you well. You dance, you play music, you ride and hunt, you're conversant in the classics … your singing voice isn't the best, but then I've heard worse.'

'There is nothing wrong with his voice,' cut in the countess. 'He sings pleasingly. And besides, just look at how he has grown. He is a head taller than you and look at that hair. How could a young man like this fail to capture hearts?'

'I'll grant you we've turned out a fine young man. Well? Harry? Are you not a fine young man?'

'Yes, father.' Standing poker-backed whilst his parents measured him, Darnley's own interest was piqued. He had heard only salacious tales from his mother about Elizabeth's bastardy, wretchedness, dubious parentage, and reprobate Court. 'But the English queen – what is she really like?'

'Oh, a vain, arrogant jade. Likes to think herself feared, far more than her sister ever did – it's why she boxes her servants' ears in her father's manner. Be sure to charm her but keep off politics – she doesn't want that from young men. She's a sharp one, though. Too sharp by half for a woman – so watch she does not trip you. Avoid begging favours unless she's in the mood to grant them. Oh, and be wary of the other young bucks – they're not likely to greet a new pair of antlers without raising their own for a fight. But do you want my honest opinion?' He leant in. 'Do you wish to know what you'll find in that queen?'

'Yes, father.'

'You'll find a lost young lass doing a poor player's impression of what she imagines her father to have been. Aye,' he slapped his knee, 'a mummer acting at being the Great Harry! Think on that if she frightens you. A woman playing a boy playing a queen playing a king. And not even well, at that. And Harry,' Lennox continued, lowering his tone. 'There is something else. I've had a mind to have with talk with you since you returned. Madam, leave us,' he said without taking his eyes off his son.

Margaret hesitated, before dipping her head and gliding from the room. Darnley swallowed. Had his father heard some news of his shenanigans abroad – was he to receive an admonition? Did that mean his mother knew? Raised mainly by a succession of governesses and tutors, his parents had always been remote, awe-inspiring figures. Disappointing them was a detestable thought.

'Come, let's sit. It does my old neck no good to crane up at you.' He steered Darnley to a green-cushioned seat by one of the room's tall windows. Rain tapped against the flattened animal horn, the window a milky eye dotted with grey. They sat, Darnley's black-stockinged legs folding under the seat.

'You see, young man, I wasn't lying when I listed your good qualities. We really have laboured with you.'

'I know, father. I appreciate all that you have done for me.'

'Yes, yes. But I want to give you a fair warning. The Court

of England is and has always been a pit of vipers. I spare your mother this, knowing her heritage and pride, but it is so. I've seen Courts: Scotland, England, France. They're all cesspools. But in those cesspools great jewels lie buried and can be a wise man's for the taking. You may find yourself, as I've found myself, splashed with the shit of those cesspools. The stains can be indelible and it's not pleasant to make your way in the world stained and stinking. But mark me – you must not let yourself become mired. Do you understand me?'

The inflection of a question brought him back into the room. He had barely been following his father's lecture. Metaphorical speeches by old rhetoricians – even his father – bored him to tears, lacking as they did the sparkle of an exciting tale well told. Still, he lowered his lids and nodded. If his father had something to confess, and his tone suggested he did, he ought to get on with it. He focused on his nails. They needed trimmed.

'Good. That's good. Do you know, I've been criticised for what fate has had me do? Oh aye. They call men like us traitors and ambidexters; they say we deal with both hands. What of it? Where does the pig-headed man make his end? On the block; at the end of the noose; butchered like a cut of meat, entrails torn out and burned.' The violence brought Darnley back into the room. He looked up, now beginning to catch the drift of his father's advice. 'Keep your own counsel. As soon as your name becomes known they'll seek to put you in a chest. They'll mark that chest "Catholic", or "Protestant", or "heretic". You mustn't let them, do you hear me? I've seen good men suffocate in those chests. Avoid religion, unless it's to your advantage to embrace it – I've seen the turbulence it causes. Have faith in yourself and show God you serve Him by serving His high offices. In France, they call men like us the *politiques* – and that's no insult, eh?'

Darnley felt a little relief, and he smiled at his father, ever the good son. He had no strong religious feelings. Each morning his mother still insisted on the household hearing illegal Mass. He mouthed the responses, but there was little room in his head for theological debate. He had never been able – not that he had spent much time attempting it – to square his own life in rainy England with the fire and brimstone of the Bible. Born too late to remember the glory days of English Catholicism and uninterested in the nuances of Queen Elizabeth's religious settlement, he found his father's advice an exercise in sagacity. What's more, it was sound – being boxed up for professing feelings that one needn't even feel was stupid. A secret conspiracy of indifference would therefore be ideal – and yet he couldn't bear the thought of his mother finding him out. He was just on the verge of telling his father this when the old man put his arm around Darnley's shoulder, gave him a half-amused, half-serious look and said, 'And son – one more thing. Few women are permitted at Court. Forbear lifting the skirts of any of the pretty young slatterns. You'll only get the pox for your troubles.'

Darnley blushed and looked shocked, as his mother had always instructed him to do when his father made bawdy jokes. But it didn't last; he burst into laughter at his father's grin. It was always less easy to fool his parents than he assumed.

'Now off with you, Harry. Go and instruct your brother.' Darnley stood up and skipped from the room, humming to himself.

Once he was out of sight, the countess slipped back in to join her husband on the seat her son had vacated. 'Well, husband, what think we?' Her tone was business-like. 'Shall he make a king?'

'Of course he will. Look at him. Do you doubt it?'

'Indeed not!'

'But I do worry …'

'About?'

'The boy is idealistic, Madge, easily led, a dreamer. We've given him the best of everything, but his head is in the clouds. There are practicalities he may not grasp.' The countess pulled a sour face at the hint of criticism.

'I fail to see how the best of upbringings can inhibit a man.'

'Don't be sore. As I said, he's a fine lad but soft. Too many books and not enough living will do that. He has the temper I had as a lad, too, you remember? Poor fellow. But he lacks my craft. You'll have to watch him. He'll bend to the will of any strong mind. With me outside the Court you must make sure that that will is ours. The Lord only knows what he might have been induced to get up to abroad. My brother's family are not known for their chastity.'

'I cannot think what you mean,' sniffed Margaret, her bottom lip jutting out.

'That is for the best – the loose living of the French isn't for a lady's ears. Besides, an unmarried youth is free to do as he likes. Until he takes a wife and settles down, anyway.' He put an arm around the countess's shoulders. Her posture remained stiff, and she glanced around in case any servants peered in.

'And his marriage prospects?'

'Glorious,' said Lennox. 'He'll make a great marriage.' He took her hand, flesh growing over the rings, in his hairy one.

'I do not doubt it. But there must be love in it. I wish our boy to be as fortunate as us,' she simpered, cosying into her husband's embrace.

'Love waits on marriage. It'll find him afterwards as it found us, sweet. Who could fail to love the boy?'

'His Scottish cousin, perhaps.'

'A full-blooded child herself. It is not the Queen of Scots

who worries me, little Frenchling that she is.'

'Who does?'

'The Scots. You know them as well as I. If he goes north it is as an alien. He's both Scottish and English, belonging in both countries and neither.'

'You speak as though our son is an aberration.'

'I speak of what I know. He may not be able to serve our turn so easily. You recall when your uncle wished Mary wed to Edward? The Scots wouldn't accept an English king any more than the English would accept a Scotsman. The nobility of Scotland is suspicious of anyone English-born who lacks the money to advance their personal ambitions ... as I can attest.' He tightened his arm around his wife, chuckling. 'His blood is great, my Madge. No man can boast greater. We must pray it does not become his greatest liability in that viper's nest.'

3

The sun was reaching its zenith when their wherry began its approach to Windsor's long lawns. Squinting into the reflected dazzle of dozens of tall windows, he could see what appeared to be a vast array of buildings competing for height and importance, towering above trees and ornate gardens set out in concentric lines. A path lined with statues of gilded beasts led towards them from the dock. The complex looked official – important. Whereas Settringon had looked and felt like a small country seat, and his cousins' French chateaux had been frothy, delicate, fairytale pleasure palaces, here was a seat of government where important things happened, harried secretaries rushed back and forth, and the uninitiated had no business.

'Windsor is just as I remember it. Is it not a goodly sight?' The countess's eyes were brimming with emotion, one hand shielding them from the sun.

'Aye, not changed from the old king's day,' said Lennox, sewn into a new satin doublet and hose. 'You half expect him to come stumping out of the place, dragging a lame leg. What do you think of that, my lord? A home from home?'

'It is very big.' His hazy memories of the English Court consisted only of endless corridors and busy rooms.

'I should think so.'

'No, I how do we find our way in such a place?' The sense of being overwhelmed, of being swallowed, was strong.

'Hold fast to your mother. Just remember it's all a great game, and our name assures you the winning hand. Such places were meant for you, and you for them.' Darnley's hand instinctively reached up to smooth the fluttering feather in his cap. He twirled it with one finger to give it fresh bounce. The rowers had halted the boat and were turning it around to align it with the wooden jetty, dizzying him. Already a boatman was readying a set of steps to disembark. 'Ho, now,' said his father, 'here we are. And I daresay that those mounts have been sent down by the Master of Horse to speed the queen's loving relatives to her side.'

***

Darnley had not been wrong about the size and business-like atmosphere of Windsor. Although it was the dining hour, clerks in their dark robes moved swiftly from building to building, their heads down. Others were deep in animated conversation, heads shaking; some held rolls of parchment, pointing with fury at the dense, spidery script. Few took notice of the latest addition to the ranks of their superiors.

Upon the family's arrival at the castle, a servant of the queen's Steward, betrayed by his robes of office, informed them that the Court was at dinner – this was not surprising, given the hour. However, the Lennox Stewarts had been expected – expected for some days, the snooty official said with inflection. Darnley felt they should explain themselves, but his parents seemed to think an imperious look would suffice. Mother and son were to be housed within the castle precincts. At this, Lennox and his wife looked at each other with something their son could not catch. Was it approval? A hint of satisfaction?

They were conveyed into the wood-panelled hall and told that here, within the same building as the queen herself, was their lodging. Their luggage was already being brought up by castle porters, and those servants not lodging with the earl would be shown to their own rooms. The Lord Steward's servant bowed and excused himself, bidding the family a gracious welcome to Court and informing them that the queen would receive them in her Privy Chamber after dinner: a servant of the royal household would be sent up to fetch them. Their time was their own until then. When he had left, still bowing, Margaret grasped her son by the hands whilst her husband surveyed their surroundings.

Windows – clear, expensive glass, not horn – looked out on one side down towards the outer gate through which they had been led: on the other, onto an internal courtyard filled with small, delicate trees. Around their new home hung vibrant tapestries depicting a hunting Diana, armed with her crossbow; Hestia, modestly veiled and kindling a hearth; and Astraea, fleeing the corrupt earth and ascending to celestial divinity. These goddesses looked down on the latest inhabitants of the Court with challenge in their stitched eyes.

'Husband, said his mother, 'you know what this signifies. We are not impoverished courtiers; we have not been invited here to humble ourselves in repentance before a gloating queen. She recognises us as her peers at last, as her blessed sister did, God rest her.' She crossed herself at the last.

'Aye, and no mistaking it. You will be very comfortable here.' There was a sniff in envy in his voice. 'Well, I shall be better placed for the London posts and the north when it needs me. Much better that one of us is on the outside. But the Privy Chamber, did you mark it? No jostling for her attention with the rabble. And all before she's even laid eyes on her handsome young cousin.' Darnley laughed. His parents' mood was intoxicating. He began to feel that Court life was not the daunting experience he had supposed. Who could feel inadequate knowing that they had the queen's ear, shared her lodgings, and could call these richly-appointed rooms their own private sanctuary?

'Away, Harry, and stifle that grin,' said his father, aiming a mock blow at him. 'Away and see your own room and have a care for your old father languishing in a poor house out of the sun.'

Darnley needed no encouragement. He swaggered off, stretching his legs with confidence in the high-ceilinged chamber, and opened the connecting door to what was to be his own suite. Here there would be no stooping to avoid doorframes.

The scent hit him first. Fresh, perfumed rushes had been strewn on the floor – at least, he noted, on those parts of the floor which were not adorned with thick Turkish carpets. An enormous bed sat against the wall on the left, a pallet bed for an attendant at its foot. Charlie flashed through his mind, wandering, bouncing about. How he'd love this great playground.

The oak-fronted walls of his room were also hung with tapestries: not the Greek goddesses of the entrance chamber to the new Lennox lodgings, but a more curious mix. Here Narcissus looked longingly into a pool that reflected his image; there Eurydice was dragged from Orpheus for his impatient desire to look upon her; by the bed, Adonis was about to be gored by a wild boar. If Elizabeth was attempting to signify something it was in vain; his love of the stories of classical mythology did not extend to the domestic dramas of lovers and goddesses but was limited to heroic battles between martial men and monsters. In the corner of the room were arranged several musical instruments: a lute, a viol, a decently-sized virginal. These were practical: these he could use. Picking up the lute absently, he plucked it and found it to be in tune.

He sat down on a cushioned window casement, the afternoon sun streaming onto his back and illuminating the white feather in his cap. Suddenly finding inspiration, he began to play an old melody, his foot tapping the rhythm.

After several false starts, he got the tune and began to sing in a shaky but high and clear voice.

***

When Daphne from fair Phoebus did fly,
The West wind most sweetly did blow in her face.
Her silken skirt scarce covered her thighs.
The god cried, O pity! and held her in chase.

***

He abruptly stopped and looked up; his parents were standing in the doorway watching him. How long had they been standing there, the sneaks? His father had his arm around his mother's shoulder, her head rested on his.

'Pray do not stop.'

'I did not know anyone was listening,' said Darnley, jutting out his bottom lip in a pout that would make his mother proud. 'Damned fine recital,' said Lennox. 'And you need not be precious about people listening to you play – in fact, you'd better get used to it. The Court's finished dinner. *She* wishes to welcome you, and Hell mend you if you fail to impress. Aren't you glad you managed to reacquaint yourself with the lute now?'

4

To reach the queen's Privy Chamber, one had to run the gauntlet of what Lennox had contemptuously, if not inaccurately, described as being populated by the rabble. Like the castle itself, the queen's receiving rooms were arranged like a sanctified temple, with a guard chamber blocking entry into the Presence Chamber. That room was open to anyone received at the royal Court, but beyond it lay the Privy Chamber, to which entry was barred to all but the queen's coterie of favourites.

For the first time since their arrival at the castle in the morning he became aware of people now beginning to take notice of him. Stares he was used to: the very tall attract admiring glances, even in opulent, high-ceilinged rooms. As he and his parents entered the Presence Chamber, however, he noticed that the huge room, filled though it was with chatting courtiers, people playing dice and cards at tables, and gentlemen discussing their fortunes, began to emit a lower buzz of conversation. The height of the room created a strange echo, and the whispering voices became almost eerie.

Everywhere people were eyeing the new arrivals. Their identity must be known, he thought: the grapevine of close-packed humans is always fruitful. His parents were already notorious, and he himself was far from inconspicuous. Very keenly he felt the weight of his upbringing: country, country, country. These Court-dwellers might smell the Yorkshire air on him. Fool! he told himself; you outrank these hangers-on. Show them what a real courtier is made of. The self-recrimination worked, and he raised his head in what he considered to be a suitably commanding pose. Still, he kept his eyes lowered to gauge the reception.

The men, he could see, were looking at him with barely-concealed jealousy from their little knotted groups. He had been granted what they fought and scratched for like rats in a sack. The few women, however, were looking at him with something different entirely. Older matrons and young ladies, all in black and white, shared a look of smirking, lascivious appraisal. In some cases this was disguised by fluttering fans and lowered lashes, in many cases not at all. Confidence rose like a cork. He even managed to flash some of the prettier ladies a coy look, which set those fans fluttering with greater rapidity.

His father, several paces ahead, had reached the guards flanking the door to the Privy Chamber. The doors opened on a wave of cloying damask scent. At this, many neck sinews in the Presence Chamber were strained, and a liveried figure appeared, impassively beckoning the Lennoxes to approach. They entered solemnly, supplicants before a deity. The doors slammed closed behind them.

There, on the far side of the room, seated on a raised dais beneath a great red-and-gold canopy of estate, sat Elizabeth of England. Curiosity overcoming nerves, his eyes slid over her. She was dressed in the Italian style: a cream-coloured dress shot through with gold, puffed sleeves slashed to reveal yet more gold. At her throat were ostentatious jewels, and a small, gauzy ruff encircled her neck. Sunk into her coppery-red, elaborately curled hair was a golden, pearl-studded headpiece. All of it, thought Darnley, was designed to draw attention away from a long face, sharp-featured, high cheek-boned and thin-nosed. She was approaching thirty at a gallop and looked every day of it. She seemed – at least, she affected – not to see the new arrivals, so deep was she in conversation with a sad-eyed, bearded man at her side. Others – men and women –

stood looking practised in their boredom.

He was not sure what to do. It would be unthinkable to address the queen first. A few awkward moments stretched on into what seemed an interminable time: he began to feel like a naughty child who had wandered into the private rooms and conversations of his parents, and who must sneak back out before being noticed. Just before he could begin fidgeting, the queen abruptly cut off her discussion and turned heavy-lidded, coal-black eyes on the Lennoxes.

'What is this? Ah. My Lord and Lady of Lennox. I am pleased to see you have obeyed our summons. Welcome. What say you?'

Lennox removed his cap, revealing his bald head. It shone ridiculously in the light pouring in from the room's tall, diamond-paned windows. He fell to his knees, his son following his lead. His wife dropped a curtsey, one knee issuing a crack, to which no paid the slightest attention. Darnley bit his tongue.

'Dread sovereign, we thank you most humbly for your welcome,' said Lennox.

'That is gracious of you, and we have quite forgotten our last dealings. I trust you have found a home suitable to your station. At a respectable distance.' She raised him from his knees with the flick of a hand. His son followed suit. Overcome, the countess forgot herself and spoke. 'Gracious Majesty, you are most kind. We-'

'We have *quite forgotten* our last dealings.' The queen's voice was clipped. 'Now, you are settled into your lodgings, my lady? We would have our kinfolk close, they having come under the scrutiny of our late parliament.'

'We are, your Majesty. You do us great honour.'

'I do England great honour as its wife and protector, madam.' The man at her side threw back his head in a show of weariness. She ignored him.

Darnley resisted the urge to shuffle his feet. Instead he let his eyes wander the room, following the twisted vines sprouting pink-and-gold flowers that were painted on the walls. The queen seemed to be making a point of ignoring him; she had not so much as glanced in his direction. Instead, she addressed herself to Lennox.

'Tell me, my lord, what news do you bring out of our northern counties?'

'All is well, your Majesty. Peace reigns over great Elizabeth's England.'

'This is not what I hear, sir. I hear there are great tumults in the north.' Lennox was clearly at a loss. The queen's tone was light. Was there, he wondered, some great plot afoot of which he had no knowledge? Had his family been invited south with some expectation that they had secret news?

'My lord,' continued the queen, her eyes glinting with malevolent humour, 'From my northern frontiers, news reaches me that you are growing giants in England.'

Finally, the queen swivelled her head up to look at Darnley. She barked laughter, and, as though jerked by strings, her courtiers laughed too. He blushed. The little reserves of confidence he had built up during his strut through the Presence Chamber emptied, their container burst open by the jagged laughter around him. He smiled, but behind it he thought viciously that the old cat had been stalling him, keeping him on edge. He noted with distaste and some vengeful satisfaction that her skin was waxy and imperfect, not the milky white of a beauty.

'Come forward, my fine, tall lad. Let me look upon you.' He did as he was told. 'Yes, you are very well proportioned. Clearly the seed of our stock has flourished in you; you are a mighty oak. Quomodo vales?'

'Valeo, most triumphant and gracious princess,' he began, sweeping his own cap from his head to reveal his mass of wavy blonde hair, 'I must humbly render my thanks unto you for the kindness you have bestowed upon me; the apartments with which you have provided us are much too good for our little needs. You would do me greater honour to let me thank you in any way you see fit. I am from your obedient servant to command.' The words had come unrehearsed: he had simply recited half-remembered snatches of conventional platitudes in an uncoordinated mishmash and hoped for the best. But the speech had come out so well he couldn't understand why the hand which held his had was quivering, its feather betraying it.

'Very pretty, very pretty,' nodded Elizabeth in unsmiling approval – whether of his speech or his person, he neither knew nor cared. If she caught the quivering cap she did not expose it. 'We are not displeased to have you. And we shall find you some occupation that is not without use to us. Of that you may be in no doubt. You have not met, I do not think, the Lord Robert Dudley?'

A distinguished-looking gentleman stepped forward from the small knot of people who had been monitoring his performance. He was dressed in fine, silvery-lilac, a pearl-studded black hat on his thick, dark hair. Unlike the jealous, hostile looks Darnley had drawn from the male courtiers in the Presence Chamber, Dudley had a surprisingly kindly look on his swarthy face. He smiled without guile. So, this was Dudley, the great wife-killer? He looked more like a noble hero from an Italian romance. 'My Lord Darnley,' he said with a bow, 'it is a pleasure to meet Her Majesty's kinsman.' Darnley began to offer his own smooth salutation. The queen's terse voice cut in.

'Robin, you will look after our young cousin.' It was a command, not a request. 'You need looking after, do you not?'

'I ... am ignorant in the doings of courtiers, your Majesty.'

'Aren't we all?' She drew a ripple of laughter from the room, playing it. 'If you will excuse us, we have much to discuss with Master Secretary.' With that, Elizabeth turned her head from her audience and resumed her conversation with the bearded man as though there had been no interruption. Voices began to rise again in the small room as the assembled courtiers, who had watched the entire scene, returned to their own conversations. Lennox patted his son on the back in approval, before swaggering over to an old companion. His wife adopted an almost manic vivacity, greeting a couple of older matrons as though they were long-lost sisters.

Dudley had been eyeing him with an appraising look neither calculating nor malign; if anything, he thought, the older man seemed to be considering him with a measure of gentle pity. He spoke quietly. 'You shall get used to this kind of life. I am sure it is a world away from life in the north.'

'It is rather,' said Darnley, smiling. 'For one thing, everything is much larger. There are so many people here, such life. We had no one else at home.' It was not hard to speak freely with Dudley, who was nodding in sympathy.

'I sympathise. Like your parents, I have known disfavour. I know what it is to be the son of men who know the value of their sons and how to use it.'

Darnley was momentarily confused; was Dudley insulting his parents? No, his open face and matter-of-fact tone suggested he was simply being honest. 'My parents are good to me.'

'Oh, I am sure of it, sir – I meant no disrespect. I know a great deal about your parents; oh, a *great* deal. But you need friends at Court, especially with your father lodging without. You need people who will protect you, promote you ... and keep you out of trouble.' The last came with a wink. 'Hold fast to me. We are not all like that vicious-looking mob through which you have run.' Darnley laughed. 'And worry not: no lectures, no sermons. I am not such an old man myself; I have not forgotten what bores and what pleases young men fresh from the country and eager to see something of life.' As simply as that, he had a real friend, older and more chivalrous than even his gone-to-seed father.

'You are very kind.'

'I am not in the least kind. I am a selfish knave, and an ambitious one at that. I am not half as bad as the cot-queans of this Court would have you believe, but then I am probably more stuffed with sins than I ought to be.' His dark eyes clouded a little, but soon returned to Darnley. 'But I am a judge unparalleled of a man's nature, and I know who deserves a friend.' He clapped the younger man on the shoulder. 'I am running myself dry. We do not lock ourselves up here just to flap our jaws. Do you play?'

'Oh yes, I can play the lute, and the viol, and-'

'The lute; that will do. It is as quiet as a tomb today, and the Lord knows my voice has lost the sweetness of youth. Here,' he indicated a large table opposite the queen's dais that held a selection of musical instruments not dissimilar to those which had been left in his room. Darnley obediently retrieved the polished lute and began to play. Not Daphne and Phoebus, this time, but another old tune, and one that seemed fitting.

***

Pastime with good company
I love and shall unto I die

***

The queen's voice cut in, 'Well chosen, my giant. Play on, play on.' He played on. Dudley and Elizabeth's gaze met, a silent message passing between them. This, for the moment, was her new pet, to be denied nothing. The other courtiers made encouraging noises.

***

Youth must have some dalliance,
Of good or ill some pastance;
Company methinks then best
All thoughts and fancies to dejest:
For idleness
Is chief mistress
Of vices all.
Then who can say
But mirth and play
Is best of all?

***

He had arrived.

5

In the following few weeks, Darnley was introduced to the gentle, agreeable rhythm of life at Court. In fact, he and his mother became virtual – albeit willing – prisoners in a golden cage, their sentence a strict life of ceremony and ritual. Bubonic plague had broken out in London not long after their passage through the city, and a swath of hideous death had followed in their wake. Thankfully his father had slipped away, abandoning his wife and son to luxury. The queen gave orders that the city was to be quarantined, and anyone attempting to approach Windsor from the city of the dead was to be hanged.

Whilst a thousand domestic tragedies wreaked havoc with life in the city, the Court played on.

Mornings were invariably spent hunting and hawking in the parks which surrounded Elizabeth's country retreats and the estates of her obliging courtiers. Dinners were sometimes spent in the Privy Chamber – always a rare honour, for the queen dined in private. At each dinner, over a dozen dishes were brought before her, before being passed down to her closest friends (and from thence removed to her less-favoured courtiers). Everything was spiced, jellied, or sweetened, and presented with aplomb. Miniature castles made of Madeira sugar were served; songbirds were roasted and could be eaten in one bite; great pies were baked to resemble enormous golden crowns. But the real meat and drink of the Court was gossip. Who was writing verses full of ardour to whom? Who was short of money? New clothes in the latest styles could be ordered and tailor-made – the queen would allow no slovenliness to offend her eye. Dandiness was encouraged, with the clothing of the men outshining that of the women, in whom sartorial sombreness was demanded so as not to deflect from the lady herself.

Afternoons were a never-ending round of masques, dancing, dicing, parties for visiting ambassadors and dignitaries, and musical recitals. Church services were regular: not the incense-filled, mystical Masses of Settrington, but dull, wishy-washy sermons in English read by timid, sincere preachers hoping for advancement. These boring protestations of faith, bolstered by one of Elizabeth's latest religious policies, were merely to be got through, the promise of excitement afterwards giving Darnley something to think about when the preacher's monotonous voice threatened to cause him to nod off.

Evenings were given over to private parties and gatherings in the rooms of courtiers, some of which Elizabeth graced with her semi-divine presence. All the senses were unfailingly inflamed: at Court, the food was richer, the scents sweeter, the outfits, surroundings, and countryside more ostentatious, beautiful and cultivated.

To his further – and even greater – delight Darnley found himself first a rising star and then an almost permanent fixture in the firmament of the peripatetic Court. During his daily processes through the Presence Chamber he was continually pressed upon. Dewy-eyed women, their bosoms heaving dramatically, would ask him if he would ask a favour of the queen – a loan for a brother; a position for an ailing father. Those gentlemen who had looked on him with spite on his first visit began to mask their jealousy and, knowing that he had the ear of the queen, would pay him the most outrageous homages in their desperation to be remembered to her. It was gratifying.

Those first few weeks of revelry stretched into months in a flurry of masques, dances, plays, hunts, and receptions. Full of idle, indolent luxury, it passed with all the hazy quality of a dream. Gradually the smell of rural Yorkshire was overpowered by the rich aroma of refinement and acceptance.

When 1563 turned to 1564 Darnley, his mother and the full complement of Elizabeth's courtiers were in residence at Richmond. The threat of plague had abated and the monstrous, swollen, pus-covered bodies of the dead had been buried: hundreds of lives ended and covered over with dirt. It was deemed safe for the flower of the nobility to progress closer to London. An elaborate mix of soaring, domed towers, bricks and glass, Richmond didn't suffer the atmosphere of a bureaucratic outpost, but instead absorbed something of the vibrancy of city life. Darnley's latest apartments were just as well furnished and his year in the service of the queen had seen his favour grow rather than subside.

Now eighteen, he was one of her bright young things: the glamourous, talented men at Court who could always be relied upon to play a merry tune, dance with grace and flatter anyone, matron, or ambassador, until their cheeks reddened, and they left his company thinking themselves as tall and magnetic as him. Elizabeth asked little of her gentlemen. Politics she reserved always for her ministers and men of state. They were welcome to it. She wanted wit, charm and diversion from handsome men, not dry, dusty policies. Although her barbed comments and acerbic jokes could cut to the quick, the queen honoured Darnley more than ever. She delighted in having her 'giant', as she insisted on calling him, welcome new guests to Court, and he began to feel keenly what his mother had always assured him of: he really was one of the great men of the kingdom. The fearsome Elizabeth had even granted his father, who was quite willing to live in the city as long as its airs did not harm him, access to Court. Provided, of course, he did not dare attempt to bed and board with his wife under her many roofs.

One evening in September he lay casually on his bed reading a sheaf of sonnets aloud, one arm tucked behind his head like a Roman emperor dictating letters of state. He had been working steadily on his writing – his penmanship, he fancied, was masterful – and oral recitation, and his words had gradually developed a honeyed power. A small group of adoring single ladies and their matronly chaperones (for Elizabeth kept a virtuous Court) were grouped on cushions and on low stools around the bed as he read. He was careful to address his words of courtly love to all and none of them.

His only really close friend at Court remained the avuncular Robert Dudley. Unfailingly thoughtful, it was both a disappointment and a delight to Darnley that Dudley's dark reputation had been so exaggerated; it was somehow more interesting to imagine the worst of people – to picture licentious, amoral lives were there existed only cordial normality. The queen's Master of Horse encouraged him to find comfort and pleasure in the fairer sex – provided, of course, that there was no hint of impropriety. Of this lesson Darnley had been an earnest student, although he felt sure that any one of his little harem would have made a willing bedfellow had he ever given a signal.

His friendship with Dudley had been the lynchpin of his life at Court. There was rarely an evening in which he did not join a gathering in the older man's apartments – always tantalisingly close to the queen's – or Dudley one of his. The two men had formed a bond new to Darnley: they shared interests, goals, and dreams. Robert – Robin, as he liked his friends to call him – was frank in his dealings. He was eager to disabuse the young newcomer of any preconceived notions of his dark past, and he did so without self-consciousness. His wife, he told Darnley, had been a sad, sick, and withdrawn woman: but she had died alone, either by accident or – perish the thought – by her own design. His reputation was the product of jealousy; and oh yes, he loved Elizabeth and she him, but without impropriety. He scoffed at the idea, joking that it would be about as possible to get Elizabeth alone as it would have been to convert her sister. In Dudley Darnley also found a sympathetic mind, and a fellow he did not feel the need to impress. Above all, he never felt that Dudley had one eye on Darnley's use to him. Feeling liked for himself, for his own thoughts, was something new. And welcome.

He finished reading and reached for a cup of light ale. He looked at his ladies as he sipped. He had been tempted, of course, but Dudley's advice had taken root. He had avoided heavy drinking, and so not encouraged any temptation. Going without carnal relations after a brief awakening was not so difficult – he had not fallen, as some men did, into a lack of self-restraint. Besides, these ladies were not Gallic whores. Like his mother they were Englishwomen, unassailable however much bosom they revealed. They had become idols of admiration who admired him in return, not sweaty, willing bodies to be used and forgotten after frantic coupling. No, he had no wish to rob them of their virtue. It was enough to have a group of admirers, sweet in their words and sincere in their praises. What delightful, senseless things they were – it was the least he could do to promote the interests of their fathers and brothers when he could.

The door to his chamber flew open and his father strode in, barking something. He looked at the apt women with disapproval and shut his mouth. When he did speak his tone had turned jovial and roguish. 'What is this, my son the Moorish prince, attended by his faithful bevy of wives?' The ladies giggled, matrons included. 'And what beautiful wives too. Away with you, ladies, before you turn my head.' They got up and began to file out. Lennox made as if to spank them as they left, grinning mischievously. This caused another outbreak of laughter, with which the earl joined in. 'And don't let me catch you here again, lest I forget I'm a married man'.

His laughter abruptly stopped as the door closed behind the last of them. Anger was written on his face when he turned to his son. The boy had been displaying a worrying level of independence since they lived apart, the hero worship he had confidently expected to last forever softening under this coddling by women. It was a shame there would be little time to sway him with old tales of his paternal derring-do – they usually worked a special magic over his son's fertile imagination and brought him back into wide-eyed admiration. 'What is this, my lord? Is this what goes on in my absence? Your mother has warned you about surrounding yourself with young wenches.' Darnley yawned. 'You know how gossip and rumour fly around this place, and you know Her Majesty objects to her young men paying court to her ladies.'

'They were all chaperoned, father, as always. Or do you think I now chase the skirts of old lady Parry? Shall I be seeking after Mrs Ashley next?'

'Don't get smart with me, my fine young lord, you're not so grand as all that. And not nearly as sharp as you think – else why would you favour the company of such pretty little spies as those?'

'Spies?' said Darnley, scoffing. 'They're well-born ladies.'

'Aye – and aren't they the most mischievous kind of spies. Who do you think your "well born" minxes go slithering to with news of your thoughts, of your likes and dislikes? I'll tell you. Some will go dutifully to the queen, some will sell everything you say to the highest bidder. It is not you giving favours here, boy, but those young wenches selling them. You are cousin to the queen and an English-born male at that –

God's teeth, being native-born alone makes you a better heir than some of her relatives. Every word you breathe will be worth something to someone. Each action will be reported. I've not met the woman who'll not happily unbridle her serpentine tongue for a jewel or a new gown, and Hell mend you if you allow it. All of this from living with ladies! Ach, but let's not argue.'

'Well, father, you have no cause for anger. We have been here for a year. Has there been a scandal about me? No there has not. I live more chastely than any monk ever did. I do not eat or drink to excess and have not even been tempted to compromise any of the vixens that stalk me, nor even speak scandalously to them. But what brings you? What news?'

'" What news"? Only news that could affect my – your – all of our futures.' Darnley sat up. It was not like his father to announce things of no importance; Lennox had his ear to the ground, and the city fairly shook with rumour.

'You know how hard I've been striving for the restoration of my estates in Scotland?'

'Oh,' said Darnley, nonplussed. 'That again.' The affair of the Glasgow estates had been rumbling on all summer, from London townhouse to Court to Scotland. His father was like a dog with a bone, endlessly agitating his wife to harass the queen to press the Queen of Scots for his restoration. The rival queens had batted the ball back and forth, neither committing to Lennox's return to Scotland in honour, neither demurring. There had been lots of false starts and stops. Darnley cared little: what was Scotland when life at the English Court was so comfortable? Nevertheless, it had only increased Lennox's desire to regain Glasgow. His appetite had been whetted. 'What of it?'

'Youths these days, how you talk to your parents – I'll wager you have a softer tongue for your courtier friends, male and female! Yes, you bold imp. That again. Queen Mary has accepted my innocence and Queen Elizabeth has released me from England. I am to go north, to my homeland, and I go in favour.'

'You are leaving?' A stab of panic hit him. 'Do we go with you? Are we leaving England?'

'Soft, Harry. I go alone. The Queen of England hasn't yet tired of her giant.' That was alright then. 'But your mother may not be happy.'

'Mother likes it here.'

'Aye, she likes it well enough, but you're forgetting yourself. Your mother still harbours dreams of a crown on your head, and a Scottish crown at that. You can hardly win the bonny hand of the Scottish queen when you're paying court to her English cousin. And her English ladies.'

So that was still the game: his parents wanted him packaged up and sent north for Mary of Scotland to unwrap. 'Well, father, if I must stay I must stay, and that's that.' There was relief in Darnley's voice and he settled back on his cushions. He would miss the old man, for all he had grown used to seeing him infrequently. It was good to have a father around, someone with whom one had more license than the rest of the Court's great men.

'For now, perhaps. But that's not all.'

'Oh?'

'No. Other news is flying about the Court. Her Majesty, they say, intends to honour your friend Dudley, the rogue.'

'Oh really? What is he to become?'

'We don't yet know, but should you not ask yourself why he's likely to receive such honour?'

'Why?'

'Isn't it plain? The higher he is raised the more attractive he shall be to a prospective bride.'

This stabbed at Darnley a little. Dudley was his best friend and practically an older brother; their minds, he thought, were open to one another. But Dudley had never once hinted at their being any woman to whom he would pledge his heart other than Elizabeth herself. Could the old rumours be true?

'He is not to marry the queen?'

'Perhaps not this queen; but I believe he is to marry a queen: the Queen of Scots.'

***

Marriage, marriage, marriage! All through the summer of 1564, it was all anyone could talk about. It almost promised to take the shine off Court life; any subject, even one of interest, can lose its lustre with repetition. Would the queen consider an Austrian husband? A Frenchman? A Swede? Could she ever make an Englishman her equal? A few wags even considered Darnley himself – but as puffed up as he was with Elizabeth's admiration and regard he found this idea laughable – even distasteful.

By September, when the ennoblement of his friend was not only certain but scheduled, it was old news in the Court that Dudley was to receive his reward for loyal service in preparation for a still greater reward: Scotland. The Countess of Lennox, for her part, was in a great tumult about the whole affair. Being too proud and too sly to admit the failure of her schemes to her fair-weather friends in the Court, she had only her son on whom to vent her overflowing emotions. All her hopes for Darnley had evaporated, and she could almost feel the crown of Scotland slipping from her grasp and being deftly caught by Dudley.

For once she was at a loss as to what to do, her mind quickly turning to the possibility of any other matches that might provide glory for the Lennox Stewarts. Nothing announced itself. What could rival a crown? Darnley tried to console her – this was her loss, he felt, not his. But even with his best efforts he still frequently found her cloistered in her own apartments with the curtains drawn, weeping, and kneading her forehead. Without Lennox she was like a songbird without its mate, no answering warble to complement her own. She spent a great deal of time writing poetry about fortune's wheel – usually a favourite pastime – but it was uniformly dreadful and ended up in the fire. Her talents had fled with the prospect of a sovereign son.

The wheels of diplomacy were already in motion for union between Dudley and Queen Mary on the day that Elizabeth's Master of Horse was to be made the Earl of Leicester and Baron of Denbigh. Naturally Darnley was in attendance in the Great Hall at Westminster to show support for his friend and patron and, as Elizabeth's most distinguished relative, to bear the sword of honour. He had a magnificent view and, he fancied, the Court had a magnificent view of him. The old palace hall itself was not splendid, except for its colossal size. Spartan and chilly, it sported only a few tapestries and almost seemed to revel in the stark, dignified look of stone walls and hanging oak rafters. It made up for a lack of glamour with an air of ancient importance usually reserved for cathedrals. It even *smelled* historical – like old water and dust and candlewax. It was a fitting place for ennoblement, and Darnley felt that his presence would help strike an agreeable balance between the old and the new.

A relatively new face at Court was also in attendance. Darnley immediately spotted the figure of Sir James Melville, a representative of the Scottish queen. He rolled his eyes at the sight of the busybody. Like many veteran ambassadors he was a gossip; these creatures, thought Darnley, loved nothing more than to ingratiate themselves with the great only to draw out their secrets and report them home. Melville's charm – and he could be charming at the drop of a hat – appealed to the queen. Frequently Darnley found the man's searching eyes on him; occasionally he spotted him scuttling from Lady Lennox's apartment when he was returning to his own, although she kept whatever they discussed to herself. As an honoured guest, Melville had been given pride of place in the front row of onlookers, resplendent in a jewel-buttoned doublet and short cloak.

As the ceremony began Dudley knelt before the queen, his head bowed, solemnity written on his face. He had dressed in his best – no mean feat, given his extensive wardrobe – and, to Darnley, he had never looked more the part of the consummate courtier. Every eye in the room was trained on him and his sovereign. This was a moment to be watched; he was, after all, Elizabeth's reputed lover, and here she was bestowing great honours upon that would make him fit for her cousin's bed. What was going through that sharp mind? After she had read out Dudley's new titles in a sonorous voice – what a sense of the theatre the woman had – she conspicuously leant forward and tickled him under the chin, her long, thin fingers brushing his neck. Murmurs ran through the Court like a ripple on still water. The queen took no notice. She affected to pry her eyes away from her favourite with some difficulty. They fell on Melville.

'Well, my lord, how do you like our newest peer?' Her voice echoed up to the rafters, between which her predecessors stood in recessed niches, listening with carved, deaf ears.

'Your Majesty, he is a worthy subject, and one lucky to have such a gracious princess who will reward good service,' called out Melville from the crowd.

'Well said. Yet I think you prefer yonder long lad?' Without warning her bony finger shot accusingly at Darnley. The eyes of the Court followed it – and the unexpected politics of the unusual turn of events – raptly. Darnley swallowed. A sudden heat descended on him, an itch rising from his starchy collar and creeping up his neck. He had not expected to be thrust into such an active role – his purpose was to be ornamental.

'Madam', replied Melville after a deep breath, 'no one of spirit, man or woman, would prefer such a pretty, beardless, lady-faced youth.'

The queen erupted in laughter and her courtiers followed suit. Darnley took an involuntary step backwards, nearly tripping over his own long, gartered legs, the sword on its cushion almost overbalancing. His refined manners and the cool, urbane confidence he had built up so carefully over the last year that he felt it was intrinsic and inviolate melted away. He was made ridiculous, an actor in princely clothing disrobed to reveal a countrified clown. Even his mother was managing a red-faced titter. The only person not laughing was Dudley. Instead his friend looked angry at his moment of elevation being overshadowed. But worse, his expression also had sympathy in it. Darnley felt childish tears begin to nip at his eyes. His automatic grin was fixed, idiotic and incongruous. It fooled no one. His scarlet cheeks gave him away, and only deepened the Court's laughter.

6

Dudley – or rather Leicester, as he was now styled – was pacing Darnley's apartment. It was now late November, and Darnley had found himself spending almost every evening and as many afternoons as possible eschewing the company of the Court in favour of time alone or with his friend. The humiliation at Westminster had pricked his pride and he felt reduced, humbled, and foolish. One day in the Presence Chamber he had actually heard derisive laughter and caught the words, 'lady-face' and 'long lad'.

He had immediately turned around, determined not to let them see him redden again, and stormed back to his apartments where he picked up and hurled a dish of comfits at the wall. He had cursed and cursed, wishing painful deaths upon the smirking, arrogant fools, their wives, their children. He hated them – he hated them all for laughing. He had thought he belonged at the Court, was a star in it, but it had been an illusion, no more substantial than a dream. It had taken Leicester, who had made a point of visiting him often to warn him about letting the scornful remarks of bitter, vindictive asses touch him, to cool him down.

Now it was Leicester's turn to vent his spleen and Darnley intended to be there for him. He had never seen him in such a frenzy; Leicester was always so calm, stoic, and imperturbably aloof. Now he was driven to frustration: a result of his future being tugged between two rival women, each trying to one-up the other. It was no surprise that he was fraying.

'I tell you, she won't have me. And I thank the Lord for it. The Scottish queen sees no advantage in having her cousin's favourite share her bed – not if Elizabeth refuses to recognise her as her successor in return. I am cast on the rocks, neither good enough for one lady nor the other. I am a courtier – not a great man of state – and I shall likely never be anything more. And by my truth, I would not be forced into a marriage with an unknown lady. None know better than I that a hasty marriage breeds unhappiness for both and love for neither.'

'They are using you dishonourably, Robin. Things have come to a fine pass in Britain when these fickle, grasping ladies treat their loyal servants so. It ought not to be borne.'

Leicester looked at him, sudden appraisal on his face, and Darnley felt quite the wise councillor, their roles reversed. 'Besides,' he continued, 'why would any man seek marriage with either lady? I shall be no great queen's lapdog, petted and spoiled and then whipped raw when my mistress feels the urge. In any marriage I make I shall be master, as God intended.'

'You are changed, Harry. You are turned cynic. But with the Scottish queen's ardour for me cooling, does your good lady mother know about this sudden scepticism?' Leicester was amused by the serious look on his young friend's soft, childish features.

But he had a point. Darnley's mother, who had reacted to the stalling of Leicester's Scottish alliance with cautious optimism, like a politician careful not to say or think too much, would not rest until Mary was sharing his bed, or someone else's, or dead.

'Mother schemes, Robin, but her plans come to nothing. My father shoots at the same mark. Even now he bombards the queen with requests that I join him in Scotland to help him with legal matters. Fancy an old Scotsman needing his son to help him negotiate the finer points of Scots law.'

'Ah, you cannot blame them. Unless you make another match here at Court they will shoot for the stars.'

'Tchhh, a match here at Court. I am a running joke. The queen's 'giant': her pretty, lady-faced lad. I might have pissed myself before them all. They were certainly doing just that. Robin, may I ask you something?'

'You may.'

'Why do you pursue the queen so?' He looked around, as though expecting spying servants to have materialised. They were alone, but still he lowered his voice. 'I find her rude, offensive and defensive.'

'Ah, my boy. It will come to you in time, an understanding. Her Majesty and I were young together, in trouble together. It is not for ambition I seek her out. Oh, very well – it is not for ambition alone. In truth she enchants.'

'Surely not with that tricky tongue – she has more the wit of a man than a woman.'

'You see only what she wishes you to see. Alone she is different. She can trust no one, and so she fears everyone. Everyone, I hope, save me. When a woman is so doubtful, so lonely, it fair brings out in me the desire to protect. God's blood, she did not ask to be what she is any more than you did. Or I, the son and grandson of traitors!'

'Right now, I confess I would rather be anyone else, and anywhere else.'

A strange look came over Leicester's face, a thought dawning on him. 'Then leave,' he said. Without thinking, Darnley started to stand up. Leicester shook his head, laughing. 'No, no. I mean try and leave England. It will please your parents no end if you attend the Court of Scotland – you need not fall in with their schemes, but you will spare your ears your mother's entreaties. I shall help her in this.'

'Robin, she hates you.'

'Which makes me the more determined to win her. Besides, a change of scene might do you good, Harry. You can already speak the language like a native, thanks to your parents.'

'It is not so different.'

'It is different enough. And think on. There are other ladies in Scotland than its princess. It's a fine-looking country. And its men of state are always eager to keep the favour of the English, we being –most of us being – their friends and natural governors as the greater part of Britain. I am sure I can convince our gracious queen – even if it means doing your mother's work. You see, I have no mind to continue as bait for the Scottish queen and you have no mind endure taunts here. So we help each other. Is friendship not a grand thing?'

Darnley considered it. He had begun to feel stifled by the life that had started out with such promise. Without the warming glow of constant adoration and uncritical attention, living like a Eunuch under the constant, unwavering gaze of his mother had lost its appeal. He had ceased to be an exciting novelty in the English Court and had instead become another decorative minion. In Scotland his family had estates; he had roots. All his adult life, he had associated that northern land with his cousin, the willowy Scottish queen. His parents had forged that link, and now it seemed impossible to break it and see the kingdom as anything other than a large, tombstone-like altar. Yet Leicester had a point. There must be more to Scotland than its mistress.

'Your words hit home. But no matter where I fetch myself, I promise you that I will not be batted about by inconstant women. Anyway, here are we discussing my future when you have come to seek friendship. It is my turn to give you advice and bid you take heed. Robin, do not let either queen unman you, nor let them bat you back and forth like cats with a mouse.'

***

The effects of the Earl of Lennox's entreaties to the queen, combined with his mother's hectoring, seemed to be warming Elizabeth to the idea of his leaving during the winter of 1564. Darnley turned nineteen in December, and the countess did not waste the opportunity to inform Elizabeth that it would delight her son to visit his father and see, for the first time, his Scottish inheritance. Elizabeth had tartly replied that her Court could not possibly prosper unless it was supported on the strong shoulders of her giant. Lady Lennox countered by reminding Elizabeth that she had a younger son who could be called down from Yorkshire, and who promised to fill the void with rapidly developing shoulders of his own. To this Elizabeth fetched heavy, theatrical sighs, stating, 'the lad is no prisoner' and that all of her birds eventually fly the nest. Thereafter she kept the countess dangling with vague, circumlocutory answers pregnant with promise. And so it went on.

For Darnley's part, the idea had begun to take on a pleasing shape. Leicester's words had had an effect on him and the idea of a new life in a foreign land became more attractive every time he sensed a malicious look or thought he overheard railing laughter. A foreign country – it could be like France. His father's recollections of Scotland seldom failed to include dolorous tales about the influence of the old French regent, Queen Mary's mother, and her influx of French courtiers and soldiers. No doubt Mary herself would have brought home a French retinue, and poor little Scotland would be thinking itself quite the place. Further, it was a small Court, full of canny Scots governed by a glamorous young widow. His arrival, surely, would only add to a chic atmosphere. These thoughts swirled as Christmas approached and passed. Throughout the freezing, pitch-dark evenings, it became a pleasant occupation to sit plucking his eyebrows before a looking glass, preening himself for no one in particular, and imagining riding Scotland's glens, once more adored.

The Scottish queen also began to enter more into his thoughts. As winter blanketed the country in hard, brittle frost, fantasies of Mary presiding over her northern Court in baronial fortresses helped to lull him to sleep in his great bed, chilly even with a crackling fire. His images of Mary, first as a child bride and then as a statuesque and remote widow, had started to fade. In their place she became a tragic and submissive princess waiting to be rescued from a life of bleakness by a confident, smiling hero on a white palfrey.

It was especially fun to indulge his imagination when he was under a coverlet. He found it easy to envision himself playing a starring role in one of the great romances of royal history. Mary's father, engulfed by passion for an unseen bride, had flown from his Scottish throne to France to seduce the tragic Madeleine de Valois. Unable to contain his infamous ardour, Henry VIII had sought out the unfortunate Anne of Cleves upon her arrival in England, donning a disguise in order to glimpse the lady unofficially. Henry VII had taken his short-lived son, Arthur, to gaze upon Katherine of Aragon before their marriage, disregarding Spanish protocol. Darnley did not dwell on the disastrous outcomes of these impassioned and impulsive gestures of romantic zeal. Why spoil a pleasingly soporific flight of fancy?

The festive revels also seemed to work wonders on weakening Queen Elizabeth's resolve to keep Darnley ensconced in her Court. Plays and masques were performed throughout the Christmas period, and for Darnley the Court almost began to recapture something of the magic that it had had before Leicester's investiture. Courtiers danced around on hobby horses and the young lawyers of the Inns of Court, accompanied by actors, invaded to declare misrule and demand that queen submit to their ordered disorder. Food was in greater abundance and elegance than usual – the queen even overdid it and took to her bed for days, recuperating swiftly and eager to laugh and play harder than anyone else to flaunt her constitution. It was so pleasant to hear people laugh – when they were not laughing at him.

His mother went everywhere with an almost frenzied sense of nervous energy, never still or content to remain long at any occupation. Her obsession with her son's appearance and fortunes had become more intolerable than ever as she tried to imagine seeing him as his Scottish cousin might see him, grown up and a potential suitor for her hand. Her dreamy, romantic notions were as annoying as they were infectious, and Darnley actually began to understand Elizabeth's vindictive delight in exciting her hopes only to dash them.

But such a game could only be played for so long. In late January Darnley was finally summoned before Elizabeth in her Privy Chamber. At last, he thought, the malicious old harridan was to grant him permission to leave, so rejuvenated was she by the fun and frolics of festive misrule – or perhaps worried that her brief Christmastime sickness had caused too many eyes to drift inexorably towards him again. He did not tell his mother, and for once the news of an express summons from the queen to her son did not make its way via the Court grapevine to her twitching ears.

By now he had come to recognise a particular habit of Elizabeth's. She delighted in appearing deep in business when her courtiers answered her summons – business which she was required to break off in order to attend to them. Her attention must always be seen to be a great favour, her callers a nuisance. He bowed before her raised platform until she fixed a black stare on him.

'My Lord Darnley.' Her tone was curt. No nickname. 'We must profess we are astonished to see you still here.'

He was thrown off guard, and so he kept his silence. It was undoubtedly her intention.

'For some time now your parents and my Lord of Leicester have entreated us to release you. They must think us a gaoler – an accusation one of our experience finds most distasteful. I defy any man to prove it of us. Are we a gaoler, sir?'

Beyond the windows the sun briefly retreated behind a cloud, the quality of light in the room shifting. Darnley found his voice. 'Your Majesty – as God is my witness you are no gaoler.'

'How kind of you to say, having willingly waited on us like a good Stewart for over a year', she replied, smiling at her own pun to reveal neat, discoloured teeth. 'And having dined off our table, enjoyed our company, basked in our sunshine, and ignored the ardent desires of your father to repair to our sister's northern kingdom to support him in regaining his fripperies. Well, you may go, if you will go, and get you gone. Your loving pater has need of you. I do not expect to see your face for three months. Attend your affairs in Scotland, and we are resolved that you will then return home to serve us once more. Three months, my Lord Darnley. You may go.'

'At once, your Majesty.' He bowed deeply, crunching hard on the inside of his cheek to kill off an unbidden smile.

'And Harry.' He looked up. Her face had softened, the harsh lines of her mouth relaxing. 'Touching the matter of your travels, we would have you remember that you are our loving subject and a representative born of this proud and ancient realm.'

'I am always yours, gracious majesty.'

'We are pleased to hear it. Now you may go and give the news to your mother. I fear the sorrow of your going may kill the poor woman stone dead.'

This time Darnley could not stop his smile from breaking

out – it was an open, guileless smile, full of humour, youth, and freedom. It caught Elizabeth, who smiled herself, and suddenly the two were laughing like a pair of mischievous children. The queen had a curiously youthful laugh. She made it a mark of honour to share it with those for whom she had a genuine liking. He could almost forgive her infuriating unpredictability, her streak of spitefulness and her love of patronising people. When she wanted, the old nag could be very witty. If only she had never turned that catty tongue on him.

'Off with you, away before I really do turn gaoler.' Without rising she waved him off with exaggerated gestures, and he left her chamber to begin directing his packing. As he strode back towards his chambers, whistling, he felt lighter, the weight of recent months falling away and the prospect of a new beginning moving from dream to reality.

7

It was in February that Darnley found himself making the journey north with five of his father's men. Thus accompanied, he really could feel himself a well-served gallant, backed by retainers, on his way to win the heart of a fair and willing maiden. Still, the trek was not an easy one. It was one of the coldest, cruellest winters anyone had ever known. His reluctant riding partners were full of baneful stories picked up along the route of people found frozen to death on the outskirts of London or drowned in the thaw that followed an unremitting fortnight of snow. The whole world seemed quilted by that acrid odour borne on winter's breath. It smelled like childhood and past days, the bittersweet tang of seasons long dead and half-melted memories. It was strange how beginnings felt like endings.

His mother had been incandescent when he had told her the news, and full of advice on how best to present himself before his Scottish cousin. Though she drank no more than heavily watered wine, he would have sworn by the countess's behaviour after receiving the news of his leaving that she was constantly in her cups. Though he was secretly pleased to escape her clutches and the claustrophobia of Elizabeth's Court, it was with a heavy heart that he left his one good friend. Dudley had roughly embraced him and reminded him of his own words of a few weeks earlier: 'do not let either the Queen of Scots or of England bat you back and forth, like cats with a mouse'. He wouldn't forget. Besides, the pretty Scots queen was Frenchified: a frivolous, lovely bauble in a hard land. She was waiting for someone strong and powerful to ride to her aid and shine her up. As he turned his back on the sprawling city of London, so frequently touched by death, his poetic mind turned to the life and vitality that lay ahead of him. He rode hard into icy blasts which numbed and refreshed.

The flat, featureless lands of Elizabeth's midlands, still carpeted with melting snow, were gradually succeeded by the dramatic, hilly moorland of the north. Here, ugly blackened tree stumps and desiccated roots poked out of dustings of white, like scorched skeletons trying to claw off their funeral shrouds. As he passed through northern market towns, the great city of York and eventually the imposing castles of Alnwick and Berwick-on-Tweed, he could not help but notice the growing wildness of the land, brought into relief at intervals by the flat, emotionless iron sheet of the North Sea. The world beyond Yorkshire carried a different air – one apt to breed hardy, tenacious people. England's timbered cottages and red brick manors gradually gave way to grey, stone buildings and thatched shacks. There was little money in Scotland, but it seemed to Darnley, whose tastes were dandified even by English standards, that what there was clearly wasn't being spent on beautification. What manner of man was content to brood in fortified stone towers, behind thick walls, peering out at a feral landscape from tiny, untrustworthy windows?

The Scottish landscape too rose up in windswept hills and passes, yawning high and wide to swallow the small cadre of horses and men who sneaked out of England's postern gate. Wherever he looked he saw a land of distant horizons so mountainous, misty and wild that they seemed eternally unreachable. It was a fairy-tale land in a story. He had been raised to believe it was his place to be part of something great. And what was greater than a story? But the nine days' ride gave him the opportunity to turn his mind to weightier matters.

Liberated once again from the charm of his father and the

fussing attentions of his mother, he was free to ruminate on the reasons behind his journey and his own role in this exciting caper. It was not a task he relished. Accustomed as he was to the outward trappings and manifestations of rank and protocol he found it increasingly hard to reconcile his own wants with a world that was just an expansive stage on which men must play the roles written for them. His parents had written his as their parents had written theirs. Yet during his time in London – perhaps it had even begun during his visit to France – resentment of their machinations had joined fear of disappointing his parents. What had once, when he had known nothing else, been worship of two infallible titans was now something altogether different. It was inescapable duty to a pair of loving, smothering, imperfect, tiresome old people.

He must, he knew, use all the wit and charm of his arsenal in order to win favour with the Scottish queen. This was the reason for his journey, and it could presage great things for his family. But would he enjoy the company of this much-storied lady? Would she welcome and fete him or would her attitude be that of her cousin: Sphinx-like, fearsome, imperious? If he failed to impress her where would his future lie – in England or in Scotland? Was he a pawn in the power games which kept the world moving, or a willing participant? The answers to these questions were not easy. He decided to let them lie.

As his horse put one foot in front of the other, subservient entirely, he decided to give way to fate. He was escaping one queen's jurisdiction and entering another's. He would meet with and find security in his father's lands; he would meet the Queen of Scots, his kinswoman and almost as much a stranger in her country as he would be. How could he fail to capture her favour and enjoy it as Leicester enjoyed Elizabeth's, if not more? Nearness of blood bred and fed affection. The difference would be that he was in control and wouldn't be toyed with. Nevertheless, an irritating voice in his head kept pace with the beating of his horse's hooves – what are you doing in this unfamiliar land? Why are you here? Similar thoughts, he remembered, had assailed him when he first travelled to France. No answers had come then either. The voice only quieted when he had passed through Haddington and begun his approach to Edinburgh, the sight of which encouraged him to take off at a gallop. His valet Will Taylor, a Yorkshire boy who had been practically a gift from a family glad to see the back of him, turned to his fellows, perplexed. 'What's 'e in such an 'urry for? There i'n't anythin' 'ere we couldn't get easier and better in England, queans included. Well, we'll be makin' do with Scotch lasses for now.' He spat over his horse. 'Take your time, boys. Who wants to bet 'e'll be draggin' us all't way back afore a month's out?'

Scotland's metropolis was a curious combination of large frontier town and traditional royal seat. It had, Darnley knew, been burned the year before his birth when Henry VIII had ordered that Scotland be brought to its knees until it acquiesced to the marriage suit of his son Edward to the infant Mary. Old Henry, Darnley thought, must have pursued his unfortunate son's marriage with the aggressive vigour that had marked most of his own courtships. He liked to think of the town as growing as he would grow – a down-on-its luck noble on the road to recovering its birth-right: a phoenix of ancient stock rising from the ashes of dishonour and ill fortune. He could belong here.

If he became a person of means and influence in Scotland he would, he vowed to himself, help it pick itself up, dust itself off and rise to equal the power and prestige of Elizabeth's famous capital. As his horse cantered into the city – little more than a large town comprising competing burghs – it seemed to him a playground. London was a gallimaufry; it was too big, graceless, and unmanageable. Edinburgh would be suited to a young man finding his feet. He wanted a good look and so turned his back on Holyrood and entered the town through its old northern Netherbow gate, a route which allowed him a view up the High Street and back down the Canongate, the unmistakable road to Holyrood and its royal residence.

Due to its relatively recent misfortune the lawyers, diplomats and preachers who thronged the town mingled with a slowly expanding populace still wary of the dangers of invasion, violence and the hungry flames of marauding soldiers. People followed royal Courts. With Mary's return and the subsequent flocking of ambassadors, courtiers, petitioners and the curious, demand in the town had grown for inns, marketplaces, prostitutes and food. Everywhere construction work was in evidence. Buildings new and old were in various states of extension: new accommodation was needed for merchants, seamstresses, embroiderers and upholsterers. The narrow, winding streets were overhung with hastily-built, crooked upper floors. Gutters were frozen with waste and the vomit of workmen tasked with refashioning the town, but apt to spend their time huddled in the many dank taverns which are always the first places to be re-established after upheaval.

The people of Edinburgh – poor and slovenly, Darnley had been warned – had not achieved the worldliness of Londoners. Here and there a few of them were braving the mid-morning cold and leaden skies in the pursuit of business. Merchants in furred robes kept their heads down in their collars as they made their way to and from the Market Cross. Somewhere a woman's voice cried, 'and dinnae bother comin' back!' from an upper window, and an exasperated man let loose a stream of invective from below. Some long-faced, plump housewives led small battalions of servants out to stock up on food, new silks, and scandal about neighbours. He smiled to himself.

Edinburgh was not so different from any number of English towns. Yet there was one difference. Everyone eyed him with more suspicion than interest. The grey town, brooding under the sightless eyes of its ancient citadel, was heavy with secrecy. Clinging to the side of a dead volcano, it was a place where one could imagine dark happenings in shadowy alleys.

All this would change. Mary, he knew, had been causing a sensation in a country accustomed to belligerent old men jealously wrestling over the reins of power. By joining a Court of young beauties and gallants he would help sweep away the old guard of Scotland's governors on a wave of fresh young life. This, of course, depended on their mutual attraction. That lay in a favourable impression. In the days before his departure his mother had tried to coach him in the correct way to woo a princess – but her notions of seduction were hopelessly outdated, trapped in the manners and customs of a less refined generation. Only her parting words echoed. She had cupped a hand around his face and said, 'Harry, remember that you make your end in the way you make your beginning.'

Turning back on the High Street and the Netherbow he rode across the icy, cobbled Canongate towards Holyrood, rehearsing the modern, elegant phrases and platitudes with which he intended to catch Mary's affection. Scots was a distinct language from English, incomprehensible to most south of the border. 'Richt guid greetings and commendacions frae the men o' Lennox, baith faither and son, tae yer belovit majesty' would work.

He was suitably attired, a new suit of clothes under his heavy outerwear. As he and his retinue arrived at the gates to the old abbey of Holyroodhouse – or rather the palace, as Darnley knew it was becoming known – he was alarmed at the silence. There was little to signify the presence of a royal Court in the building's blank, snow-drifted windows. It appeared to be sleeping, towers and walls comfortable in their relaxed, lethargic beauty.

Calling for a gate guard, he wondered whether he had made a mistake by coming directly to Holyrood without sending an advance warning. An impulsive arrival, begrimed, but not too begrimed, from travel had seemed a romantic means of presenting himself. It lost something of its ardour if the lady was ungracious enough not to be present. A chubby man bundled in furs, a red nose protruding over a thicket of black moustaches, appeared from the gatehouse.

'Greetings, friend', he called down in Scots, his voice pluming in the air. 'I have come to see Her Majesty, Queen Mary, and bring messages from England's Elizabeth.'

'All the way from England to see our queen? Well that's a sin. Her Majesty's from home.'

'What? Well … where is she?' Darnley replied, confounded.

'No' here.'

'Well that's obvious. Where might I find her?'

'The Court's on progress. Master Robert Stewart is in residence.'

'Robert Stewart', he muttered. Was he kin? Of course – he was one of Mary's army of bastard half-siblings, the result of her father's taste for mistresses. So this half-brother was acting as caretaker of the place whilst she was on progress. And a progress at the height of a monstrous winter – was that folly or extravagance?

'Eh?'

'I … nothing. I thank you. Please give our commendations to our cousin Robert, and tell him we are come to rest before we seek the Court.'

The little man looked up at him with bemusement, and Darnley silently bid him do as he was ordered, lest his ability to command and be obeyed be compromised at the town's first hurdle. His first interaction in Edinburgh was rapidly threatening to descend into farce. Attempting to recapture an air of nobility he tugged the reins to turn his back on Holyroodhouse but succeeded only in making the horse shy at the air. A further yank turned him around and he could hear what sounded like a chuckle at his back. Trotting towards his groom and attendants, who had caught up with him whilst he embarrassed himself, he announced, 'Gentlemen, we are arrived in the capital. Welcome to your new home.'

He hoped that his wavering voice, almost lost to the chill wind which was picking up, carried cool authority. It began to rain. The frozen feather in his cap drooped under the weight of a fat droplet of water and fell forward, smacking his right eye and making him jerk in his saddle. 'God*damn* it!'.

8

Fighting back sneezes and resisting the urge to wipe his dripping nose, he was led into the Abbey-turned-Palace of Holyroodhouse by a member of the household staff fetched by the gatekeeper. The new man, at least, seemed jovial, and Darnley was pleasantly surprised by the opulence of the place, which was a refuge from the biting cold even if it lacked the heat of courtly activity.

He was shown into a small, wooden-floored withdrawing chamber in which three men were talking and warming their hands in front of a roaring fire. The flames made the golden designs painted on the ceiling dance and shimmer. Scenes of hunting and hawking lined the walls, and the sense of cosiness was welcome. One man, short and puffy-cheeked, extricated himself from the group and came towards him. He looked like a jolly, overgrown child.

'Welcome, welcome. I'm sorry we're so small a number – none of us was expecting you, young master. You must be cold.'

'I thank you', he said. It was always easier to be confident as long as one had a sympathetic face to focus on. 'I am Henry Stewart, Lord Darnley, come to greet the fair Scottish queen on my way to meet my father.' He gave the little assembly a bow, removing his sopping hat.

'The young son of Lennox, and a head taller than the elder. We'll have none of your English Lord Darnleys here. You're the young Master of Lennox in Scotland.' The man's youthful face crinkled in a broad, open smile. 'I'm Robert Stewart, our fair queen's brother. We're a small company left to tend to the abbey whilst Her Majesty and the Court are in Fife, but we're pleased to have you.' At this, he stepped back, gesturing to Darnley to come forward and meet the men with whom he had been staving off the chill.

A dark-haired man of about forty raised a thin hand and dipped the brim of his hat minutely. He had a neatly trimmed beard, through which were many greying hairs, and when he spoke his accent was unmistakably English.

'Lord Darnley, allow me to introduce myself and welcome you to Scotland. I am Thomas Randolph, ambassador of your mistress, the mighty Elizabeth. I represent England and England's interest here, and I am, I think, a great friend of both sovereigns. They have always told me so.' Darnley smiled to hide his contempt. He had no time for ambassadors. He nodded his head equally minutely, keeping his own hat pressed respectfully against his chest.

'Please, call me Harry. I'm just a poor stranger come to attend my father and see something of his native country.' Again he focused his attentions on Robert. He was conscious of his own accent, English with a soft Yorkshire burr that he had been unable to eradicate in either France or London.

'A poor stranger?' asked Randolph. 'Is that so? Do you not come with a suite of attendants?'

'I have five men with me.' His chest puffed out in imitation of his father's bravado and bluff.

'Five only? Well I daresay it is always up to royal Courts to furnish eager young visitors who require assistance, and to extend their bounty to those in need.' Darnley's smile stayed fixed. So the English ambassador to Scotland was a snob, despite his polished manners. Immediately his resolve stiffened to make the man repent his nasty aspersions. The inflexible dislike beneath Randolph's unctuousness manner was disconcerting; people always liked him. But that was just too bad. Great men, his father always said, excited the dislike of lesser souls. It was the way of the world. Randolph could stew in his own gall, and so could any man who disliked him on sight.

'I am sure the Scottish Court is a fountain of charity, even to such poor scraps as I –' Darnley sneezed without warning and offered apologies. Turning a sheepish grin on Randolph, he spoke with mock solemnity. 'I pray you, Master Ambassador, do not relay that to our mutual mistress. I fear she will tell my mother that Scotland has given me a chill, and you might know that Lady Lennox worries.' Randolph held up his hands; Robert laughed; the third man did nothing.

Robert, over whom the sarcastic exchange between Darnley and Randolph had passed unnoticed, cut in excitedly. 'Oh, Harry, this silent fellow is your kinsman, James Douglas: the Earl of Morton and Scotland's Lord Chancellor. Impressive, hey? He's your mother's cousin. Or are you her uncle, Morton? Ach, I've no head for these things. He's a Douglas, Harry. Is your mother well?'

'She is very well, my Lord of –'

'It's Robert; if you're Harry, I'm Robert.'

'She is very well, Robert.' He turned his most ingratiating smile on the remaining stranger in the room and felt it falter. Morton was a different proposition from the open Robert Stewart and the supercilious Randolph. So he was the Lord Chancellor – the highest office in any land except England, whose queen had inflated the dreary, administrative role of secretary to elevate base men to great power. Aloof and distant, Morton offered a hand that was as listless as his cornflower-blue eyes. For kin, he was not particularly friendly or familial. It was unnerving. Family ought to make one feel welcome, at ease, comfortable – not like a stranger. Yet he was far from hostile. Rather he appeared to be a cold fish.

'Young son of Lennox, I'm glad to hear that your mother

does well. A fine flower of our ancient stock. Commend me to her, won't you,' he said in a rust-coated voice. If he smiled it was impossible to tell: the lower half of his face was lost in thick, sandy-red hair. 'I'm sorry that the Court's not here for your arrival. You'll have only the company of some old men and servants until we can speed you to the queen at Wemyss.'

'Wee-eems?' he asked.

'A pretty place over the river. But if you've a mind to it, I'm sure Robert will be happy to play host to you for a spell until you've sent word to your father of your arrival. You'll be needing fresh horses too?'

'That would be kind, cousin.' He did not think aureate language and easy-going charm would impress Morton. Randolph spoke up again. 'I have a team of horses stabled. You are welcome to them. As I said, we must show kindness to the needy. They are good horses. Oh, certainly this weather displeases them and with so few people here their welfare is probably not well handled, but –'

'Thank you, Master Randolph.'

'It is no trouble I assure you. But I must second Morton's invitation to honour us with your esteemed company. It would also do us a service. I hope to entreat our royal hostess to consider her marriage to our own mistress's candidate, and you are, I hear, great friends with the Earl of Leicester.' Well, thought Darnley, aren't you well-informed. 'You can join me in deciding how best to bring off the matter. I have some ideas. Her Majesty must be assured of his lordship's very good qualities. You can help me there. He is a great man. I have met him, you know. Did he ever mention me? I suppose not. Though he esteems good service – oh, he demands service unparalleled. And of course –' The man was a chatterer. If he composed his dispatches as he spoke, Darnley thought wickedly, his mistress would have little time to be a haughty bitch to her courtiers. Probably she had sent him knowing his blabber would accomplish nothing but delay, keeping Leicester by her side. He interrupted his ramblings.

'I'm at your disposal, Master Randolph.' He smiled again. His cheeks were beginning to develop a tic from the enforced glee. So Randolph was still aiming at pushing Leicester's suit to Mary. That would be something to watch. Seeing the man's project founder might even be fun.

'So we might detain you a space, Harry?' asked Robert.

'If you will have me, I will be glad to enjoy your hospitality, and will look forward to the day when I can repay it.'

***

Darnley spent the next four days getting acquainted with the charms Holyroodhouse, its majestic apartments, red-rimmed doors, reception rooms and, when muffled against the cold, its sprawling grounds. Robert Stewart proved to be a fountain of knowledge on the history of the place. He enjoyed recounting it with pride, undoubtedly due to the rich income he received from its lands, which had been granted to him by Queen Mary. He may have been the product of one her father's mistresses, Robert said, but the queen rewarded family loyalty, bastardy or no bastardy. Darnley liked him immensely.

The pretty palace had been built in front of a much older abbey. It had been modernised by James IV generations ago and the royal apartments had been a project of the queen's – and his own – father, Robert explained. But the palace had been damaged during the bellicose Henry VIII's assault on Edinburgh and there had been damage to some other parts of the building during the recent religious debates. Robert carefully skirted his lecture on the latter.

There was something different about Holyroodhouse in comparison to the palaces of England, thought Darnley, and it was not just the relative quiet of a building without a Court in residence. If it lacked the flamboyant glitz of Windsor, Richmond, Whitehall and Placentia, it boasted an immeasurably stately ambience, like a secretive, fairy-tale palace. It was asleep in a deep freeze, waiting to be woken and given life in spring.

During the course of his stay he was introduced to a small number of Scottish lords and retainers, some of whom had heard of his arrival and, not having followed the Court, sought to meet the young Master of Lennox, fresh from England and so near in blood to the queen. He turned the full force of his charm on all comers and was rewarded with glowing reviews.

Amongst them was a curious little monkey of a man named David Riccio. He had sidled up to Darnley one afternoon after dinner had been removed from the inhabitants of the palace with great ceremony and introduced himself as 'Signor Ree-zzio', a musician in the queen's household and, he said, Her Majesty's friend and secretary. Riccio had to bend his neck to look him in the eye, and Darnley caught him doing so frequently and surreptitiously. The little man made himself a virtual servant. Darnley, much flattered, accepted the fawning attentions of the swarthy little Piedmontese, enjoying the novelty of having an older man listen to him with rapt attention. Chiefly Riccio provided him with conversation about modern music, about how rebecs were out, and viols were in: it was something he missed had missed sorely since leaving England.

He had time also to speak more with the Earl of Morton, whose manner changed from glacial circumspection to something approaching stiff and formal friendliness. Morton, it seemed, was eager to take the young Darnley under his wing and sought to advise him on the importance of family ties and the absolute, unassailable need for the young and inexperienced to act under the tutelage of older kinfolk.

Darnley listened, torn between an eagerness to be well-thought-of by an older and wiser head and a suspicion of the sandy-whiskered older man's motives in continually beating the drum of guidance, respect and the greatness of Douglas blood.

It was not until the following Saturday that he finally availed himself of Randolph's offer of horses, crossed the river and set out for his first meeting with the Court, which had by now been made aware of his arrival. His planned pretext was his desire to extend his greetings to the royal cousin he had not seen in years before going on to meet his father to discuss the business which had brought him from England.

***

Darnley wiped his nose and removed his wet, mud-splattered riding clothes. The sleet which had fallen throughout his few days at Holyrood had turned again to rain. There was little he could do about his damp hair, but he caught a brief glimpse of himself in a tall looking glass in the castle's entry hall and was pleasantly surprised at the way the exhausting ride through a Scottish winter had brought a red glow to his cheeks. A few of the harried servants bustling about the room cast curious glances up at him and he smiled back.

'Will,' he said, turning to his glum-looking valet, 'go forth and announce to Her Majesty's household that I have arrived.' He wished he had brought one of his father's household heralds northwards to announce him in style, as a man of means and importance. He took another sidelong glance at himself. He would, he decided as Will trooped ahead dragging wet feet, have to do.

The Great Hall of Wemyss Castle was a familiar enough sight – bright tapestries covered its walls and small huddles of well-dressed people were grouped around its rush-strewn floor. As he was announced, these groups made a path down the centre of the hall and every eye turned to him. It was all familiar. At the far end Mary rose from her throne under its canopy and turned a bright gaze towards him. Even from a distance he could see full, crimson lips part in a welcoming smile. For a moment Darnley paused, irresolute, his practised smile frozen and his confident swagger reverting to the awkward, gangly gait of his younger years.

Somehow, he had pictured the Scottish queen as she had been when newly anointed the Queen of France: very young, very graceful, but no more substantial than a fairy. Here, however, she was in her element: the equal – no, the better, of England's proud Elizabeth. Only a few inches shorter than him, perfectly proportioned and wearing a shimmering green, high-necked gown, Mary was dazzling. She stood with her head tilted towards him, her shoulders back. Her hair was a burnished golden brown and the delicately-perfumed air of the room hung about her like a haze. Her almond-shaped, lash-fringed eyes twinkled as she called, 'My Master of Lennox. Harry, my faithful cousin and friend. You are welcome to the Court of Scotland.' Her husky Scots had a musical French lilt to it. She reached her arms out like an actor portraying a beckoning angel in a morality play.

Essaying confidence, he marched forwards and bowed, taking his cap in one hand before reaching forward to kiss hers. This was no Elizabeth. This was no terror. He had intended to do so lasciviously, before turning upwards to give her a knowing look. Yet suddenly the stuff of chivalric romances did not seem appropriate, self-consciousness crept in and the audience of courtiers was a palpable force behind his back, willing him to provide it with intrigue. Instead, he lightly touched her hand with his lips and then looked up into a pale young oval face and warm amber eyes that sparked and flared in the flickering candlelight.

Her smile was unreadable. He had a sudden urge to stretch out his hand, release her hair from its artificial curls and headpiece and brush a strand of it behind her long neck with the back of his hand. If he ever really did have to be married this was exactly the kind of lady who could really make a man proud. All thoughts of this magisterial princess melting at the sight of him faded, and he suddenly felt ashamed of them – and above all glad that he had not confided his supreme self-confidence in his ability to melt a lady's heart to anyone else.

'My lord,' she pouted, 'are you not ashamed to stand nude-headed before me?' Darnley stared dumbly. She giggled, not unkindly. 'It is the custom in this realm that our great lords may keep their hats on in our presence. She leant forward, wrenched the cap from his hand, and set it on his head. 'Continue.'

'I did not,' said Darnley, his voice breaking. He recovered, buoyed by her smile. 'Most gracious sovereign Majesty, I am overjoyed to lay eyes on you again. I bring greetings from the Court of our mutual cousin, Her Majesty the Queen Elizabeth of England.' He was unsure how to continue but was mercifully rescued by Mary's interjection.

'Oh, my sweet sister, Elizabeth. I love her well. We write often, you know. She is very kind to advise her sister queen on many issues. I hesitate to choose a gown without knowing it would please my dear cousin. How does she?'

'Her Majesty is well, my lady, and wishes the same for you.'

'And does Her Majesty send news, or does she send my beautiful cousin Harry only to write me poetry and ornament the Court of Scotland as he has ornamented England?'

Once again he was at a loss. The flirtations of a queen, especially a Dowager Queen of France, were to be expected, but he did not like being caught out, nor being out-matched by a woman whose education in the arts of courtly love were superior to his own. Mary was, he noted, at least direct and engaging.

'Your Majesty, I come because the gracious lady Elizabeth has restored my father to favour and allowed our coming north into your own dominions. I could not set foot in Scotland, however, without paying homage to the most beautiful and mighty princess on this island.'

That was poor, Darnley knew, but he hoped the implied comparison with Elizabeth would win favour with the elegant Scottish queen. Women, he reasoned, set great store by weighing up their own beauty against that of their rivals. Somewhere behind him a distinguished gentleman in English-cut hose, who had been milling around a crowd close to the queen's stage, raised his head and an eyebrow. Mary's eyes danced, her little white teeth showing in a grin. She caught sight of the man and called over to him, 'My Lord of Moray, come and greet the Master of Lennox.'

Moray. So this was another of Mary's illegitimate half-brothers, and how different from Robert. He was tall – though not, Darnley thought with satisfaction, as tall as himself – and he carried with him an air of stately elegance. Why, he is the kind of man that portraiture was made for, thought Darnley distractedly; he looks like a Roman general who has stepped out of history and into the present. Like Morton Moray had a cool, calculating gaze, but it had a stronger appearance of intelligence and nobility. When he spoke it was with a clear, refined accent that seemed to come directly through his long nose.

'Lord Darnley,' he said, not subscribing to the Scottish form of address. 'Your good reputation precedes you and I am pleased to note that you do it justice.'

'Thank you.' He was unsure what to say to this semi-royal brother. The man discomfited him. The queen, still brimming with a pleasant vibrancy, spared him the trouble.

'Harry, mon cher, shall you be staying with us?'

'Madam, I would be honoured to spend the night. But I must away tomorrow to find my father, who wrote me at Holyrood that he's staying with family at Dunkeld.'

'Ah, so you come and go like Apollo across the sky. Your father is a charming man. I hope you will both attend on us after you have seen to business.'

'Again, madam, it would be an honour to attend so fair and generous a queen for as long as time endures.' Moray's jaws tautened as he digested Darnley's words.

'You turn my head, my gentle cousin,' she said, cocking it to one side. 'It has been a long space since I was flattered with such gorgeous words. But you must be tired. Travelling in this cold saps the energy. Your face is quite red. Please see my steward and he will find you apartments. You must ask him for refreshments also.'

She extended her hand once more and he took it in his. It was warm, the fingers pale and the nails exquisitely shaped. He bent over it reverently and made his farewell before backing out of the room. Mary watched him, her right cheek dimpled in a smile, her speculative gaze lingering unashamedly on his legs. Moray watched him too, one hand resting arrogantly on his hip, an eyebrow arched in something between a noble sneer and a look of amusement.

So that was the Queen of Scots who had haunted his fantasies for months. Not a shy, blushing princess trapped in an inimical, barren Court, but a glowing jewel in a small and slightly shabby crown. Here was a woman of some passion and personality. Here was a Gallic Scotswoman quite unlike the haughty cynic who sat spinning at the centre of England's web. The thought of getting to know her was exciting, and Darnley knew that his indulgent fantasies would take on a new complexion as he sought sleep in Wemyss Castle that night.

***

He rose early the next morning having woken several times in the night, as he often did when being awake offered exciting opportunities to allow his imagination free rein. The queen, he learned, was already hearing Mass, and his early start would mean missing the opportunity to see her that day. As he was giving instructions to his attendants in the entrance hall of the castle, however, a less welcome face appeared.

Sir James Melville, the diplomat who had seemingly taken great pleasure in ruining his life at the English Court during Leicester's investiture, approached him as he prepared to take his leave of the Court. It was all he could do not to spit at the man, who spoke in his customarily smooth manner.

'My lord,' he said, raising his hands, palms facing Darnley, 'I am glad to see that you finally escaped the English queen's realm.'

'Melville,' he nodded. He had no intention of wasting charm or friendliness on this insect who buzzed between royal households, stirring up trouble for men who had done nothing to offend him.

'Ah, I see you have conceived a grievance against me.'

'A grievance?' exclaimed Darnley, his anger flaring. 'A grievance because you insulted me in front of the English Court? A grievance because you made a shipwreck of my honour? A grievance because you made me a laughing stock? You are damned right I have a grievance!'

'I do not blame you. But allow me grace to explain a little and you shall understand better of me.' His tone was not quite wheedling, but it sounded contrite enough. He had been anticipating this meeting for some time.

'Explain, sir.'

'You are, my lord, an esteemed personage. Within you flows

the blood royal of two great nations. No impertinent remark can touch one of your heritage. But in your importance lies the reasoning behind my actions.' Taken in by the flattery, he inclined his head for Melville to continue. He did, choosing his words carefully. 'The Queen of England knows your worth.' Darnley tutted and rolled his eyes. 'Indeed, she is always sensitive to the power of those near her in blood, and never more so than on that day, when you bore the ceremonial sword before her as the first man in the kingdom.'

'And so you desired to cut that man down?'

'In a sense.' Darnley's eyebrows furrowed. He had not been expecting Melville to admit that. 'Do you believe Elizabeth would have permitted you to come north had I agreed with her that my own royal mistress would have favoured you as a suitor? No; that would be bootless. And it was imperative that you come.'

Confused, Darnley mumbled. He had fostered ideas of humbling and humiliating this man, or riding in to Scotland, securing the queen's favour and enjoying a threatening power over him, like Damocles' dangling sword. In all good stories the wronged hero got his revenge on the snake-tongued churl. Yet his speech sounded sincere. And, after all, was he not now in Scotland as a result of his embarrassment in England?

Sensing that he was making headway Melville quickly continued. 'If you do not believe me, my lord, I can perhaps offer something in the way of both proof and apology for the impetuous manner of my … well, my *reducing* of your status in Elizabeth's eyes. I will make bold. I intend to do what I can to advance your cause here. No, you need not deny it; I know that you must be here with some hopes of recovering the royal rights to which your birth entitles you. I think you will be good for Scotland. *If* you wed yourself to its cause in the world, and its cause alone.'

Darnley raised his chin. Perhaps he had been wrong. This man, loathsome as his behaviour might have been and his occupation certainly was, seemed earnest enough. He nodded politely, a signal for Melville to continue to make his case.

'We need a man in charge here. It is my belief – my *suspicion,* based on good counsel – that the English queen cannot produce heirs. Yes, I have sources: ladies close to her body. And she could be carried off by the illnesses borne on London's foul airs at any time. Our queen is healthy and vigorous and needs a husband, and a husband who is strong enough to fight for Scotland's advancement in the world and give us heirs whose rights across this island will be undisputed. We have too many here who would have our kingdom another pearl in Elizabeth's crown, provided she gives them the money and power they crave over their own people. It is rumoured that some of these advise our sovereign and would advise her that the two realms be joined in a band not easily dissolved. Any such yoking together would leave our nation at the mercy of its larger neighbour and like to be swallowed up.'

Mollified, he deigned to favour Melville with a cautious smile, gleaming white. As usual when he offered someone a smile, he got one in return. 'I am prepared to trust you in this, Master Melville. Your words have moved me. They make sense.'

'That is all I ask. But perhaps I can offer you a little more.' He looked around the hall. It was relatively empty; those who were not at religious services were busy with household duties. 'The queen made it quite clear to me after you retired last night that she is well disposed towards you, not only as a good kinswoman should be but as a young, unmarried lady might be. She finds you one of the most well-proportioned men she has ever met, and can scarcely believe that she has never given you the thoughts that a vigorous young man of your standing deserves. Persevere, my lord. Persevere and you might have all.'

With this, Melville bowed, rapped him lightly on the shoulder and retreated. Well, thought Darnley, from a caustic enemy to a friend in so short a time, and all it took was the favour of a delightful woman who had been married only once and to a weak, sickly child. A husband who will fight for Scotland: a man whose loyalties will be to the advancement of this northern kingdom. Of course he might be that man.

'Will,' he called. 'Will Taylor!' His valet came loping out of a window casement from which he had been eavesdropping, with a broadening grin.

'Are the horses ready? We're leaving,' said Darnley. He could not resist adding, for his own benefit, 'you see, absence and a little distance knit hearts closer together.' As he left Wemyss, the word 'persevere' rang in his head.

9

The Earl of Lennox was in apoplexies of joy at the sight of his son in Scotland. He was full of questions: how was Lady Lennox? Had he any news of Charlie? What did he think of the country? Above all, however, he wanted to know again and again how he had fared in his brief visit to Court. What had he said? How had the queen reacted?

The line of questioning was so tiresome that Darnley, despite the guilt that withholding information from his father gave him, refrained from sharing his chat with Melville. It would, he knew, only lead to another barrage of questions, and he'd had quite enough already. The only useful information he got in return was a warning about Moray. He had been right to be suspicious of the man. According to his father Moray was a forward whoreson who believed himself to be the real ruler of Scotland, the accident of his birth being an inconvenient fact that could be effaced by his use of Mary as a figurehead. With the assistance of the services of Scotland's principal secretary, Maitland of Lethington – a man who, according to Lennox, was a veritable Machiavelli dressed like a boring legal clerk – Moray had the run of the commonweal. Each kept a finger perpetually in the air, ready to gain mastery of whichever wind blew. Mary, for her part, provided the glamour.

As expected the administration surrounding his father's recovery of his Glasgow estates hadn't really required his presence, although he was able to provide his signature to a small pile of legal documents that he didn't bother reading. He sat at a broad wooden desk in Dunkeld, a Stewart family stronghold owned by the Earl of Atholl, a bear of man whose tremendous, musclebound frame was belied by his friendliness. He scratched around with his quill, dipping it aimlessly in and out of ink, trying to think of someone to write to. Now that he had arrived in Scotland and the thrill of a long journey was over, loneliness threatened to creep in again.

Inspiration hit him. He began composing a letter of gratitude to Leicester for so successfully persuading Elizabeth to give him temporary leave, which he was beginning to believe might really extend into permanence if he had the courage to persevere. He sat back after finishing it and admired the sincerity of his thanks to his 'good brother and friend'. He had taken extra care and the letter looked beautiful. He was, he fancied, a very accomplished writer when he set his mind to it. Writing, however, left him out of sorts. Words laid out on a page, no matter how beautifully, were a poor substitute for real conversation. No matter which rhetorical tricks and literary quirks one employed, a lifeless block of words could never really construct or capture presence. He really would have to find friends in Scotland. Why else had he ever wanted the freedom to enjoy life if not to share that enjoyment with other people?

His father intruded on his musings and caught sight of the letter. 'Writing to Leicester? Very good. Always worth keeping up with the competition.'

'He is my friend, father.'

'Aye, aye. But a man in your position cannot afford to such friends. What you need is a wife, someone who can have your trust and won't dare to betray you.'

'Yes, father.'

'I hope you haven't become too comfortable here.'

'Comfortable *here*? You jest, surely.' He looked around at the bare stone walls.

'Less of that – Scotland is not all palaces and modern luxuries.'

'I know. Anyway, I have only been here one night. What now?'

'Now we strike whilst the iron is hot. The Court is returning to Edinburgh and you and I will be part of it.'

As welcome as leaving the Spartan conditions at Dunkeld would be, and as eager as he was to see Mary and her lively Court again, he sighed. Freedom and liberty he wanted, but being a knight on a chessboard was exhausting.

'Well, if we are to make good speed and reach it, we had better make haste.'

Darnley sealed up his letter and took it with him to send from Edinburgh. He thought of Leicester, whose unwanted marriage with Mary was being pursued by that high-toned snob Randolph. Leicester had warned him not to marry without at least hope of love. Love, he had once said, was like a growing thing – it needed a spark of life, and thereafter to be nurtured and tended to prevent it from dying. Leicester himself had professed that his relationship with the Queen of Scots, whom he had never seen, had no spark to make it bloom. Darnley, who had seen her, wondered if their propinquity in the Court would provide a hothouse.

***

Having rejoined the Court – and how welcome did Mary make father and son on the short journey across the river – Darnley found himself installed once again in Holyroodhouse in a fine room in the southern range. As he had imagined, the sleepy building had awoken at the call of its sparkling mistress. It was refreshing it was to find a Court so open. Though formality reigned, with Mary at its core there was a cosiness and friendliness that Elizabeth's Court had lacked.

In almost constant attendance was Signor Riccio whom, it seemed, Mary had appointed to keep Darnley unobtrusively stocked with money. Embarrassingly he had no income of his own. His straitened finances and reliance on handouts from his father were, he suspected, a source of great scorn and amusement for Randolph.

Riccio's low-profile movement of money from the Privy Purse into Darnley's coffers, in order that he might continue to delight the queen, thus had an extra spice. Randolph, he heard, was furious, and absolutely desperate to discover the source of his loathed compatriot's funds. Unsuccessful, he simply had to watch in seething silence as Darnley's relationship with Mary blossomed whilst his own attempts at matchmaking between the queen and an absent and uninterested Leicester made him look increasingly buffoonish. This made Darnley laugh even more than the old iron-beard's covert attempts – related with glee by Riccio – to seduce the queen's ladies-in-waiting.

As he walked back to his apartments after a supper party with Mary one night, it was to Darnley's surprise that he found Riccio beneath a staircase, piling straw mattresses on a chest.

'What ever can you be doing?'

'Ah, I'm but a poor musician, my lord. I bunk where I can, not where I list' said Riccio, shuffling his feet sheepishly.

'Like a common attendant in a country house? But you are a friend of the queen's.' He was struck by pity. In his childhood homes it had been common for lowly guests to bed down wherever they could find a convenient spot – beds were rare and expensive– but this was a great palace.

'And I shall wager in the chest is everything you own. And as a consequence, everything I own.'

'Sì, my lord.'

'Well, I cannot leave you sleeping under a staircase. It is unmeet. Come with me.'

'You are a kind boy, and a very fine one, sir, very fine.'

He escorted the embarrassed little man, still clutching his things, to his own apartment. Mary was certainly not mean with Darnley; he had been given a great bed equal to those he had lain in at home and at the English Court. Four people could have fit quite comfortably in one. In fact, his brother had occasionally woken up from nightmares, eluded his sleeping nurses and climbed in beside him. Often Darnley didn't even realise until he spotted the little bump in the mornings. With much gratitude and effusive, Italianate thanks, Riccio accepted the offer of sharing a real bed. As they walked to Darnley's room he turned to the humble musician, who moved with a stoop. The poor fellow's years of deference must have left him unable to attain his meagre height.

'I must say, it is good to meet someone who is as much of an alien as I.'

'An alien, sir?'

'Foreign. Different. I am still trying to find my place.'

'Ah ... You feel you are ... *different*?' There was a strange, searching look in Riccio's eyes as he latched onto the word.

'Naturally, being born out of the realm. Tell me, Signor Riccio, what think you of your new home? How do you like Scotland?'

'Oh. I see. It is a fine country,' he answered, the sharpness in his gaze fading. 'The queen is kind to me. She is a sweet, generous lady.'

'Well said. You do not miss Italy?'

'I wander, sir. I go everywhere. Piedmont, Savoy, Nice, all Europe. I'm used to travel. But I do miss my family. I send my brother money. It is all for him and my mother, what I do. They have little. Our name fades.'

'You have a brother?'

'Sì. Younger than myself. Him I miss.'

'I am possessed of one myself. And I miss the little dunce.'

'The cost of bettering oneself, eh?'

'Bettering oneself? You mean you hope to improve their lot

or your own?'

Riccio paused mid-step, his brow furrowed in concentration. 'These are the same in this new world. This country is beautiful. Its people are friendly. It deserves just governors and wise rule. I hope one day to do what I can to help it achieve greatness and bring honour and wealth to my family. It is a fine thing for a man to be what he makes himself rather than what he is born.' Darnley nodded politely but absently. A man was what he was born to be. They took the rest of the short trip to his room in silence, each thinking his own thoughts.

As he lay under the covers that night – sleep was as elusive as ever – he felt Riccio's hand wander over and rest on his buttocks, squeezing them gently. Darnley's eyes shot open and his mouth went dry. Gently but firmly he reached down, took hold of Riccio's wrist and removed his hand.

He should have thought of just such a possibility. Perhaps he had given the wrong impression, or perhaps the servile Riccio had actually thought that he was expected to pay for the luxury of a bed for the night, the poor wretch. Such things were not unheard of. Leicester had warned him before about the proclivities of men would take to passionate extremes the love needed for friendship to flourish. 'Do not think this unmeet,' he had said, 'and do not let it frighten you, but there are men at this Court who fear and dislike women, and still others who worry that consorting with women will lead to disgrace. Instead, they will try and take their pleasure elsewhere. It might be that some of these men fancy you have a handsome face and will try and take it of you.'

When asked how to discourage these attentions, Leicester had casually told him that breaking the arm of the would-be seducer usually sufficed – but that the warning might be enough. The thought of breaking Riccio's arm was beyond the pale, but nevertheless he was thankful that nothing else was attempted. In the morning neither acknowledged the incident, and if Riccio was either embarrassed or angry at being rebuffed, he never showed it. Thereafter things continued as normal, with the musician as prepared as ever to promote his pursuit of Mary.

Pleasant weeks were spent in this pursuit, undertaken against the glittering backdrop of Holyroodhouse. He began to bring gifts – nothing ostentatious, but little love tokens. It was how things were done, he knew, in France. She delighted in them all: rings, gloves, perfumed handkerchiefs. He came upon the queen strolling in the Gallery one day and professed that he had lost something, and had she seen it? 'What is it?' she asked with concern.

'My heart,' he answered. She giggled and pretended to hit him with a handkerchief.

He paid court also to her gentlewomen – that phalanx of ladies which surrounded a female monarch, defending her against men and discouraging over-amorous suitors. Bribing these ladies with gifts – and money – earned him knowledge of Mary's tastes. It was a remarkable thing, he thought, that it was much easier to know a woman through the gossip of her friends than from her own lips. One of her ladies – at the cost of a pair of gloves – told him the queen liked nothing more than dogs. Another – for a brooch – that she liked nothing more than dancing. For a length of lace he was assured that her abiding love was her family. A purse of small coins won him the news that she hated politics, whilst a purse of larger coins rewarded him with the guarantee that she was mistress of the art of policy, a graduate of the French Court, and valued nothing more. If any, all, or none was true, he did not hear it from the queen herself, who, butterfly-like, evaded his questioning.

One day he playfully broached the idea of marriage. He even produced a ring given him by his father in the hopes that it would one day appear on the queen's finger. It was a pretty thing, heavy gold and very old. It had been in the Lennox family for decades. She affected great offence, turning on him vehemently. Why, she asked, would she be interested in marriage? Why must a good friendship be ruined by talk of marriage? Would one of his rank have been so bold as to approach the Queen of England so? When he tentatively responded that he was the nearest prince of the blood in England she had stormed off as though he had slapped her, her ladies flocking to her with tuts, sighs and shaking heads.

Afterwards she rejected his company for two whole days, sending only a message to forbear his suit. He affected an air of tragic loss. After that brief frostiness she once more linked arms with him when she saw him taking a morning walk in the palace gardens and behaved as though she had never met a man more charming, desirable or suitable as a partner. It was all part of the pleasant dance of courtship.

Neither made any attempt to know the mind of the other, so content were they to enjoy constant revelry and a shallow romance. At times it seemed to him that there was little else of Mary that was knowable. Her preferred topic of conversation was Darnley's life and background, which he was happy to impart. What was life like at the English Court? What were England's customs? What was the queen like? How did she speak to her ministers? How did she treat his mother? How did she treat him? Did she show him especial favour as her natural cousin? The woman seemed fascinated by the smallest details of Elizabeth's attitudes towards everything – especially him. 'I am like a criminal being interrogated,' he said, and she made a little moue. 'But what a happy prisoner.' The lady had a remarkable talent for making a man seem popular, like he was the very centre of things, like his words and thoughts were valuable.

The one Scot he knew would not be susceptible was Moray. Mary's half-brother certainly affected friendliness. In fact, he had been seeking Darnley out, giving him constant advice on what to say and do, on where to go and when. At first it was welcome, and the prospect of a Scottish Leicester briefly flared in Darnley's mind, but it quickly became irritating beyond measure. The man was just too frosty. His every look cried out, 'I will never approve of you; your mind is beneath mine.' Yet Riccio – ever vigilant to rumour and happy to relate it back – assured him that Moray was happy only as long as Mary and Darnley proved tractable, obedient children who would conform to his wishes and allow him to continue to frame Scotland's policies in accordance with directives from Elizabeth, of whom he was said to be in frequent correspondence and in great admiration.

In early March Robert Stewart was eagerly – he did everything eagerly – showing him a map of the kingdom which was spread out across a huge desk in a Holyroodhouse antechamber, a candlestick at each corner acting as a paperweight. He had pointed out the area of Darnley itself, near Glasgow in the west. To the far northeast was Inverness, and beyond that the country grew increasingly barbarous, full of fierce-tongued wild men, mountains and lochs haunted by water-horses. A strong hand would be needed if ever the whole of Scotland was to be brought into peaceful unity, as all strong nations must be. Darnley's eyes flitted from place to place, from town to town, following rivers and ancient highways.

'And where lie the Earl of Moray's estates?' he asked.

Robert dutifully pointed them out, with much cross referencing and drawing his finger back and forth across the map. He had to stretch over the table to show it all.

'All of that? One man owns so much of Scotland? Ye Gods, he must have made himself richer than Croesus off the Roman Church's old lands. Surely that is too much for any one subject.' Moray, he thought, must be one of the richest men in Scotland. No wonder he was such a committed supporter of the Reformation.

Robert's reaction was unexpected. He burst into laughter, thumping his hand on the map so hard the unlit candles wobbled in their sticks.

'Too much! Aye, and maybe it is at that. You wait till I tell him he owns "too much" of Scotland, Harry. He'll rage and won't that be a fine sight! My brother can't take to bastardy. Doesn't realise it gives you all the good cheer and no need to herd the vipers. The more he can get his hands on, the better he feels!' He laughed again. 'Too much, man. You're too much!'

Darnley frowned. He hadn't been joking. And he disliked it when people laughed at him. Furthermore, he wasn't entirely sure that Moray would agree with his brother that it was a witty observation rather than a criticism of his monopoly on a country that he had been treating as his personal fiefdom.

***

Darnley had been right to worry about how Moray would take his words and he cursed Robert without any real venom; the man was too innocent and naïve. Still, his comments caused ructions. Mary begged him to apologise, which he did with glib insincerity, but Moray not only avoided his company, he cut him dead if he happened to pass him at Court.

Many courtiers, sensing a drama, began to organise themselves into factions, some according to principle, others according to ancient grudges against men with principles. The Douglases, as kinsmen of Darnley's mother, naturally fell into line behind the Court's rising star. This gave him the saturnine Morton, whose support he was happy to have, given his earldom and the fact that he had been his first would-be mentor when he had arrived in Edinburgh. Moreover, he sensed that Morton was not a man he would want to have against him in anything.

Backing him up also was the Earl of Ruthven, a cadaverous old scarecrow; the Earl of Atholl, who had hosted him at Dunkeld (and who clapped him on the back with a great paw for showing up Moray); and Lord Lindsay, a Protestant who was married to a Douglas and disliked the extent of Moray's religious zeal. On that Darnley had to agree. During Moray's attempt at appearing to be a caring mentor in Darnley's first weeks in Edinburgh, he had invited him to hear the famous cleric John Knox thunder a sermon. Darnley had been nonplussed by the booming, doom-laden prophecies expounded by the unpleasant preacher. His service was neither the theatrical, mystical performance of his familiar Catholicism nor the trite readings of Elizabeth's clergymen. Knox preferred to frighten. These men each pledged their loyalty to the younger man and gave him confidence that his pursuit of Mary and Scotland was no longer a dream to be chased solo, but one to be cheered on by those who had bets riding on it.

In March the tide turned perceptibly in his favour. A letter arrived from Elizabeth, and on receipt of it Mary summoned him to her red-and-gold decorated bedchamber, reached through the outer and inner chambers at the top of the public staircase. There was nothing sinister in it; she did, after all, have a curiously French practice of allowing private council meetings to go on in her bedchamber, unlike Elizabeth, who reserved hers for her ladies to piece her together. He found her collapsed on her seat under its royal canopy, red-eyed, her head in her hands. The jubilant and animated mood of recent weeks had reversed.

'Sweetheart, what has happened? Are you uncles harmed?' He knew she was sensitive to any family news, and her French uncles were never done bombarding her with gloom. She was so upset she could barely speak, the words catching in her throat.

'Elizabeth ... England ... she ... has ... fooled ... me ... ohh,' she choked.

'Now, it cannnot be as bad as all that.'

Only the queen's constant companions, four ladies also called Mary, were present. They looked at him as one, all wearing the same frown, as though he had said something incredibly stupid.

He went to her, taking her in an awkward embrace, and rather than try and draw sense out of her he extracted the damp missive from her with one hand and began to read it aloud. She broke into fresh paroxysms of grief, as though hearing Elizabeth's words somehow conjured her frosty presence into the room. Fighting the urge to roll his eyes, he read on. After months of dangling the carrot of succession to the English throne as long as Mary acted on her marital advice Elizabeth, it seemed, had grown weary of the game. Now she claimed that she would not recognise Mary's right to succeed her unless she, Elizabeth, decided definitively whether she would marry, and with whom. It was a neat trick. The English queen would undoubtedly drag out her own marriage negotiations for years before settling on a candidate and had thus strung Mary along knowing that she would be unable to choose a husband until she herself had made some public pronouncement of her own intentions. What a crafty coney-catcher Elizabeth was.

'Oh, sweetheart. That withering beldam wants to keep you as joyless and lonely as she. But forbear distress; this is not the end of your hopes.' She looked up at him dully, a child seeking comfort. Her eyes, a bloodshot amber, were trusting. 'Do you not see, now that she has made this plain she has set you free. There need be no more hoping and wishing that the great Elizabeth will approve or advise – her approval and advice mean nothing. No ruler of Scotland should wait on approval from London before they can marry, any more than they do before they can wipe their backside.' He squeezed her and she smiled. 'You are now free to do as you wish. Freedom is always important.'

'Freedom,' she repeated, meekly. 'C'est important. I shall taste it. I think I shall like it.'

Her racking, convulsive sobs slowed. She smiled up at him. It was the first time he had seen her look less than lovely, her face puffed and liquid at her nostril. He immediately felt a little ashamed that this was the first thought to run through his mind as she looked at him, and he held her a little more tightly as if to excuse his ugly thoughts. Her Marys pretended to be suddenly interested in her private apartments' tapestries. Each knew what this closeness meant. Soon the world would know the path on which their mistress appeared to be setting her foot.

10

When he saw Mary the next day she was a changed woman again. Both the girlish, flirtatious princess and the grief-stricken tragic heroine were gone. She was taking the Court to Stirling Castle to the northwest, because the airs of Edinburgh – and the news carried on them – had ceased to please her. Darnley was to ride at the vanguard of the procession. This was mixed news: since his arrival in Scotland he had been battling with a cold exacerbated, he was sure, by the constant toing and froing in the short days of winter. Now that they had lengthened into spring – a time, he reminded himself, for beginnings – he could only hope that the necessary ride across the hilly country would blow the lingering chill out of him.

Stirling reminded him, happily, of Edinburgh in miniature. Its castle, with palatial apartments liberally painted in an eye-catching king's gold, clung to its own tall crag. The little town lay below it, a clutch of buildings nestled under the protection of a golden eagle. Unlike Edinburgh, however, the modern palace was not across town but housed within the sturdy walls of the castle itself. Scrubbed stone walkways and crenelated ramparts gave an illustrious façade to well-furnished, carpeted and brightly-coloured inner chambers. The royal party arrived at the end of March and breathed life into rooms that could rival the best of France's rural chateaux.

Darnley, the queen and the Court had barely settled into life within the walls of Stirling – a steady round of Masses in the mornings, enormous dinners, and some afternoon riding or indoor entertainment – when he collapsed in the castle courtyard, his legs buckling and his head suddenly overcome with lightness, a team of servants racing to his aid.

'Bonté divine! His face ... il est très malade.' The words drifted into his consciousness as if from a great distance. It was a man's voice, heavily accented. Darnley struggled to hang on to reality but felt himself losing his grip again. 'No danger of death, but sure to cause a high fever' chased him as he faded. He did not have the will to open his eyes and see where he was, or who was talking to whom. He only knew that his body was hot and shivering and a strange, maddening itch was breaking out on his face, neck, armpits and groin. His arms were too leaden to scratch himself; it was all he could do to lapse back into unconsciousness.

When he finally came to his first thoughts were that he had somehow caught the plague which had ravaged London for years and must have blown north to Scotland, Death chasing him again. He cried and whimpered at the thought, drawing his legs up to his chest. He was swaddled in bedclothes in his own room, the windows shuttered. Several of his attendants came at the sound of his wakening. They told him that the queen's personal physician had examined him, and it was only a minor case of measles. But none of them seemed able to look at him directly. He demanded a mirror and when he saw his reflection he screamed.

***

Trying to sleep that night was an ordeal, the horror of what he had seen in the mirror raw. Violent headaches began to assault him and the physician was again sent for. Darnley was provided with a quantity of some strong liquor which succeeded in knocking him out.

He dreamt that he was walking through a tiny ornamental garden next to a fast-flowing river. It felt strange, the atmosphere oppressive and foreign, the air ancient. The sky was a dark purple, with moonlight eerily illuminating the vague shapes of carved statues. He followed a narrow, winding path between them, noticing with rising fear than they resembled waxen funeral effigies, oddly moulded into sitting and kneeling stances, heads bent downwards as though in prayer. Strange, long-leaved plants sprouted between the uneven cobblestones, spreading long, dying tendrils around his ankles.

With horror, he realised that what surrounded him were not statues, nor were they effigies. This was no garden of sculptures; it was a cemetery in which the corpses were not encased in winding sheets, buried in unmarked graves and forgotten, but were on display, twisted perversely into their seated and standing positions. He wanted to be out of it, to escape, even just to find sanctuary in the church that must belong to this grotesque place. Trying to stick to the winding path, he bumped into one of the propped-up corpses and it fell forward to embrace him with fish-like limbs. As he shoved it off in revulsion it fell to the side and dislodged its neighbour, which fell forward too, arms outstretched, smooth, slimy, rotten flesh brushing against him. What had first seemed like faces of marble or wax were revealed to be swollen and grey-green, with leering, lipless smiles and eyes that looked at him with rapt blindness. He woke up moaning, sweat pouring down his red-spotted face, his back and his thighs.

The next day Mary came to visit him and at first he refused to see her. His burning face was thick with ugly, weeping spots. But she insisted, and neither he nor his attendants wished to refuse the queen. His illness, he thought bitterly, could not have been more inopportune, when their friendship had been blossoming so much that it had really seemed the start of something substantial. And so she was permitted access to his sickroom.

She made no mention of his blotchy complexion. Instead she fussed over him, full of concern, enquiring about his night's sleep and the medical prognostication – two whole weeks in bed at least – and then put on the mask of light-hearted gaiety she had worn when he had first arrived at her Court. She settled herself down on a chair by his bed, her hands clasped demurely on her lap.

'My brother Moray continues to sulk. I do wonder that he did not take your apology in good part. Robert told him you spoke in jest. It is really too bad of him.'

'Um.'

'And little Riccio is very busy here – he sends his regard and heartily bids you feel better soon. He wishes you to join him in a game of tennis. Do you think you will be up to tennis soon?'

'Um.'

'Oh, and you know Randolph?' He mumbled sulkily in the affirmative. 'Yes, of course you do. Well, I do believe the old fox is trying to make love to my own Mary Seton. He bores her ceaselessly.' She nodded to emphasise the scandal.

That was interesting. So Riccio had been right and the English ambassador really was desirous to cast aside his pretensions and seduce the queen's ladies. It was always useful to know what was hidden behind men's public faces. 'And on the subject of Randolph, I am afraid we are neither of us his favourite people.'

'Why is that, your Grace?' he asked, speaking properly for the first time, still conscious of the workings of his face under its outbreak. Talking almost felt like it would pop spots and lead to more weeping sores.

'Because, my lord, I have graciously decided to accept your suit.' She spoke whilst looking up coyly from under thick, lowered lashes. He could think of nothing to say, and his mouth hung open stupidly. 'Bonté divine! Is that any way to celebrate the acceptance of your betrothed?' She pursed her lips playfully. Still he could not understand what has happening; it was too sudden. 'My answer, mon coeur, is yes.'

'Your ... Mary? Can this be true? Am I still in fever?'

'Non. I assure you, this is the wisest course of action. Our cousin Elizabeth and her man Randolph may think and do as they list. The sovereign Queen of Scots shall not play their games. One queen has as much right to accept the suit of her man as another. I am not made for widowhood and have fashioned my heart to you. I now humbly accept your offer of marriage, and will enter into the contract with you most willingly.'

'Oh, sweetheart,' he said, drawing out the words. 'This will do more for me than any arts your physician or a whole guild of apothecaries could provide me.'

'I am glad. Alas, I am afraid that we cannot seal this pact with a kiss until you are well.'

They both laughed, the itchy pain forgotten. Instead of kissing they gossiped about the latest intrigues and scandals in Scotland and beyond, discussing the means by which Mary would elevate him to a status befitting alliance with a queen regnant, all of which lifted his spirits.

As she chattered he began to look at her with a new and awesome sense of proprietorship. This attractive woman with her flashing white smile, dimpled cheeks, lavish clothing, elegantly-coiffed hair and easy manner was really going to be his. This princess, a jewel sought by the great princes of Europe, was to be his bride, to do with as he pleased. He alone had drawn her eye and was being offered her crown. All along his mother had been right: kingship was his destiny, and at only nineteen.

The question of Mary's own motivations in choosing him never entered his mind. It was enough that she had done so. There was no reason to try and peer behind the shifting guises of a charming, perplexing lady – she had succumbed to his confident, youthful charm and that was quite enough. The part of the blushing bride-to-be suited her best of all. Still, he thought as they talked, it was curious that neither of them had spoken of love. The thought of bringing it up seemed somehow awkward, embarrassing, even obscene.

When she rose to leave she announced that she would have to play the part of the suitor, taking his hand and brushing it with her lips. That night he slept well, and when he awoke he had almost convinced himself that her visit had been a dream and that waking up in stuffy, itchy discomfort was the only reality. That eased when his attendants addressed him in unusually hushed, reverent tones, and disappeared entirely when Mary, announcing herself, giggling, as 'the king's wife', arrived to see him again that afternoon. She did the same the next day.

As he recovered the pair spent two days of relative intimacy. Darnley's illness and Mary's acceptance of impending marriage to him eliminated the need for games and small talk, and without the ability to ride out the two had only conversation, wit and the mutual charm of youthful exuberance to entertain them. Mary had moved with consummate grace from a hunted young nymph to the dutiful wife of an ill husband and seemed to be revelling in the role.

Letters poured in from the outside world, from all those whom the queen had made privy to her plans. Letter after letter from Lennox arrived, full of bluster, of joy, of the most outrageous flattery, continually begging to see him. Darnley did not linger on whether he would welcome a visit from his father or dread it: the excuse of his illness and subsequent attendance only by servants and his fiancée delayed him having to see the old man for the moment.

On the third day, however, Mary brought news of a much less welcome kind. With professions of sympathy, she broke it to him that his mother and little brother had been imprisoned, the family estates seized by a vengeful Elizabeth, furious at the temerity of one of her subjects in daring to enter marital negotiations without permission.

Further, Elizabeth had warned that unless what she called a foolish, fond caper was ended immediately, both the Countess of Lennox and little Charlie could look forward to punishment of a more permanent kind. The message to Darnley was clear: Elizabeth had been disobeyed. She had his family in her stranglehold and she would not hesitate to squeeze.

***

The pleasant gloss which Mary had painted over his prescribed inactivity was at an end. The knowledge that his mother and innocent brother were likely destined for the Tower of London had bred in him anger and dreams of revenge which his incapacity caused him to release in impotent violent rages, flaring temper the surest means he knew of effacing shattered confidence.

His attendants frequently found themselves chased from the room by flying tankards. The faithful Will Taylor bore the brunt of his master's conniptions, resigning himself to them and praying that putting up with abuse would pay off in the end. When his fellows quailed at the sudden and unwelcome ill treatment, he sighed wearily and encouraged them to take no notice.

The bullying offered Darnley no comfort. When he had shouted himself hoarse those same servants were the only people obliged to listen to his woes and self-pity, and he needed to talk more than he needed to shout.

To take his mind off thoughts of his family languishing at the mercy of Elizabeth he allowed full rein to his fantasies, which were now on their way to becoming reality, albeit with agonising slowness. When he sat at the top table, when his peers were the mighty sovereigns of Europe, only then would he be able to demand his mother and brother's release. Let Elizabeth consider him a wayward subject when he had the full might of kingship behind him. Let that heathenish, bastard daughter of a witch and a musician look down on his untainted royal blood then.

In the meantime, he could do nothing to vent his rage or to advance his cause. He was caged in a sickroom. His apartments had become foul, shuttered as they were against sudden cold blasts. The sour, foetid smell of bodily odour fought against heavy, overly sweet perfumes and spicy unguents, producing a stink that was at least novel in its offensiveness.

Try as he might, he could not blot out even the fouler image of his mother crying with fear as she was rowed to the Tower, the prison she had long claimed nearly drove his father insane. Still worse was the image of Charlie being dragged in the night from his home, treated like a felon, not understanding why, only to be cast into a dungeon in grubby, crooked London. Why hadn't he taken the time on his mad dash to Scotland to call at Settrington and see the boy? He had had from him only infrequent formal letters undoubtedly dictated by a tutor for more months than he cared to remember.

His father was attending to business in his restored Glasgow estates (and undoubtedly posturing as the father of a future king); Riccio had returned to his favourite haunt of Edinburgh after only a brief visit to Stirling; his only conduit to the outside world was Mary. His attendants told him little, suddenly fearful of the rough edge of his tongue and an aim astonishingly accurate for a sick man.

He had no idea what Scotland thought of its prospective king, of undoubted Scottish stock but born and reared in England and attuned to French manners. From the windows of his apartments he could not even see the silent, indifferent town, sitting closed-lipped beneath a rising and setting sun that he was unable to feel on his face and body. Mary was apt to shield him, still engrossed in her role as a protective lover. Her fawning attention lost the charm it had had before the news of his family's arrest. Now he sought to reassert himself, belatedly remembering his own pledge not to be fed and petted by a queen. And yet he found himself trapped within his sickroom, within his own body, once again at the mercy of a powerful woman's favour.

As the second week of his enforced immurement began more unwelcome news was brought to him. The Justice Clerk, whom Mary had told him would confirm his elevation to the Dukedom of Albany – a stepping stone on the road to Scottish kingship – arrived to tell him that he was dreadfully sorry, but there was no question of the ceremony taking place immediately. For his troubles Darnley put a trembling hand on the hilt of his dagger in as deadly and authoritative a gesture as he could muster and announced, 'shit upon my infirmity and your excuses – get out of here!' Shocked, the Clerk pawed at his great, brown beard before fleeing the room in a panic. Darnley laughed stupidly at him, then at himself. Then he caught side of himself in the little mirror: still red but scabbing and swollen. He thrust his dagger into it and little cracks radiated out from the blow. His reflection was lost in the convoluted tangle.

By the end of his second week of confinement his temper had cooled, his anger and frustration replaced with a strange kind of fervid energy. As soon as he was free to leave his sickroom – he was not, he was assured, contagious – he took off alone, riding hard and fast around the bright countryside of Stirling. The spots had disappeared, but his skin remained a smooth, shiny red. It continued to itch but, as far as he was concerned, without the embarrassment of suppurating blemishes his body must be sufficiently healed to be seen in public and to withstand the rigors of a fine Scottish spring day. Like his sickness, the last remnants of winter had finally been shaken off. He breathed in the good, wild smell of the air and closed his eyes. For a moment he was a child again, wandering too far into the woods near the old Lennox home of Temple Newsam; getting lost amidst the trees and streams; wandering and wondering; being found and spanked by his governess, but then petted and hugged when he cried.

But memory was the fragile seat of imagination. He opened his eyes and the illusion dissipated as a cold, hard rain turned the sky grey. He was back in his sickroom after only an hour's riding, once again balling his hands into fists and cursing himself, his room and his indisposition.

Dutifully Mary had continued to visit him despite his rages. She told him, as though he did not know – and in truth he had not given it much thought – that it was crucial that she canvass international support. Her remarriage had been the talk of many Courts, and to announce her choice to be the British queens' mutual cousin would require everything from the acknowledgement of France, where both bride and bridegroom were known, to a dispensation from the Holy Father in Rome. 'But,' she warned, 'our problems are not across the seas. Our problems are here in our kingdom.' Since she had announced her intention to marry the sick young boy who lay festering in a sickroom in Stirling some of the Scottish nobility had begun to murmur. To prevent that murmur developing into a full-throated shout she decided to meet the problem head on.

Once Darnley's appearance, if not his strength, had recovered, she summoned Moray to a meeting in his sickroom. She hoped, she forewarned him, that the sight of the young queen and her innocent husband-to-be would move his sympathy and remove any opposition he was brewing. Darnley did not know whether to roll his eyes or openly tut at her naivety, but he agreed to the meeting all the same.

May arrived before Moray. When he did turn up at Stirling to attend the queen and a supine Darnley – who had adhered to Mary's desire for him to appear as docile and pathetic as possible – he was as unreadable as ever. Mary began the proceedings from a gilt chair by Darnley's bed, close enough for her to reach out and touch him.

'Mon cher frère, you know now it is my intention to marry this man and to make him Scotland's king.'

'I have heard, madam. You know how rumours fly, good and bad, especially on fair winds.' One of Moray's hands leant on a padded hip, half in provocation, half in disinterest. His other arm stretched across the garlanded mantelpiece, a study in practiced coolness. Absently he plucked a flower and began rolling the stem back and forth between his thumb and forefinger.

'And you do not approve?'

'I neither approve nor disapprove. Your choice of husband is yours alone. Though I would think it the privilege of your servants to offer you counsel. I have been a good servant, I think. You have had no cause to doubt me before.'

'Then you shall have no trouble signing a declaration of approval, knowing my choice?'

'Madam, I neither approve nor disapprove. I can sign nothing without having time to devote my mind and prayer to the matter. I am sure you would not have me act in haste.'

'You play with words. You have had time enough. It is your queen's will that you should sign, and *that* is enough. Why … why … the King of *Spain* approves this match. On what grounds can you refuse to approve of the choice of your sovereign?'

'On the grounds, your Majesty, of religion. This matter touches it too near. I cannot in my conscience consent to your marriage with one of whom there is little hope of becoming a true follower of our faith. This man has shown himself to be rather an enemy than a friend of the Kirk.'

'Now cease there, Moray,' said Darnley, sitting up on an elbow, his pretence at continued illness forgotten. 'There is no truth to that. An enemy of the Kirk? Did I not accompany you to hear friend Knox speak?'

'Have you not accompanied the queen to her Catholic Masses?'

'I am permitted by the laws of this nation to have my household worship as I see fit,' put in Mary.

'Indeed you are, madam. But I am aware of no law or act of parliament which allows for a Catholic king to rule here. The commonweal will not have it.' Moray's eyebrow arched smugly.

'Moray, you cannot hide behind the law,' said Darnley. 'You approached me as a friend and now you hate me as an enemy. Religion, law – these are things a man will shoot his venomous arrows from behind.'

'And you cannot pull them down. Madam, you will not have my approval. But I will give you my warning. Marry this man and by him you will lose a kingdom. I can only assure you that I will do whatever necessary to defend the Kirk from any threat, including those posed by a young Englishman who thinks it his right to rule a country of which he knows nothing. This boy is a dreamer. Nothing more. Why, he has no understanding of our barbarous highlands, our islands, our religion. He cannot have the slightest practical notion of how best to secure our future with our friends and neighbours. He has scarcely set foot in the country and yet he hopes to have it for his own. I will not concede to give it up to an aimless green youth looking for a cause.' He crushed the flower in a fist, releasing a small cloud of sickly scent. Dejected petals fluttered downwards.

'And no doubt you plan to defend it with English support and English gold,' said Darnley. This was a guess. Ever since Melville had implanted in his mind the idea of Scottish nobles being in the pay and service of the English queen he had made it his mission to ferret out exactly who was implicated, who profited from undermining his own country's nationhood. 'The only thing you defend is your own privilege; you think to rule all here. Tell me, Moray, do any of you "proud" Scotsmen shrink from collaborating with the English to enrich yourselves?'

'That,' countered Moray, 'may be a question better directed to your child-killing father. After all, is that not how you were begun?'

'Bastard! You lying, dirty bastard! You dare speak of other men's births?' But Moray's shaft had hit home. Nationality had always sat lightly on the Earl of Lennox, and he was not above selling out his country and seeking denizenship in another. It was something he had tried – not always successfully – to push out of his mind in recent weeks. 'Ah, there is the pang pinched,' smiled Moray. 'Sister, your young man has some fire. A fair Prometheus, in fact. I pray you do not get singed.'

The conversation was becoming too heated for Mary, who by now seemed unsure of what her role in the fracas was. 'Ça suffit!' she announced. 'If you will not offer your approval, brother, then you may not offer your counsel. But you may leave. I shall have the freedom to do as I list.'

'Yes, get out, Moray. You'll be sorry for this.'

Moray gave a brief, sarcastic bow and strode leisurely from the room. His head was held high, his expression that of a bored aristocrat, weary of the amateur theatricals of subpar players. He made as though to stifle a yawn as he went and let the heavy door slam behind him. Once outside he removed his cap and ran a hand through his hair, the practised boredom dropping. Servants pressed themselves against the walls as he stormed out of the palace, their eyes downwards.

'You should have him arrested,' said Darnley, shouting the last word after Moray and punctuating it with a pillow thrown at the door.

'We cannot arrest people simply for disagreeing with us. But Moray, le bâtard, and his friends' opposition to us, it unsettles me. To oppose their anointed queen, mon Dieu. They must be radicals, little better than republicans.' She shivered at the word. 'This may yet become a bigger problem.'

11

Following the altercation with Moray that bigger problem grew in magnitude: it became a great, pulsing boil. Finally allowed back into courtly circulation with a clear face and robust energy, Darnley found himself at the head of an emerging party of Scotsmen who rallied behind his and Mary's marital banner. His supporters in his first feud with Moray – Ruthven, Morton, Atholl and Lindsay – were behind them. So was Riccio – indeed, the musician seemed to think himself a confidential adviser on all things nuptial, sending letters full of advice to Stirling – and the guileless, merry Robert Stewart, who sided with his sister rather than their brother.

Gathering behind Moray were the Duke of Châtellerault – that flabby, middle-aged Hamilton who had long feuded with Darnley's father and felt threatened by the rise of a Lennox Stewart king – and the Earls of Argyll and Glencairn, whose motivations, they attested, were religious. Never having threatened Scotland's Kirk, he scoffed at this. Did they think him a crusading Jesuit? Nevertheless, he knew that these men commanded the loyalty of vast swaths of Scotland, could muster arms and munitions on a whim, and by publicly opposing the royal marriage declared to the world that Scotland was divided on this most important of issues. Recalling Robert's map of Scotland, he could envisage by these men's titles the considerable portions of the nation that opposed the marriage, the dividing lines drawn thickly.

When he had resumed his place at Court it was no longer as a favourite of the flirtatious queen but as a king-in-waiting, and everyone knew it. He had stepped from a noisome, stifling sickroom into an emerging Scottish summer, and basked in its warmth. Good weather had come surprisingly early. That made for a bad winter, an annoying little countrified voice in his head chirped. Darnley's father had rejoined the assembly of courtiers as soon as he could, and danced attendance on him. It was uncomfortable. Moray had not only pointed out that his father had taken up arms for England against Scotland but cast up that it was public knowledge.

Ingratiating nobles lined up to seek his friendship and offer their support, amongst them the aloof Maitland of Lethington, who had been Moray's right hand when he had enjoyed proxy administration of the nation. To Darnley Lethington was like all bureaucrats: a dry, serious man, whose disinterest in Court life and fun was an indicator of his intelligence. His domain was the country's administrative network, his mistress an eternally-pregnant inkpot and his children a legion of documents, notes and secret files. Only his terrier eyes prevented his appearance being completely colourless, and it was these that made Darnley wary. Still, having Lethington supporting his cause was a positive boon, not only for the blow it dealt Moray, but for the quiet, serious glean it gave to the marriage.

Meanwhile, an oppositional faction comprised of those who disliked Mary's foreigner-filled, pleasure-seeking Court aligned themselves publicly with Moray. Chief amongst them was the entire clan Hamilton, which Darnley had been told from childhood was a semi-demonic race, generally insane and indefatigable enemies of the Lennoxes. In their madness, the family fancied itself rather than the Lennox Stewarts the natural successors to Scotland's crown. Their leader, the Duke of Châtellerault was, Lennox assured him, a fat sweaty pig who had too long evaded slaughter. The effect was that a pall was cast over what should have been a time of joy and excitement.

In the middle of May his eagerly-awaited elevation to the Scottish peerage took place with great ceremony at Stirling. Gravely he was created the Earl of Ross and Lord of Ardmanoch – highland regions in which he had never set foot – with the promise of greater honours to follow. As the titles were bestowed on him, he thought of poor Leicester's investiture: ennobled for a queen he did not want, by a queen who did not want him. How much more felicitous was his own position. He smiled angelically as he swore always to be true and loyal to his 'princess and sovereign lady, the Queen of Scots'.

There was much celebrating in Stirling's Great Hall that evening. Masques were performed, and a company of minstrels played romantic ballads and sang more upbeat tunes from their little gallery. At Mary's insistence he took the opportunity to confer knighthoods on his friends – including dear Robert Stewart, who became Sir Robert, and celebrated it with increasingly loud whoops, cheers, and cries of 'refill this cup, man – I'm a knight.' Darnley tried his best to convey his idea of a strutting, commanding presence, pacing and posing under the great hammerbeam rafters. His model was Leicester, whose chivalric appearance had raised him as high in Queen Elizabeth's favours as it had brought him low in the opinions of his peers.

***

A month later the Court passed through Edinburgh on its way to St Johnstown to be hosted by his supporter, Ruthven, whom Darnley could only imagine living in a crumbling garret attended by goblins and sprites. On the journey he was able to see with fresh eyes the city he had rode into a few months earlier as a hopeful but indigent and landless young Englishman seeking his destiny. It was now to be his capital –

the centre of justice, law and order in the nation he ruled. Mary asked whether or not he saw his city differently. He laughed and told her that he had found it a wounded, sleeping lion; together they would rouse it and make it roar so loudly the whole world would hear.

In the middle of June a letter finally arrived from Elizabeth. It did not, as he had hoped, contain news of his mother or brother. The spiteful English queen would not deign to write to him. Instead it commanded Mary to provide passports to Lennox and Darnley and immediately send them back to her jurisdiction, that her disloyal subjects might have their obstinate wilfulness curbed with her bridle of authority. They both laughed at her ineffectual anger. Darnley threw the letter to the ground, loudly proclaiming that Elizabeth's threats and demands would neither weaken her cousins' resolve nor break their will. She would, he convinced himself, do nothing to harm a hair on either his mother or his brother's heads. She had for so long been used to commanding and being obeyed that she had lost sight of her own limitations, and forgotten that her realm was England alone. He was winning and would win yet.

His father did not tell him what he himself had been told for fear that the shock may send him running back to England as Elizabeth wished. The countess's months of house arrest at Whitehall were at an end. She was already being conveyed to the Tower of London. In Lennox's estimation the news could wait until its breaking would yield more useful results.

To show Elizabeth the seriousness of their intentions Darnley and Mary embarked on wedding preparations with great aplomb. As they sat cloistered in Mary's scarlet-and-gold-decorated apartments at Holyroodhouse, she suggested that they summon the Court's resident poet and request his help in producing the most elaborate wedding procession and ceremony that Scotland had ever seen.

'Will he aid us?' asked Darnley.

'Master Buchanan is an old sweetheart, and a Lennox man to his last hair.'

As soon as Buchanan arrived it became apparent to Darnley that Mary had spoken honestly.

'Classical.' was his judgement. 'It must draw inspiration from antiquity,' the old man announced when Darnley had asked him if he would consent to lend his great skill and learning to the little matter of a wedding. He was balding, but he made up for it with a trim beard, sharp and white. He was anyone's image of a Greek philosopher, and Darnley was struck by a desire not to say too much lest the man judge him a dolt.

'If Scotland's Venus is to make history and enter into marriage with Adonis we must have a suitably classical backdrop against which to show the world Scotland's reshaping of our classical knowledge. And horses – we must have horses. Can you fetch me the best horses in Scotland?'

'Mais oui, bien sûr,' laughed Mary.

'We can.'

Buchanan dismissed himself; his age and wisdom, Darnley fancied, gave him license to behave a little irreverently. He stalked off, muttering about how to build Olympus.

'He's a remarkable old goat, is he not?' said Darnley, shaking his head and smiling. This wedding really would leave all others in the shade and let the whole world know that Scotland was being reborn as a new utopia.

Mary's habitual smile had disappeared after Buchanan left and she shivered. A tiny line appeared between her brows. 'You do not wish a great classical wedding, sweetheart?' She was not looking at him. She was not looking at anyone. 'Mary?' He nudged her hand.

'Hm?' She had crooked her forefinger to her lips and was nibbling on the tip, lost in thought.

'Are you well? You shall soon strike bone.'

'Oh,' her eyes focused and looked at her damp fingertip, then him. 'Someone must have walked over my grave.' Her smile returned, as though she had suddenly remembered she was supposed to be an effervescent young woman planning her wedding. 'Only, Harry ... do you wish to wait?'

'Wait? Do you mean you wish to delay the nuptials?' His own smile disappeared, and thunder threatened his brow. 'You do not want me to take my place? You–'

'No, no.' She shook her head. 'No, I mean can you bear to wait for all of this ceremonial to be organised? Would you not like to make declaration of our union before God more quickly, before we must declare it to the world?' What, he wondered, was she getting at? 'Peradventure we could be betrothed in secrecy; would it not be a mad caper?'

So that was it – the woman who had married as little more than a child in the great cathedral of Notre-Dame now wanted to try her hand at playing the madcap romantic, enjoying a secret and semi-illicit betrothal. What on earth had she been reading? he wondered, beginning to consider how tiring it might be to be married to someone whose moods and ideas were so slippery and mutable.

'Sweetheart, I will marry you now if we have a willing priest. Do we have one in the palace who will do his duty for two star-struck lovers trapped felled by Cupid's arrow?' He said the last loudly, glancing around. There, he thought, that was suitably pedestrian enough to appeal to her sense of daring, whimsical chivalry.

***

Mary's sudden desire for impetuosity was not a passing fancy, and Darnley was happy to encourage her. Less than a month later, on the 9th of July, the couple visited Seton Palace, outside Edinburgh. It was, he reflected with some amusement, the last place he had stopped before first arriving in the capital: where he had beautified himself in preparation for what he had thought would be his first chance to parade himself before the woman who was now to be his bride.

In the sprawling house the pair were formally betrothed, and thus married in the eyes of God. She would, she assured him, now inform the sympathetic members of her Privy Council that he was to be addressed as their king, and the rest would soon fall into line when faced with the reality of a ruling king and queen. She was too tall to pick up and carry to the bedroom, as he had done years ago with a small number of lascivious Frenchwomen, but Mary was no less willing.

The bedchamber in which they were to spend their first night together was small but well decorated. He had been undressed by Will and a nightgown thrown over him. Sweat filmed his forehead. He had not been with a woman in years. He had never been with a woman who struck awe into him. When he pulled back the curtains of the bed she was already there, smiling nervously in a chemise of her own. She reached up and touched his face. He lifted the nightgown over his head and she slid her hands across his chest and down his stomach. As she did so he felt a jolt run through his lower body. He touched her hair, the side of her face, the swell of her breast, and leaned down to kiss her. He pulled back a little and was about to speak, but she shook her head, put a finger to his lips, and pulled him down again.

Thereafter, they were truly married. Darnley, however, was unsatisfied – not by the willing young body of his bride – but because he knew this was only the enjoyable prelude to a more lasting glory and pleasure.

To Mary the adventure of secret marriage and lovemaking

seemed to spur on the pursuit of still wilder excitements. The morning after their betrothal she shook him awake early and demanded that they ride for Edinburgh. It was now her intention, she declared, that he be proclaimed as royalty before their wedding: a public wedding for a former Queen of France must only be to someone of royal status. As she lay in his arms, she looked at him intently. 'You are so beautiful,' she said, brushing his face with the back of her fingers. 'Our children will be as beautiful in form as they are noble in blood, with a king and a queen as parents. Une belle famille royale, mon coeur. The prophecy fulfilled, an heir to Scotland on the throne of England.'

Ah, he thought: perhaps the seemingly daring caper of the previous day and night had not been as impulsive as she had made it seem. He looked down at her appraisingly, half-thinking that he had in some way been hoodwinked but unsure how, and surprised that the results were so very much in his favour. Certainly, he could see no flaws.

After they had dined that morning at Edinburgh Castle, she insisted on borrowing a suit of Darnley's clothes. He acceded on the promise – requested and given in much mirth – that she not force him into a gown. She had her Marys pin her into the ludicrous outfit and dragged him out into the city at the height of the afternoon, where she had them call on merchants, look in on taverns, and pose as a pair of impecunious noblemen seeking news of the Queen of Scots and her future husband. The disguise fooled no one, but he did not have the heart to break this to her. A scattering of people laughed at the foolhardy young couple enjoying a jape; others shook their heads about the mindless pleasures of the wealthy and aimless; still more spat behind them, disgusted at the vulgar and ungodly display of vice exhibited by a woman in male garb and the glaikit young Englishman who encouraged it.

The merrymaking continued for over a week, when Darnley received an honour that was, to him, higher even than sharing the bed of the queen. On the 19th July he was created the Duke of Albany, a title which in a stroke made him the first man in Scotland. He was, he knew, now bound to his adoptive kingdom, and henceforward every move he made must be calculated to the advantage of the nation whose titles he bore.

It did not surprise him to discover that Mary's fevered displays of frivolity had a necessary political function. His reputation, which had been spotless, was being deliberately tarnished by the most bizarre and invidious rumours set spinning from the camp of Moray. The Scottish people, like Scotland's courtiers, enjoyed the thrill of the misdeeds of their governors; they were therefore suitably enthralled, appalled and intrigued by murky claims that the young Englishman had bewitched their queen and the pair had been engaging in the dark arts. Most deliciously abhorrent of all, the licentious pair had embarked on a murderous conspiracy to kill the Earl of Moray for nothing more than his respectful, conscientious reservations about a hasty marriage.

Darnley laughed uproariously when the rumours reached him. Mary, however, was in no mood for levity. Instead she was furious at the insinuation that she would be complicit in an absurd assassination attempt. 'Do you think it befits the honour of a monarch to be slandered,' she asked him, and he sensed the rebuke. 'Libellous tales leave bruises that do not fade. Would the laws of England allow such slanders of the sovereign to go unpunished?' He had to admit that they would not. It was important, she insisted, that the couple be seen to be bright, friendly and blithe, to show the world that they were neither murderers nor black-hearted scoundrels.

Two days after his elevation to the dukedom the marriage banns – those public declarations that a wedding was to take place – were published in Edinburgh's Kirk of the Canongate. It was crucial, she had rather reluctantly said, that they make concession to Scotland's official religion by allowing the Kirk to publicly announce their marriage. Riccio, whom Darnley suspected had given her this advice, argued that it would also make the wedding more palatable to the people. After all, the service itself could take place by Catholic rites. Darnley was more interested in the public nature of the wedding than its religious complexion. Still, he consulted with Riccio himself on what might be the best way for a King of Scots to proceed.

'It would be best, your Grace,' (at this he started – Mary must have told her musician about the betrothal) 'if you are seen to leave after you are wed. Before the Mass.' Darnley had smiled at that. Masses had always bored him to tears. It was the public vows that were to be the highlight of the day.

On the 28th of July, Mary issued a royal proclamation. Nailed to Edinburgh's Market Cross, it read:

We intend to solemnise and complete the band of matrimony, before the Holy Kirk, with the right noble and illustrious Prince Henry, Duke of Albany: in respect of the which marriage we will ordain, and consent, that he be named and styled King of this our Kingdom, and that all our letter be in the names of the said illustrious Prince our future husband and us as King and Queen of Scotland conjunctly.

***

He had been behind the wording, and she had agreed wholeheartedly. They were not only to have parity of status, but no one reading the announcement could fail to notice that it was the soon-to-be King of Scots who was given precedence. There was now no stopping matters.

12

Darnley barely slept on the night before his wedding. His things had all been moved to new apartments in the Palace of Holyroodhouse's northwest range. These were extravagantly decorated in royal blue and gold, with heraldic carvings and gilded fleurs-de-lis painted over the fireplaces. Tapestries of ships rearing up on tempestuous seas, and others showing hawks gliding through azure skies adorned the walls. Lush blue carpets sat on a polished wooden floor. A prince's rooms. They lay directly below Mary's own apartments and were laid out along the same lines: outer chamber, bedchamber and closet.

It was impossible to sleep knowing that he was on the brink of making a daydream come true. At the very least he had imagined, even if he had not admitted it to himself, that he would likely have his allotted three-month sojourn in Scotland, make an impression, and then return to England hoping that the Scottish queen would remember him and invite him back.

And here he was in late July trying to get enough sleep to energise him for elevation to kingship. And it had all been so easy. It was difficult under the circumstances not to see the hand of God in it. The sanctity of monarchs, God's deputies on earth, was an idea which had been inculcated in him since childhood. Even the English queen, his mother admitted to her chagrin, had been anointed, the ritual confirming that God had favoured her with his touch and effacing all trace of the Lady Elizabeth. And now he was on the road to it himself, the Almighty having sped up his progress due to some unknowable desire to have his position confirmed with all haste. He had been chosen to rule Scotland and the path had accordingly been cleared for him. To Darnley it not only made sense but had the ring of revelation.

Having turned these thoughts over in his head for hours he rose at five in the morning and his attendants, who slept where they could find comfortable spots around his apartments, rose with him. None of them, it seemed, had given the night over to sleep either, and they bustled about, sprucing up the clothes of their station as much as they dared. It was a strange, exciting hour at which to rise, on the silent border between morning and night. A strange, pearly half-light filtered through the windows of his rooms. The sky above the palace was a vivid palette of orange, pink and red, bleeding upwards into a lightening purplish blue studded with pale stars. Above that darkness lingered, resisting the rising sun and the coming dawn.

His servants dressed him in the finest garments the influx of wealth from his new lands could purchase. For once Will Taylor even managed not to jab him when pinning together his sleeves. His doublet was a rich cream, interwoven with cloth-of-gold, the buttons pearls. His padded breeches were white velvet and he wore a white cap with several white feathers. Gemstones were sewn into his sleeves, and, on his fingers, he had rings so heavy that he had to rest his hand on his breeches. The whole rig held him upright, his posture regal and statuesque. Riccio had been behind the costume, being possessed of a remarkable eye for what made a man look good, and eager to restrain the childish excesses of the new king's ideas about what made a prince. Had he been given free reign, Riccio joked, Darnley would have more jewels in his ears and through his nose than a Moorish plunderer. In return Darnley had mock-punched him. He looked in the mirror and drew breath. It was not a nervous young man about to become a husband who stared back at him. It was a powerful, commanding, fearsome king. The image of a ship in full sail struck him, he laughed with delight, and the effect was lost.

It was in this attire that he was escorted to the Chapel Royal in the Palace of Holyroodhouse. There Mary and a small company, including his beaming father were waiting for him. Absent were the Earl of Moray and his erstwhile allies. She had skilfully arranged this herself by issuing orders severely limiting his movements and company until the next meeting of the Privy Council, which would not take place until two days after she had been irreversibly yoked to Darnley in marriage.

The small chapel felt bathed in the warmth of approval, soft candlelight tinting the stone violet. The air was thick with burning incense. Mary was dressed in her mourning garb; this was, after all, her second marriage. A thin, gauzy white veil covered the top half of her body, under which was a tight-fitting black bodice, skirt and sleeves. She stood serenely; this kind of wedding she was familiar with. Taking his place next to her, the priest took her right hand and placed it in Darnley's. He recited the line his mother had hoped to hear him say for nearly twenty years, and to the woman whom she hoped would hear it, even if she herself could not.

'I take thee to my wedded wife.'

'I take thee to my wedded husband,' replied Mary.

Together they recited, 'In the name of the Father and the Son and the Holy Spirit.' He placed three rings on her fingers – one for each of the Holy Trinity. They knelt. The priest read prayers in a portentous voice. She removed the veil, her eyes a dazzling honey. He kissed her.

And with a kiss, she signed herself and her country over to his authority and will. He was the King of Scots.

***

Darnley did as he had been advised and left the chapel immediately after kissing his wife. He did not see her again until after she had finished hearing Mass. Thereafter he could preside for the first time as host over his Court. In the Gallery of Holyroodhouse there was dancing. To his delight, the custom of which he had hazy memories in France was revived: the city's heralds cried 'largesse' to the gathered crowds of Edinburgh citizens and well-wishers, and newly-minted coins were thrown to them. The coins had embossed on them the profiles of Darnley and Mary and the inscription, 'Henry and Mary by the Grace of God King and Queen of Scots'.

For their wedding feast the couple elected to dine alone, both of them waited on by those Scottish earls who were in favour of their union and who realised the benefits of supporting their new king. There was yet more dancing after the feast. The whole day passed in a strange, dreamlike whirl. He did not know where the time went and was conscious only of the obeisance paid him; it had not yet really sunk in that now, despite his youth, he had supreme power in the kingdom. Nor did it enter his mind that he also had supreme responsibility.

Before he knew it the laughter, singing and dancing were at an end for the day and the royal couple were served a light supper. He could not eat it. Instead he took her to bed. Both were to have their own private apartments; but on this, their wedding night, she was to share his. They were undressed and then left alone in their nightclothes.

'Well, husband, it will not be our first night together, but I hope that will not rob you of its pleasure.'

'Well, wife,' he said, and they both giggled, 'the pleasure you have given me today has over-topped any I ever thought possible.'

'I am so glad.' They sat on the edge of the bed. 'It is unnatural to be unmarried, and to have no hope of children to inherit our throne. It is the duty of a queen and a woman to provide for the future. And they say it makes a woman peculiar, living singly.'

'That is something that need no longer concern you, sweetheart. Scotland has a king now. God has willed it and the people will rejoice in it.' She folded herself into his arms and they lay down on the bed.

***

The next day another proclamation appeared at the Market Cross in Edinburgh, and a small number of Scottish peers circled it as the heralds, accompanied by trumpeters, cried out for attention. They read out the words Darnley had written: an invitation to celebrate the ascent of King Henry and to welcome the first year of his reign. The Scottish lords in attendance, the majority of whom were adherents of the Earl of Moray, refused to answer the call to celebrate, and instead stood in calculated, ominous silence.

The citizenry, always eager to observe the incomprehensible antics of factious nobles, merely shook their heads and carried on with their business, uninterested in playing the games of the realm's governors. A lone, gruff voice rang out, 'God save his Grace!' It was the Earl of Lennox, who had got wind of the Moray faction's plans to stand malevolently around the heralds and thereby discourage public displays of affection and support for the new King of Scots, and let the public know that there was aristocratic opposition to their new ruler. Darnley's sedulous father had determined that his son would have at least one voice of endorsement. He looked around the marketplace, hoping for some support. Heads were hastily withdrawn into timber-fronted shops. He did not tell Darnley about the noonday standoff.

At Court the celebrations continued. Buchanan's much-awaited festivities were scheduled for the day, and it was with delight that Mary, Darnley and their loyal courtiers processed out into the fine, sunny gardens at Holyrood and watched his scripted masques and pageants from hastily-erected stands. The queen's four Marys had been suspiciously absent since dressing her in the morning, and everyone soon found out why. They were given starring roles in the 'Masque of Gods', in which a Court lady playing Diana complained about the power of Love stealing her chief Mary, the queen. Love was declared the victor, Diana's complaint dismissed.

This was followed by an equestrian performance in which various Knights representing Olympian Gods challenged one another for the right to bestow praise on the married couple. Darnley, however, found the performances less amusing and enjoyable than watching the stage management of Buchanan himself.

The old man had transformed into a monster, tramping back and forth like a theatrical impresario, issuing orders and criticising the performers. On several occasions, he could be heard hissing, '*Third* conjugation, you fool, not second' and once, 'I know Cupid's blind, but the prince of love doesn't ride a horse arse-backwards!' 'Damned *butchers*! This is what *Courts* produce!'. It took some skill, Darnley thought, grinning, to say something so loudly under one's breath.

Most edifying of all were the final verses read to the Court. A child dressed as an Angel and strumming a lyre piped in a high, clear voice,

***

Thou chiefly, Henry, placed at Scotia's helm
On whom suspended hangs a powerful realm,
Thou from those cares thyself canst never free;
The law which binds us on our loyalty
Thee too constrains – that none unscathed may dare
To trample on our rights whilst thou art there.

***

His heart fluttered. He now stood at the helm of Scotland, a powerful realm. After a lifetime of chasing the approval of others – his parents, his tutors, the English and then the Scottish queen – he would now be the object of everyone else's supplication and petition. It was an exhilarating thought.

He was now the sovereign Lord of Scotland, the equal of Elizabeth and in a position to demand the release of his mother and brother, one monarch to another. His mother, his father had told him, was languishing in squalid conditions in the Tower of London and would not be freed until Elizabeth could be browbeaten into it by a fearsome and undisputed king. His childhood homes were being dispersed. Charlie, spared the Tower, was caged in the household of some rough men of the north: men, his father said, who would not hesitate to beat the boy black and blue until he conformed to their will, their religion and their hatred of his family. The child, he warned darkly, was being breeched in the cloak and colours of the Lennoxes' enemies.

If Elizabeth dared to refuse him he could write to their fellow monarchs. God knows, he thought, the heretical Queen of England is not popular, and any number of powerful potentates would back him in demanding she behave with dignity and acquiesce to the Scottish king's reasonable requests. If she continued to vex him she could never be sure when hostile forces would smash through her nation's back door: Scotland could be a dangerous friend to the enemies of England.

Mary had taken his hand. He resolved then to take advantage of her – of *his* – extensive new library at Holyroodhouse. There he would discover the realities of his nation's past. If he was to provide a model for its future, to bind the loyalty of his people, to defend their ancient rights and herald a new, golden age, he must fashion himself for Scotland. And then he could fashion Scotland for himself.

13

'If the bastard daughter of a concubine will not accept me, what am I in this realm? What hope does my brother have, does my mother have, caught in that deceitful harridan's web?' Darnley was fuming. He had broken out in an itchy sweat and was pacing Mary's bedchamber. She sat on her throne making sympathetic noises. Once he had finished railing on Elizabeth she ventured, 'Well we must see her man. We might yet persuade him to convince her together.'

'Even so, for the monarchs of Scotland to have to seek the acceptance of that ... that leathery, red-haired old bollock purse – it will not stand. The Scottish crown is in no English prince's gift, whatever she might think.' Mary bit her bottom lip, battling a smile at the insult.

'She is not so very old,' she said with false innocence and wide eyes, as though prodding for more mockery. He was in no mood to be witty.

Only a week after their wedding the realities of his kingship began to sink in. He had written to and received congratulations from other heads of state. These had gratified him, and he took great delight in signing his letters 'Henry R', in his own immaculate hand with its flourishing curlicues.

But Elizabeth expressed nothing but contempt, treating him as an insignificant joke. He could envision her, sitting in her Privy Chambers or breezing majestically to her Council meetings, barking orders in her clipped, shrill voice. He could see her reading his letters and braying with laughter as she tried to foment trouble in and exercise influence over his kingdom. Elizabeth, he suspected, fancied herself the Protrectress of Scotland: a feudal overlord of the country's own monarchs. Even now that he was king he had a dread of her, her slick ways and the length and breadth of the webs she spun from London.

He had attended his first meeting of the Privy Council as its leader. This was an opportunity to cement his place as a just and powerful monarch before the assembled nobility of Scotland, including those of Mary's old guard who had opposed the coming of the new regime. Yet it was diminished in one way: Moray, who was called for examination for his outrageous recent behaviour, failed to appear.

Eager to begin his reign with a show of patient justice, Darnley had insisted on not recognising this defiance as open rebellion, but on pursuing Moray for non-appearance. In an attempt to show his wisdom, he also insisted that armed men be summoned to accompany the newlyweds for a planned progress through Fife, lest any of Moray's followers decide to take up arms. It was a warning, he thought, to any in the Privy Council who might be sympathetic to the pig-headed earl. He was now clearly possessed of the full paraphernalia of state. But still Elizabeth refused to acknowledge him as anything other than a bumptious little upstart.

After the days of dancing and revelry had died down an envoy appeared from England. He carried urgent messages from Elizabeth and was invited to meet with Scotland's rulers. As soon as he arrived Darnley had pressed him for news of Charlie and his mother. He had been completely ignored, the curly-bearded messenger not even looking in his direction. He had shouted his demand louder and was about to get up from his throne and shake him when Mary, who was the only one he would acknowledge, called a halt to the audience and asked the man to leave, to be recalled when he had found his tongue. Having vented his spleen and reached a state of calm, Darnley agreed to a second meeting.

The messenger, Tamworth, re-entered the chamber and once more bowed to Mary, silently cursing his awkward and embarrassing commission. This time, however, he had thought better of his stonewall approach and gave a curt nod to Darnley, who had recognised him instantly on his first audience. The man had been a servant of Leicester's, his dispatch north by Elizabeth a crude attempt at driving a wedge between her favourite subject and her former.

'Your Majesty,' he said to Mary reverently. 'My Lord Darnley.'

'You are behind the times, sir,' he said. 'I am the Lord Darnley no longer.'

'Forgive me, my lord, but I have instructions from Her Majesty, Queen Elizabeth, that the pretended titles of her subject are not to be recognised and will not be recognised by my queen or country.'

'Your queen is wrong. Your queen will regret this,' said Darnley. He turned imploring eyes to his wife.

'Indeed she will,' added Mary, rising from her throne. 'And if you and yours refuse to recognise the Scottish state and the sovereignty of its monarchs, you will leave it immediately, you vulgar knave. We shall even be pleased to speed you on your way with a passport, which I am sure my sovereign lord will be happy to sign himself.'

'Gracious princess,' said Tamworth, twisting his cap in his hands, 'I will accept nothing signed by the hand of a pretender. It is your Majesty alone my queen recognises – in *all* things.' He had been told to leave no doubt as to his meaning, and he let his eyes lock on Mary's.

'Then you will go wanting one.' Darnley's voice rose to a shout. 'Get out. Get out of my kingdom. Go, scurry back to your blind queen. A worthless slave you were in England and a worthless slave you are here. And let my mother go! I command it!' His heart was racing with anger and excitement.

Tamworth ignored the outburst. 'Your Majesty, I take my leave of your Court and Scotland, and wish you well.' When he had left, Darnley turned to Mary.

'The impudence of the man', he said, 'to acknowledge the queen and not the king on the orders of that hateful woman. And after she showed me such favour in England as her nearest male relative and natural heir. I see now she thought to rid her Court of the nobleman who might one day succeed her but is now in greater fear of the threat I pose as a king. Neither she nor her creatures can bear to countenance it. We shall call the Justice Clerk', he added. 'I intend to have that man arrested before he leaves our soil.'

But his wife was not listening to him. On her face was a pinched, pensive look. When had that appeared?

***

A few days later he was in the library at Holyroodhouse, a small room secreted in the western range, thick with the good smell of old books, of peace and solitude. Thick volumes were shelved horizontally along three walls, the more expensive chained. The entire room thus shone gold, the books' spines hidden, the gilded edging of their pages on display. It befitted a treasure trove. After attending to Council meetings and state functions he had begun to spend a good portion of his afternoons surrounded in these felicitous surroundings, invariably followed by long rides, archery and impromptu tennis games with Riccio, who was always keen to compete with Darnley to improve his own game. When active and sporting he was able to mull over the implications of what he had read.

He had settled himself down with a number of volumes on the history of Scotland, which he had been assiduously working his way through, when George Buchanan came in.

The old man was surprised to see him; he normally had free access to the library when he wished it – it was a favour granted him – and he seldom found anyone else consulting the royal collection.

'The young king,' he said, a look of amusement on his face. 'You have turned scholar?'

'I am making an attempt,' Darnley answered, returning his smile. Buchanan turned an inquisitive eye on the stack of books piled on the desk next to the room's lectern.

'The history of our nation?'

'I thought it best to understand Scotland if I am to rule it.'

'Wise, wise. But you will not find much history in these volumes.'

'No?'

'No. Boethius?' He looked at the embossed leather on the topmost book with scorn. 'It is of its age, but the realm's lineage requires the attention of a modern scholar, one with more care than Master Bellenden. It is for us to construct lessons through the parallels, patterns, deeds and misdeeds of the past, so that we might fashion better rulers, nations and citizens.'

'You fancy yourself the man for the task?'

'I do. It has long been an ambition of mine to turn my hand to a modern history of our land. We must study the past so that we do not repeat the mistakes of it.'

'And you think yourself ready to write such a study?' Buchanan drew back at this, a comical look of insulted pride on his face. Darnley quickly corrected himself. 'What I mean is do you think you have the time to devote to it at present?'

'Ah, of that I am not sure. It is premature to write a history when one has, I hope, many years to watch unfold.'

'That is true. I do not suppose I might prevail on you to provide me with lessons in the story of this kingdom? I would feel at quite an advantage with the Court's scholar to tutor me in a subject in which he has a special interest.' He held his hands up. 'The history and sovereignty of Scotland has become, I confess, an obsession with me. I would like to know it all.' Buchanan smiled at him again. His look was almost fatherly. The opportunity to help fashion a monarch was a rare gift, and to have a man willing to learn rather than a child who required his lessons beaten into him would be so much more pleasant for student and schoolmaster.

'Do I detect the irregular pulse of a Scottish heart in an English body?' He chuckled. 'It would be my pleasure. I consider Scotland to be in the vanguard of education and political theory, even as some other nations go backwards in making fearsome idols of men – and women. And you are in a unique position. A monarch must be mindful of his people, treat them well and safeguard their rights, for it is the people's love on which a monarch prospers. For too long the monarchy has produced princelings unable to rule, and the avarice of the nobility has resulted. As a leader of men, I implore you to abjure tyranny, do not be arbitrary and do not deign to be flattered by titles. We are more sceptical of such trifles in Scotland than our neighbours in England. "Your Majesty, your Grace, your Highness",' he mimicked in a shrill, craven voice, waving a brown-spotted hand dismissively. 'Bah!'

'Then you must call me Harry,' he said, a little taken aback by Buchanan's sudden animation. 'But I warn you, my wife will call you a republican. The queen fears republicans.'

'Act as good Christian people – people, not gods – whose duty is to protect the state and its subjects, and she shall never have reason to fear. Remember humans make events, humans make policies, and humans make history. To understand the present and the future, you must know something of the past. Part of that is understanding that you are the King of the Scots, of the people. Shall we begin?'

Thus in the first few weeks of his kingship he took to devoting hours each day to listening to Buchanan give rousing lectures on the history of Scotland, from the Celts to the Wars of Independence, from the first High King to the rise of the House of Stewart. Together they debated Boethius' history and Bellenden's translation, judged the merits and failings of Cicero's *concordia ordinum*, and read the 'The Complaynt of Scotland', Darnley narrating Dame Scotia in piping tones.

Frequent enmity with England was a commonplace. As Buchanan spoke in his strong, rich accent of the injustices done and the cavalier, resolute spirit of Scotland's past, Darnley found it easy to imagine himself as the latest in a long line of warrior kings, fighting for the prestige of the ancient kingdom he had been chosen to lead. He wouldn't fall into the trap of the battle-slain James III, who had locked himself away from his people, leaving them to suffer injustice whilst courting England's favour.

As Buchanan implied, Darnley had become a part of it all. The old scholar even helped him compose verses dedicated to Mary on the good governorship of Scotland. He would be just to the poor, strong as a lion against rebels, listen to counsel and know God. His name would join those of Robert Bruce, who had ended Scotland's vassalage; his own great-great-great grandfather, James II, a military hero who fought to enlarge Scotland; and the young James IV, who had perished at the hands of Henry VIII's forces. Hitherto he had seen kingship as the height of all earthly ambition. Buchanan impressed upon him the glories of being a King of Scots, and a strong, benevolent one at that.

What struck him most about these uniformly Catholic dynastic heroes was their sole sovereignty. None of them co-ruled with a queen regnant. None were merely king consorts.

That, Buchanan pointed out, was because they were kings in their own right: their kingship did not derive only from marriage to existing queens. Darnley pressed him a little, asking him particularly about the means by which, in his opinion, he might force Elizabeth to recognise him as king. It was Buchanan's opinion that the granting of the Crown Matrimonial and sacred anointment as king would leave her unable to dismiss him. Anointment was, after all, all that had kept Elizabeth on her throne when the world knew that her parents' marriage was legally invalid and that legitimate claimants to the throne – including both Mary and Darnley – existed. Moreover, it was Scottish tradition that a king's coronation saw him sworn publicly to his people. That sacred touch made the recipient untouchable. He digested this quietly.

He knew the scholar was a Protestant, but to his surprise he did not attach much importance to religious history. Buchanan gravely assured Darnley that he judged men not by their faith or even in their actions, but by their value to the common good, and what he perceived to lie in their hearts. The old man had been a godsend. As a result of his gift of time and knowledge, Darnley felt himself to be as versed in Scotland's history as any native, and better placed than any native to chart its future. If Buchanan had his own agenda, Darnley didn't question it.

***

Not all of the new king's subjects were as accommodating. At the end of the first full week of his reign the Privy Council, finally exasperated with Moray, had him declared an outlaw. That afternoon was one of glorious sunshine without even a threat of clouds, and Darnley joined Riccio in a game of tennis in Holyroodhouse's court. The Italian, a born showman, was constantly on the eye out for opportunities to give Darnley a public profile and always seeking to please the royal couple –

it was, after all, good for his own prospects.

These had taken an upwards turn. Lethington, who had professed himself wholly behind Mary's marriage, had begun to absent himself from Court on one pretext or another, allowing the talented Riccio to slip into the role of an informal secretary of state in charge of a small army of clerks. The Italian had been right, Darnley thought: it really was possible in Scotland for a man to rise by ability alone.

As they called it a game a panting, beaten Riccio threw down his racquet. 'Good game, sir. But you are playing the best, so do not be downcast. I would advise you to keep your eyes as well as your hands more alert for the blows to come. Defence, Davy – defence is the thing,' said Darnley, shaking the little man's hand.

'Ah, I will beat you someday, and then you will not be smiling.'

'Unlikely.'

'We shall see, we shall see. But your Grace, I was a thing distracted today.'

'Oh?' Riccio appeared to be working his way up to something. 'Out with it then; what ails you?'

'Well, it is the business of Master Knox.'

'That old pest,' said Darnley, already bored. The preacher, who commanded the attentions of many of Edinburgh's citizens, had been running his mouth off for weeks about the dreadful excesses of the Scottish Court. Mary outright refused to have anything to do with him, claiming he hated her because he bore a grudge against her mother.

'The same,' said Riccio, mopping his brow with an embroidered handkerchief. 'It is, I think, for you to let the public see that the royal couple are no idolatrous monsters but headed by a worthy young king willing to acknowledge the status of the Kirk. The people, they murmur. Such men as

Knox, you see, will stir them up unless you show yourself a friend to their Kirk.'

'If they are stirred to mutter against their king by a dirty old firebrand then they lack enough to do with their time,' he replied smoothly. Riccio tucked away his handkerchief and bit his bottom lip. He began worrying a loose thread on his damp shirt with both hands, muttering like a fussy old woman about Knox's influence, his reach, his Kirk. 'Ah, very well,' said Darnley, exasperated. 'I will go if it will spare your clothing. And if you think it necessary.' Riccio dropped his gnarled little hands from his shirt and gave a very eager and somehow very foreign nod. Besides, though he did not relish the opportunity of listening to a fiery sermon, Darnley surmised that it might provide a great opportunity to show himself off to his subjects. 'And you see if I don't charm the obstinate old fool out of his imagined grievances.' Riccio threw back his head and barked with laughter. Darnley bristled. 'Have I said something comical?'

'Ah, haha, your Grace,' he replied, shaking his head. 'It is only the thought of anyone charming Master Knox which makes me laugh.'

'Is that so? We shall see.'

Duly, he found himself seated on a specially-set-up throne in the cool cathedral in the third week of July listening again to the much-ballyhooed John Knox. He could not get comfortable on the stiff-backed throne of estate, but the discomfort was offset by the feel of the heavy, gilded wood beneath his fingers. This, thought Darnley, was power – and with pride of place in St Giles the whole congregation would know it. He looked around. On the outside the building was impressive, a monument to Catholicism that had since become its Scottish sepulchre, in which its assassins now gleefully celebrated its demise. Inside it was an exercise in bare, stony austerity. Knox evidently did not just detest idols; he wanted nothing to distract his audiences from the full force and fury of his rages.

His theme was, predictably, the debauched nature of the Court. It was rank hypocrisy, thought Darnley, from a filthy old pervert who had married a child and had been required, Mary had told him, to sue people in the past for entirely-believable slanders regarding his weakness for Edinburgh's prostitutes.

Knox gripped his lectern as he spoke. His voice, English-accented, rose and his eyes became saucer-like as he recited from memory his sermon on Isaiah. Frequently he raised a fist and brought it thudding down. His thinning hair stuck out wildly, his beard as unkempt as an Old Testament prophet.

It was all, he thought, bordering on parody. Everything was engineered to inflame and arouse the imaginations of the gullible, with Knox choreographing his performance to appeal to the weak, the frightened and the ignorant. He would not be cowed by this shabby man and his tricks.

'Ahab, as it is written in the book of the kings, received many notable benefits of the hand of God, who visited him in divers sorts, sometimes by his *plagues*, sometimes by his *word*, and sometimes by his *merciful deliverance*. He made him *king*, and, for the *idolatry used by him and his wife*, he plagued the *whole of Israel* by famine,' screeched Knox, raising palms that were criss-crossed with thin, white scars, the reward of years of enforced slavery on French galleys at the command of Mary's mother.

He paused to turn his artfully wild eyes on Darnley, who felt himself colour. The eyes of the congregation had also begun to slide towards him. Despite segregation according to sex, age, station and trade, all looked at him with similar aggression, some with fear. There were children near the front, eyes as wide as Knox's, suspecting that the king now sitting above them must be a harbinger of death and disease. It was preposterous – he had done nothing – and yet he could read anxiety on their faces as plainly as illuminated type. They would believe anything. Their preacher's words hung in the air like a cloud of poison, invisibly infecting their minds and hearts.

Sweat began to prickle up on the back of his neck, and he had to resist the urge to scratch himself. This wasn't the kind of attention he had anticipated. Knox continued, warming to his theme. With mounting indignation, Darnley saw himself as they all must see him, these good Scottish Protestants: a red-faced young Englishman arrayed in overblown, alien finery, who might at any point terrorise or repress them. He was no more to them than an arrogant Ahab. These people didn't love him: they didn't know him. He felt anger rise, an antidote to embarrassment and weakness.

'But *how* did Ahab visit God again for his great benefit received? Did he *remove* his idolatry? Did he *correct* his idolatrous wife Jezebel?'

He sat through the whole thing red-faced. He listened to Knox liken him to a proud tyrant – he who had never authorised an execution, drawn blood or even threatened this vile man and his Kirk. Knox's audience listened raptly, and Darnley was disgusted. Knox must know that if he pressed his lies long and hard enough they would acquire the veneer of truth. Darnley felt vindicated in this assessment when Knox went on an hour longer than was usual, the better to fully humble and humiliate his royal guest.

After the morning's sermon he didn't return to Holyroodhouse immediately, but rode around the countryside, first imagining the gruesome tortures a king might inflict on a slanderous sower of sedition, and then, cooling down, considering the more realistic, legal means by which he could punish the preacher.

One did not have to ride far out of Edinburgh before the terrain turned rugged, crags and spent volcanic ruins littering the landscape. It was easy to imagine breaking the heads of wicked men with those rocks. But whenever the city came back into sight during his ride about it, sobering civility regained control. When he did return to the palace he ordered a meeting of the Council, bathed with care, and had Knox summoned to answer for his audacious language. Mary gave this over to him. She had had, she told him, her fill of trying to pull out this particular thorn in the flesh of the body politic. 'Then I will do it,' said Darnley, the image of a shining knight errant passing through his mind. She looked bemused. 'You may try,' she said. 'As I have tried. In my youth the Estates gave the Kirk power to rival, to overtop mine, and make me its creature. When I rule England and its church I shall have a stick strong enough to knock Knox about his pate. I will avenge my mother then.'

'You have no need to wait for that. You have a husband now.' This would be his opportunity to prove that he would not go weak-kneed and girlish when confronted by an old and powerful man.

When Knox arrived before the Council he had discarded his wild-eyed, proselytising persona. His hair had even been brushed, his beard smoothed and combed. Nevertheless, the man stank, and was apparently proud of the sweat he had worked up earlier in the day. Darnley pitied his poor young wife and wondered at the life she must lead at home, servicing the wants of this dirty old fanatic.

'Sir,' said Knox, 'have I offended you to be so called?'

'Your reek alone offends,' snorted Darnley under his breath.

'I beg your pardon?'

'Ha! Pardon is exactly what you should beg, Master Knox,' replied Darnley. 'For you have offended us.' Knox stood silent, his head held high. 'Do you believe that your sermon today was acceptable?'

'The word of God is always acceptable to those who have faith,' answered Knox in low tones.

'Undoubtedly. And you think it acceptable to preach to the people the benefits of resisting, of rebelling against the sovereigns whom God has called to this high office?'

'God encourages us to resist and disobey the ungodly rulers and proud tyrants which the Church of Rome produces. The word of God frees us from the obedience of a cruel prince.'

'Are we tyrants? Do our people cry for release?' Knox one again held his tongue, and Darnley began to falter a little under the aged, battle-worn gaze. He latched onto the humiliation he had felt earlier and let his anger flash. 'No doubt you hope your radical theories will gain currency. But I will not have it, Master Knox. Your God is not my God.' At this, Knox raised his bushy eyebrows, and Darnley felt the advantage again on his side. 'My God,' he continued, 'is the true God. The God who deputises the ruling of the great nations of the earth to those he has chosen. He has chosen me, and he has chosen my wife. And as a subject of the same you will obey our commands, and you will cease from the wicked, seditious practices in which you have hitherto indulged.'

Knox began to launch into a justification of his sermon, attempting to fire up his oration by railing on the on the Catholic Church as a haven for the venal bastards of the aristocracy, but he had been caught off guard. The old devil is not so sure of himself when he has to deal with a king and not a frightened girl, thought Darnley. He had done it. He cut him off, focusing authority into his words. He stood, so that Knox could appreciate his full height.

'It is our express command that you forebear preaching for a space of fifteen days. I recommend that you use this time of leisure to search your soul, Master Knox, and find in it the necessity of obeying your sovereign lord and lady, giving thanks to God for not sending tyrants to correct you by violent means and providing a stable, orderly realm. Good day, Master Knox.'

Uncharacteristically lost for words, Knox stomped from the room, red-faced, clutching the front of his clerical robes in a vice-like grip. Darnley was surprised to find that his legs were shaking, and he sat down gratefully.

***

Mary was delighted with his handling of her bête noir. That night when she came to his apartments she threw herself into his arms. He took the opportunity broach to her the idea that had been simmering in his mind since Buchanan had explained it all to him. Full of excitement, he asked her how much more strongly and confidently he could rule Scotland, and how much lighter her own cares would be if she granted him the Crown Matrimonial and had him anointed as king. To his surprise, she did not embrace the idea as he had expected.

'Are you not sufficiently honoured?' she joked.

'It is not a matter of honour. I have been making a great study of the history of the realm.'

'Your sessions with Master Buchanan?' she asked. Her tone was sardonic. He ignored it.

'Yes. I have learned a great deal. For one thing, the Queen of England would no longer be able to so wilfully scorn my existence, nor to treat me as a runaway from her Court. I would truly be her peer ... in some eyes, her better.' He thrilled at the impiety. *His* mother was no traitorous courtesan.

'The Queen of England will accept you. I have written to her explaining that our marriage was intended only to cement amity with England.' Mary's face reddened after she had spoken, as though she had done so unguardedly. Her finger came up to her lips and she nibbled nervously at it.

'You have done what, madam?'

'I mean – naturally a dry, unmarried spinster could never understand the ardent passions of young lovers, of Selene and Endymion.' He narrowed his eyes. Her revelation of correspondence with Elizabeth gave him the distinctly unpleasant feeling that secret things were happening all around him, just beyond his view – that he was one small panel in a larger, hidden tapestry.

'Oh, and am I then to be only the Queen of Scots' consort, the product of her carnal lust?'

'You are the king. You rule jointly.'

'But not equally. Not in the eyes of the law. Without you I have nothing. Should the unthinkable happen and you predecease me, what then? My name is dead and my line extinct and Scotland open to bloody civil war. Is that worth having the English queen's goodwill and amity? Heretofore you have not seemed so particular about securing it. Your uncles have made sure you have never ceased styling yourself the rightful Queen of England, free of bastardy. You cannot suddenly be worried that crowning me will mean your displacement as Elizabeth's heir. Sweetheart, take your eyes from the English succession and look to your – to our – country's future. A crown may make me the legitimate king England seeks, but you shall continue to be its true queen, as you will be Scotland's. You shan't lose anything by granting me a crown. We are united, we are one: one soul, one heart, one love.'

Her eyes darted around frantically as she searched for words. 'Mais bien sûr,' she said, an idea evidently occurring to her as she focused on him, 'you must realise the Crown Matrimonial cannot be granted without the assent of parliament. Remember,' she added, 'we are not tyrants.'

'You were not so nice about calling parliaments when you conferred royal titles on me. No, you simply coudn't marry someone who was not of the right degree. You desired someone to rule jointly, and I am he. I've proven it today, haven't I? Or did you think to marry only to show Elizabeth you could, with no thought of what follows? Did you think to strengthen yourself without strengthening me? I tell you it's God's will that I'm anointed king.' She cocked an eyebrow, her expression somewhere between amusement and scorn.

'And we must render to God the things that are God's?' she asked.

'Do you not see, only when I'm crowned king can I rescue my family.' He was aware of the querulous tone creeping into his voice. 'Ach,' he said, sensing futility. 'You can't understand. You've been a queen regnant almost since birth – you know nothing else.'

When she spoke, her habitual girlish tone had been replaced with steel. 'I see it is true that men are slower to recognise blessings than misfortunes. You are right to recognise all that I have done for you, and the means by which I have done it. I expect gratitude, not greed, from one who has everything by me.' The last two words were given emphasis. He looked at his benign, docile wife with horror. How had the conversation taken such an unpleasant turn? He had been so sure she would leap at the chance to share her rule with someone of the same status as her first husband, but with the power, ability and willingness to make full use of it. He was at a loss as to how to continue.

'We will think on the matter, Harry. But consider the importance of parliament. A crown granted by parliament would have legitimacy far beyond anything one poor woman can bestow. And remember you are yet young – parliament might well look more favourably on granting the Crown Matrimonial if we wait until you are twenty-one.'

'Yes, as it looked favourably on granting it to your late husband. When he was fifteen. Your Stewart forefathers have always ruled in their minority.'

She pursed her lips before speaking. Her voice always became more lyrically Gallic when she was in a passion. 'Vous devez apprendre à avoir de la patience, mon cher. Haste makes waste. Our late parliament last year made plain that twenty-one is the perfect and lawful age for princely majority. Your mother and brother are in no danger. You have said yourself that Elizabeth will bluster, she will bluff, but she would never harm the kin of a monarch. It would hit her too near. At any rate,' she yawned, 'I am afraid that I have pain in my side. I will retire to my apartments now. Alone.'

'Mary …'

'Bonne nuit, your Grace.' With that she swept from the room and up the winding private staircase that connected to her own suite, a whisper of her scent hanging in the air like a musical note.

The next day she was her usual self, bright and sunny. But she did not visit his apartments that night. He was far too proud to ask her why, or to demand her presence as his bedfellow. Neither did she come the next night. Or the night after that. He was ready to apologise for his presumption after three nights without nightly comfort and pleasure when all thoughts of their first marital affray were driven out by the news that Scotland was at war.

14

The Earl of Moray had been gathering support and arms since the Privy Council had declared him an outlaw. Friends flocked to side, and with friends came political opportunists, hopeful profiteers and troops of men sworn by fealty to answer the call to arms given them by their territorial lords. A rebel army of hundreds had gathered and was prepared to take up arms against Mary and Darnley under the fig leaf of protecting the state religion. These desperate men were, they claimed, seeking to right the disastrous wrong of Mary's marriage, and to prevent the proud young tyrant who had seduced her from destroying the kingdom.

Here, felt Darnley, was his opportunity to prove his abilities. But this rebellion would also show the world that his rule had begun weakly, was dividing Scotland, and was not universally recognised even at home. He simply must, he concluded, show a firm hand, rout the rebels, crush their cause, and establish that King Henry Stewart was the unquestioned, divinely-appointed King of Scots.

All his life he had reached his goals by taking the most direct path. Obstacles in that path invariably cleared themselves. The honour due a King of Scots would be his once these rebellious lords had been curbed of their insolent resistance to his authority. The flurry of activity which the news had precipitated had allowed him momentarily to put to the back of his mind the persistent, dark images of his family in England. He had a new goal.

As the Privy Council made preparations he issued directives of his own. Chief amongst them was the commissioning of a gilded suit of armour: a king clad in bright, shimmering gold could not fail to lead the royal army to victory. Who, he wondered, could fail to love a golden prince, mounted on a white warhorse? Their argument forgotten in the exciting crisis, Mary took to his ideas with alacrity. If Darnley was to be the heroic Ares, she must be Athena, clad in a steel cap and breastplate. On the evening of the day news of the rebellion had reached them, a bright-eyed Mary had returned to his apartments, full of passion and vigour. She continued to come to his room throughout that week.

One night he had drifted immediately and unusually into a contented sleep after they had exhausted their bodies. He awoke soon after and was surprised to find that she was still in his room, sitting in the window casement, staring blankly outside. Strange, he thought; normally she demurely and discreetly returned to her own bedchamber, allowing Will re-entry – usually with a sly smirk on his face – for the night.

He went over to her. She seemed not to notice him. He put an arm on her shoulder and she started. Her face was emotionless, drained of colour in the moonlight. She looked like she had been crying. 'What ails you, sweetheart?' he asked. A terrified look came over her as her eyes focussed on him, two gold coins coming into sharp relief. She shook off his hand and abruptly rose, running from the room and back to her own apartments. In the morning she was herself again, the unfathomably low spirits of the previous night forgotten and unmentioned. He did not chance a recurrence of inexplicable sadness by questioning her. It was true what his old nurse used to say: there was nowt so queer as folk.

***

As the couple prepared to fight so too did the rebels. News reached Edinburgh that printed material was pouring from unknown presses, warning of the king and queen's intention of overturning the Kirk. Mary had burst into tears at the news.

'What they seek,' she sobbed, 'is to do to us as they did to my mother: to use religion to drive us from power and into our graves. It is how these same wicked men achieved the Reformation they now pretend to protect.'

Darnley, however, was furious, not only because of the rebels' lies, but because the royal proclamations declaring his and Mary's disinclination to return Scotland to the Catholic fold were being undermined. They were reissued, and he ordered it to be declared in every town and city in Scotland that anyone immediately desisting from support of or sympathy with the rebels would be forgiven and welcomed back into the open arms of a just king and queen. To illustrate their benevolence both monarchs signed a public pardon of the Earl of Huntly, a poor, stammering fool of reputedly mad stock who had been languishing in prison for years for the misdeeds of his father. They signed also the formal recall of the Earl of Bothwell, a Protestant military strategist who was fiercely loyal to Scotland. This, Darnley realised, was to be a war of words as well as a war of swords. And words could be villainous and persuasive things.

The rebels and the small army they had amassed were reputed to be encamped on the west coast. Word came that they were gaining in numbers and expected still more to be provided from the Earl of Argyll, who commanded countless men in the western highlands. If the reports were true then the rebels, with Moray as their figurehead, were not far from Lennox-country. It was there that the royal army marched towards in the moody, oppressive weather of late August.

His father rode in the vanguard of the army; the saturnine Morton marched, ramrod straight, with the main body of men summoned to fight for the king and queen; and Mary and Darnley rode with the rear guard. It was a calculated manoeuvre. In the pursuit of the rebels he insisted that they not be seen to drag their men away from their wives and children but ride with and alongside them.

Although they were cheered out of Edinburgh his enthusiasm and exhilaration began to wane almost immediately. Despite studying maps of Scotland, he had not stopped to consider that trooping across even the lowlands in stifling humidity would be an unpleasant job when encased in heavy, gilded metal.

Grassy plains, recently-harvested fields and wooded hills stretched interminably, an endless sea of yellows and greens. Even with his visor down sweat poured into his eyes. The pieces of armour chafed with every step of the horse, and the chafing began to rub off chunks of skin, leaving his sweat to pour into raw, lacerated wounds. He was thankful that no one could see the blood and bruising beneath the metal. By the time they had reached Stirling he was exhausted and fed up. By the time they reached Glasgow he was thoroughly miserable and had to be scrubbed down with soft sponges like an old horse.

During that interminable march along the highway the royal army had swollen as men rallied to the royal banner. Gangs, mostly comprising the young and the old, some carrying homemade weapons, left their crofts to the more able-bodied to join the established soldiers. Old women, children and young wives turned out to watch the troops, waving their aprons and throwing flowers plucked from the bushes on which their laundry lay drying, interested in the brief novelty of something happening. It did not hurt, Mary told him, tapping the pistol she carried on her hip, that they both looked the part. The couple waved graciously to their spectators, each movement cutting fresh bolts of pain through Darnley's armoured arms.

He had heard about Glasgow since childhood; his father,

after all, had allowed the recovery of his estates there to become a personal fixation. The town sat in Scotland's hilly, verdant west country, encircled by smaller villages and in command of the frigid Clyde. Away from Edinburgh, the main diplomatic thoroughfares and the regular rotation of the royal Court, Glasgow's inhabitants retained a fierce sense of pride in their town – really a sprawling collection of buildings, a university, churches, castles, orchards and park lands. In the coming war they were determined to be on the side of their young and vibrant Lennox Stewart king and his queen.

The agonies of the long march were momentarily thrust aside as crowds of Glaswegians came out to cheer the arrival of the army with cries of 'God Save King Henry and Queen Mary'; 'God Save Scotland'. Just as Darnley had never seen Glasgow, Glasgow had never seen him. Forgetting his pain, he waved his golden arm in genuine pleasure at the warm reception and its corollary – the fact that they liked what they saw.

The day after arriving in Glasgow word came from scouts that the rebels had gathered around Paisley, a little village set in rich, fertile hunting lands around a Hamilton-owned, partially-ruined abbey. Paisley was close by Glasgow and overlooked by a range of hills called the Gleniffer Braes, high enough to view both the small village and its larger neighbour. A sharp-eyed spectator up on the Braes might have witnessed a large swarm buzz around Paisley, eluding its pursuers by flying south and then east.

Darnley was not disappointed at the lack of a battle. Although he had wished in childhood to be a great soldier, he had not been prepared for the realities of broken skin, bleeding, sweating and restricted movement. A hasty meeting, which he insisted on calling a 'Council of War', was called in a sooty merchant's house on the lands that were his namesake, with Darnley, Lennox, Morton and Mary in attendance. 'Undoubtedly,' he began, 'these men have avoided battle in order to run to Edinburgh, where they might think support forthcoming from those sympathetic to the English policy they caparison as an aggrieved defence of the reformed religion.'

'These men will have support not just from the English queen, your Grace, but from the highlands,' said Morton. Mary looked at him with distaste and Darnley noted something on her face that he had suspected for weeks: his wife did not particularly like his relative. He could not blame her. Family or not, the man had an unsettling air about him. It seemed to come from his staring, near-sighted eyes. He always held one's gaze longer than was necessary or comfortable.

'Argyll has not yet given them the men they need. I suggest we let it be known that if he refrains from doing so, he will not suffer for his sympathy,' she said.

'A just thing, madam,' said Darnley, smiling at her. 'But they will take their money and men from Elizabeth, with or without Argyll and his highlanders. These traitors are well-used to receiving English money, given freely as long as it causes tumults in Scotland.'

'At any rate, your Graces, if they capture Edinburgh Castle, this war'll be over before a shot's been fired,' said Morton. 'And not in our favour. On that we agree?' There was murmured assent, and it was then that he noticed that his father had stood off to one side during the discussion, twiddling his hands and staring downwards. Darnley did not want to know what the old man had been thinking about.

And so the tramp back towards Edinburgh had to begin before his wounds from the circuitous westward march had closed up. As the royal army prepared to backtrack the close, stuffy weather that had persisted throughout August broke with a flash of lightning and the low groan of distant thunder.

The brief glory of the Scottish summer was at an ominous end and with it came a furious storm.

***

If the approach to the west had been painful the return journey was akin to torture. It seemed to Darnley that nature itself was roaring in outrage at the unnatural rebellion within Scotland's borders. Ferocious winds blew in all directions, whipping people and horses, making conversation impossible. Words were snatched away by the more forceful air of the maelstrom. And on the winds came gusts of rain that fell with such force it felt as though huge flagons of water were being thrown at the royal army. When he put down up visor he was almost drowned, sometimes by water, sometimes by the fury of the wind as it robbed him of breath.

The luxuriant greenery that Scotland boasted at the height of summer quickly turned an ugly, muddy brown. Long grasses bent as one to the competing wills of turbulent winds. Scrubby little black bushes were ripped out by the roots and carried off. Frequently his horse lost its footing, sending Darnley lurching forward, his heart pounding wildly from the sudden shift in balance.

In an attempt to rally their own dwindling strength and courage, Darnley and Mary chose midway through the march to take the vanguard, relieving Lennox to follow with the rear troops. It worked like an invigorating tonic. Riding at the head of a royal army, facing down wind, rain and thunder was like issuing a direct challenge to the designs of nature. For a time he could forget the unpleasant realities of sore and bloody limbs, the constant struggle to breathe and the pointlessness of the march across the country. Instead he could imagine how the opening engagement in this battle for Scotland's future might be written, and how he might appear in it.

When they stopped at Callendar House to let the storm blow

itself out a bedraggled messenger arrived. The rebels had reached Edinburgh ahead of them. Yet he was keen to assure them that the castle still held out and was in the hands of their loyal subjects. In fact, he had been told by the castle's Lord Keeper to request permission from the king and queen to fire on the rebels and force them out of the city. The messenger, soaking wet and covered in mud, was invited to go warm, feed and dry out the clothes of his office whilst Darnley – now out of his armour, which was left to languish with the army's ordnance supplies – sat shivering across from Mary in front of the house's great fireplace.

'We must have the castle bombard them. These men are evil,' was her immediate pronouncement. She sat hunched, with a finger nestled between her chin and lip, her elbow on her skirts.

'We cannot launch cannonballs into our own city. We are prepared to fight on the field of battle.' He was horrified at the sangfroid with which his wife was prepared to endanger countless lives.

'I know these men better than you. Nothing will dislodge them. Nothing will stop them.'

'We will! You and I, and my father, and Morton, and Atholl, and now Huntly, and Both-'

'Non, non. That is not enough. Never enough. They will continue to lead us by the nose.'

'We have the men – we have the superior forces – loyal Scotsmen. That is why they flee from us.'

'Since our marriage these great earls have fled from *me*.'

He blanched. 'Are you saying that our marriage has done this, that it should not have taken place?'

She gazed into the fire. Her face glowed as heat and warmth returned to it. 'No. No, these men seek an excuse to agitate. This was inevitable unless I did as our cousin Elizabeth does and remained alone, playing on the hopes of everyone.' He relaxed, pacified. 'However,' she continued, 'now that it has happened, these devils must be crushed, or else we will never sit on the throne of Scotland without knowing when le serpent might creep again from under it.'

'And we will crush it. We will drive them from Scotland–'

'Non! It is not enough to drive them out. They must be stopped entirely or their plots will be made elsewhere. If they escape we will not know when they shall return, nor what help they shall bring in the furtherance of their wickedness.'

'Then we will destroy them on the battlefield.'

'If we can meet them on the battlefield.'

'They cannot run forever.'

'They cannot run if they are dead, or imprisoned. Only one of these will stop them. These men must not run. They must be arrested and locked up. We will turn the guns on them.'

'We will not.'

'I tell you it is the only way. The people have already noted, you know, that my courage waxed manlike these last weeks. Where is yours, sir? I did not seek nor do I expect a weak husband who expects me to rule as the courageous king whilst he plays the queen.'

He stood up, dropping a tankard of some warm, spicy confection that he had been given to heat him up. 'Nor did you get one, although I am beginning to think that it is exactly what you want. And neither did you marry a bloodthirsty tyrant who will take the lives of the innocent.' His bottom lip jutted out.

'It is no tyranny to blast cuckoos from our nest, par Dieu. If they have already infiltrated Edinburgh, they must be blown from it in smoke and flame.'

His eyes widened at her matter-of-fact tone, his brow furrowing. Crises did something to this woman. They transformed her from gracious girl to remorseless brute. Perhaps the one always lay behind the other, the lion inside the lamb. He thought of Edinburgh, his capital, which had been reduced to flames the year before his birth; the city which was even now still rebuilding, trying to recover the glory which had been taken from it by rapacious invaders.

'No. I will be no part of this. I forbid the keeper of the Castle to train his guns on our capital city.'

When she responded her voice was low but implacable. It carried in it contempt. 'Harry,' she said, glaring up at him, 'you cannot prevent it.'

15

Even gazing from the dizzying, windy heights of Stirling Castle's battlements it was impossible to see much over the Forth. All that stretched ahead were vast, undulating plains, hills, and the grey snake of the river. Huge patches of land were bathed in sunlight, others left to languish in dullness; periodically they would switch at the whim of ever-shifting clouds. Darnley spent hours staring down at his country, willing some news of the affray to manifest itself.

At the start of September, the whole royal army was at Stirling awaiting news of Mary's campaign of cannonading. He tried to avoid her company and she made no further effort to explain the reasoning and necessity behind training the guns of the castle on the rebels – and therefore the people – of Edinburgh.

At Stirling the smell of hundreds of men and horses living in wet, cramped conditions was overbearing. It rose up from the town, where some lodged, to the castle, where still more did. It became too much for some, who began to melt away, suspecting that this war was in name only and that there would be no battles fought.

Around Stirling the countryside was already beginning to turn a burnished orange-red, the rusty colour of drying blood. The rain had ceased but the wind kept up. The air carried the clean smell of damp grass and wet stone whilst the sky was a cloud-filled slate. The rebels might have been killed, smashed into bloody pulp. They might have stormed Edinburgh castle with their troops. They could have escaped and be on their way to fight. It was impossible to know.

When news did come it was mixed. They had been repelled

from Edinburgh and the odious Knox had fled with them, abandoning his flock to the cannon. No, the messenger assured him, there had been little damage to the city and little bloodshed. But that meant, of course, that Moray, his cohorts and his followers had escaped to fight another day. The civil war would rumble on.

At least, thought Darnley, the indication was that Edinburgh had remained loyal. Still, other heralds arrived to inform the couple that there were still ongoing defections. The apparently weakening position of the rebels had only added piquancy to their cause. These greedy, opportunistic men, he stated during a Council meeting at which he and Mary were encouraged but refused to make peace and end the whole thing, would be kings themselves. They aimed at claiming the crown of Scotland, breaking it up and fighting over the pieces. It was all so impossible to fathom, this racing back and forth across Scotland, trying to keep track of the shifting loyalties of men.

He began to wish for it to be over. It was becoming apparent that the glorious field of battle, an idea he had cherished since childhood, was a hollow fantasy. War was an exhausting, confusing, frustrating thing, even without bloody action. Caesar's Roman campaigns, the feats of Alexander and the books of chivalry that had so impressed him in childhood were just stories, and stories with the monotony of life stripped out.

Eager to escape the confines of Stirling and to give the army something to do, it was decided that the royal forces would return once again to Glasgow. He did not wear his armour.

They reached the city in the first week of September, where an assembled group of the western nobility signed a bond of allegiance to the king and queen, pledging their loyalty and their commitment to supporting the crown in military action which, Darnley and Mary declared, was surely anticipated given the liberty of the rebels and their undoubted support from the kingdom to the south. He assured the remaining army that the families of any men who should be killed in armed conflict under him would be provided for out of the Scottish treasury. Muted cheers answered him.

In the hopes of snapping his father out of the strange reticence he had shown to play the role of a loyal Scottish patriot he appointed him Lieutenant-General over swaths of western Scotland, particularly around Glasgow. He had been hesitant about floating the idea with Mary given their recent disagreement, but she had been surprisingly sanguine at the prospect. 'He is a Lennox man and this is Lennox country. What more could we do to ensure that its people remain loyal to us than elevate one of their own? The rebels will find their western bases less safe hereafter,' was her laconic reply.

To his greater surprise was the wording of the formal declaration of Lennox's new powers, which she drafted herself. He and anyone acting under his authority were to be 'discharged of all actions, criminal or civil, that may be moved or intended against them if they happen to hurt, slay or mutilate the rebels.' Freedom from prosecution was also granted from anyone who spoiled, destroyed, burnt or cast down the homes and goods of rebellious subjects. It was chilling. Conflict, it seemed, brought out an unexpectedly tough and unforgiving side of his wife. Flexing his new muscle, Lennox immediately commanded that the tenants of Argyll and Glencairn, Moray's loyal partisans, disarm or face the full force of his newly licensed wrath.

With that they left control of Glasgow to Lennox's appointees and once more prepared for a cross-country march. They reached Fife in mid-September, where a further bond was signed, this time by the lesser nobility eager to pledge their duty to the king and queen. It was, Darnley and Mary managed to agree, crucial to destroy support for the rebels wherever it had been rumoured, even if the traitorous lords and their men continued to play the mischievous mice. That accomplished they would have no alternative but to appeal to England as supplicants, begging English men, money and arms to attack loyal subjects of Scotland. He hoped it would come to pass, and that the traitors would reveal themselves to be what he knew they were: opponents of Scotland and Scottish sovereignty.

As the new strategy of roaming Scotland to win declarations of loyalty continued, a face unknown to Darnley answered the summons which had been sent him at the beginning of the conflict. The Earl of Bothwell was a man he had been keen to meet. Mary had spoken of him in glowing terms – a heretic, but a man who detested the English and was an adherent of Scotland. This notorious hatred of the English offered some trepidation, but he was sure that he could win over any defender of the Scottish state when the perfidy of some of the native lords was made clear. Yet Mary's commendations aside, he had heard from his servants and others around the Court that the man was reputed a vile lecher, a practitioner of buggery who spared neither woman or boy his irresistible advances. He was certainly well known for entering places he shouldn't – he had even been imprisoned in the Tower of London for trying to get into France illegally during his year at the English Court. That alone made him interesting. Darnley considered befriending the man and asking him about the true conditions in the place, or whether there was some knowledge he would be happier not having.

Bothwell arrived when Darnley and Mary had returned to Edinburgh, from where they could direct orders across the realm and to where all news, visitors and rumours swiftly made their way. The two were enjoying a brief respite in Mary's bedchamber at Holyroodhouse when he was announced, and the man whose coming he had looked forward to with apprehension and excitement strode into the room. He was a disappointment.

As he did with all young men – and Bothwell's strange features placed him anywhere between twenty and forty – Darnley measured him up as a potential threat and instantly discounted him. If this man was truly an untiring seducer, it must be through force. The barrel-chested Bothwell looked to be about two full heads shorter than Darnley and reminded him of the aggressive bulls that were bred on the farmlands of Yorkshire. He had pictured and feared a potential rival, someone powerful whose friendship he would have to win in the pursuit of the common goal of Scotland's statehood. Here was an angry-looking lout.

'Your gracious Highnesses, I am pleased to be recalled, and pleased to join the fight for Scotland.' Bothwell's voice was as much of a surprise. It was soft and cultured. 'My Lord of Bothwell,' gushed Mary, 'bienvenue, bienvenue. We have great need of you. Our brother Moray, your old enemy, has revealed himself to be a rebel and worse. We require your support in bringing him to heel.'

'Bothwell,' was all Darnley could think to say, with an attempt at an imperious nod. But Bothwell did not look the type to be impressed by imperiousness, and he cursed himself for feeling such a child before this ugly hulk.

'Your Grace, it is a pleasure to meet you. Scotland has been without a king since I was eight years of age.'

'My late husband was–'

'Never resident,' Darnley interrupted. 'The realm has been in need of a king, my lord,' he said without looking at his frowning wife.

'In need of both a strong king and a strong queen.'

'And we are they.' Amusement threatened Bothwell's fat

lips. 'I may have been born out of these dominions, but I have come to love Scotland as much as any native. And more, I think, than some.'

'I am glad to hear that. From an Englishman.'

'As you have returned to us, may we rely on your support? The queen assures me that you are a man of sound strategy.'

'Her Majesty does me great honour. I have seen much of the world, and I think I have learned something about handling traitors. I will serve Scotland in this as in all things.'

'We thank you. And we expect to see you in our next meeting of the Privy Council.'

Bothwell bowed, before coming forward and kissing first the ring on Darnley's hand, then on Mary's. He walked backwards from the room, his head lowered to hide a look of distaste at the daft, plummy-voiced foreign chit who now expected fidelity. King of Scots, indeed.

'An ugly brute, but a very charming one,' Darnley said cheerfully when the door was closed. She did not answer immediately but gave her husband a look so withering that his smile faltered.

'It does not befit a sovereign to focus always on the gleam of a diamond when its hardness shows its value. You must concern yourself less with what the eye sees and more with what can be seen in the eyes. We will have your "ugly brute" lead our army. He is well trusted,' she said, smoothing her hair.

'Madam, my father leads the army.'

'Your father led the army. He has been gifted extensive new powers, I think you will agree, and must be free to discharge his duties in the west.'

'His duties are already deputised. He is with us still. I see no reason to withdraw his post.'

'As you saw no reason to train the guns on the rebels,

without which we might not be sitting here, oui?'

'My father stays,' said Darnley, his teeth beginning to grind, his lower lip protruding.

'Bothwell despises Moray. That can only be a help to us.'

'My father is as strong in his hatred of the traitor as anyone.'

'Very well,' she sighed. 'Your father can continue to lead the army as it is marches from town to town in search of ghosts. The Earl of Bothwell can swear his allegiance to you as king, as have the other earls who are still willing to acknowledge us. We will see what he makes of a Scotland in which the oldest advisers of the sovereign are in disarray, lesser men are promoted and the royal army built of petitioners. Ah, quel monde. Perhaps he is indeed the man to judge the loyalty and prowess of the new King of Scots.'

'Perhaps he is.'

***

With the lack of armed engagement persisting, the start of October filled him with enthusiasm that the skirmish would soon be over. Mary was keen to turn to what would be done with the rebels when they acknowledged the failure of their treacherous rebellion.

He begrudgingly had to admit, even if not to his wife, that she had been right in her claim that the old guard of noble advisers had melted away. 'To the Devil with them,' exclaimed Darnley, hoping he sounded convincingly flippant. But his wife was more inclined to lament the loss of so many experienced statesmen. Even many who had not taken up arms with the rebels absented themselves from the Court in silent sympathy.

Morton too was rumoured to be flirting with the idea of deserting his kinsman and the queen in the presumed belief that, with the rebellion lost, Moray and his friends deserved support from their coreligionists. To Darnley the old man alleged that he was simply getting too old to traipse around the country in pursuit of men who had no wish to fight, when reconciliation could be sought much more cheaply and easily. It was, Darnley thought, an odd kind of way to win a war.

The royal army, hearing rumours of rebels to the south of Scotland, made ready to troop towards it, to be followed by the northern men of the Earl of Huntly, who had been restored to royal favour with Bothwell. Darnley nominated himself to lead what was hoped would be at least one decisive battle. Still October drew on and on. Plans were made, men were moved, strategies were considered, discarded, and news of the rebels' hiding places was awaited. A bloody farce without blood.

It was not until the third week of October that definitive intelligence finally reached the king and queen. The gruelling weeks of marching to-and-fro were at an end. The war was over. The rebels had escaped into England unnoticed near the start of the month, there to be given succour by a sympathetic Elizabeth, who had sent a stream of letters to Mary throughout the campaign encouraging her to reach a peaceful accord. Darnley decided to address the assembled men of the army that had never seen action himself. His heart was in his mouth at the prospect. They might feel cheated at being denied action in the field. They might see through him as a leader who had led them nowhere.

'Friends,' he began, sitting on his horse, free of his armour, 'We come before you to announce that God has given us victory. The traitors have been chased from Scotland, to seek refuge under petticoats of England's Elizabeth.' He waited for the bawdy laughter to subside, and his jangling nerves settled. 'Proud men of Scotland, we now thank you for your service to our country. God has seen fit to spare us the horrors of war, and we thus give you leave to return to your homes; your wives; your children. Not a hair on any man's head had been harmed, and yet you all go home victors, safe in the knowledge that your country, king and queen have been safely delivered from the poison which has lately infected our realm.' There was a polite, if not an emphatic cheer.

The civil war was over without a battle being fought. A quiet murmur broke out. He could see men laying down the weapons they were carrying. Others removed helmets. Some slouched into relaxed positions, spitting and scratching themselves. As his men began to shuffle off, talk to one another and debate the usefulness of the whole endeavour, his mind turned to his golden armour. It was still being carried with the munitions. The wounds it had caused him had begun to scab over. They itched but, as always with pain, the memory of it was difficult to recall. He imagined the armour being carried back to Edinburgh, to be locked away and gather dust, never having achieved the purpose for which it had been created.

That night, when he and Mary were alone, she abruptly said to him, 'Do you know what they are calling this war? They call it "the Chaseabout Raid."' He laughed.

'They have got it right. The "Chaseabout Raid", that describes it.' It was delightfully on the mark. She set her mouth in angry little lines. 'It is not a matter for jest. It is not a matter for laughter at all. If they laugh at a rebellion then they laugh at us. If they laugh at us, then where is our authority?'

'Mary, the rebellion is over. We won. Give losers leave to laugh. The rebels have shamed themselves with this foul flight.' She was, he thought, making something of nothing. Had she always been so humourless? He was sure she had not.

'You listen to nothing, mon enfant' she said, tutting. 'I told you that if my brother and his friends escaped they would be free to do mischief elsewhere. We need their lives in our hands, to destroy the source of evil. Did Heracles kill the

Lernaean Hydra by banishing it, or even by removing one head? No sir, he prevented them all from multiplying lest they continue to spread poison. These are the simple rules of statecraft. I suggest you learn them.'

He said nothing. He had grown used to her irascible tone and would have enjoyed giving her the rough edge of his own tongue if only she would stop being so calmly detached from his barbs.

But was she right? Was it not a risk to have dangerous men hostile to him and the governance of his country find refuge in the realm of a woman who would not even recognise him? It was more crucial than ever that he be anointed and invested with Crown Matrimonial with these traitors possibly drumming up support in a foreign land. If they ever did come north again it would not be a toothless king consort who greeted them but an undisputed king in his own right, all lingering doubts about his unworthiness crushed by a crown.

But he would not bring it up with his wife in her current mood. Who knew what belittling reasons she might find to refuse him? It was enough, he thought, to try and forget her attempts to ruin his sense of relief and victory and appreciate that the days of uncertainty were over.

He had rid his country of wicked men, and those who remained would prove loyal. Even Knox had gone. Now, he thought with a smile, he could have Catholic Masses sung right within the walls of St Giles if he wished. It would be worth it to hear about the fanatical Knox's reaction. Besides if the "Chaseabout Raid", as these wits were calling it, had done nothing else, it had given him the opportunity to begin work on his beard.

16

Darnley stood preening in front of the mirror at Holyroodhouse, stepping back to admire the effect of the regal, manly beard with which he was attempting to strengthen his jawline. It was wispy and flaxen, but it was a beard all the same. No one would ever call the King of Scots lady-faced. It was November, and in the weeks since the end of the civil war (which he still insisted on the skirmish being called), he had felt curiously out of sorts. At the start of the month Mary had been struck down by a bout of vomiting in the morning and briefly confined to bed, leaving him in charge of government. Yet he noticed that in Privy Council meetings, now reduced to a small rump of lords, his voice was often given polite hearing and then ignored. Conversely, recent attendees Bothwell and the nervous, jittery Huntly were given undue respect. In response he had tried seeking out his lords individually to give his opinion on matters man-to-man but was barely humoured. His father had returned to Glasgow, ostensibly mopping up lingering rebel support, leaving him with no partisans. He was crestfallen. He had hoped to see behind the veil, to glimpse the mysteries and secrets of power. Disappointingly, its true source seemed to be a fiction, always deferred, fragmented and deputised.

Where previously Mary had been an enthusiastic bedfellow she now came to his chambers to do her marital duty only sporadically. At first he assumed her illness was to blame, but she made no attempt to resume the regularity of her visits after being released from her sickbed. He missed her. After years of sexual inactivity, he had enjoyed the private aspects of married life, and enjoyed equally the private talks afterwards, before she returned to her own rooms. And David Riccio, who had been a poor, humble little wretch when Darnley had come to Scotland now paraded around in finery, the little traitor having all but abandoned their friendship to spend his time in the queen's shadow. These were strange times indeed.

He gave himself a final pout in the mirror then crossed his eyes and stuck out his tongue. He was running late for a Privy Council meeting, hoping to keep them all waiting. He had come to his rooms to be pinned and laced into a new suit in the hopes that a bolder outfit would turn some attention to his opinions when he made a grand, belated entrance. He went in a cloud of aniseed and perfume towards the Council Chamber. To his surprise, before he could reach it he found his councillors pouring out of the north range of the palace.

'Your Grace,' Atholl nodded. The lumbering bear, usually so jocular, averted his eyes.

'My lord. We are to be in council.'

'The Council has taken place, your Grace.' This was Bothwell. 'Her Grace was insistent that it not be delayed.'

'Her Majesty cannot do that. Meetings of the Privy Council must await the presence of the king.'

'I suggest you take that up with your wife.' Bothwell did not smile, but his eyes glittered with nasty humour. 'And, your Grace, have I leave to speak?'

'Yes?'

'The beard is very becoming.'

Darnley did not answer the impudent ape.

Instead he burst into the Council Chamber where Mary still lingered, talking to Huntly. Seeing him, she politely dismissed the man with a gracious tilt of her head. He left, mumbling a greeting with his eyes as downcast as Atholl's had been. Riccio was gathering up papers, seals and ink. Around the room Scotland's kings glowered down from their portraits at the scene before them: at the latest in their line being robbed of his regal authority.

'What is this – a great Council of the king's lords lacking the king?' He thumped his fist on the table for emphasis. Riccio did not look up from his task.

'You were late,' she said.

'The king cannot be late. Council cannot sit without him.'

'The Council did. You need not concern yourself with these meetings. You are perfectly at liberty to do as you wish with your afternoons. Read your histories with the scholars – I know how close to your heart stories lie. Hunt, if you list. The governance of the country is a tiresome business and need not detain you. Unless you have developed a sudden and undisclosed interest in the issuing of coinage, or feuding in Annandale? Avez-vous?'

She spoke so calmly and serenely that he could barely comprehend the force of her words. 'But, I am needed. Of course I am needed.' He looked down at the pile of needlework that sat on the table before her throne. 'And,' he added, nonplussed, 'I see that your *own* interest in matters of state hardly commands your full attention.' He felt he had scored a point and paused while it sank in. 'Besides, you cannot provide the royal signature without me. Official business cannot be transacted without the approval and signature of the king.'

'That has been taken care of,' she said, her face impassive. She reached over and plucked something out of Riccio's little secretarial box. She held it up to his face, like a mother showing her child a new toy. 'Comme tu vois.' The little metal object had a wooden handle and on its flat bottom were some curiously familiar squiggles.

'What is this?'

'An iron stamp. It was made from an imprint of your

signature. Now you do not need to spend your time in these meetings. You can do as you list; Signor Riccio will administer this only with my permission.'

His mouth went dry. 'You cannot do this. It is … it is illegal.'

'Do not be so theatrical,' she said, returning the stamp to its box. 'It is entirely legal and entirely sensible. You once told me that freedom is very important. Now you are free to make your own time. My brother Robert is staying with us and the Earl of Morton asked me to commend to you your mutual kinsman George Douglas. They are both gamesters. Why not spend some time with them? Amusez-vous bien.'

'You shan't get away with this. You cannot treat me as a child.' Realisation dawned on him. 'Have you been concerned that the country did not grind to a halt when you were a-bed? Is that it? Do you resent the king governing alone? It is not so easy to relinquish the reins of power as you imagined, eh?'

'Oh, Harry. There is no need to make something of nothing. This is simply a means of saving time and allowing you to conduct yourself as you wish without the tedious burdens of state. Important papers will still require your hand. After mine. But you are entitled time at leisure, are you not, following your taxing military engagement?'

His cheeks flaming, he brought his arm up underneath the box Riccio was holding, sending it skyward and tipping its contents to the floor. Ignoring Mary, he glared at the started secretary. 'A fine friend you have shown yourself. Turncoat! Caterpillar!' Still Riccio avoided his eyes. He then turned on his heel and stormed from the room to seclude himself in his own blue-emblazoned chambers, which at least felt like the apartments of a king. The unwelcome memory of Leicester's investiture intruded. He had handled that humiliation by hiding away and then leaving escaping queen and country. That was a luxury he didn't have here, wedded as he was to both.

On the heels of the memory came a desire to write to Leicester to let him know of this latest affront. But it would not do for a King of Scots to write to a foreign earl, especially one whose allegiance must always be to a foreign queen. Besides, Leicester had some fool ideas about Scottish monarchs owing homage to English sovereigns. He would like to have disabused him of that notion, but it was a regrettable consequence of his high marriage, he knew, that it had severed him at a stroke from his old friend's confidences. A king had no equals and must lean only on his courtly advisers and noble intimates.

That night he decided not to wait to see if Mary would make one of her rare appearances at his bedchamber door. Instead he found himself sneaking up the back staircase to beg entry into her private apartments. He had avoided supper in embarrassment and wanted to speak to her alone. He knocked on the door and waited. Nothing. He knocked again, louder. Still there was no answer. He turned to leave and then changed his mind. He beat on the door and shouted, 'Mary! Mary! Open up!'

He heard movement and the click of a lock. The door opened to reveal Riccio in shirtsleeves, a robe of some rich fur draped over his shoulders like a cape. Without thinking, he grasped the little man under the arms, lifted him off his feet and pinned him against the wall, a forearm against his chest. Riccio wriggled, his feet kicking the air above the steep stone steps. 'Your Grace!' he spluttered. 'Please!'

'What do you mean by being in my wife's inner chamber in your nightclothes, you little rat?'

'I brought business – only business!' His voice was strangulated, gasping. He began making inarticulate sounds, his Scots deserting him, his eyes popping out of his head.

Darnley let him down, instantly regretting his reaction. He almost apologised to the cringing Riccio but bit his tongue. Instead he hissed, 'Get out of here. If you have urgent business in future it belongs to the morning. And it belongs to the king as well as the queen.' Riccio fled down the stairs, through Darnley's own rooms and out of the royal apartments without looking back. Darnley looked at his wife's door, still open. He would be within his rights to storm in, threatening to spill blood if she did not spill answers. Instead he turned around and stalked down to his own rooms.

It was possible, he thought as he tried to sleep that night, that Riccio had been telling the truth. Urgent news certainly did come in at all times, and he knew the hours of a secretary were strange and unpredictable. Still, his thoughts kept returning to his first stay at Holyroodhouse, and how he had offered the Italian a place to sleep. Riccio had been willing to share his bed. Was it possible that, having been rebuffed, he had now sought to take his wife's? Could the man really be such a shameless and amoral libertine? And could Mary, married to a King of France and now to a King of Scots ever be so base as to allow a glorified musician to take pleasure of her? It was absurd. And yet Queen Elizabeth's mother, Anne Boleyn, had wronged King Henry by dallying with her musician, begetting Elizabeth in the act, so his mother said. That same king's child bride, Katherine Howard, had even elevated her former music teacher to the position of secretary so that she might continue cuckolding her husband. It was possible. After all, when the candles were out all cats were grey. Like a sharp blade, pain sliced through his head, so sudden and acute that he cried out.

He shouted for his servants, disturbing their sleep. He demanded strong liquor, which he usually avoided. He had long heard that it could numb pain, bring on sleep and stave off the unpleasant thoughts of waking hours. The dulling of pain and the inducement of sleep would be enough.

***

He woke with a new resolve. If his wife wanted a puppet for a husband, a man whose authority, ideas and power could be encased within a little stamp, then she would feel the realities of one. He felt like a child excluded from play who could only peep through clouded windows at the shadows of his former playmates. Passive resistance to the corruption of good order was the only sensible option: Scotland would have the world's first *secessio regis*.

He took her advice and invited Robert Stewart and George Douglas to his apartments. George, lascivious and rat-faced, was in his thirties, a hard drinker who called himself 'the king's good uncle' and funded his wild lifestyle by performing occasional services for the Earl of Morton. Darnley was simply delighted to be the handsome one. When George came into the apartments, he looked around and then whistled. 'What a place you get as a reward for lifting the queen's skirts!' Darnley was stunned, unsure whether he should berate an older relative. Robert came to his rescue. 'Shut your mouth. You're speaking of my sister, as well as your sovereign, man. Harry, ignore this horse's arse. He's uncouth.' George barked laughter.

'And you're a pig! Look at your shirt – filthy and frayed. You're standing very close to my lord, your Grace; can you smell the animal?' He held his sharp little nose.

'Better a pig than a black sheep.'

'How ever did you two become friends,' asked Darnley.

'Friends with this worthless twat? You insult me!' said George.

'And me,' added Robert, elbowing him. 'The slave's fond of his ale and so am I, and that's the all of it. Believe me I would not sit with him in sober or civil company. No offence intended, Harry,' he winked.

The insults, good-natured and given with laughter, bounced between the pair for some time. Darnley said little himself, letting the unbridled banter wash over him The trio went hawking outside Edinburgh and then, at George's insistence, asked Will whereabouts in town three chaps might enjoy good sporting and cheer. He gave them the names of several taverns, some of which Robert already knew and all of which were familiar to George.

The three men sat in the king's apartments that evening calling for hard liquor and strong wine. For the first time Darnley allowed himself to get steadily drunk. As he did all the secrets of his heart came pouring out, his thoughts getting more and more fanciful. He had to speak more slowly and loudly with each drink just to make himself legible, even in his own head. Robert and George, who were getting merrily drunk too, agreed with everything. Of course he should be crowned. Of course he was treated disrespectfully. And George especially was keen to concur that Riccio was *absolutely* an untrustworthy, treacherous, climbing little shit.

When they left to enjoy Edinburgh's nightlife the trio were already in their cups. The awkward, gangly walk which Darnley had as a younger man made a curious and unexpected return, to the hilarity of his new companions. He also found it funny. As they marched through the town, Darnley towering over his fellows, they sang old Scottish songs. Here was a novel way to shown himself off to his people, who, curiosity overcoming them, joined the revels. He was keen to tell them all about his relatively recent knowledge of Scotland's history, its independence, and its future. They would all have important roles in that, he assured them.

The night got gradually blurrier. Even as king – his height betrayed him wherever he went – the proprietors of

Edinburgh's hostelries were not keen to serve a man in the company of the bickering Robert Stewart and George Douglas. But money was money and he was their king, as the coins proclaimed. The swelling group found tiny drinking and gambling dens, and bid yet more strangers accompany them.

Dirty tankards were constantly thrust in front of him, and he tried to impress the company by standing up and downing full drinking horns of beer, whisky and wine. They cheered and he felt himself quite the lad. The stink of the taverns – stale ale, cheap food and unwashed bodies – was blotted out as his senses were dulled. At one point he vomited, which gave him a moment of strange, sobering clarity. It soon passed.

Women were also pressed on him. George seemed to know an extraordinary amount of buxom young women – nearly all Douglas women – who were happy to sit on his knee and laugh uproariously at everything he said. How clever it would be to give lavish praise to these ladies and let the news filter back to his wife that he was desirable to other women and might well take up with one. But inevitably they drifted off when he launched into a diatribe about the harpy he'd married and the injustices done him. He tried to thrust his lips onto a girl no older than himself only for her to squirm away, laughing.

He lost all concept of time – the night seemed to pass in a blink. He woke up in his chamber late the next morning. Memories of singing in the street, of vomiting in the street, of telling Robert Stewart and 'Uncle' George Douglas all manner of private thoughts without even a semblance of shame or circumspection hit him hard. Robert, naïve and disingenuous, had turned stupid and incoherent in drink, falling constantly; George had turned nasty and shouted insults at strangers. He felt sick again, and curled himself up into a ball, wincing at inexplicably skinned knees. It was hard to believe he had behaved as he had, and yet it had seemed so natural at the time. The loss of control and reason was frightening. He needed something to drink, but all that was to hand was some stale wine. The thought of it made him feel like vomiting again. If these were the wages of hard drinking, he thought, then it can go to Hell. He did not even have the strength to shout for his servants, much less to stand up without the room spinning wildly.

But the day passed in a sluggish nightmare of sleeping and rolling about his bed, and he felt steadily better. He called for spring water and told his attendants to let it be known that he was indisposed and would not be dining in state or attending to any business that day. No messages came in reply.

***

His shame at his own behaviour and his determination to avoid humiliating himself in drink again did not last long. This time it was Robert and George who approached him. Amazingly, the two laughed about their behaviour and his; they had had, they assured him, a great night, and were keen to outdo it. In particular, they were eager to outperform him in downing great jugs of spirits. They even laughed that they could remember little of the night, which they took to be a measure of its success. Their enthusiasm was infectious.

Darnley thus found himself embarking on a new campaign to replace the old military one. This was an assault on the public houses of Edinburgh. He took to it with gusto. Throughout the remainder of November he signalled his fury at his wife's outrageous behaviour in arrogating his power by absenting himself, as many an earl had done. Whilst she governed he would usurp her place in the affections of the common people. Let Mary and her pretentious nobles, with their petty little private disputes, have the commonweal. He would have the people.

What sprang up was a mutually beneficial relationship: drunken friends and strangers would aggrandise him with fawning praise and he would buy drinks and make valiant promises about the favour he would bestow on them. He even began to sympathise with the rebels, having been stuck with such an ungrateful and ill-conditioned royal mistress.

Given time, he was sure, his absence would attract attention, and the actions of a Privy Council comprising a woman's favourites and an Italian social climber would fall into national – even international – disrepute. To her misfortune, the old ache in Mary's side flared up and she took to her bed for days, leaving the Council to cooperate with a stamp wielded by Riccio. If she had assumed a little stamp would safeguard her supremacy over her husband against any bouts of sickness, she would soon be sorry. Before long the Council would be begging him to come back. In an ironic way, he mused, she had been right. He could well look on this as a brief break before his presence and authority were once more required at the heart of Scottish politics.

In December the plan seemed finally to have worked and his days of merrymaking – which had already begun to lose their lustre – seemed likely to be at an end.

He had taken a small party of his newfound cronies to Linlithgow, a large *maison de plaisance*, when a messenger arrived to tell him that the queen was being brought in a horse-litter. His immediate thought, uncharitable though he knew it was, was that she was feigning illness to save face when begging him to return, her mutinous lords having grown weary of a sickly woman, a secretary and a stamp.

As he waited, he thought about how best to indicate his willingness to release her from the yoke of power. It would not do to look too eager. He must be reluctant in giving up the lifestyle she herself had forced on him. And of course there could be conditions. For one thing he would demand to be crowned. He would also demand that she join him in writing again to Elizabeth to release his mother and brother, on pain of being denounced to the world as a harbourer of traitors and a meddler in the affairs of another realm. It would all be his for the asking.

When she arrived she did look peaky. Her colour – always a little ruddier than Darnley's – was like wet chalk. She got off the litter and stood up with some difficulty, her Marys present to support her and bring her into the palace. In spite of the recent frostiness between them he felt some concern. He had not imagined that she was genuinely unwell.

She was conveyed into a private chamber where they could speak without being overheard. No, she did not want refreshments before they talked and no, she was not quite well.

'I am sorry to see you are unwell. I had not imagined it.'

'Thank you,' she said, looking sullenly at him.

'Do matters run well? I mean with administration and … everything.'

'Quite well.' He had not expected that.

'Then what brings you here? Surely not to take in the air as a restorative?'

'I am in no need of a restorative.'

'Oh?' He wondered at her meaning, and terrifying thoughts came into his head. She was dying. She was gravely ill. He moved towards where she sat and bent down on one knee to her. He brushed a stray hair from her face and she winced. He drew back, embarrassed at his own attempt at being tender.

'I am in need of nothing, because I am in a happy condition. Un condition heureuse. Ha! Mark my joy, sir; remark upon it! For you shall never again make a woman so happy.' There was no humour in her voice; it was strained and odd. His brow creased as he tried to work her out. He did not have to.

'You are to be a father. Scotland is to have a little Prince or Princess.'

17

A boyish grin spread across Darnley's face. It faded when he noticed that his wife's expression remained gloomy. This was not the look, he thought, of a woman in the first flush of expectancy, nor was it the look of a woman who had done her duty in securing the future of her kingdom.

'Madam,' he said, 'this is no time to be downcast. God has smiled upon our marriage. You can no longer deny it.'

'Cease with the pretended piety, Harry. I am with child because we are young and healthy.'

'I will thank you not to confuse your own lack of faith with others,' he said. 'I know myself to have been blessed. My position proves it. In fact, the Lord has once more given us proof that you must now call parliament to grant me the Crown Matrimonial.'

'And why should I do that? What is your reason this time, other than to harp on your favourite string?' Her voice was weary.

'You think I require a reason? You cannot govern alone. You are with child. Your only duty is to protect and nurture it whilst your husband governs. That is clear to anyone.' He was beginning to become frustrated – she could not deny the logic.

'I cannot govern without the support and unity of my *nobility*. I reigned alone without wars and division and the loss of counsellors for years before your appearance, sir. And I cannot believe that God now wishes a drunken, boorish child to govern.' So she had heard of his frequent drinking sessions. What did she expect of a man who was denied any serious occupation?

'Drunken! It's no crime to drink, madam – I would think

that any number of Scotsmen will testify to that. And what else am I to do with my nights, married to an icy bitch who sees me more as a rival for the throne she has and the one she covets than as a husband? You deny my rights for fear I will outrank you in the eyes of Scotland *and* England.'

'Ha! You? Ça c'est drôle. A man who indulges in night after night of wenching, diverting himself with common women like a gutter whoremaster?'

'A whoremaster? You may be right – after all, look what I married. A queen who would rather spend her time doing heaven-knows-what, closeted with a cheap Italian servant.'

'Signor Riccio is my secretary and more fit for business than you have shown yourself.'

'More fit for your bed too, I suppose? You … you *whore*.'

She gasped. Tears began to flow and he felt a stab of regret. But he couldn't take the words back and wasn't sure if he wanted to. He had succeeded in making her feel something. Besides, the notion of Riccio seducing her had been preying on his mind and become a common complaint when he was drinking. Even when sober he could not leave it alone – like prodding an abscess with his tongue, he kept envisioning the two together despite the pain it caused. For reasons he couldn't account for his feelings for her had deepened from superficial attraction with the idea that she had taken to lavishing her affections on someone else, someone cheap and beneath him. Jealousy mingled with revulsion and possessiveness were emotions too complex and contradictory to understand.

'Ah, Mary, how has it come to this? You should be happy. We should be happy. The throne of Scotland is secure. And the boy – it will be a little boy, the latest in a proud line of Jameses – will need a strong father from whom to learn. You have said yourself it is not right that a queen play the role of a king – what lesson will that provide our son? Else why did you wed me, if not for this? He deserves to be born to two anointed rulers. It is all laid out, I tell you – if you ever doubt our marriage, know that I have been called to this high office as you have to provide Scotland with heirs. And if, God forbid, anything should happen to you or the baby and I am not truly king, who knows what ill omens will result. I doubt those inclined to rebellion will be equally disinclined to fight if the throne of Scotland is vacant.'

'I do not know, I do not know. I will think on it.'

'You have had a long space to think on it. Now you must step back from government and rest, and let me put my head in the yoke. It will do your child no good for you to be daily concerning yourself with the business of state.' She opened her mouth to interrupt, and he forestalled her. 'It is my child too, I know. I misspoke. We can call parliament any time – few Scots will be celebrating Christmas. I can-'

'Leave me alone,' she said.

'What?' He was taken aback by her sudden vehemence.

'Sortez.' she said through gritted teeth. 'Out! Out! Out!'

He was driven from the room by a torrent of racking, sobbing screeches.

***

The winter promised bitterness, and Darnley reflected that it was only a short year since he had been entombed in the English Court, a figure of fun. Now he was the uncrowned King of Scots and about to become a father. So much had happened in one year that it was impossible not to believe that his meteoric rise would continue unimpeded in the year to come. Who knew where he might end up?

Since Mary had visited him at Linlithgow he had returned to Edinburgh but found that, even when he attended meetings of the Privy Council, he was treated as an irrelevance at best, a pariah at worst. It was infuriatingly impossible to fathom – he had done nothing wrong, save try and convince his wife to grant him the honours due him: the honours she had happily granted her first husband, a fifteen-year-old weakling whom she would have let absorb Scotland into the kingdom of France. The unfairness of the situation led him to believe that there must be someone, or some people, hostile to him.

His immediate thought was Riccio, but for all he had come to distrust and dislike the haughty braggart it made little sense that a man who had been so supportive of his marriage would also want to reduce his status. Bothwell and Huntly were also under his suspicion – but as he methodically tried to work out exactly when the incipient discord between him and his wife had begun, he found that it predated their arrival. It all seemed to have crept in during the fruitless months of war.

Mary had been less than sanguine about his coronation and anointment as king in the first weeks of their marriage. He continually returned to her claim that she had not wished to marry a man who made her king and himself queen. He agonised over whether she had revealed more than she had intended. Did she see him as Henry of England had viewed his wives: disposable, ornamental creatures to be used for the purposes of begetting heirs and then discarded once the duty was done? Or perhaps he was intended to be like the Yorkist Elizabeth, married by Henry VII for her pedigree and womb and then confined to pretty, powerless obscurity. Could his wife really have been callous, calculating and cynical enough to wed a fellow heir of England in order to keep him in check, to humble him? Had she wed him not to unite their claims to England but to strengthen her own whilst abrogating his? But no. It could not be so. He knew her. If he encouraged invidious thoughts and suspicions they would set up home and breed.

But why – why had she married him? He could not understand her; he could not read her; he could not work out her motivations. And that made him even more determined to gain access to the enigmatic woman who had, by now, stopped coming to his bedchamber altogether, claiming the infirmity of pregnancy.

He resumed his drinking and carousing but cut it down to two nights per week, combatting the resultant nausea and exhaustion with rich food the following days. The rest of the time he took jaunts around the countryside, read whenever he could find company in the library, and played golf. Life fell into a routine of the same activities, the days invariably rainy and grey. Robert and George – and even Will the valet had become an eager drinking partner, continuing his fruitless quest for a woman – would have happily roistered about the town every night, but he felt there were limits to what a king should do, even if he was still waiting for his status as a real king rather than a mere king consort to be conferred. What really curtailed his drinking sessions was that he was becoming a bore, and worse, he knew he was a bore. Prior to drinking he always promised himself that he would not resume his familiar, hackneyed diatribes about his wife, his suspicions, the unfairness of his treatment. After several drinks he returned to these themes with the readiness of a tiresome drunk. He had begun to irritate himself.

He was pondering what to do with his day one morning when Morton came to visit him in his private rooms. He was clad in black, the clothing of an elder statesman. With a presumable nod to the approaching winter he had let his moustaches and beard thicken more than usual. They lent him a wild, untamed look at odds with the clothing: a scarred old lion dressed in finery for battle in the arena. His watery eyes remained as cool and detached as ever.

'How fares the king's grace? I hear you've been enjoying the company of young George.'

'Good morrow to you. We are friendly. Your uncle George knows something of Edinburgh.' Morton chuckled at this. It was an unpleasant sound, like fetid water full of dirt being sucked down a drain. His teeth were yellow, gaps between each one. His breath smelled bad.

'I'll believe it. Ach, you're all yet young. It's good to see the young enjoy themselves.'

'What news brings you, my lord? Am I being invited to a meeting of the Privy Council?'

'No … and yes. Might we speak alone?' He had been voted the man to broach a difficult subject, and he would not speak his lines well with an unwanted audience. Only Will was in the room, wiping invisible dust from a clothes chest.

'Yes, of course. Will, have you something useful to be doing?'

'If I in't needed 'ere, your Grace …'

'When are you ever needed? You can go into the town and find something to do.'

'Uh … Can I take the 'ole mornin', sir?'

'If you wish. Your duties are light, Lord knows. Why?'

'I … well … I got a girl, your Grace.'

'Do you, Will?' asked Darnley, amused in spite of himself. 'A pretty one? Who is she?'

'I don't know as you'd say "pretty", your Grace. She works in't pantry. She's a big lass. We walk up and down't courtyard though, for exercise.'

'Very good.' He went to a little silver casket and extracted a couple of coins. 'Here,' he said, holding them out to Will. 'Go into town and buy her something. And behave yourselves, both, or you shall have a thumping for it.' Will grasped the coins eagerly, nodding his thanks. He strutted out of the room, anticipating his purchase. Something non-fattening. Some cosmetic, perhaps, that would disguise a profusion of acne.

His master was welcome to the spooky old earl.

'Well, sir?' asked Darnley, turning his attention to Morton. 'Speak your part.'

'Yes. Your friends. Robert and George are good boys,' he sighed, 'but hardly serious-minded enough for grave matters. So I've come as your kinsman to discuss the important matter before us and beg leave to advise you. It can't continue now, can it?'

'I do not follow,' said Darnley. He was curious, but suspicious. When an older relative visited him he always suspected that it was either to give him a dressing down or to impart bad news.

'I may sit?' Darnley nodded, and Morton eased himself into a gilt chair much too dainty for his bulk. Darnley took his adjacent, canopied seat.

'The situation in Scotland. It's unprecedented and it portends no good. Every commonwealth needs a strong leader who shares the goals and policies of his nobility. But we've a king who's removed from government and a queen who is with child and allows all access to her person to be controlled by a common, foreign-born musician. One, incidentally, who does far more than offer her his instrument and make her sing.'

'I am unsure of your meaning.'

'I am unsure if you are unsure... It's an affront to our custom and our privileges as much as yours. God's foot, the man even advises her on her *wardrobe*,' said Morton, scandalised.

This was interesting. Darnley began to really listen. 'What read you of their relationship?'

'By my truth, your Grace, I judge it to have some dark potential. No man's wife should be so wantonly familiar with another. You must control our queen – your *wife* and *household* – if you hope to control our realm.'

'And what do you propose?' That, he thought, was clever.

He might be able to manipulate Morton into some confederate solution.

'What your Grace needs to do is assert your authority.'

'By which means?' he asked, a little disappointed. 'I have already made clear to Her Grace the importance, the necessity of granting me the Crown Matrimonial. It is crucial for the status of our child. She dislikes the idea.'

'The queen is in thrall to the Italian. You must remove him. Every day he proves himself an enemy of the state, an adder ready to strike at our breasts. It is he who poisons Her Grace against you.'

'But why? To what purpose? He was as supportive of our marriage as you.'

'That is because he hoped to control you, to make you his creature. He played Pandarus to make you beholden to him. When he realised that he'd be unable to keep you in his clutches, in his debt, he decided to ensure that the queen rules all and he rules the queen. Tell me, did the villain try and ingratiate himself with your Grace?'

He thought back and it all fit into place. Riccio had indeed tried to make him his creature; he had tried – and failed – to make him reliant on his support and advice. Now he was never out of the queen's company, and the queen had never been more at odds with her husband, nor so protective of the authority of which she once sought to relieve herself. 'Yes,' he said simply. 'He was a false friend.'

'The type of which a king needs none. Not when he has loyal men of real rank and pedigree. Now I'm no Knox, your Grace –'

'Thank God for that.'

'No, I am not. I don't fear a woman's rule. But we have in Scotland a king, young and healthy. It's fitting that he bears the weight of government whilst his wife bears the weight of her child. In no land should the hen crow before the cock.' He winked. 'It's against nature and it makes for a strange and disordered world. You see, you're a victim of the poisonous fruit of the musician's unnatural labours, as we all are. Now our queen rules before our king, and the base foreign interloper holds precedence over the ancient blood of the realm. It is dangerous, don't you agree?'

'Yes.'

'And you may have noticed that your wife, though a fair and virtuous woman, is inconstant?'

'How do you mean?'

'Only this: when she's happy and gay, things go well. But without cause, without reason, she'll often fall perilously low in spirits and no man can reach her. No business can be done. Her motives and her wishes cannot be deciphered. You've seen this?'

'Yes.'

'It is no sure way to govern a country. We can't rely on a woman, however virtuous and good, whose humours are so volatile. Especially not when we have a king. Besides, the queasiness and water pangs, the burden of her sex will be on her soon. You are needed.'

'But what can I do, cousin?'

'I believe,' said Morton, sitting back, the chair groaning under his weight, 'it is first necessary to rid our kingdom of Riccio. Any ruler ought to flush the body politic of poison. He is Scotland's Cromwell. You know of Cromwell, your great uncle King Henry of England's evil counsellor? He sought to enrich himself from meddling in the affairs of his betters, and he was not spared the axe despite pleading for mercy as all villains do. The Tudors have always been partial to wielding the axe against enemies of the state. The Italians favour poison. In Scotland we've other means.'

'How do we do it? How do we remove him? The queen would never countenance his arrest, to say nothing of a trial. Might there not be some bloodless means of separation,' he said, still hoping Morton would be his creature, would think and do for him.

'A merciful thought, but there is none. You must rid yourself and your wife of him forever. The man used to solicit your royal company for tennis, did he not? You might challenge him anew, discover him cheating and duel him then and there. Or when you and George next go fishing, ask him along and George will happily push him from the boat.' Darnley almost laughed at this, and Morton read his incredulous expression. 'Ach, there is more than one way to beat a Jack. We'll find it. But what I also suggest is that you consider allowing the return of Moray.'

'That traitorous dog? That rebel? Never! He will not set foot in Scotland as long as I breathe!'

'Peace, your Grace.' Morton closed his eyes and shook his head slowly, raising a finger to his lips. 'There are things you don't know.'

'Such as?'

'Such as the reasons behind Moray's rebellion, which he admits was rash and foolish.'

'You have been in communication with the rebel?'.

'I ... Ach, some letters have passed – private letters, personal. Old friendships, acquaintanceships, you know ... He has a king's blood, whatever his errors.' He shifted uncomfortably. He had been hoping for few questions, to keep to the points he had memorised. 'He bewails it even now to the English queen and your old friend Leicester. He regretted it before it had begun. That's why he avoided open battle. It has been his single great folly, and every man is entitled to one.'

'Neither rashness nor foolishness make treason tolerable.

Leicester will know that,' said Darnley, but he was thrown into confusion. The pages of history were littered with unfortunate kings who had rashly forgiven bad men. Leicester would know that. But then Leicester was a long way away, in a different world.

'Perhaps not; I mention it only in passing. I shan't press it. Let Moray make his own obeisance and demonstrate his own penitence. He's none of mine. Riccio is the problem, your Grace, as he's been the problem for all of us for longer than I care to recognise. The shame is in it taking so long to become clear.'

'We shall think on it,' he said, mustering up some regal presence. 'We thank you for coming and look forward to hearing *your* ideas on solving this problem soon.' There, he thought: with ease, he had played the compliant old man like a lute, sending him to work and relieving himself of a problem he hadn't even been able to see clearly. Morton got up with a grunt, gave a stiff bow and left the room. Too late Darnley remembered to dismiss him with a flick of the hand.

The thought of ridding the Court – the kingdom – of Riccio remained after Morton departed. Could the solution to his problems really be as simple as getting rid of jumped-up little man who may well be meddling with his wife, and who was certainly meddling with Scotland?

18

Christmas was approaching in a flurry of snow. The aspersions Mary had cast on his religious convictions had stung him, and Darnley resolved to make a greater display of his devotions in the darkening days of December. Throughout the month he made a habit of hearing Mass before dawn. He found that sleepless nights were better spent inhaling incense, hearing comforting Latin orisons and giving unthinking responses than tossing and turning. Besides, the Church allowed him something he was increasingly inclined to do – apologise, confess and be forgiven for anything and everything that he did. In return, the priest bestowed mercy, forgiveness and everlasting life. It was a good deal.

Religion had sat lightly upon him for too long, he realised. Since childhood Catholicism had always been something sneaky and covert – a private passion of his mother's. He could now see why she felt it unfairly suppressed. It offered comfort and redemption where Knox and his ilk offered damnation and doom. People began to wonder what the young king's sudden religious frenzy might mean. Some welcomed it. Some were horrified. He did not care. He had come to the uncomfortable realisation that his father had been wrong to treat religion as no more than an overcoat to be thrown on and cast off according to circumstance. It was too old, too heavy, too conspicuous to be treated so.

As well as proving the depth of his belief in God's plan for him, kneeling before the priest and receiving Communion also allowed him time to speak to God in his own way. He offered prayers, as he had always been taught to do, for his ancestors; for his wife and child; for his parents; for his brother; for his brothers and sisters who had died in infancy. He prayed also for divine guidance as to what he should do to save his family, gain his crown and provide for his son. Please God, he thought as hard possible, show me what you expect of me and grant me the strength to do it.

'Benedicamus Domino, alleluja,' answered his thoughts. Bless the Lord he would – but he needed something a little less woolly than that.

Nothing was forthcoming. He spent the rest of his time hawking and drinking when he had companionable lads who wanted him to go out and join them. His birthday came on the 7th – he was now twenty: a fine, bearded man – and Mary's twenty-third followed on the 8th. They did not celebrate together. Instead, he went out with his friends, toasting his birthday happily and his wife's sarcastically.

As a gift to himself he took the opportunity to indulge in another pastime: penning carefully-written, grovelling letters to allies he was courting in Europe. He wrote especially to the King of France, expressing his grief at the precarious state of Scotland, the heretical men who continued to enjoy influence, and the lack of respect shown the king. He declared his hearty desire to return to France and meet his fellow ruler. As always, he signed himself a good friend, eager to resurrect the alliance between his country and King Charles'. Writing to a fellow monarch always lifted his mood.

On Christmas Eve he sat playing cards with Mary in her apartments, where he had gone to show himself solicitous in the spirit of the season. It was not late. He sat across from her at the little card table and looked down at his hand. He had her beat. He smiled sweetly.

'Madam, I think our game is at an end. I will retire now, or else I might miss the morning's services.'

She looked bemused. 'And the king must not miss Mass,

oui? It would be a mirror of his wedding.'

'One of Scotland's princes must, I think, show some loyalty to the true Church. It would be a terrible weight on the conscience to do otherwise. I myself could not turn my back on the faithful, and my face to heretics. Some people are less sensitive. Although I see that double dealing does not ensure success. Goodnight.' He leant over and kissed her cool, smooth cheek. She did not flinch. But as he was leaving she called after him, 'Have a care, husband. One good hand does not win the game.' She lay down her own, stronger cards and he flounced from the room.

Still, he noticed, she did not attend Mass at the break of Christmas morning.

***

At the reformed Scottish Court there was to be no festive revelry. Troops of travelling entertainers and theatricals would not be welcomed as they were at the Court of England. The traditional twelve days of misrule would be a muted affair, without great paper dragons and bawdy pipers. Many Scottish Protestants, particularly of the nobility, were filled with the zeal of recent converts, and even without Knox to fire them up they would dourly point out the lack of Scriptural basis for celebrating the birth of Christ on the 25th of December. To them it was a day like any other, unworthy of note and not fit to be recognised.

Disdaining the prospect of a Christmas period of joyless austerity Darnley took off with a small retinue of servants to the borders town of Peebles, in hunting country. He had not even a royal guard, disliking the distance it would put between himself and his subjects and the lack of trust in them it suggested. That disdaining one would offend his wife's dignity only added cream to the pudding. Lennox was to meet him there, the old man having been as much out of favour as his son. It was time, he knew, to let his father know about his coming grandchild, and he did not want him to strut and swagger in Edinburgh on receipt of the news.

He had not been so far south in his new kingdom since coming into it from his former one: the land he had now come to think of as one of subjection and imperial aggression. Nearly a year of living well and travelling in mild – even if wet and windy – weather had fogged his memories of the difficulties of Scotland's borderland terrain in the depths of winter. He had travelled to Linlithgow and was heading south when fat flakes of snow began to fall. They landed on his eyes despite his cap. His hands were numbed.

As the snow got heavier the world became a whirling blizzard. Frequently he had to call his little troupe to a halt whilst he warmed up and reassessed the route. His riding cloak was sodden and heavy. In such weather it would be possible to be riding around in circles. It was odd, he thought – whenever he ventured near the borders freezing weather threw icy hands around him. It was as though the country which had once tried to keep him out and failed now feared he might leave and fought to keep him in.

It was a strange feeling also to be so close to where his brother still languished under house arrest, to the nation in which his mother was imprisoned in a dungeon. He had written her several times, but always his letters were returned by a spiteful Elizabeth, accompanied by commands that the pretender cease writing to a prisoner who was not permitted correspondence.

He now thought of England as a foreign, cruel land – a refuge for Scottish traitors and apostates. He no longer thought of himself as English. He spoke only Scots and French, and his Yorkshire accent was almost gone – something he had never thought possible. He had ceased to even *think* in English;

Scots words and phrases formed in his mind and marched to his tongue as a matter of course. Only his scrawny valet clung to his northern English patois – claiming the ladies loved it – despite his master's insistence on pure Scots. Now more than ever he wanted his brother and mother released, not so that they could resume their lives under Elizabeth's yoke, but so that they could come north to his kingdom.

They were bound for Peebles' old castle of Smithfield, a disused rural outpost of the Earl of Erroll in which they had been granted permission to lodge. Undoubtedly it would take time to properly heat and provision. As they trotted towards the town the likely state of the place and the paucity of victuals they had brought were beginning to play on his mind when a figure clad in muddy brown staggered towards them out of snow that had died from a whirlwind to a confused and aimless flutter.

'Stop, and let me do you service.' The stranger had a high, reedy voice. But in his hand he held a rusty, pitted dagger. He was a common ruffler: a brigand. Darnley reined in his horse and looked down at the pathetic figure. He could not have been more than thirteen. Whichever uprightman controlled the boy had probably sent him out to bring back spoils or die in the attempt leaving one less mouth to be fed.

'Lad, you are speaking to the king.' The boy looked up. He was emaciated and his sandy hair was thin, his scalp pink from the cold. His eyes, unfocused, were ringed by dark smudges. His mouth worked stupidly; he looked like he was about to collapse, though whether from shock or exhaustion it was hard to tell. He presumed the latter. The lad looked too defeated to be shocked or surprised by anything. His dagger fell. Sliding from his mount, Darnley pocketed it and hoisted the boy by the armpits. He signalled for his retinue to take control of his horse and steered the wasted form towards the town. His feet, wrapped in cheap cloth, took aimless, dragging steps.

He took the boy to a tiny, gloomy tavern in which no one would claim knowledge of him. The town had not been expecting a noble visitor. No one seemed interested. He paid for something hot to eat and drink, and some scanty cold fixings were produced. As the surly proprietor, giving every impression that service was an imposition rather than his trade, brought them over, he grumbled about the state of the town since there had been no useful wars. Darnley ignored him, uninterested in the sullen complaints of a man not happy with his lot. He set the food before the boy, whereupon he seemed to come to his senses. His eyes opened wide, and he jumped up, uncomprehending. Darnley tried to grab for him but he wriggled away, making incoherent grunts in which only the occasional Scots swear word was decipherable. He flew out the door with astonishing speed.

Darnley followed, intent on pursuit. His servants were tending to the horses. No ostler had offered to stable them. 'Where did the boy go, Will?'

''e took off.'

'Where, you fool?' Will was a loyal soul, but a dull-witted one.

'O'er there,' said Will, gesturing vaguely in the direction from which they had come: a world of greyish white sky and land blended together in a chalky palette.

'He'll die out there.'

'Give over, 'e's just a thief, your Grace. Nowt to concern yourself about.' Will, Darnley noticed, had been steadily giving himself more and more airs since he had been allowed to join his royal master in the occasional drinking session. From a respectable Yorkshire family, he thought himself quite the man-of-the-world in Scotland. He would have to do something about that.

'He was a child.'

'Aye, well, there i'n't nowt but thieves down 'ere,' said Will, sniffing and shivering simultaneously. 'Me dad always warned us of the border folk. Thieves, footpads, free-booters and reivers: there's stacks of 'em. And not a woman worth lookin' at neither. Can we get inside afore we freeze to death, do you think, your Grace? It's colder than the Queen of England's paps and I'm wringin'.'

'I'll slap your face,' said Darnley without much heat. Instead he looked around, turning in a circle. They could certainly expect no welcoming cheers from the local burgesses. The place was a shanty town. Empty barrels topped with snow lay neglected in the High Street. The windows of the rough wood and stone dwellings on either side of the road were stopped with wadded up cloth. The whole place was devoid of the noise of human presence – no children laughed, no merchants shouted their wares, no dogs barked. The only sound was the wind which occasionally issued a whiny, high-pitched blast.

***

Smithfield Castle, he had been told, could not be missed on a road off the High Street. It was certainly unmissable, but for all the wrong reasons. It was a grey mausoleum, like many of those of any age dotted around Scotland looking like it might stand forever or collapse, dejected and exhausted, tomorrow. Its windows were suspicious, defensive slits, admitting little light, giving and receiving no view. The circular interior walls were bare, as cold on the inside as the outside. What furniture there was – some cushionless wooden chairs, some mouldy bare bunks, and a chipped and battered desk – was sagging and ugly. Perhaps the people of the town or the roving vagabonds outside it had been in at some point and stripped anything left that was worth taking. Forgotten, abandoned places attracted forgotten, abandoned people. He began to doubt the wisdom of his hunting trip.

The royal party had brought little with them and so Darnley thought it prudent to explore the town to find provisions. What he saw horrified him. He had known there was poverty and hardship in Scotland – he unfailingly tossed silver groats to Edinburgh's myriad beggars to buy ale when he was revelling – but nothing had prepared him for the sight of children in rags staggering like silent ghosts through piles of drifted snow, nor for the faces of old people who had never known anything but struggle and starvation. He had never seen real poverty before, or never paid it any heed. The poor were simply there, ordained by God to be poor in his great chain. But ... but ... God also wanted great men to be charitable. Might it be, he wondered, that the poor were a test? That he had been guided here as a test? Well, God would not find the King of Scots lead-footed and uncharitable.

For days he and his servants lived like nomads. At night they huddled on and under blankets and delicate cloaks through which the cold, uneven floor sent waves of penetrating chill. But when hunting he could enjoy the sensation of the freezing air on his face, the feeling of freedom and control – over himself, over nature, over his horse. His hunting parties encountered no one out on the high, frozen hills: no brigands, not the boy who had so pathetically tried to rob them – and not, he thought gratefully, any bodies. The world of intrigue, of politics and power struggles, might have been swept from the earth by the icy winds.

He was beginning to grow accustomed to the relative simplicity of a pastoral lifestyle when a procession of horses drew up to the dilapidated castle, breaking the spell. The Bishop of Orkney, with servants of his own and abundant stores of food and drink, had come and was horrified at the primitive conditions under which the King of Scots was living, despite Darnley's lying that it was a short break intended to be one of fasting and discomfort.

'It is not meet, your Grace, for any royal person to live in such a manner,' said the Bishop, gesturing dismissively around dingy castle's main hall, thick greying hair jutting out from beneath a furred hat.

'Lord Bishop, it is not meet for anyone to live as the people here,' replied Darnley.

'It is terrible, yes, but the poor will always be with us, alas, alas.' He rolled his eyes skyward and raised chubby white hands in the air. The man had a theatrical manner and a face settling merrily into alcoholic flab.

'I note that meat and drink is what you have with you.'

'Indeed, with which we shall be happy to provision you.'

'See that you tend to the people here, Lord Bishop. They require of it.' He had expected some demurral from the bishop and set his jaw lest the old man cow him with age and experience, but instead the small, fleshy mouth twisted in a smile.

'Your Grace, I have enough to provide against the poverty of the town for a time. When I visit my property here I always bring sufficient supplies to give succour to those in need. I see the hand of God in directing us both to this place.'

For the remainder of the trip he oversaw the bishop, whose chins nodded eagerly, in tending to the people of the desolate border town. His initial altruism, however, faded at the sight of the food and he helped himself to the finer provisions carried in the ecclesiastical train; he had, after all, ruined a perfectly good cloak on the trip and deserved some comfort. Still, he was well pleased that the royal will had shown itself bent to recognising and alleviating appalling suffering. When he was a child and had been good, his parents had occasionally employed local balladeers to entertain the family after supper.

Invariably their lyrical tales involved a percipient prince appearing amongst the downtrodden in lowly disguise, only to throw it off and intercede to thwart and shame villainy, bring justice, restore order and allow the abused to triumph. Listening to those stories, no matter how poorly sung or unlikely they were, he would hold his breath and bite his bottom lip, eyes wide, just waiting for the prince to appear and save the day. Now he was just such a king. He expected – hoped for – pathetic gratitude. But the denizens of the border town were beyond even that. Like animals they greedily fought over the food that was given them, stuffing mouths and pockets with as much as they could.

When his father arrived to hear the news his son had promised him he was as overjoyed by it as he was nonplussed by Darnley's continued efforts to be seen out and amongst the needy of Peebles. Whilst he was here, Darnley thought, he cared little for the earl's worldly concerns. 'When the king goes a-hunting, dark forces a-mass,' Lennox kept repeating, proud of his aphorism. He insisted passionately that they must return to Edinburgh, to shout to the world that God had smiled on the Lennox Stewarts after all, making them unquestionably faithful sons and natural governors of Scotland. But Darnley had seen something of real life beyond the rarefied airs of Court and city, and his father's persistent pressing of him to demand his royal rights did not seem quite so vital. He also turned a deaf ear to Will, who had found the town's female residents even more disinterested in him than Edinburgh's.

Darnley kept thinking of the boy who would have robbed him. He was probably dead – frozen solid in a foothill. Looking at the blunted little dagger, which he had set on the lodge's desk, he realised he had taken his only means of income. He decided to keep it. If he could never return it, it could serve as a reminder that there were things in Scotland that needed fixing, and worse things in the world than his own cares.

He dreamt again of the mysterious, corpse-littered cemetery by the river. Now, however, the grotesque monuments were snow-covered. The body which fell towards him, nearly pulling him down, was the young brigand. His eyes were gone – the blank sockets two broken windows revealing nothing.

19

Darnley returned to Edinburgh after the twelve days of Christmas. He threw himself once more into his devotions. He prayed for God to banish nightmares from him and grant him a peaceful sleep. He prayed for the lost and desolate thief.

After one of his early morning observances he bided his time until after dinner, a plan forming. The Privy Council was meeting in the afternoon and he decided that he would appear, unexpected. Since he had returned to Court he had heard the latest gossip – that the queen, in his absence, had shown signs of forgiving the Duke of Châtellerault, the fat, wheezing Hamilton traitor who had joined in rebellion with Moray. Evidently, the Queen of England was working on Mary to forget the civil war and welcome back into the country the men who had been chased from it.

Fired up with religious zeal he threw the door open and made his entrance. All heads turned to him. The Protestant Bothwell's was not far from the queen. Only Mary did not seem surprised to see him. Her expression remained bored, curiously like her brother Moray's.

'Gentlemen,' he announced, 'I understand that there is talk of inviting back our kingdom's prodigal son, the devious duke.' No one answered him. 'Your king will have none of it. In fact, we have decided to make a stand against the heresy of this nation and tolerate the ancient Roman faith for any who do not subscribe to our Kirk.' Bothwell's jaw tensed. He looked like a grizzled, angry bull. Darnley held his gaze, lifting his chin. 'In fact, in the interests of accommodation and tolerance, I believe we should have a Mass celebrated in St Giles. What think you of that?'

Only Huntly, the faithful Catholic Huntly, answered. 'Your Grace, I b-b-believe our religion to be sufficiently re-respected by Her Grace's policies.' He met no one's eyes and immediately wished he could have the words back, that he had not drawn attention to himself.

'Do you, indeed? Well, let us test the extent of that respect. I suggest you – all of you – join me in attending Mass on the morrow.'

'Never,' said Bothwell, disgust at the Papist English child animating him. 'I'll see any Scotsman who pledges the crown to *any* foreigner – petty Pope or not – *dead* before I'll see him put us under the boot-heel of Rome.' His hands were flexing in and out of fists, the knuckles turning white and red. Here, thought Darnley, was a hint of the temper the man usually glossed over with affable or sardonic urbanity. He wondered what it would take to unleash that chained beast.

'Is that so, my lord? And will the queen be equally obstinate in neglecting her faith?' He turned his gaze to her. She was dressed in white, without ostentatious jewellery. She looked at him with challenge. When her temper rose the soft amber eyes kindled.

'On the contrary, your Grace. We think it an excellent idea. We shall be most happy to hear Mass. Is it not so, my lords?'

It was evidently getting too much for those on the Council. Once again it was Bothwell who stood up, and rather than siding with Mary in the battle of wits with her husband he swept the documents which were laid out in front of him away with a thick arm. 'I said never.' He stood up without being asked. She was momentarily flustered. Ha! he thought – she was expecting her little gaggle of servants to fall in line behind her and out-bluff their king.

Smiling, Darnley held up his hands. 'Pax,' he said. 'I see that there is no taste in Scotland for the members of the

Council to listen to either king or queen in matters of religion. What a people you are. Well, I shall leave you locked in disagreement and hope that the key is lost. Good day, my lords. Good day, your Highness.' He poured as much scorn into the last word as he could, and bowed before leaving the room, a grin on his face.

Bothwell's expression had been worth the commotion – as had the reminder that he existed and that he would not be silenced. He had not forgotten the smirk on the brute's ugly face when remarking on his beard, which was now neatly trimmed and golden.

When he returned to his apartments he found a letter from the French Court, full of hearty greetings from King Charles. Further, it gave warning that France was sending an ambassador to invest him with the ancient Order of St Michael. The French king claimed to value the friendship of the King of Scots, reputed to be one of the most beautiful and accomplished princes in Europe. He held the letter to his chest. The kingly fraternity of Europe had embraced him as one of their own.

***

The ambassador Rambouillet and his train arrived at the start of February, and a week later Darnley once again knelt in order to be awarded titles and honours as a favoured friend of the Catholic French Court. For over a month he had continued to flaunt his faith and Mary had begun competing with him. There was something enjoyable about watching her respond to his goading, the feeling that he was driving events, making her do things, incredibly exciting and vital. As a result of his out-praying her she had declared her intention to increase Catholic toleration. In response to his recognition by the French king she had declared before the visitors that she was the true, Catholic Queen of England. It was a game of wits and one-upmanship, and for once he felt like they were really playing together, even if it was as opponents.

For the occasion – which felt tantalisingly close to a coronation – he wore a scarlet and black robe of satin trimmed with gold. He swore before the Court – what remained of it – that he would be loyal and true to King Charles as far as was possible given his loyalty to the queen. The words came easily, as much as it galled him to swear allegiance to a woman who had shown little respect for him and who seemed to have ceased to have much liking for him.

After the ceremony a Council meeting was held at which Darnley's presence was required, as much for appearances before the ambassador as for anything. Rambouillet, a thin, slight man with a hooked nose and long, twirled moustaches was given the honour of speaking first.

'And what arms should be bestowed? I must know so that they can be emblazoned on the armoury of the Order.'

'The arms of Scotland,' said Darnley, pride in voice. 'There can be no other.'

Bothwell spoke up. 'As parliament has not yet granted his Grace the Crown Matrimonial, I fail to see how that can be. The arms of his Grace's dukedoms are fitting.' He sat back in his chair, pleased with himself. Scottish dukedoms granted to an Englishman were ridiculous enough, to his mind.

Darnley could only stand dumbly, unwilling to embarrass himself any more than Bothwell had done. Rambouillet already looked uncomfortable. Ambassadors he knew had a nose for disharmony and conflict. Lennox, who had returned to Court with his son and was determined to be present at all meetings of the Council even if his son was usually excluded, added in what he supposed was a deadly cadence, 'Only the arms of Scotland will suffice for a King of Scots.' Rambouillet looked pleadingly to Mary, his moustache twitching.

'Give him only what he is due. No more.'

'Ah, um ... I see,' said Rambouillet, clucking his tongue and wringing his hands fussily. 'And so ... well ... then the arms of Albany and Lennox shall be sewn onto all insignia, until such a time as the ... uh ... king ... is anointed and crowned.' He seemed torn between enjoying the domestic dispute and heartily embarrassed at being forced to participate. His eyes flitted between Mary and Darnley as he tried to read their reactions. This was the meat and drink of his profession.

The day had been ruined. Darnley was seething, belittled again and in front of a man who would return to France full of the lack of respect given the King of Scots. He stormed to his rooms after the Privy Council meeting, elbowing servants out of his way. He could feel them staring after them but determined they would not seem him red in the face. Once there he tore off his robes and threw them to the floor. It was all becoming so hideously clear. His wife was fighting a war of attrition. Having promoted him she had immediately denied him his crown and now sought by degrees to diminish him bit by bit until he was nothing in his own country. At every turn she would have him lose face.

He thirsted for revenge, for some means of humiliating her, of humiliating the whole, stinking pack of them. They must all be repaid in their own coin; but how? An idea began to come together in his mind and a sly smile twisted his lips.

***

Days of feasting and revelry in honour of the French guests followed his investiture. The lords of the Council took part in masques; Darnley and Mary performed; there was much music and dancing. Throughout it all he behaved admirably, displaying the courtesy and geniality which had won him the good opinion of the King of France. He presented the ambassador with an ornate, golden dagger, which he solemnly said he hoped would not be the only thing by which the French remembered him and his country.

The last day of Rambouillet and his attendants' stay in Scotland was to be the most magnificent. Dinner in the morning was held in Edinburgh Castle. Afterwards the royal couple and their guests processed through the city back to Holyrood to the sound of a gun salute fired from the castle. At Holyroodhouse a majestic farewell reception was to be held. Once they had all arrived back at the palace and were seated at well-appointed tables in the Gallery, Darnley stood up to offer them his own goodbyes.

'Honoured guests and friends,' he said. Voices died down. 'It is with sorrow that you are to leave our home, but with that joy that you shall remain in our hearts.' There were murmurs of approval and agreement. 'As this is our last night with you, we beg you partake of our finest *aqua composita*: the bonniest liquor our nation has to offer.' He held up a delicate wrought-silver cup of amber liquid he had requested earlier but not yet touched. He gazed at it intently, turning it in his fingers. 'Friends, let us have good cheer,' he said at length, tilting his head and his cup at Rambouillet.

A bevy of serving men, whom he had had Will tip off before the banquet was begun, had raided the royal kitchens for every drop of the strongest liquor that could be found. When they had gathered it all they brought in more from the city and were instructed that it should be kept flowing into the mouths of the French guests. Darnley's farewell was their signal to start pouring.

There was general cheering at the prospect of the whisky. Rambouillet professed himself greatly pleased to be given such a fine drink in the midst of such a sharp winter. Darnley threw an arm around the scrawny man, favouring him with a smile and another drink. More and more drinks were poured, with Mary becoming increasingly alarmed at the rowdy state of her guests and her courtiers. Time seemed to speed up. The banquet which began as an afternoon reception roared on until after nine o'clock. He indulged himself, enjoying the warming glow of the spirits almost as much as he was enjoying the unravelling occasion.

One of Rambouillet's men vomited in a corner of the Gallery leaving a puddle of brown liquid dotted with chunks of half-digested food. Some of it splashed up onto a tapestry. Several courtiers, lower-ranking nobility, decided to engage Rambouillet himself in a game of drinking, downing vast quantities of whisky and falling about laughing. The noise in the room was reaching the city itself: crowing laughter, angry shouts over nothing of consequence, agreements and détentes as old enemies became best friends. The ambassador's thin face was bright red as he hacked and coughed, was clapped on the back and commiserated. His moustaches drooped. 'I cannot', he spluttered, trying to catch his breath, 'I cannot … I cannot.' But whatever he could not do was forgotten as he slumped face-first onto a table and closed his eyes.

Mary stood up from her throne heavily, gathered her skirts and left the room, her head high. Riccio scuttled after her. He had followed her lead in avoiding the alcohol. As she was leaving George Douglas crept up to Darnley, nudging him lightly in the ribs. 'The queen takes to her bedroom,' he said, a leer on his thin, ratty face, 'with her crookbacked lover. She may as well hang garlands on your cuckold's horns to advertise her misdeeds. Well, some mares like to be worked hard when in foal. Never mind, your Grace – the king can take his own pleasure elsewhere.' George always turned vicious on the drink, his rancid breath matching his words in aggression. Normally he disliked having to do duties for his pompous cousin Morton, but when he was given license to drink to excess, insult the stuck up and encourage a bit of vice, they became a pleasure.

Darnley ostentatiously turned his back on his departing wife and her creeping secretary. If she would publicly impugn his honour, showing the world that he had no authority in the realm or in their marriage, he would not spare her reputation.

For Darnley the day had been a triumph: his wife's elegant reception had been ruined and the Frenchmen would have quite enough humiliation of their own to worry about before letting slip to their king the private shaming of the King of Scots. He was on a high, delighted with the success of his scheme. Skipping merrily through the carnage, he found Robert Stewart drinking contentedly with some of his friends. 'A banquet unparalleled,' he said, beaming, 'much more to my taste than masques.' Darnley laughed.

'Come on,' he said, 'let's go out and enjoy the night before the smell of vomit spoils the taste of the drink.'

Darnley, Robert and a group of drunken lords and nobles tore out of the palace intent mischief. As they caroused through the city, others joined the Saturnalia. As always Robert managed to pick up some women. Darnley didn't know whether he knew them; he didn't care. They played at eluding the city watchmen – a pointless game, given their status – and eventually passed out of their jurisdiction, much to the watchmen's relief.

Somehow they acquired some little boats and were rowing out into the Forth for Inchkeith Island, a tiny, secluded mound. It all seemed like a marvellous idea. Darnley swayed in the boat, stood up, nearly capsized it. The women were screeching. A little voice in his head kept trying to sound reasonable, to tell him to calm himself and be sensible. He stifled it. They crashed up on the beach. Someone was sick. Someone told him that they should all strip, and he threw off his clothes and crashed into the icy water, howling yet not feeling it. When he clambered back out, coughing up spurts of dirty liquid, he saw Robert halfway up the hill, scrambling around some scrub with one of the women. Her clothes had been torn. Yet she was shrieking with laughter rather than fear or anger. Someone had lit a fire and he could see her and Robert frolic and gambol in the flickering light like two grotesque, semi-clothed fawns.

'Harry,' Robert shouted over to him, his voice thick and punctuated by hiccups, 'Harry, come over and join us, you great coy maiden! Let her have a great king as well as a wee bastard!'

He collapsed to his knees, sinking in the sandy mud. He was hooting laughter again as he gouged his hands deep into it and threw clods of the muck at Robert and his wench.

20

He woke up with a grunt. He was in his own bed, in his own apartments at Holyroodhouse. The bed-hangings were open and dishevelled. He was naked and he had no idea why, nor how he got home. His last memories were of falling about the streets of Edinburgh, though he thought he remembered being on the water. His head was still light and buzzing; the alcohol was still giving him the 'good cheer' he had called for the previous night. He had no idea of the time. Instinctively, he looked around for his clothes. They had been neatly arranged on top of a clothing chest, presumably by his servants. They were caked in mud. But they were all there. He wrinkled his nose. Someone had been in – they had filled bowls with fresh flowers, the sweetness of the blooms making a poor job of counteracting the stuffiness of stale fireplace smoke and an unemptied chamber pot. Chilly fingers of wind to groped their way in through open windows.

When he stood the room rocked crazily and he had to screw his eyes shut. He threw on a clean nightshirt and thought about waking Will, who was still sleeping on his pallet bed. Had Will been drinking last night? Darnley thought he had. He had the strange idea that if he continued to drink he could maintain the pleasant glow which still enveloped him. There was an attractive logic to that. There was a jug of wine next to his bed, half-full. He must have had some when he got home, he thought, frustrated at the gaps in his memory. What had he been saying to people last night? He couldn't remember and didn't think he really wanted to know. Hopefully, he thought, his company would also have been too drunk to remember whatever nonsense he had been blurting out. He picked up the jug and swirled the wine, sniffing at it. It was sour-smelling, heavy and vinegary. He took a swig, holding his breath and rocking on his feet.

There was a knock at his door. He shook Will awake. The boy's eyes, which usually had the sly look of someone who thought they were much smarter than they were, were bloodshot. He bade him answer the knock and tell whoever it was that he was unwell. Grumbling and rubbing his eyes, Will obliged. Darnley went to his mirror and jerked back from the sight. His eyes were bright red, unfocused, and there was something dry and crusty around his lips, flaked through his beard. He ran his tongue over it and tasted the bitter tang of thrown-up alcohol. His blonde hair stuck up at odd angles, like little sticks of broken wheat. I have never looked less like a king in this mirror, he thought. It struck him as funny.

Someone came into the room behind him. 'You might as well go back to bed, Will,' he said, turning. He blanched. It was a bowing Morton. He was carrying a sheaf of papers under his arm. Darnley cursed his own blithe assurances, given time and again, that he embraced the Scottish tradition of any man of standing having free access to his private chambers. Damn the man. He could certainly pick his moments. 'I told Will to let it be known that I was indisposed.'

'I can see that, your Grace. I took the liberty of sending your Will away to combat his own indisposition with some nourishment.' Morton's eyes were twinkling in what passed for him as good humour. 'I've been indisposed myself.' He sniffed at the air and smiled almost triumphantly. 'And I suspect your morning's draught will have loosened your pipes. This will not detain you long. May I sit?' he asked, already settling himself down on the edge of Darnley's bed. He remembered that Morton had been circumspect at the previous night's reception. In fact, had he even seen the man later on in the evening?

'It is no day for business, cousin.'

'Every day's a day for business when you rule.' That shut him up. He retreated to the bed himself and lay down casually, annoyed that the position forced him to look up towards his cousin. But there was no help for it; standing was making him feel dizzy. 'Monsieur Rambouillet and his friends also had difficulty shifting themselves this morning I gather. Well, no matter. I'll come to the point; I'm a straightforward man. Your Grace, I've been appalled at how you have been handled these last months. Touching the matter that troubles you, I've since given its resolution much thought. As have others.'

'The matter?'

'Riccio.'

'Him,' spat Darnley. 'That enemy of the state: that Italian Cromwell.'

'The same.'

'And what have you and others been saying?'

'We've devised, your Grace, a way of removing the usurping scoundrel without staining your or our honour. In fact I've been given these bonds. They're signed. They declare the support of the loyal men of Scotland, friends to you and Her Majesty.' He brandished the papers he was carrying in the air.

'Who are these loyal friends?'

'Moray ... Argyll ... Glencairn ... Roth-'

Darnley cut him off. 'The rebels.'

'They were the men involved in the late broils, aye, but men of great blood and experience. You must understand, your Grace, they bore you no ill will. They believed – falsely, as they now know – that your marriage to the queen was being managed by Riccio, and that he hoped to use you to abolish the Kirk. Not to tolerate it, but to overturn it. This is still what we believe he aims at, and what he hopes to achieve by stirring such discord in our land.'

'I have no wish to banish or overturn anything,' he said. He could hear the meekness in his own voice and buffed his pillow in a sham of irritation. Morton had not been present at the Council meeting at which he had bragged about ordering Masses at St Giles, but he had surely heard of it. To his surprise, Morton smiled. 'And so the rumours about you and your saucy mates declaring in the streets that the old religion was back are false?' he asked.

His mind raced. Had he said that? When he drank to excess he was apt to anything that sounded impressive and grand, and then either to forget it or blanch at the memory. Such was the price of a lads' night out. But wait – suddenly he recalled ladies leaning from a window in the town; he had called up that he was the good Catholic King Harry; they had giggled and jiggled their bosoms before pulling closed the shutters. It had been a jest. Morton spared him the need to answer. 'No matter – we're all braggarts in drink. Hard liquor makes even the timid chick a strutting cock. The problem is your wife's inclinations, and the intolerable power enjoyed by the man encouraging them. Your private worship is your own concern provided you let the Kirk stand and accept the friendship of the realm's old blood in finding a solution. Together we can restore order and stability, have things as they were – loyalty to the crown throughout the realm and respect from the crown towards its great and loyal men. And with your help the world will see this is no intolerant religious killing, no aping of French and Spanish butchery.'

So it had been Riccio guiding Mary's actions - and to think he had flattered himself as having influence. What a fool he had been. What an unimportant nobody everyone must think him. 'I cannot forgive rebels,' he said. 'Their crimes are too great. The queen,' he added weakly, 'would never forgive me. I could say farewell to any hopes of receiving favour, to say nothing of my crown.'

'Your Grace, the queen has already forgiven Châtellerault.' That was true. She had slapped his and his family's faces in doing it. 'She'll forgive the others in time. Trust me; I'm an old statesman as well as your blood relative. I've seen these things pass before. I know of your belief in Scotland – I share it – but I see peace and amity with our neighbours as essential to a stable nation. And the Queen of England wills it, and to that end has offered to recognise you if you look favourably on Moray. Lethington has seen to that for you; and he has almost as much reason to resent the usurping alien as your Grace.

'Moray made a mistake in rebelling I grant you, but he feared a greater and bloodier disagreement in the future. Mind, he did all he could not to come to blows. That's why I come here as your kinsman, to offer you the opportunity to seek pacification first, so that you might extract the best deal you can from those who'd seek your favour. If you support us in ridding our country, and your wife's bed,' - Darnley flinched – 'of this serpent, we'll do all in our power to support you in your aims. I want to see one with Douglas blood wearing a crown as much as your Grace. But that crown will only be safe in an orderly realm. What is your will?'

He tried to think, but his head was still fuzzy. The will of Elizabeth? Had she and Lethington been in secret correspondence? The English queen certainly loved secretaries and shadowy men of business. It should be no surprise that Lethington would be trying to direct matters from beyond without raising his head or his voice, but what did it signify?

'I wish ... I wish to be crowned. If you pledge to support me in that, I will think of joining you.'

'Is that all?'

'No,' he said, 'I heartily desire you all to labour for the liberation of my mother and brother.'

'Naturally,' said Morton. 'I'd do that as a matter of course, as your dear mother's cousin.'

'Only ... what help do you seek from me? A signature? I will sign anything if you pledge me your support.'

Morton tutted, shaking his head. 'Ah, would that it were that simple, your Grace. You are a great king, are you not?'

'I am.'

'And a defender of Scotland?'

'You know I am.'

'Well then I'm sure you'll be as eager as we to help eliminate this wicked serpent. Her Majesty must be shown what a strong king is. The wretch must be removed from her protection. Otherwise what is Scotland but a despoiled Rome, where Sejanus rules whilst the Emperor is left to pursue idleness and vice?'

'You want me to strike him dead myself?' asked Darnley, his head spinning. Was Morton suggesting that he was a pleasure-loving Tiberius, whoring on Capri whilst his realm was left to the depredations of a powerful servant? Is that what people were saying? Morton was an unlettered man; he must have had that from someone. He had half-hoped that his kinsman would have gone off and dealt with Riccio himself, his regal indication that he was unhappy being enough for matters to be taken care of.

'We seek your authority for his death and immunity from punishment for the act. But we find it fitting that the cuckolded man recovers his own honour. What could be more natural?'

'Death! Where? When? And if I cannot?'

'You said you were a defender of the realm,' answered Morton. 'We know that the great senators of Rome did not forebear to take up their daggers and slay Caesar when he became a threat to the state: and Caesar was once their friend. Little Edward of England, a younger sovereign than yourself, was not afraid to make the corrupt Duke of Somerset shorter by a head when he sought to take power for himself. It's womanlike to be weak, fearful and submissive, your Grace. Brave monarchs make these difficult decisions with courage. Why, even the queen has ordered executions for the good of the realm. Are you not a man, as other men? Are you not a statesman equal to your wife?'

'Yes,' he said. His head had settled to a dull throb.

'Yes?'

'Yes, I am the equal of my wife. And yes, I understand that the proud, perverse man must go.'

'Must go,' repeated Morton.

'Still, I should prefer some gentler measure. I wish that known.'

'We would all prefer some gentler measure. I would much rather be at some gentler *occupation*, tending my gardens or finding my girls husbands.' He stroked his whiskered chin ruefully. 'Alas, I've been called to this business, and we must do what we must to make the world secure for all our children.' He tutted sadly, and Darnley wondered if that calling was from God or some other. 'The Tudors, as I've said, are fond of using the law and the axe to remove enemies of England. In Scotland, we use these bonds.' He waved the papers. 'And the dagger. That's the way of it sometimes. If you're with us you're part of us. And we're part of you. You wish a place in noble company, do you not?' Darnley nodded imperceptibly, wishing he could knead his temples. 'Good. I have here a promise to protect the state and its religion and provide clemency and mercy to those men who fell into error. In return it pledges our support in all your endeavours. You may sign and keep a copy, and I'll take one to your friends, who'll put the execution of this business in motion.'

'But ... no trial?' he chanced. 'We must proceed against him without trial?'

Morton sighed impatiently. 'Treason trials are not held to prove guilt or innocence. They merely demonstrate for the public the means by which a man's guilt has already been established.' Darnley frowned in confusion and Morton pressed on, leaning closer, his voice becoming more animated. 'Am I not the Lord Chancellor? When it comes to justice, I know whereof I speak. We'll demonstrate guilt without the ignominy of publicly humiliating your Majesty in a courtroom.'

'How do we do it? Do we seize him silently? He is never alone.'

'That's for you to say. But if you wish the advice of one with experience-'

'I do, please.'

'Then we take him from the queen's presence. How more clearly and honourably can your Grace demonstrate proven guilt than by taking your wife's seducer from the very scene of his crimes? You must be seen to reclaim your wife and your honour. What greater way can there be to show our sovereign lady that we're removing from the heart of Scottish politics a malignant growth, eh?'

Darnley's throat was as dry as Morton's sheaf of papers. It made sense. Riccio was indeed a wicked, amoral beast and Morton had reminded him of the bitter jealousy he felt whenever he pictured the brute scurrying from Mary's room in his nightshirt. Simply trapping them and exposing their proximity in court was useless; like the adulterous Aphrodite and Ares in their golden net, public exposure would only entangle them further. The domestic dramas of antiquity, rehearsed in childhood, were more useful than he had once imagined. Separation and dispatch were needed, the rightful vengeance of Odysseus rescuing Penelope from the men who had made merry in their home and would do so with her body. Perhaps when she saw her husband order the corrupt satyr from her she would even appreciate that she had married a strong man rather than a womanish boy. He could see himself punching the little fiend, kicking him, stabbing him. The dark fantasies he had enjoyed when he thought she might be sleeping with him could come true. What was the life of such a twisted, perverse thing, an enemy of the state, when innocent people died every day from lack of food and warmth? No great king recoiled from meting out justice to the iniquitous.

'We will take him from the queen. We will drag him away from her forever. We will free her from his malign and pernicious influence.' He spoke slowly, giving weight to each word, wanting to be convinced by them himself. He was conscious of his sour morning-after breath. He half-remembered thinking he had been cunningly manipulating Morton into solving his problems for him; now he felt vaguely that he was part of the puppet show, not its master.

Morton nodded, his eyes downcast in earnest reverence as though he was hearing the pronouncement for the first time from a grave judge. 'Would you like to meet with the men who have pledged themselves to you, and to whom you have pledged yourself? Would you like to explain your grievances and hear theirs? I, uh ... I don't read so well myself – no need for it, you know; a man of my station has menials enough for papers.' Though his tone was light, his eyebrows briefly knitted and then disengaged. 'But your friends and I will be happy to meet and speak plainly with you if you sign your name.'

'Oh no, please – if I sign, won't you meet with them for me

and tell them?' He cursed the rising pitch and weakness of his voice.

'I'd be pleased to. You let your old kinsman take things in hand for you. Sign these bonds of remission and association now, and I shall deliver a copy to your loyal friends. I shall return when they know of your favour with their names attached to the warrant of execution so that you may sign that also.'

Darnley stretched out a quivering hand and took the papers. He rolled off the bed, stumbled to his desk on watery legs and set them down. He did not read them; the spidery writing was blurry. He took a quill and unstoppered a pot of ink. He rifled through, finding where spaces had been left for his name. To sign the prelude to Riccio's death he had to grasp the wrist of his writing hand and hold it steady. His signature was shaky. As he looked at his hands he noticed for the first time that they were filthy. The backs of both were coated in a thin crust of sandy-coloured dirt and the tip of each fingernail was trimmed with black.

21

As the following weeks passed Darnley tried to clear his mind and reflect on the enormity of what he had committed himself to. He cursed himself for being so pliable, for not demanding more time to think before agreeing to the rebels' return. But there was no going back. By signing, he had written himself into the unfolding tale and must see it through to its conclusion. He must frame his mind to it. This was his chance to prove himself as a man and a king – and he must not shirk it with pretty doubts. His spirits rose somewhat at the news that the smug Randolph, who had never forgiven him for foiling his mission to wed Mary to Leicester, had been ordered from the country after being found to have helped fund Moray's rebellion. Randolph's parting shot, delivered with tiresome prolixity, had been to refuse to accept any passport signed by a false king – and so he tarried at Berwick, probably stirring up local trouble. But there was one less pair of spying eyes at a Court pleasingly quieter without a garrulous English ambassador.

Seeking confidantes he approached Ruthven, the stalwart supporter of his marriage, for advice. He was the oldest ally other than his father Darnley had; his knowledge and opinions could be relied upon. The old man, whose throat rattled from deep within when he spoke, was delighted at the prospect of eliminating Riccio. It was, he claimed, how things ought to be done in Scotland, a country which had lost its way under a woman's soft rule. His father concurred, telling him that it was high time that he did something concrete to gain his crown, and if that meant forgiving men for past sins, well, who had never erred? He did not need to seek out his Uncle George: he knew all about the plan and professed that he would support his friend at all costs in the violent pursuit of the villain who was cuckolding him. Offhandedly he had told him that it was a well-known fact that some women reached a stage in their pregnancy of uncontrollable, voracious sexual appetite, despite the well-known dangers of intercourse to mother and child. At that stage women were as strong as oxen but as wild and witless as young bulls. She might well be satiating her hunger with Riccio every night. Why, removing Riccio from the queen's embraces would, said George, safeguard the life of the unborn bairn.

Morton eventually returned on the first day of March to make sure of his agreement and understanding of what was being proposed. He brought only one copy of the final bond, the declaration of the intent to dispatch Riccio, and took it with him after getting it signed. He wanted, he assured him, to leave him in no doubt that this was an honourable bond of brotherhood equally agreed upon for the good of Scotland. He left Darnley's chambers feeling decades younger. It was a difficult job well done, and he was grudgingly grateful for Moray's stock of precedents, which he'd had read to him until he felt himself, for the first time in his life, quite a scholar. The bairn, as he always thought of his king, had swallowed the old tales and was in his pocket – almost literally. As he strode out of the palace, he kept patting the breast of his doublet into which the bond had been slid, the feel of it crinkling against his heart reassuring him that it had not somehow slid out and escaped. It was proof that he was safe, his allies were safe, and his country would be safe in the hands of the old and ancient-blooded.

***

Now that the course of action had been decided Darnley was eager that it should be carried out. Rashness, he decided, was no bad thing if it produced positive results. Morton and the rest were right – no one supported Riccio except the woman he was seducing. A canker had been allowed to fester and it needed to be removed by the swift hand a strong and skilled surgeon.

The jealousy had intensified since his agreement with his new supporters, and self-pity rendered him unable to bear the Mary's presence even during their dinners and days holding their little Court in the Gallery. Perversely, he sought her out whenever possible. He was more desirous of her cold and hateful company than he had ever been. If he could be with her at all times, if he could keep her under his gaze, the musician could not meddle with her. She was appalled by any moves to spend time with her. The more he thrust himself into her company, the more she spurned him. He had even taken to giving his servants money to pay hers for information on what she said to Riccio; what he said to her; what they did together; whether he made her laugh and if so by what means; or whether he stirred any other emotions within her. Did she talk about him? Laugh about him? Not knowing was too troubling. He began to dream incessantly of her. Invariably he would confront her or be confronted by her: always they were fighting, always she would flaunt her cuckolding of him, always he would wake up fearing it had really happened. But only in those dreams did he have the liberty to say all that was in his heart.

The neutered frustration, the tension between desire and anger, found its outlet in grim and violent daydreams. He would slit the oily little bastard's throat; he would kick him as he lay dying; he would decapitate him and dare Mary to kiss his ugly, frozen features. The idea that he could butcher Riccio, illustrating his mastery over the unworthy wretch, and then expect her to accept and return his feelings did not seem at all incompatible or incongruent. He would have won the battle for her and she would know that he had won.

By the 9th of March, a Saturday, Darnley and his newfound friends and allies had worked out a plan that involved him entering his wife's apartments and announcing his intention to arrest a traitor. He would be backed up by Ruthven and his accomplices, including his Uncle George. Riccio would be arrested, read a list of his crimes, and marched from the queen's presence by a triumphant Darnley, who would end the tyranny and cuckoldry of the musician by executing him with a dagger thrust into his black heart. And to think Morton had wanted him pushed off a boat – that was funny.

He sat in his bedchamber, going over the plan again and again over a strong, resolve-stiffening cup of beer. All day he had been on edge. Mary had not seemed to suspect anything was afoot at dinner or throughout the day. That was funny too. He himself felt constantly on edge. How could she not feel the thickly charged atmosphere? It was like the unnatural calm before a lightning storm, the air heavy with the promise of noise and violence to come. It was late. The palace was quiet. Outside his window nothing could be seen in the indistinct dark – even the lights of the city were muted. There were no stars. A brief tattoo was beaten on the doors of his chamber.

It was his signal that everything was in readiness. He took one last swig, swallowed, and took the private stairs up to her apartments on unsteady legs, gripping and ungripping the hilt of the dagger at his belt. Its solidity was reassuring. The wall sconces cast skittering light and made odd patterns on the stone. The door to her rooms was unlocked. He opened it and went in to the little cubby off her bedchamber. He did not expect to find what he did.

Working himself up to this night he had pictured bursting in on Riccio and Mary locked in a lovers' embrace, their tongues in one another's mouths, their clothes loosened as he had begun to see in his nightmares. What he found was a companionable supper taking place, several people present. To his horror, his friend Robert was there, as was his and Mary's half-sister Jean, a handsome woman in thirties. Two of Mary's manservants were also seated. Robert grinned at him – they had not really spoken since the night of the French ambassador's farewell reception. Robert was no part of this. He should not have been here. Clearly *his* wild habits did not perturb the queen. 'Harry,' Robert said easily, 'I hadn't expected to see you here.'

Darnley's throat tightened. He could not think of what to say. He nodded a greeting. Riccio was seated at their old card table on which was set a large candelabrum, its dozen points of light dancing. More light spilled in from the main bedchamber. He was being looked at with suspicion and curiosity, Riccio's dark eyes the wariest of all. He sat down next to Mary and put an awkward arm around her. She squirmed away but sounded amiable enough when she spoke. 'Have you supped?'

'Aye, thank you.' The feel of her shrinking from his grasp hurt; it made him feel nasty and unclean.

There stretched out an uncomfortable silence. Whatever happy conversation had been taking place his arrival had killed it. He had no place here. What he had planned for the night would not work. There were too many people.

Then the heavy sound of clunking on stone steps came echoing up and through the closet, the insistent thuds of an uninvited guest. All eyes turned towards it except Mary's, which looked in her husband's direction, full of mistrust.

A grotesque apparition propelled itself into the doorway of the stairwell. It was clad in black-painted armour, an absurd nightgown draped around its shoulders. A sunken, skeletal face grimaced from it. It glared around at the assembled company. Jean Stewart gasped in horror, covering her mouth with one hand. It was Ruthven, his breath rattling. One armoured arm extended to point a claw-like finger at Riccio.

'Your Majesty, yonder man, David Riccio, is called out of your company, where he has lain too long.'

'What? What has he done? What is this? Expliquez-vous,' said Mary. She was beginning to grasp the magnitude of the affair and the reason behind Darnley's appearance.

'He has offended your honour, which I dare not be so bold to speak of. As to your husband's honour, he had hindered him of the Crown Matrimonial, which your Highness promised him, besides many *other* things.' Darnley's face felt hot. She was close enough to him that he could feel her body stiffen. 'He is an enemy of the state,' Ruthven continued, his voice gaining in strength, 'and he has shown himself to be a haughty, proud slave. He has enriched himself and sold favours. He has-'

Ruthven's litany of crimes was cut off as Mary abruptly rose, her chair scraping on the floor. Riccio, who had been listening with barely-concealed horror made his move, throwing himself towards and behind his royal mistress. At the sight of their sovereign rising Mary's two household gentlemen jumped up and put their hands to their daggers, drawing them in her defence.

'You men stay away from me,' cried out Ruthven, 'I'll not be touched.' His voice had risen and his epicene declaration clashed ridiculously with his grim appearance. He had done his part. To Darnley he shouted, 'Sir, take the queen, your wife and sovereign to you.'

He panicked: things were not going as planned at all. There was a great clatter of sound and movement behind Ruthven. A shrill, inconsonant sound filled the air as the caged pet birds Mary often kept in her bedchamber to entertain guests after supper began squawking in alarm. Everyone looked over Ruthven's shoulders to see men begin to pour into the closet, pushing past the company and out into the bedchamber, where still more had entered through the main entrance to Mary's rooms. He recognised George Douglas. He had come up behind Ruthven and was scanning the small, dim room for Riccio. He spotted the dark little head peeping from the floor next to Mary's skirt. He pushed into the closet and made a grab for him. The little dining table was knocked and began to fall over, its candelabrum sliding with the sudden shift in gravity. Light and shadows danced crazily. A scream rang out as Jean Stewart lunged for it, catching it by the stem and lifting it from the sinking table.

Mary was jolted this way and that, unable to move because of her clothing and her expanding belly; she must be about six months into her pregnancy, thought Darnley; it was easy to forget. The rush of movement had startled her. Ruthven gave her a hard, graceless shove into Darnley's arms, but she wriggled and wriggled. He had to hold her in a tight grip, the muscles in his arms straining. He could feel his heartbeat in his fingertips as they dug through the cloth of her dress into her flesh. *Now you're touching her again*, he thought wildly as he made soothing noises.

Strong arms were now beating at Riccio. His hairy little hands still clutched the queen's skirts as he screeched. Darnley could not see who was grabbing at him, only that someone had his wrists and was bending back his fingers until he released Mary. Other men were pressing into the small room, pistols drawn. A gun pressed against her distended stomach by the crush of bodies. In the low light he could see his uncle George standing close by. There was a ruthless look in his eyes as he reached down to Darnley's waist and slipped his dagger from its scabbard. There was no friendliness or collaboration in

George's contemptuous expression. He looked at him with scorn, a rodent baring its sharp little teeth.

George called a halt and the men holding Riccio released him. He lay on the ground next to the upturned table, whimpering like a whipped dog. 'I do this,' George called out in a stentorious voice, 'in the name of the king'.

'No!' screamed Darnley, 'take him out! Take him away, get him out of here!'

Ignoring him, George raised Darnley's dagger up high and brought it down towards a screaming Riccio, who threw up his right hand to ward off the blow. The sharp blade pierced the soft flesh of his palm, bit through it and emerged, bloody from the back of his hand. In the flickering light, the blood appeared black. Riccio's scream became piercing, the awful, deafening sound of a castrato. With the terrible benefit of his height, Darnley had a clear view. A moan escaped his lips. Mary let out a guttural wail.

George tightened his grip on the hilt of the dagger and jerked it back, but that only succeeded in jerking Riccio's arm with it. It was stuck. Grasping Riccio's wrist with his left hand and holding it steady, he then yanked the dagger back through the impaled flesh, grunting at the effort. Riccio's terrible cries had now become the expressionless howls of a mortally wounded animal. Darnley thought he was going to faint. He swayed on his feet, the beer in his stomach souring. None of this was right. This was horror: sickening, disgusting horror.

In the bedchamber men now fell towards the closet and the prone form of Riccio, who had ceased to struggle or plead. He was in shock. A multitude reached out and grabbed him by the feet, by the calves, by his clothes. They began to drag him away from the closet and he resumed his screeching, holding his wounded hand in the air. Darnley could see them dragging him across the bedchamber towards the outer room. Those who could not contain themselves were already stabbing at him as though to shut him up. Riccio's groin was stabbed. His stomach was burst open. Someone sliced into his ribcage, breaking bones and bursting internal organs. He coughed up blood in large bubbles as he thrashed. Over his screams the wild, frightened chirping of Mary's birds went on until one of the assassins threw a cloak over the cage. Mercifully Riccio disappeared from view, croaking and yelping.

Mary had stopped wriggling. She stood in front of Darnley, who had relaxed his grip when he had begun to feel dizzy. Both had borne witness to the full horror of the attack. He could not believe he had thought he would have been capable of taking part himself. He had never seen violence. He had not been prepared for its reality or for the bloodlust which overtook its participants. These were men he knew, ordinary men, transformed into beasts. He had wanted Riccio gone but he hadn't wanted this.

Gently he took her arm and began to lead her out of the closet. They had to step around splashes of dark blood which desecrated the gleaming wood and carpets. In the macabre light it looked like streaks of pitch on burnished orange. On the floor were also the scattered remains of the supper that was being enjoyed only minutes earlier. It was hard to believe that had been the case. He wondered at what he had invited into the room.

She collapsed in a padded chair in her bedchamber. Tears began to flow. The crowd of killers had fled back down the stairs, their bloody mission accomplished, Mary's servants giving chase. Robert looked at him, shock and confusion written on his face. With some difficulty he detached the candelabrum from his sobbing sister, set it down in the bedchamber and led her from the room, patting her head and whispering softly whilst she mewled. Only Ruthven remained.

Mary ignored the old man, looking up at her husband instead. 'Why,' she asked him, 'why have you done this? S'il vous plaît expliquer pourquoi.' Her eyes were meek. 'I have given you everything. I took you from your low estate and made you my husband. What cause have you had that you would do me such shame, that you would cause me such hurt?'

He was stung. He hadn't meant to hurt her. He had meant to rid her of a great evil. When shame burned, self-righteous anger was the only means he knew of dousing it. 'I've done this for you and me,' he said. 'Since that fellow came into familiarity with your Majesty you have not looked upon me, regarded me or trusted me.' She looked at him with uncomprehending disgust, her eyes narrowing and her forehead wrinkling. 'Don't you remember you used to come to my chamber every morning or night and pass the time with me? It seems a long time ago now. And whenever I come to you, you shrink away from me. You keep – you kept – that man about you at all times.'

'It is not the duty of a wife to go to her husband's chamber but for him to visit her,' she said. It was his turn to narrow his eyes. His hackles were up.

'How can you say that? You used to come to my bedchamber nightly until this musician rose in your favour instead. I do not know if you have hated me these past months, or if my body disgusts you of a sudden. Or have you conceived some other horror of me? I have been willing to do all that becomes a good husband. What offences have I done you? Where have I been deficient? Yes, I might well have been of a low estate, but I am now your husband. You promised me obedience, and that I should be equal with you in all things. But you have used me otherwise, by the persuasion of this slain servant.'

'Ha,' said Mary, beginning to recover her own passion. 'Je ne peux pas croire mes oreilles! I am the only one offended, as you well know. And for this unforgiveable crime, I shall be your wife no longer, nor lie with you ever. My lord, I shall make you a new promise: that I shall not rest until I have caused you to have as sorrowful a heart as you have given me.'

Ruthven had watched the altercation without interest. He now collapsed into an empty chair and attempted to cut the domestic scene short by announcing, 'I'll have a drink, for God's sake.' He helped himself to a cup of wine from a silver jug on her desk. 'Pfft,' he rasped after sloshing it around his hollow cheeks. 'Bloody women's wine, weak as a nun's piss.' Mary turned her attention to him.

'How dare you, sir.' she exclaimed. 'If I or my child dies, you shall have the blame. You will suffer for treating your sovereign so. Do not forget what I am. I shall write to the King of France; I shall write to my uncles; I shall write to the Pope!' A loud knock at the door silenced her. What now? Darnley wondered.

It was Lord Gray, a loyal queen's man. 'What news?' she asked him. He looked at Darnley and Ruthven as though unsure whether to speak in front of them. She gestured impatiently for him to do so.

'Your Grace, the Earls of Bothwell, Huntly, Atholl and others are doing battle in the grounds of your palace, against …'

'Yes?'

'Against the Earl of Morton and his company: those calling themselves the king's men.' Darnley bristled, shifting uncomfortably and looking down at the ground as though he could see through the floors of the palace to the fighting going on below. He then made a move to leave, to find out what was happening.

'Stay, your Grace,' wheezed Ruthven. 'Give me a moment and I'll go down and broker peace between these zealous lads. No doubt their blood's up from the fighting that has been. Ah, to be young and full of fight.' He tilted his head and sighed. Darnley padded from the room and through Mary's outer chamber to see what was left of Riccio, careful not to step in any of the scattered patches of gore. His dagger was still jutting out of the chest, and one arm was stretched ahead as though reaching towards the public staircase for aid. He looked away quickly and returned to the bedroom where his wife was still sitting, her head in her hands. He tore a sheet from the bed and went again to Riccio, throwing it over the body. Parts of it started to bloom a dark claret. The hilt of his dagger formed a little white peak.

He returned to his wife but did not tell her about the proximity of her dead favourite, now lying like a broken puppet not far from where she sat weeping. Nodding in approval, Ruthven heaved himself up, panting, and then, absurdly, hobbled over to Gray and took his arm as though going for a stroll. Still in his nightgown and armour, he said weakly, 'Now, if you'd be kind enough to show me to these boys.' Gray did as he was bid, too dumbstruck to object. Together they left, looking for all the world like a man taking his elderly grandfather on an evening walk. Darnley and Mary gawped after them.

22

The sounds of the fighting between Morton's faction and Bothwell's – a cacophony of swearing and yelling – died down. Ruthven managed to pacify them and saw everyone back into the palace, from which the squat Bothwell and the hulking Atholl, having professed themselves the royal couple's loyal servants, escaped through a back window.

However, the sounds of madness had carried out of Holyroodhouse, over its walls and into the city. Darnley and Mary could hear the thunder of an approaching crowd. Ruthven had returned, bringing Morton and his friends, to warn Darnley that the city had risen up, alerted to trouble and fearing for the queen and her husband. His mouth turned down at the reference to himself.

At the walls of the palace the Provost of Edinburgh had arrived at the head of a troop of townsmen. On behalf of the city, the Provost demanded to be given proof of the safety of the queen. She began to rise, her face foxlike and sly. Darnley put a restraining hand on her shoulder. 'No,' he said, fearing what she might shout down to an armed band, 'I'll pacify them.'

Her bedroom, like his, was at the front of the building with a tall window overlooking the approach to the palace. He opened it, struggling briefly with the latch. Many of the men carried torches. There were dozens of them bobbing up and down at the outer walls and gate. He shouted down to get their attention – he could not make out individuals. 'Good people,' he cried in a shaky voice, 'you know me. I am your king. Her Grace is safe and well. Go on now to your homes, I command you.' There was a rabble of discontented, distrustful voices but he could see from the movement of the torches that the group was beginning to disperse.

Mary made a last, desperate attempt to get up, but was shoved back into her seat by one of Morton's men who growled in a low voice, 'if you want to see them so much, we can cut you up and throw you over the wall in collops.' Her eyes widened, her mouth working abortively. Darnley had heard the threat and moved to stand in front of her, arranging his face into a mask of savage protectiveness.

The men who had come with Ruthven set about removing Riccio's corpse. They rolled it in the sheet with which he had covered it and dragged it by the feet from where it lay sprawled half in and half out of the entrance to the royal apartments. He heard a grunt as someone kicked it down the stairs. A voice crying, 'Now throw the bastard in the midden; but watch out, he's dead heavy!' followed it. She closed her eyes and put her hands over her ears, drowning out the hooting laughter of her friend's killers as it reverberated through her rooms.

Once again husband and wife were left alone. At a loss as to what to say, he made to leave the room for the second time. 'Wait, Harry,' she said. 'Please, stay the night. I … I do not feel safe alone here.' Her expression was doe-like and simpering, but there was something wild behind it. She frightened him.

'I'm sorry. I have to go to my own rooms. I give you my word of honour that you will be quite safe. I would never let any harm befall you. I am sorry for what you have had to see tonight. I would have had it otherwise. But,' he added firmly, 'I know that in time you will see the necessity of what had to be done, even if the means will never be excused. Goodnight.' She turned away from him.

Darnley finally left her rooms for his own. He was surprised to find that a guard was stationed outside the private entrance to her bedchamber. For her protection, the man explained. All entrances to the queen's rooms were to be guarded. Who are they trying to keep out, he wondered – or are they trying to keep her in?

He was undressed by silent servants who would not meet his gaze, then collapsed on his own bed and tried to sleep. The image of a thin dagger being dragged backwards through a skewered palm came to him every time he shut his eyes and his customary night-time headache appeared like a vicious and unwelcome old friend. He wondered if his wife was plagued by similar torments after watching the noose tighten and the axe fall on the necks of those she had had executed. How could such atrocities spring from a signature? Did a man turn murderer for sanctioning death? Like a child he had shrunk in horror from the execution, appalled by its excess. He was no fearless Guy of Warwick, no Orlando, no literary hero who wielded sharp dagger and sharper tongue in the face of danger and then carried his swooning wench to bed to make love to her. Lying on his side he pulled his knees up to his chest and folded his arms tightly around his head.

***

He woke up; he must have slept. It was still dark. The events of the night before seemed unreal, like a hideous nightmare. But it had not been a nightmare, and he would never wake up and be rid of it. The sense of wrongness was like an enveloping mist that he hoped would fade into nothingness, taking the horror with it.

What had he been thinking, leaving the woman carrying his child alone, guarded by men who had threatened her? What had he been frightened of? Disgusted by his own cowardice he jolted up from his bed and raced up the private staircase, still in his nightshirt. The guard – he was not sure if it was the same man as the night before; he had barely paid attention – nodded at him. He let himself in.

She lay sleeping on her bed, its curtains open and inviting and he went to her. He touched her face lightly and she opened eyes that were red and swollen. 'Mary, I should not have left you. Please forgive me. Shall I stay? Are you harmed?' She murmured in the negative.

Sitting up, she said, 'I have been imprisoned. I have been imprisoned in my own palace.'

'It is not imprisonment, never that. Things are unsettled. You must be kept safe.'

'Oh, Harry. You are such a child.' Her voice was gentle. That was disconcerting. Something acidulous lay beneath. 'Always seeking the approval of older men. But you have misjudged. It is imprisonment. These rough men care for nothing and no one. It is a mistake to trust any of them. They sow sedition, to reward themselves with the richest pickings from the wreckage.'

He did not know what to say to her. 'Try and sleep, sweetheart,' was all he could think of.

'Pray grant me something.'

'Anything.'

'Have them return my women. I cannot manage by myself.'

'Of course. I shall do it now.'

He patted her head awkwardly and strode out of her bedchamber and towards the door out of her rooms. A guard was posted outside. 'Your Grace,' he said, his face expressionless, 'you have been summoned by the Earl of Morton to the Council Chamber.' He was perplexed. He had hoped to find his confederates, but for the king to be summoned by an earl?

'I will go when I will it,' he said as haughtily as he could. He was damned if he would rush to discuss the disaster of the previous night in his nightshirt. He returned to his own rooms. She had her eyes tightly shut. He did not see one open a crack to watch him. He was changed into the protective armour of rich, clean clothing before striding through the quiet palace to find out what was happening.

***

Morton was sitting in the Council Chamber, not in Mary's elevated throne at the head of the table but next to it. Ruthven and others were around him.

'Your Grace,' said Morton without much interest, only briefly rising.

'My lords,' nodded Darnley.

'We've much to discuss now that the head of the serpent has been struck off.'

'You mean after last night's butchery?'

'I mean,' said Morton, 'after the king's will was done. We'll return your dagger once the filth's off it, incidentally.' He smiled crookedly, and Darnley frowned at him, saying nothing. 'We've this morning already drafted a royal proclamation,' he continued, tapping a document on the desk. 'It dismisses the parliament Her Highness convened at the beginning of the month without your authority. We can call a fresh riding and charge the new parliament with considering your claim to the crown later. You see, I keep bargains. I'd not betray blood. It awaits your signature.'

He tried to think, to see if he was somehow being trapped. It all seemed correct; Morton and his friends were keeping their word. It was impossible to think with such an assembly of flinty eyes boring into him. He took the proffered quill and signed his name at the foot of the document.

'I have a request,' he said, cursing himself for not having asked before signing. Morton simply raised a bushy, coppery eyebrow. 'I have an order. Her Highness requires the attendance of her ladies. It is not fit that a queen should lack gentlewomen.'

'No.' Morton and Darnley turned to Ruthven, who had croaked out the word. 'Where there is a band of women there is a band of plotters and schemers. The queen is a sharp one. She must be kept from mischief.'

'Now, now,' said Morton, 'I'm sure we can trust Her Grace's ladies to use their good sense and keep her from any rash course of action. Fair dealing must be seen to be done. We'll allow this. Let the Dowager Countess of Huntly attend her. She, at least, is too old to furnish the good lady with means of escape.' Escape? His mind latched on to the word. So Mary was the prisoner.

'And she knows that any attempt will see her sliced up and given her liberty in pieces,' said Ruthven, a devilish, gummy smile on his hideous face. Darnley started trembling, wondering what he had unleashed in Scotland.

Dinner that morning was a sombre affair, with even the horn blown to announce his arrival sounding flat. The usual chatter of the lower members of the household was hushed. The petty jealousies and enmities amongst the servant hierarchy had been forgotten: pages, grooms, ushers and secretaries were united in horror at one of their own being slain. As he aimlessly shifted oozing chunks of gristly meat about his trencher with a knife he wondered whether he should visit his wife after the meal. The barely-touched food was being removed with cold ceremony when a stricken herald arrived. Darnley's immediate thought was that Mary had been murdered.

'Your Grace, the queen is grievous ill. There is great danger to the unborn child.' He jumped from his seat, jolting the table. He raced through the palace and found her writhing on her bed, sweat sheening her body, staining her clothes. The stately old Countess of Huntly was sponging her forehead but stopped and stepped back when Darnley leant over the twisting form.

'Mary, can you hear me?'

'She cannot answer. The pain is too great,' said the countess. Darnley looked up at her, and was surprised at the repulsion written in the old woman's fine features. She eyed him as one might eye a cutpurse. He shrank from the look. 'The Earl of Morton's already been informed. I suggest you plead with him for proper attendance on your wife and child.' He needed no more convincing.

Finding Morton – who had evidently been on his way to inspect the queen's condition himself – on the public staircase, Darnley told him about Mary's sickness. 'It must be the shock of the night. Oh God, I shall roast in Hell for this – it is my fault!' Tears stood in his eyes.

'Peace, your Grace. We'll send for a woman skilled in midwifery to attend on Her Grace. And if she keeps the child we'll remove her to the safer confinement of Stirling.' Morton's voice was emotionless. 'But I've other news for you. The Earl of Moray has arrived back in Scotland and will be here this evening. You'll have much to say to one another by my reckoning. Aye, there'll be much to discuss.' With that, he turned and went back down the stairs leaving Darnley, still full of colour and dismay, standing at the top of the flight.

He sought out his father, needing the sight of a familiar, friendly face. Lennox had resumed occupancy in his own, lesser apartments in the palace. He was alarmed when he heard the news of Mary's health and paled further when he told him of the imminent arrival of his old enemy. 'Don't worry, my son. I'll come with you. You'll not be cowed by a rebellious earl and his cronies. I won't have disfavour touch this family again.' He hugged the old man tightly, as he had done when he was a child in need of comfort.

***

When Darnley and Lennox went to the Council Chamber they found it already full. Moray and the friends with whom he had fled to England were being embraced back into the fold. Some of its occupants bowed, other inclined their heads, others did nothing. He was not surprised to see that the dry, barely-noticeable Lethington was back, ready to resume his quiet and unobtrusive management of the dull, daily processes of government with the skill of a Florentine banker. He distrusted his capable, administrative air more than ever. He had been a signatory, a mover in all that had happened. But he had been careful to remain well away from events as they played out. The expressionless drab did not even look up from his papers, his cheeks sucked in in concentration at whatever he was reading. Already Moray was leading discussions. When he saw Darnley and his father enter, he turned his cool gaze on them, a hand briefly touching his cap. His demeanour had not changed; still he looked like a patrician Roman, long-nosed and perpetually bored.

'Your Grace,' he announced, leaning forward, his fingertips touching. 'I am pleased to see you again, sans the fire in your belly, and thank you for your gracious courtesy in forgetting the distant past.' Darnley smiled tightly. He could not stand the man's manner or his high-toned, nasal voice. 'Touching the matter of our dealings together I will speak plainly. If you wish to obtain what we have promised you, you must follow our advice in all things. If you do otherwise, we will shift for ourselves, whatever the cost.'

Darnley clutched at his father's sleeve, pulling him to one side. 'They have deceived me,' he hissed, 'I am lost'.

'Quiet, my lamb,' whispered Lennox, sotto voce. 'You must be brazen. Don't let them see fear.'

'I tell you our lives are not safe; I have heard their threats!'

Moray cleared his throat ostentatiously. He had waited for this moment, for the reclamation of his seat at the top table, for so long he had to savour it. 'Your Grace, time is somewhat short for cheap theatrics. If you are quite finished communing with your old dad?' There was a sneering smile on his lips, masking hatred. 'We need not detain you further. Only one more thing; it is only a little thing; I barely need mention it. If you wish to speak further with your wife it must be in our presence, with our permission and only through us. To that end, we have removed your personal attendants from your rooms. I believe they have enough mopping up of blood and burial of detritus to keep them from lounging around the royal apartments. We have also granted you our own guards and retainers – you will find them at your doors – to keep you safe from incident. Now, my lord the Earl of Morton has been kind enough to invite me to supper. Good day, your Grace.'

23

Darnley was petrified. Things had spiralled so wildly out of control so quickly it was impossible to understand just how it had happened. That night he crept up the private staircase. A guard was on the door and told him that he may not see the queen, who was in any case still unwell. In the morning he tried again, this time armed with a purse full of coins. He was let through.

She lay on her bed. She looked remarkably bright and well, but when he entered she clutched her swollen stomach. It had been, she said, a difficult night – but she and the baby would not suffer for it. He fell to his knees beside the bed.

'Thank God,' he said, 'thank God. Ah, Mary, how I have failed you. How can I atone? All I can do is admit my fault, my grievous fault.'

'Lève-toi. I will not have you on your knees.'

Grudgingly he stood up. 'This was my doing, all my doing. They came to me; I did not seek them out. They promised me so much – that they would grant me the crown. They said they would force Elizabeth to release my mother and brother. They told me about Riccio's plots, about his … his dealings with you. Stories wrought this, Mary – false tales. I promised them that they may return with my blessing if they would deal for me.'

She started at the name of her secretary, her lips pressing together and paling. He could see doubt written on her face. She did not want to believe him. To do so would be to admit that she had been unaware of the schemes being orchestrated behind her back. 'I had no notion they would behave as they did, nor where they did.' That was true. He had never imagined Riccio would be struck down before her eyes but led away from her presence and informed of the verdict against him. If only he had accepted judgement like a man, and been allowed to resign himself to his fate, things might not have gone so wrong.

'They lie,' she said, without pretence. 'Such men are only interested in you for what they can gain of you. They will pull you this way or that, until you fall in with their wishes and your shared guilt gives them indemnity. Kings must not be drawn so. They lied to you, Harry. And now you have seen the brutality of which they are capable'. He knew that she spoke the truth. He had been lied to and had fallen for it because he had wanted to believe.

'Yes. They lie. And they have plans – for you, for our child. They will take you from here and lock you in some place to be delivered. And who knows what they might will afterwards.'

She looked at him thoughtfully. 'I had suspected this. Did you put your signature to anything?'

'I did – I signed a bond. Oh, I am sorry. Morton, he made it sound right, he-'

She cut him off, murmuring something in French, gnawing at a finger. 'They have this? It is in their possession?' she asked finally.

'I know not. It must be. Yes.' His face brightened. 'I have a copy of the promise to allow their return.'

'Zut! Their copy of your signature is the thing.' He fought the catty urge to suggest they claim that his signature had been forged with an iron stamp. 'What to do ... My brother! He has a tender conscience, he will not have the blame of this.' She was no longer looking at him; she was thinking aloud, staring at nothing, lips moving silently. He was watching a master tactician thrown into action by unexpected peril. He marvelled at it. Behind that pretty face her mind was as fluid and mutable as quicksilver, and as quick to spring into action under heated pressure. 'Yes ... I can wring tears from his eyes over what has brought on his return. That will temper his harsh manner, becalm his friends.' Her gaze returned to him. 'Harry, do you trust me?'

'Of course. And never again shall I have cause to doubt it.'

'Then listen to me very carefully. I have plans for our release from this place.'

'What are they?'

'In time. For the moment, it is necessary for you to have the guards removed from the entry to my chambers.'

'I will try, sweetheart, I promise. But do you not think you should provide an official pardon, in writing, for the conspirators? If you do so they will have no need to put us away.'

'That I cannot do; I will not. But it is no crime for a prince to dissemble. These men are our common enemy: a threat to our person. You may say to them what you list. Tell them the whole pack of them they are forgiven for their great evil. But you *must* tell them that you have concealed your role in this foul deed from me. Let them think you a harmless, drunken fool, who has secured their pardon and curbed his unruly wife. They will believe that.' He pouted. 'It is how they treat their women,' she explained with a smile. It had been so long since he had seen her smile. It still flushed light into her face, making a dimple in her cheek. But it did not touch her sunken eyes. 'Only private persons can lie and betray. A prince has the permission of God to say whatever need be said for the good of their estate. Never forget that.' She read the doubt on his face. 'You once said to me that freedom was very important. So it is. And it must be won at any price.'

He kissed her on the cheek and squeezed her hand before returning to his own rooms. The guard on the door looked the other way, whistling and jingling the coins in his pocket.

In the afternoon Darnley was sought out by Morton, Moray and Ruthven. The three men greeted him with surprising affection, which he did not return. They asked him to bring them to the queen's outer chamber. There the trio fell upon their knees, Morton's prearranged strategy for showing their loyalty to good order, before her and she stood, supported by two of her Marys.

'Bienvenue, my lords,' she announced, 'Welcome. We do not pretend that the late affronts have not shocked us greatly. Mais tout sera bien. In the pursuit of peace and amity we solemnly declare to you that we are willing to remit the banishment of those involved, as well as those who were present at the death of our late secretary. My Lord of Morton, my Lord of Ruthven; you may go. My Lord of Moray, we wish you to stay, as our dearest brother. Please take the hand of your sovereign lady.' Moray took it. 'Husband?' she held out her other hand for him. 'Oh, brother, how I have been treated. How in need of you I am.' Darnley's outstretched arm spasmed, and Moray looked at him with suspicion before returning his gaze to Mary, who had neither reacted nor taken her open, pleading eyes off him. But an absurd thought had struck Darnley. They were all engaged in a great game of chaseabout, pursuing and being pursued in a circle. Mary was now after Moray, who had chased Morton into leading Darnley to go after Riccio, by making him believe he was chasing Mary. It would not end until they had all fallen down.

On her lead, the three of them walked up and down the room in a curious galliard, Mary cheerfully enquiring how Moray's health had been and what ideas he had for restoring law, order and peace. They might have been old friends.

As Darnley paced his apartments afterwards, wondering again at the astounding mess that had come to pass, he was visited by another stocky little Douglas called Archibald. Morton, he realised, must have filled the palace with his creatures. The man was sullen, moody, and stank of some disgusting, cheap musk. Darnley wrinkled his nose – the stench was that of a wet, dank forest.

'Here,' Douglas barked. 'These come from our cousin Morton.' He thrust a pile of documents at him.

'What are they?'

'How the Hell should I know? Papers. For you and your woman. I've no time for her roarin' and greetin'. Get her to sign them and then get them returned, there's a good boy. That is,' he added, 'if you can get her to do anythin' after killin' her lover.'

'My wife knows nothing of my involvement in the sentence against the deceased.'

'Oh ho-ho. Isn't that a fact worth knowin'. Well, you deal honestly with us and that way it'll stay. Leastways you'd better if you ever want the mare between your legs again, eh?' He patted him on the crotch with the back of a hand. 'Get her signature on those.'

'Yes, I will get them signed.' He thought as quickly as he could. He needed time. Heaven knew what they would be forced to put their hands to. 'Only, my wife is still unwell. I would prefer not to disturb her tonight. I will have her sign them tomorrow.' He puffed out his chest at the sceptical look on Douglas's face. 'My wife does as her husband tells her. Like all women she responds to a firm hand.' He tried to arrange his face into what he supposed was a cocky smirk, playing the lout as convincingly as he could.

Douglas returned the look, grunting in assent, and Darnley relaxed. Pressing the advantage he added, 'Only you might think about removing the guards from our doors. The moment of danger is passed. I have taken the queen firmly in hand.'

'Now why would I want to do that? I've no mind to be responsible for you or your wife's skulduggery. D'you think I'm daft?'

'There will be no "skulduggery",' he said, fighting to control his temper. The man's insolence was infuriating, but he could not afford to rise to it. 'It is quite safe, I assure you. I will vouch for all. We are all now reconciled and must try to get on with matters.'

'Hmmm,' grumbled Douglas. 'Morton'll be away from the palace the-night. He's givin' Moray a supper at his own home, and invitin' the favoured men of Scotland.' He laid emphasis on the word 'favoured'.

'All the more reason to relieve his servants of duty here,' he ventured.

'Well, if I've got your word you've got the woman under control ... But if either of you try anythin', I promise I'll personally make you pay for it. D'you hear me? Anythin' unmeet happens and you pay the price, big man.'

'Worry not, cousin. Her Grace is far too ill to risk anything. She dares not stir from her bed.'

Nodding hesitantly, Douglas stomped off in a cloud of unwholesome air. When he was out of sight Darnley closed his eyes and blew out a sigh of relief, willing his racing heart to slow.

***

They slid from her chamber at midnight. She had, she admitted, feigned illness – she was in rude health and the baby was not in any danger. Despite what the midwife had said publicly, privately she had advised Mary that she had never seen a woman more suited to childbearing, nor one less likely to turn a hair when being delivered. The Countess of Huntly had smuggled out letters asking for assistance from loyal men, and they in turn had assured her that horses would be ready behind the palace if only the royal couple could reach them. He had begged Mary to let his father know of the plan. She had refused. 'It is too great a risk to spread word of this. Your father can, I think, shift for himself,' was her pronouncement. A page boy and a gentlewoman who had advised them of the best escape route were the only reliable servants they had been able to reach.

The private staircase was quiet. The whole palace was quiet. Never before had he really noticed how loudly footsteps echoed up and down the rough-hewn stone staircase. They sneaked through his rooms. He looked around them. There was nothing he wanted to take that they could afford the time to look for or had the ability to carry. They paused at the door out of his apartments. He opened it a crack. There was no around. He slid out first with a dark lantern in one hand, its light shuttered, and Mary's hand clasped in the other. In her other hand she held that of her gentlewoman, Meg. Meg, in turn, held on to the young page, and the nervous boy took note of the steps of those before him and tried to match them, as though playing an absurd game.

Around the corner to their right was the Gallery. To their left was the public staircase. Voices were drifting from it – people were ascending. With mounting panic, Darnley recognised the voice of George Douglas. '- should calm down now, mind. Morton will be happy, the old fart.' Someone grunted in assent. George again: 'Honour this and order that. O! My ancient blood! He'll not forget who did the dirty work, though, not when it comes time to open the coffers. Nor will the brains. I reckon …' He and his companion had moved too far away to be heard further.

Their escape lay ahead, through a gauntlet of interconnected butteries, flag-stoned kitchens and pantries: storerooms with which Darnley had never concerned himself. He was concerned about them now. He could see a lantern held by someone deep within them. He waited until his eyes grew accustomed to the dimness. It was a servant reading off items from a long parchment. Meg nodded in animated silence; it was the way to go, and it was safe. He tugged at Mary's hand, clammy with anxiety, signalling that their human chain, forged in fear, had to move.

The man with the lantern looked up at them in surprise. In other circumstances, Darnley could have laughed at the strange mixture of shock and curiosity on his face. He opened his mouth to speak, but Darnley put a finger to his lips. Seeing the king and queen in such a state he did as he was bid and gestured to a dank little doorway in the corner. The royal couple stooped and went through it, pulling the servants behind them, down a shallow flight of stairs that dropped to a wine cellar.

The underground rooms were dank, and cool. And empty. Little light filtered down. The smell of stale alcohol was suffocating. They picked their way through haphazard shelves, barrels and storage boxes and clambered up the steps which led from the underground storage space to a back door to the palace. Outside was the old Abbey Church and burial ground. He opened the door and cool night air washed over them. Mary shivered and he squeezed her hand. The servants breathed audible sighs of relief. There was no one around.

Darnley was not excited by the daring escape. Instead it seemed to him the last few days would not relinquish the quality of a nightmare made real. The thought of being caught or of being pursued terrified him. They pressed themselves against the walls of the looming church, their backs caressed by huge, icy hands. The sound of horses whinnying and a voice calming them carried faintly on the night air from the direction of the cemetery.

It was his turn to shiver. They had to pass directly by the old outdoor burial site and he could not help but look. He expected to see silvery-white corpses arranged in macabre lines. Instead, the moonlight illuminated a fresh mound of black dirt. It was Riccio's grave. He looked away but Mary had frozen on the spot. 'Come on,' he whispered, 'we must go.' He tugged harder.

'Please – remember I am enceinte,' she chided him, stumbling.

'For God's sake, if we are caught we are all dead: you, me and our baby. We will lose our lives and Scotland will have no heirs. Don't you want to live to have any more?'

Her loyal supporters had the reins of the horses and helped the foursome mount. They rode hard into the chill night air, swallowed up by protective, welcoming darkness, first to Seton – where they had been betrothed, he noted – and then on to the coastal stronghold of Dunbar. She never flagged. He was astounded at her dexterity. She did not complain; she did not even request a slackening of their pace. He thought of her fevered thrashings when she had been feigning dangerous illness and shook his head in wonderment. The woman was a natural-born dissembler. And it had just saved their lives.

24

In the following weeks Mary's actions were vindicated. The appeals for aid she had sent out to Bothwell and Huntly proved to be the saviour of the royal couple's governorship of the realm. Men and arms had flocked to join them at Dunbar. An angry letter came from Lennox, furious that he had been abandoned to the mercies of Riccio's killers but blaming the queen entirely. He told a dubious tale about his narrow escape from the closing teeth of Morton's coup. She ignored it and busied herself sending messages, receiving letters, organising forces and making plans.

Those who could deny involvement in the murder of Riccio were quick to do so: Moray had not yet returned to Edinburgh when it took place so he might be forgiven, although she was not ready to trust his slippery friend, Lethington; Glencairn and Argyll had the same excuse. Key antagonists in the previous year's war, Mary forgave them on the proviso that they joined forces with her loyal supporters Huntly, Bothwell and Atholl in restoring stability to the country. Although she explained to him that binding formerly adversarial parties together was good policy, she otherwise had no time for Darnley. She was not rude or abrupt but otherwise engaged. He, in turn, made no demands of her. Like a true penitent he tried to be helpful and useful, asking nothing.

An unexpected letter arrived. From his mother. He tore it open – it was the first letter Elizabeth had allowed the countess to write her son since she had been imprisoned. As he read it his heart sank. What had happened, his mother wanted to know – the rumours were swirling even in the Tower that her own dear son, who had never put a hand to his sword in violence, had brutally murdered his wife's loyal servant. He could see why Elizabeth had let it through.

In a fit of panic he put pen to paper – not to his mother, who would be denied his letter – but to Elizabeth, who would read it even if she pretended not to. He poured out the truth of the affair, underscoring that his mother had had no foreknowledge and should not be held responsible for his errors. He sent it off and then locked the letter from his mother in a little casket. What should have been an object of joy was instead something he couldn't bear to read again and yet would not destroy.

Before March was out Darnley and Mary had amassed enough support from those opposed to the treatment given them by Morton and Ruthven that they were able to march on Edinburgh. The couple rode side by side. Overhead the sun made valiant attempts to break through the clouds but succeeded only in turning the sky the colour of a yellowish bruise on decaying skin. He thought it encouraging that she had forgiven him for being taken in by the innuendoes of his fellow bondsmen. He needed to believe it was so. He needed to believe that the whole chapter could be closed, a new page turned. But the memory of it continued to haunt him, as he knew stories might haunt readers long after the books have been shelved or players departed the stage.

As they rode she turned to him. 'We return to our capital but not to what we have left behind.'

'What do you mean?'

'I mean that you must be completely severed from the men who have abused us both. You must turn your back on their conspiracies and deny all knowledge of their schemes.' He started to speak, but she cut him off. 'Remember what I have told you – a true prince must dissimulate. A wise one will abjure the company of crooked councillors and cast them out without warning, even having shown them favour and made use of them. He will close his door to bloodthirsty servants who would stain his reputation with their violent deeds and advice. Your uncle, Henry of England, had an adviser called Cromwell-'

'I know who Cromwell was!' he snapped. 'I'm sorry. I've had a surfeit of precedents.' The conjured-up ghosts of the past had certainly lost their power to sway the present. She looked at him curiously.

'At any rate you will deny all intelligence of that heinous crime.'

'But I ... I signed the warrant – the bond,' he said, suddenly recalling Morton's paper and his own signature unsteadily appended to the bottom. 'God forgive me, I signed it. They have proof thereof.'

'The spiteful fools have sent me the murder bond, as I knew they would.' Well, she had kept that to herself. 'It tells me nothing you have not, save that you were art and part of the villainy undertaken, and undertaken before me.' He started to protest, but she continued over him. 'No. Feigned ignorance shall not plead for you. I asked you to trust me and you were right to do so. These men seek discord. They hoped that giving me proof of your guilt would make me denounce you. But they were wrong. You see, I must be above the suspicions and disgusting conjectures of a jealous husband. That is why we ride together, to let the world think that there is no distrust between us. That you allowed these men back into our Court I forgive, but this other ... this murder ...' She closed her eyes, her throat catching, then slumped forward in the saddle and swallowed. After a moment she pulled herself upright and regained her voice. 'From this moment hence, you will remain neutral. You will not respond to importunity or be swayed by any man's attempts to involve you in his schemes; you have not the steel for plotting. And everything that has passed must be laid at the door of the abominable men who took that evil course of action, etc-ce clair? It ought to be. Men are clever at shifting blame from their own shoulders to those of others.' He was silent. He was to abandon Morton, Ruthven and all – to turn his back on them and use his regal prerogative to deny all complicity in the crime, leaving them to take the fall. So it would have to be. But he did not relish it.

Yet, he wondered, where was he then left? His list of enemies would simply grow longer. He had trusted the wrong men, he sought the approval and acceptance of the wrong men, and now he had no one. Those men now in favour with the queen would hate him for bringing this latest trouble down on her. Moray had always hated him. And now those out of favour with the queen would be consumed with thirst for vengeance for his abandoning them. And all he had ever done was what people had asked of him. He had never done anything so monstrous that he could be thought of as a barbarous tyrant – even the most celebrated sovereigns in history had far bloodier hands. It was not fair, he thought sullenly. It was none of it bloody well fair.

***

Predictably Morton, the decrepit Ruthven and Darnley's one-time drinking companion, 'Uncle George' Douglas fled Edinburgh promising revenge on the dishonourable king they claimed had betrayed them. Morton had taken it especially badly; to him, Darnley knew, the betrayal of blood, particularly Douglas blood, was most unforgivable of sins. He was relieved to see them go – to England, no doubt. Elizabeth would have her hands full with such men, he thought with satisfaction. She had not replied to or acknowledged his letter. That was also predictable.

Life began to resume an even tenor. The one difference was in the royal family's living conditions: Lennox, to his son's disappointment, was banished by Mary, who claimed she was not convinced of his ignorance of Riccio's murder. Darnley didn't object. He didn't want to fight. He slipped away to visit the old man once but found him claiming illness and repeating forecasts of doom if Darnley didn't seize power. He had left him in his Holyroodhouse lodgings. Neither Mary nor Darnley wished to return there. The Court now lodged primarily within the thick, ancient walls of Edinburgh Castle.

Resolving to earn back the trust of his wife he once more took to religion. He heard Mass every day and added Riccio. He was not sure that he was sorry the secretary was gone, but he was very sorry for the manner of his going. And there was something terrifying, something overwhelming about the knowledge that, thanks to his agreement, a man had simply ceased to exist anywhere except in the memories and actions of those left behind. His word had extinguished a life. It was easier not to dwell on it.

He was sorrier still for the effect it had had on his already-troubled marriage.

There was no question sharing a bed with his wife – her pregnancy was far too advanced. However, she showed little inclination to dine with him either. Again he did not press her. The thought of sitting at table with her reminded him too much of the little supper party which he had interrupted on that ghoulish night. So too did the appointment as French secretary of Riccio's brother: a shy, withdrawn young man who, despite his diffidence, seemed to be of service to Mary chiefly as a constant reminder to her husband of his misdeeds. Either by design or nature he showed none of his brother's ambition or spirit.

Husband and wife did meet in the Council Chamber. Neither Mary nor Moray or anyone else now objected to his presence, and he could almost feel that the first days of his marriage were back. People listened to his tentative, quiet suggestions and accepted his signature, only resorting to the stamp when he was unable to attend.

April and May passed with a sense of quiet contentment that had been missing from his life. Good news, of a sort, even came in the form of the death of Ruthven. The devil had been on his last legs when plotting the death of Riccio; now they had finally given way and Darnley had one less vengeful enemy. Already gossips were transforming the old monster's life into a lurid catalogue of demon-worship and wizardry. But no matter; he would not swoop like a spectral crow back into Scotland to peck at the king. Ruthven's was one soul he did not pray for.

At the beginning of June Mary entered ceremonially into her confinement. He waited with excitement. He was going to be a father, and father to an heir to the thrones of Scotland and England. Even as a mere consort he had achieved what the mighty Elizabeth never had.

His rooms in Edinburgh Castle were small and chilly but well provisioned. He had sent to Holyrood for some of the books he had especially liked in its library and spent time re-reading the histories of Scotland, paying special attention to the dates and circumstances of the births of princes. All the omens were good. He was convinced that a new James – he would become the sixth of that name – would be born, and looked forward to teaching him how to ride, how to hunt, and who to avoid trusting. The boy would have the best tutors but his father would teach him the practicalities of life. He was adamant that no son of his would repeat his mistakes. His birth would herald the rebirth of Scotland as a beacon of light for the whole world to follow.

On the 19th, he received word that Mary had been delivered of a healthy son.

He was called to her tiny lying-in chamber after dinner and found it packed. She looked radiant. A jaunty little headdress had even been placed on her head to cover hair which there had not been time to wash. The whole room was bedecked in blue taffeta and velvet. It was good to see her well attired. Since Riccio's death her dress had grown less stylish, the colours drabber and the jewels fewer.

'My lord,' she said, 'God has given you and me a son. And he was begotten by none but you.'

He reddened. There were other people present, noting her greeting and his reaction. He said nothing but leant forward and kissed his linen-swathed child. His lips brushed only cloth. She began to unwrap him, saying as she did, 'And here I swear before God that this is your son and no other man's. And I wish that all here bear witness, for he is so much your son that I fear it will turn out the worse for him.' There was a ripple of quiet murmuring in reaction to her speech and people looked from mother to father, waiting for him to chide his wife or to profess his agreement that she was guiltless of the crimes the world knew he had alleged.

Instead he looked down at the child's face. It was hard not to keep looking. The little boy's eyes were tightly closed, but he had a comical look of sincerity on his tiny features. He was as still as a doll, except for his fists which opened and closed. Darnley touched one carefully – it was soft – and the little hand closed around his finger. He felt the beginning of tears and blinked them away. He forgot the little scene his wife was causing. He had never truly suspected it not his. She must know that.

When she spoke again it was not to her husband, but to the room. 'This is the son, I hope, who shall first unite the two kingdoms of Scotland and England. Alas, it shall be he and not his parents, since his father has broken from me.' Finally, he looked up – she was not going to stop prodding him until he reacted.

'Madam, is this what your promise to forgive and forget means?'

'Oh, I have forgiven all,' she said. 'But will never forget. What if I had been shot when this boy lay in my belly, what would have become of him and me both? God only knows, but we may suspect.'

'These things are passed.'

'Then let them go,' she said, her manic smile darkening the room.

***

Preparations were put under way for the baby's – little James's – christening. Mary insisted that Elizabeth be asked to stand as godmother. Darnley was ambivalent, unsure whether it was a sign of capitulation to the English queen or would show the world that he was cocking a snook at a woman who still showed a puzzling disinclination to provide for her own nation's future – if she even could. In the end his feelings did not enter into it. Mary had already dispatched James Melville with the news and the request on her own authority.

Elizabeth accepted and wrote congratulating Mary on the birth of her son. She pointedly did not acknowledge Darnley, preferring instead to behave as though the child was an immaculate conception. Nevertheless, he took advantage of what he perceived to be her good mood by writing yet another letter requesting his mother's freedom to visit her new grandson. No reply came.

With his son born old fears surfaced in his mind. They centred on the belief that his wife looked upon him, and had always looked upon him, as nothing but a consort, married to provide the service of producing an heir. Since James had been born she rejected all friendly overtures. She even denied him visitation with his son, whom she jealously guarded and kept with her all day and night.

When he had battered on her door demanding to see his son she had spat through the wood, 'I will die before I place my child in the hands of a butcher who wished him dead in the womb.' He had been stunned. Is that what she thought? Is that what the world suspected? He cried out, 'You do not think that! You know me! You cannot think that!' She didn't reply. It was ludicrous, vile. His wife and child were his saviours. They were the only guarantors of all that he was and had. He wanted and needed them both. And of course he loved them.

His revulsion at her believing him capable of such iniquity, and at himself for inviting such contemptible beliefs, led to anger. He had shouted back hollow threats about leaving the country, about going to the Netherlands and coming back armed with European support for his rights as a father. Still she responded with silence.

She was not silent with James Melville, who had been so instrumental in ensuring Darnley's delivery to Scotland. When he returned from England Melville visited him in his rooms, professing himself moved to petition for royal reconciliation and the reinstatement of marital harmony for the good of the realm. He meant it. He liked his young king, he liked his young queen, he liked their young son, and he liked the power their united blood gave the nation. Darnley assured him that he wanted nothing more. As an inducement Melville presented his king with a beautiful little water spaniel bitch, a rich brown mass of curls. He had been immediately taken with the first creature to offer him real affection in longer than he could remember, as she licked at his hands and constantly snuffled around his feet. Word reached him, however, that Mary was furious about not being offered the pet and had given Melville the sharp side of her tongue for favouring a man she despised.

In retaliation Darnley named the dog Regina.

In a fit of ineffectual zest he turned again to his books, hoping to inspire ideas as to how he might prove his love and loyalty to his son. He landed on the determination to increase Scotland's power and visibility in the world. He would ensure that he left his son an empire, not just a kingdom, nor even – in fact, especially not – a kingdom apt to be united with its larger, aggressive neighbour.

He called for maps. He would join forces with the disaffected Catholics in England. He would land forces and take old garrisons on the Scilly Isles, whilst landing others still in Scarborough – then he would have England caught in a Catholic vice, as his native Yorkshire had been caught in the vice of Protestant Scotland and schismatic southern England. There was support for it; strange and unknown gentlemen were never done sending him letters with religiously-fuelled requests and promises. He was building castles in the sky, but he needed something to make him feel occupied and relevant, to let his little boy know he had a father who fought for him and his country.

His plans were futile, and he knew it. Their inadequacy led him once more to drinking, now with a reduced company of servants – all of long standing; he would have none of his wife's sharp eyed and sharper eared spies about him. Old friends avoided him, recognising a man in no position to provide influence and positions. Even Robert Stewart was politely reluctant to go carousing with a man so deeply in disgrace. Perhaps he was not virtuous and loving enough for real friendship and knew only men who would abandon him in adversity. Having love to give and no one to receive or return it was a lonely thing. By nights he stalked the city's cobbled alleys, his new drunken refrain being his wife's refusal to let him see his son, his lament that he was more loved in the country he'd repudiated than ever he was in the one that called him king. 'She's not even that pretty,' he barked at anyone would listen. 'Aye, she's an ugly wench, my bitch wife, have you seen her nose? Her narrow eyes?' It was perhaps not kingly or regal – but then, he had been denied the regalia of kingship for so long it hardly seemed to matter. More letters began to arrive from his mother. He thought at first that Elizabeth might really have finally relented, but he was soon disabused of the idea. His mother's letters now had a common theme – berating her son for drinking too much – which she could scarcely believe when she heard of it, he always so resistant to vice.

He sat one evening in July reading a fresh letter from the Countess of Lennox, this one smudged as though she had been crying when composing it, her tears splashing the page. He suspected that she had sprinkled the page with water to blot the ink and create an emotional effect. It was an old trick of hers. It listed the usual complaints – why was he not taking steps to secure her liberation and his crown? Why was he spending his time hunting and hawking and allowing his wife to amass support from violent men like the Earl of Bothwell? A king must rule with his hand on the reins of the state, not on his horse.

He sat reading the letter in his incongruously sumptuous rooms, taking occasional gulps from a goblet of wine. He had started to hide liquor in his room, building himself a private stock in order to spare himself the embarrassment of continually calling for it. He burped. The goblet was still in his hand and the sudden movement spilled some on to the page. 'Shit!' he hissed. His dog's shaggy ears flapped eagerly. She had become a constant companion. Her he understood. It was the motivations and minds of other people that presented a bewildering challenge.

He moved to stand up, the paper falling to the ground. As he did so he caught sight of himself in the mirror he had had brought from Holyroodhouse. His face was bloated and flushed, his nose red at the tip and his eyes bloodshot. He looked like a vagabond. Grunting, he hurled the goblet of wine at the mirror, wishing to shatter the image of a pathetic, prematurely-aging beast. But the pewter bounced off the sturdy polished steel, obscuring his likeness with veiny rivulets. He staggered to his bed, knocking over cups, a bottle, some jewellery, and collapsed face-down.

Although he tried to blot them out, his mind swirled with horrible suspicions and harsher truths. Perhaps he had played into his wife's hands – perhaps she had hoped all along that he would blacken his reputation whilst she played the downtrodden wife and responsible queen. Robert was her brother, after all, and might only have encouraged him into vice on her orders. But whether he had skipped merrily into a trap or not – and he dearly hoped, at least, that Robert had been an innocent pawn whose loose-living was merely taken advantage of by his sister – the fault was all his own. Should a man who had drank in low company, who had shouted and sang in the streets, who had loosened his tongue to anyone who would listen, ever have expected others to believe he had been ordained by God to govern them? It was little wonder he had not been granted the crown. He had expected God to provide for him even as he made a mockery of the system He had laid down for the rule of nations. Now he would have to make amends. 'It won't do, Regina,' he said to the dog, who looked at him from under her mop of brown hair. 'We'll set things right, you and I.'

The next day his mind felt clearer. He retrieved his hidden bottles of spirits and wine and sent his sodden life gurgling out of the windows and down the walls of the royal apartments.

He had his beard shaved off – it was making him look old and unkempt – and dressed with care. He then abruptly told his servants to pack his things. He was leaving Edinburgh. He did not leave word to his wife about where he was going.

25

Darnley's head broke the surface of the loch and he gasped, drawing in huge lungfuls of cool, sweet air. He had left Edinburgh intent on purging his body and mind of the melancholy humours which had been poisoning them. Accordingly, he had come to Linlithgow, where he had begun diving into the serene loch beyond the palace, making his muscles ache with the effort of swimming. He spent days floating in the water and looking up at the sky. It was crisp, clear and sunny – summer was coming into its own again after the longest winter he had ever known.

He loved Scotland. He felt the land calling out to him, and he did not know why, any more than a man knows why he enjoys debating scripture, or why he feels an overwhelming calling to write, or paint, or sculpt. God, probably, was behind such odd little quirks in a man's nature. He had wanted to fight for the country, to make it the nation he knew it could be. But at every turn he was foiled, used and humiliated by men – and the woman – who fought to keep control within their own untrustworthy band. These Protestant lords had the kingdom, and they would sell its sovereignty piecemeal in order to enrich themselves, dishonouring Scotland's rulers by making them subservient to England's. Fighting them would simply be kicking against the prevailing tide, which pulled in favour of the nation's return to vassalage when it should be rolling outwards, to friends and equals in Catholic Europe. What manner of man, he wondered in exasperation, was content to allow his nation to become a vassal? No Englishman – as his own upbringing attested – would tolerate such a thing. The English character cried out against it. Were the boot on the other foot Elizabeth, Leicester, the whole Court of England would be appalled at the prospect of their kingdom and authority being compromised. Why did this coterie of noble Scotsmen lack similar pride in their own realm? Even those who claimed to fight for Scotland, men like Bothwell, were too radical, too eager to cut the country off from the rest of the world.

For the first time he began to seriously consider leaving them all to drown in the turbulent waves they loved to churn up. Here in the bright summer sun he could turn on his back, let the water silence the world, and contemplate his future with equanimity. A ship could be made ready on the west coast and he could be on the open seas within weeks. He could let it be known that he was setting out to court European allies on behalf of Scotland, regaining its role on the continental stage. That would stick in the craw of the craven supplicants of Elizabeth's England even more than having as queen an uncomfortable reminder of the nation's Francophile past.

He had almost made up his mind to announce that he would leave when a herald arrived from Edinburgh. The man looked thoroughly confused by the sight of the king emerging in sodden, sopping shirtsleeves from the loch; swimming was a dangerous and bizarre thing to do – the pastime of madmen. Darnley smiled at the bewilderment. His message was that the queen had been dismayed by his sudden disappearance and had herself departed Edinburgh for a summer progress to Alloa. He also had less welcome news: he was not to attempt to see Prince James, who had been left in Edinburgh Castle under strict guard and in the care of his own household servants without the express permission of the queen. He thanked the man sarcastically and went in to dry himself and be dressed, calling out to Regina, who had been splashing in the water. She shook herself vigorously and bounded after him. He would find his wife and tell her his plans. He had heard once that absenting oneself from a lady without explanation would prick at her heart. But that was for common men, not kings.

***

When he reached Alloa Tower, north of the River Forth, he found Mary dancing in the company of her ladies. She dismissed them with a 'we shall pick this up again later, darlings', and they left the room without looking at him. Her smile left with them. 'I heard you have taken to throwing yourself into water. Dare I hope you wish to drown and rid the realm of a knave?'

'Such violent language, madam. Hardly befitting of a queen. I assure you I have no other wish than to cleanse my body of its evil humours.'

'A difficult task. I doubt there is water enough in Scotland to wash away your sins.' He ignored her. 'And why have you chased me hither?'

'I have come to tell you that I am leaving.'

'You have only yet arrived.'

'That I am leaving Scotland,' he said impatiently. She looked alarmed.

'You cannot leave Scotland. You are the king.'

'A strange sort of king, your Grace, by your will.'

'And so for your own jealousy and vaulting ambition you would leave the country?'

'Not for that. The country is hostile and turbulent. I have not slept well since coming hence.'

'You have done *nothing* well since coming hence,' she said, an impish smile playing across her face. She looked away from him to hide it, and when her gaze returned it was gone. 'But you cannot leave, you have nowhere to go. Where do you intend to fly?'

'The theatre of the world is unbounded. It is wider than this little realm,' he said, refusing to be drawn.

'And so you plan to flee like a thief in the night, without plans?'

'Does that surprise you?'

'I have long since ceased to be surprised by your actions. Ah, but you can be a trial.'

'No more than yourself, and I think perhaps less so.'

Her face softened. When she spoke, her voice was kinder. 'Il est une décision importante. One you must not make rashly. I am enjoying the summer. You have been enjoying it too, these last days. Run not from Scotland; join me on my progress.'

He looked at her, suspicious of her sudden change in attitude. She persisted. 'Where would you like to go?' Quickly, he mentally checked off the various castles and stately homes which littered the nation.

'Peebles,' he said at length.

'Peebles?' She looked dumbfounded.

'Yes. It is good hunting country. I was there for a space in the winter. You remember – at Erroll's old castle of Smithfield.'

'I know of it. And we cannot possibly stay there. I am surprised a fellow of your high tastes bore it at all; you have come up in the world since creeping from the wildernesses of England's north. It is poorly provisioned, a desolate place, out of sight.'

'You fear being alone with me without witnesses? Perhaps I should fear it.' He gave her a lopsided grin. She did not laugh, and his smile faltered. If his wife did not feel safe around him, what manner of man was he?

'There is a great house at Traquair – a hunting lodge. We shall be entertained there.' She seemed to be warming to the idea. 'Yes, that will do. We can progress southwards and take a measure of the hunting stocks as we go. Allow me to finish my visit with the Erskines. Amuse yourself until then; swim if you list. You may leave now. I shall rejoin you on the road. But I am afraid there is no room for you to share this roof with me. Au revoir.'

He grunted in assent at his abrupt dismissal. It was not quite what he had wanted, but it would do.

At a strange kind of impasse the royal couple and their train made the journey south in the middle of August, when the summer days were still long and illuminated the landscape in every imaginable shade of green. Mary was amiable enough on the journey but Darnley had the feeling that she did not want to accompany him as a wife, but rather as a custodian.

When they reached Peebles he insisted that they ride through the centre of the town, their servants trailing behind in quiet, disapproving bafflement. He wanted her to see it. Few people stirred in the streets. Those who did pressed themselves against the walls of buildings like wraiths as the noble company approached. They blended into the stone like gargoyles. He looked down at them, noting sadly that their faces were dirty, their skin thin and translucent.

'You see,' was her only comment, 'we could not have stayed here.' The buildings of the town looked as barren in summer as they had in winter.

'Do *you* see, madam, the poverty of your country? The manner in which our people live?'

She looked baffled. 'These borderlands are wild. My Lord of Bothwell has told me much of the lawlessness and crime which is bred here.'

'Yet we do nothing for it.'

'We leave it in the hands of our capable wardens of the marches and their sheriffs.' She was sitting stiffly in her saddle.

'And this is what they leave it to become – ragged people, starvation and thievery.'

Now she looked almost amused. 'You have become a partisan of the third estate. It becomes you. I had no idea you had hidden depths of feeling. J'approuve.' She smiled at him and reached over to tickle his chin affectionately. He was taken aback and laughed. She joined him.

'Ah, why cannot it be always like this? Might we not always be at ease, be friends?'

The smile disappeared from her face as quickly as it had arrived. They were passing out of the town now, leaving its grubby, dejected houses behind. 'You know why.'

'I know that you surround yourself with people who hate me – I might ask you why that is so.'

'I should think the answer obvious,' she said, her eyes turning foxlike. 'There is no other kind.'

'Oh, very clever. I suppose it is chance alone that your chief friends are men like Bothwell and that hateful brother of yours. He has caused us both a sea of troubles. I could kill him!'

'Not a course of action I would advise.'

'But how can we be friends, be husband and wife, as long as you keep company with such men? You even favour the service of their womenfolk.'

'Ah, Harry, mon enfant. Indeed, we are husband and wife. A most unhappy circumstance, but one from which we cannot find release.'

'One that has been profitable, has it not? We have a son, Scotland a prince. We have an heir. You might deny me his presence, madam, but he is my son and I shall have him when I wish it.'

The conversation was not going how he had wanted it; he

always seemed to say the wrong thing. Like too many of their conversations it had become a verbal duel, his tongue a blunt club against her infuriatingly subtle rapier. 'You must find other things to occupy your mind and leave off pursuit of me. Why not take a mistress? The world knows you would have no moral objections. Your face is yet pretty – that was ever your strength and your weakness. And I assure you I certainly would not love you any less for it.'

He reined in his horse, startled.

'Think on it, Harry. Without your dear maman you are starved of loving female company. An older lady, perhaps, will be a better influence than the unruly men you solicit and adopt as brothers and fathers.' She continued trotting onwards nonchalantly, the sun glinting off the pearls in her hair. He watched her go, shock at her candidness mingling with the realisation that she was right. When his friends were women, life had been peaceful, quiet and full of love. On surrounding himself with men and trying to fit their mould, on trying to please devious statesmen and find a succession of fathers and older brothers, he had come to this.

The day after they had arrived at Traquair House, a pretty white building southeast of Peebles, Mary's band of Lords arrived: Moray, Huntly, Atholl and Bothwell. She greeted her brother warmly when he was shown into the main gallery of the building.

'Mon très cher frère. We are well pleased to see you – but we hope you have come well-armed,' she said, accepting a kiss with a smile. Moray looked up quizzically. 'Madam?'

'Our husband has a hot temper and sees threats lurking all about. Only yesterday he informed us that he compasses your death.' Darnley, standing next to her, stiffened, his eyes widening. His mouth fell open, the genial smile he had worn slackening.

'Is that so?' said Moray, his head cocking to one side quizzically. 'How unfortunate. Should I beware the meals I am served here, or are they to be cooked over his Grace's dark fire?' Abashed, Darnley said nothing. He had been caught out, like a schoolboy cursing his master and being reported for it.

'Apologise to the Earl of Moray, Harry,' she said, her tone commanding. 'Apologise to our brother.'

'I am sorry, my lord,' said Darnley, in as low a voice as he could. 'I ... repent of my words spoken in passion.'

'If you do not act on them, your Grace, I am sure they need not come between us,' said Moray. He looked satisfied, like a cat which has just caught a mouse and is savouring it as it sucks in the tail.

During their nights at Traquair Mary locked her door. She did not speak to him at meals. When they rode out to hunt she showed no interest in discussing the state of the borders with him, although she made a point of asking Bothwell about improving local conditions. Darnley's opinion was not sought. When he tried to raise the issue with Bothwell himself the insolent man had sharply told him that he had the borders in hand and needed advice from strangers.

The whole trip had been a waste. When out riding, he had half-hoped that the little brigand who had tried to hold him up in winter might show his face, having survived the winter and the likely anger of his master. He entertained ideas about reforming the boy, bringing him into the royal household as a page and showing his wife what a good man he was. She would be shocked. But the boy did not appear whenever they hunted and hawked. Too many people knew about the coming of the queen and her fearsome servant, the Earl of Bothwell.

When they departed she rode ahead with Bothwell and Moray, immediately behind the royal guard, leaving him to ride with the friendly but uninteresting Atholl and Huntly. He liked the men, but he nevertheless felt the sting of exclusion. His own company was a heavyset old man who looked more like a bear than ever in his brown suit of clothes and a perpetually-nervous, eager-to-please ingénue who spoke only when asked a direct question. All the same it was curious, he noted, that the trio of Catholics were left to follow the queen and two Protestants.

They were bound for St Johnstown after stopping in Edinburgh where, she announced, Prince James was to be moved to Stirling under the protection of a force of five-hundred musketeers. He was not consulted. He realised this was recompense for his rash comment to her on the ride through Peebles about having his son whenever it suited him. The woman forgot nothing.

The rest of the summer progress passed in relative peace. Mary even condescended to spend afternoons with him at the hunt. Sometimes they played cards. Her acerbic comments declined, and she even seemed to lose her customary tone with him: that tone, full of tuts and punctuated with rolled eyes, which betrayed crabby disaffection. He never quite felt that he was pleasing her but the occasional moments of laughter and the taut smiles made him think he was making headway in breaking down the hard, strongly-built barrier of her dislike. It spurred him on in his desire to win her over, to make her his. For long stretches he could forget the death of Riccio, the political fallout, the enemies who had made him their accomplice. Together they galloped through lush, emerald forests to a choir of birdsong; alongside crystalline lochs dotted with floating leaves; they watched wild birds take flight and chased graceful red deer. Life was everywhere, smelling fresh and sweet and new. If he left Scotland he would miss this: this was the heart of the kingdom he loved. This was where he belonged.

When the first leaves began to fall and the astonishingly brief, golden summer started to succumb to the darkening amber of autumn they returned to Stirling Castle, his favourite golden palace. Both parents wanted to be close to their child. She allowed him to see James – and he had grown so much in only a few months. Now his eyes were open and he gazed up at his father in consternation. With this baby one had to put in work to earn a smile, thought Darnley as he pulled faces at the child, waggling his tongue and crossing his eyes. The boy had the eyes of his mother, tilted, and the chin of his father. He could not wait to see how he would grow, how he would speak, run, learn. He thanked Mary solemnly for letting him see him, and she seemed to thaw a little.

When she decided to return to Edinburgh to see to the running of the state – she had been visited by the sleekit Lethington, who was eager to get his hands back on the levers of power – she left him alone at Stirling. He was even permitted to see his son, albeit in the company of nurses and with guards stationed throughout the castle.

After his wife had left, Lennox arrived to see his son and grandson, sporting a new double chin. The rewards of being a fertile king's father in peacetime were good and apt to get better, and a wife in the Tower and a little boy under house arrest had not dented his appetite for luxurious public feasting. The thought – the image – of restored honour had eclipsed even husbandly love. His wife, God love her, had become a symbol of disgrace, lodged as she was in England's monument to it.

Full of pride, Darnley showed the child to him and he was gratified by the fulsome praise and congratulations. Little James, Lennox said, was the image of Darnley at the same age, and would thus undoubtedly grow up to be a strapping, blonde-haired prince, ripe to rule the world, not just Scotland

and England.

He then treated his father to supper in his chamber. 'And how are matters between you and Her Grace,' the old man asked, through mouthfuls of cold roast lamb.'

'They are ... they are poor, father.' He leant down to stroke Regina behind the ears. She panted in pleasure.

'How's that?'

'She bade me take a mistress.' Lennox nearly choked, his face turning red. Darnley leapt up and went around the table to him, clapping his father on the back. Little specks of grease flew from his lips as he finished spluttering. Shiny globules glinted in his beard. Regina, annoyed by the sudden activity, slunk off to find a quiet corner. 'I'm fine,' croaked Lennox, waving him away with hands still slick with his greed, 'leave me. She bade you what?'

'To take a mistress.'

'Sweet suffering Jesus! Has she no morals?' He almost smiled at the indignant outrage on his father's face. He looked like an aggrieved matron, scandalised by the liberality of youth. 'Son, you must never meddle with any other woman.'

'I have not.' Darnley was abashed. He had never been unfaithful, never taken another woman into his bed or been inveigled into hers.

'Good. Weak men take mistresses. You might look at other women – you're a young man, it's no crime, there's no harm – but for a married man to take the body of another woman in sin – that's for the basest of knaves.'

He was a surprised at his father's vehement prudishness, but he endorsed his sentiments.

'This business, your Grace, of having a woman rule you, rule us all ... Oh, she is a fair and noble lady,' he said, catching him before he could interject, 'no doubt of that. But I don't like it. It's not right. You are nearly twenty-one and you have a child to think about. Soon no one will have cause or reason to deny you your rights should you press them. No parliament called can fail to acknowledge the necessity of a king in his majority being granted his crown. Even your opponents will realise there is no way of halting the course of nature without bringing down the censure of the world.'

'I have told her this, father. The whole world stands clean amazed that a woman rules in right of her husband, who is treated himself as a woman.'

'Well we must find some way to remedy it.'

'To what end?' said Darnley dejectedly. 'Scotland has shown that it has no appetite to be governed by a strong king whose loyalty is to Scotland alone. Instead it belongs heart and soul to charlatans. I have been willing to give all to this realm, father, as God knows, but to no purpose. I would as soon leave and roam the world.'

Lennox looked at him, his mind working. 'If I know my daughter-in-law, she'll not wish that; oh no, she will not. And neither will that bastard brother or his friends.'

'Why not?'

'Because, my dearest boy, whilst they might have liberty to treat you like a petted, unworthy child in Scotland, they'll find that the rest of the world won't take well to a king being driven from his kingdom by a wife ruled by a band of disloyal men. It would be a bad precedent for any king to accept without outcry. You know the pride our French cousins have in their Salic law. Do you think King Charles would tolerate his friend the King of Scots being cast upon his shores a supplicant, and countenance the rights of a wife outweighing those of her husband?'

Lennox sat back, smoothing his few remaining strands of hair behind his ears with both hands. He had a point. When Darnley had sought refuge with his French relatives a lifetime ago, it had been as a fugitive evading a suspicious Queen of England. If he arrived now it would be as an exiled King of Scots. The shockwaves would be felt throughout Europe. Thrones would shake on their foundations.

'What course do we follow?'

'I shall write the queen,' he said, waving a broad arm airily over the table. 'I shall tell her that you are immovably reconciled to the idea of living abroad: that nothing can alter your purpose. You will make ready to follow her to Edinburgh, and once we have intelligence she has received the letter you'll present yourself. I've no doubt she'll offer anything to keep you in Scotland; her policies will be in jeopardy if you embark on your own abroad. Mark my words, her answer will speak for my wisdom. Have you paper?' He fetched some.

The old man began writing and Darnley called in Will and told him to let his fellow servants know that the king would be departing in a few days for Edinburgh.

26

It was the end of September before Mary received the letter that his father had laboured over for hours. Darnley allowed enough time for her – and, he had no doubt, her councillors – to ponder it before he presented himself as the closed gates of Holyroodhouse, where she was staying for the first time since death of Riccio. The sight of it spooked him. It was evening by the time he and his few servants arrived; darkness had fallen. Autumn announced its presence with gusts that howled through the eaves like ghostly screams.

The palace's gatekeeper, his old friend from his first coming to Holyroodhouse, appeared and informed him that the queen was in discussion with her Council. The man made no move to unlock the gates and admit him. Rather than degrade himself further by begging a servant to allow him entry to his own palace he strode up to the thick bars and called out, 'Come out, you men of the Council. Come out so that your king may enter without fear of his life.' The palace was deaf and blind to him. If he was to be humiliated then so would be his wife. He repeated his recitation at intervals, hammering on the gates. They rang like heavy chains. His voice rose to a scream, competing with the wind. It felt good to shout, to know that his people would hear even if their queen wouldn't listen. Ever faithful, his dog sat up in her fur-lined saddle basket and punctuated his cries with her own yapping barks. The gatekeeper stood aloof, watching the scene with bemusement.

Eventually Mary came out of the palace herself– a rare show of responsiveness – and the gates were unlocked and pulled open with a high, unpleasant screech. She took her husband by the arm, leading him through. He hadn't been expecting such cordiality. It unnerved him. He was, he said, unsure about even entering a palace where Moray lurked, but she reassured him that all was well. She had missed him, in fact. The news that he would really leave the kingdom was worrisome. She conveyed him up to her own apartments. His, she explained, were not in readiness. He had not been expected. He was even to share her bed. He could scarcely believe it.

As they lay cocooned in red-curtains that night, side by side, he made no move to touch her. The whole thing was too surreal for that – he was in no mood. They both stared at the canopy above, breathing shallowly. Eventually she spoke.

'Harry, why do you wish to depart?'

'There are reasons too many to venture. Too much has happened and nothing is as I would wish it. I have cast my mind back often. I have sought the moment when things fell out as they did between us. But it is like regarding a hole, unable to find in the pile of earth the first grain that was pulled to dig it.'

'We each dig our own grave,' she said in a soft voice.

'What?'

'Nothing.'

'I mean, it is like finding oneself at the end of a journey, and not recalling the confused paths which led to the place.' There was only the sound of her breathing. He continued. 'You see, I had so many plans – grand plans. Yet I have accomplished nothing. I am king in a country I love but I have no power to plot its path. I still have hopes. I still have dreams. I cannot stand being useless, being forgotten, unwanted. It is hard.'

'I do not wish you to go. Matters are difficult. But I would not have your son reared without his mother and father. Think of your own poor brother, locked away fatherless – without even his mother. Whatever falls out between us, our prince shall have a mother and a father who love him: who can watch him grow and rival any prince of Europe in his achievements.'

'I will think on it.'

'You have made mistakes,' she persisted. 'You do not understand this country. You only think you do. You have begun a thing that will not easily be forgotten. Blood feuds run deep. If you stay you might be protected.'

'Protected? No man would lay hands on his king. The world would stand in horror at so monstrous and unnatural an act.'

'Ah, but there are some Scots who have no respect for the divine order of the world: who think themselves natural rulers and not their princes.'

'And such men will never prosper in any Christian country.'

'Maybe. Perhaps.'

'Worry not, sweetheart. No one shall touch me. Even if I were struck down, or banished, you'd still stand guard over our child. It benefits no man to rid the realm of a king when the queen still reigns.'

Her steady breathing seemed to catch. After a pause, her voice, strangulated and odd, choked out, 'Goodnight.'

'Goodnight, my Mary.'

He fell into a fitful, uncomfortable sleep.

The next morning she was up and being made ready by her ladies before him. She told him that fresh clothes had been provided and even produced a small bowl of scented water. He playfully dipped his hand in it and flicked some at her. She giggled and told him to stop.

The royal couple had dinner together. The old ceremony was fully observed – they were waited on by their earls, with Bothwell bearing Mary's cup as honoured servitor and Huntly Darnley's. The stammering, diffident Huntly was so inexperienced he continually upset dishes. The ugly Bothwell managed to serve with a flourish, expertly manoeuvring a thick body richly attired in purple. The whole atmosphere of the palace seemed to have been restored to what it had been before Riccio's death had thrown a dark cloak over it: even, Darnley thought wryly, down to the service he was afforded being an ersatz imitation of that given his wife. She asked him during dinner to come to the afternoon's Privy Council meeting. He beamed in response. But when he entered he felt disdainful glares from all present except one, a smiling, oblivious man with a neat black moustache.

'Your Grace, this is Monsieur du Croc, the new ambassador from France,' said Mary. They bowed to one another. 'Now,' she continued, 'I am sure he and the lords of the Council would much welcome the truth of the plans contained within this letter.' She held up the letter Lennox had sent. 'Most especially are we concerned with the claims that you are to leave us without cause or consent. Ai-je raison, monsieur?' Du Croc nodded eagerly. 'Indeed; anything touching your gracious Highness's honour would benefit from an explanation.'

'And we hope we shall provide it, monsieur. Husband, kindly explain the cause of and intent behind the following.' She proceeded to read out the letter Lennox had sent. Her voice was full of reprimand, like a schoolmaster doing a duty from which he can only secretly take pleasure. She had lost none of her power to intimidate. So that was why she had whisked him upstairs, taken him into her bed – so that he would hear nothing of what was to come. Well none of them would have the satisfaction of a tantrum. When she finished she got up and approached him, her face a picture of sweet sincerity. She took his hand and said, 'now do not be afraid to speak your mind. Do not spare me; deal plainly. Do you plan to leave this realm without the assent of your queen and Council?'

'Your Highness, I have no grounds at all to leave the

country,' he said, shaking off her hand as flamboyantly as he could. 'Save for my own desire to see the world and return a better prince. Gentlemen, allow me to bid you all adieu. And adieu to you, madam. You shall not see my face again for a long time.' His voice was weary.

As he was making ready for the return trip he ordered Will to bring up Regina from the royal kennels. The boy was taking an age. Mary had abandoned Darnley to stew in her silent private rooms and went off hunting. It was quite alright for her to enjoy herself, he thought sulkily. Finally, the door to her royal apartment was nudged open.

'A fine time you've been! Do you expect me to-' His words stopped in mid-flow at the sight of Will, still standing in the doorway with the big covered basket in his arms. A single tear was running down his trembling face. In a heartbeat Darnley reached him, taking the heavy basket from his unprotesting arms. He swept the cloth from it and threw it to the floor. Will's mouth worked stupidly, his expression dazed, but he automatically bent to retrieve the cover.

Inside the basket Regina was still, her fur matted with dried blood. Her eyes were open, trusting, staring at nothing. She would never nuzzle him or come again at his call. Darnley sank to his knees with the basket in his arms, murmuring, 'Oh no.' He threw his head back and keened before scooping up the stiff body of his dog up and holding it close, mindless of the blood.

'Bastards!' he wailed, 'Bastards!' There was a deep gash across her throat. 'Who's done this? What bastard's done this? I'll see them in a noose!'

'She were like this ... they found her .... They di'n't know.'

'Evil,' sobbed Darnley. 'She would have went to anyone. Trusted anyone.'

It was some time before Will composed himself enough to

convince his master to relinquish the body. In hushed tones the other servants speculated that the exiled lords still had enough friends left in the country to send messages to the king.

***

'You demanded nothing?' asked Lennox. 'You told them all that you had no grounds for grievance?'

'What else was I to do,' he answered, his voice rising in pitch. 'She had me in front of the whole Council, in front of the French ambassador. She read your letter before them all.' Darnley had come west seeking comfort, people who liked him, and the obvious choice was Lennox country. When he arrived at the Castle of Glasgow and explained the events of the Council meeting his reception was muted by his father's displeasure.

'You should have fronted it out, boy. Why is it that you can never stand firm in anything?'

He said nothing. He had not come to be disciplined, or to be scolded.

'Ach, what's done is done. But I – we – won't give up. I'll draft another letter. It will lay out in detail – in detail, mind you – the means by which you are dishonoured. It will note that none attend you; that the nobility avoids you; that you are trusted with no authority. All will be laid bare, all. And you really shall take your leave of Scotland until she relents. Oh, and my son … I really do regret the dog. It was a valuable creature.' With untiring enthusiasm his father once again poured the litany of old grievances onto paper in the vain hope that they would this time be acknowledged and taken seriously. Dutifully he copied them out in his own hand, signed them and sent them to his wife.

To his surprise she acknowledged his letter. He wasn't sure if he'd have done so in her position. He knew by now that she could probably prompt him on his list of demands. Her reply read that the diminishment in his status was down to himself, and that if the nobility abandoned him it was because he had done nothing to make them love and serve him. He read the letter without anger, casually wondering if she was right. Mostly, he didn't care.

For the moment he was content to live in peace, almost like a private person, whilst his wife pursued and was pursued by affairs of state. He remained in that frame of mind for some weeks, until a messenger arrived to tell him in lugubrious tones that his wife was dying.

***

It was after noon when he was shown into the bedroom of the sandstone house in which Mary was lying. She had been visiting the charming little borders village of Jedburgh – a jewel nestling in a vast, scrubby wilderness – to preside over a travelling court of justice. There she had collapsed, lost her sight, lost her speech, lost consciousness and thrown up blood. If she should die there would be civil war. His son would be in danger as grasping men fought to seize control. Vivid images had flashed through his mind of the fall of the emperor known as Caligula, when the Praetorian Guard, under orders from Cassius Chaerea, had wreaked havoc in the city. The dead emperor's consort had been done to death, with the rampaging men not hesitating to dash out the brains of his one-year-old daughter.

To his relief she was not only alive but sitting up, her hair a tumble of waves. The room was wood-panelled, bright and airy. Little specks of dust drifted through the light. When she saw him in the doorway she crossed her arms and frowned. He went round her bedside, coming between her and the window. His shadow fell over her.

'Your Grace,' he said, putting a hand to his forehead. 'I heard such evil reports. I can scarce find words to express my relief that you are recovering.'

'No thanks to you, sir.'

'Sweetheart?'

'Sweetheart,' she mimicked. 'Sweet me no sweethearts. You need not have come hither. You are the very author of my misery and pain.'

He faltered. He had not expected her to fall into his arms, but he had expected some measure of appreciation for his wild ride to be by her bedside. The room dulled as clouds passed over the sun. Before he could speak Moray strode in, his boot-heels pecking at the wood and his nose in the air. 'Your Grace,' he nodded. 'As you can see, bruits of the queen's death have been premature. She shall recover. And it would be better she was not encumbered by childish squabbling.'

'You hear my brother, sir,' added Mary. 'Your presence is not desired in this place. If you insist on haunting this town you will not lodge under this roof.'

'Madam,' he said. 'I repeat that I am pleased to find you well. I apologise for any discontent I have caused. I will not tarry.' He left the room just as the sun re-emerged.

Somehow he had managed to do wrong again. Nothing he ever did seemed to come out right; always, there was some disagreement, some unexpected unhappiness. His wife was now immersed in her performance as a tragic, wronged heroine, and now she had in her brother and her friends supporting players.

He couldn't ride north in the dark. He sent Will to find suitable lodgings. Only some drab but comfortable rooms in the house of a local merchant were available. The merchant, a fat man in ill-fitting clothes at least welcomed the king warmly and with deference. He had been so sorry, he said, to hear that the queen had been taken ill in her rush to see the injured Earl of Bothwell. However loyal a servant the earl was, he would surely never have wanted his sovereign to worry after him so much that she made herself ill. Darnley's ears pricked up at this. So the local gossip was that his wife's illness was not his doing but her own intemperate ride to visit Bothwell. The woman would say anything to make him feel bad.

He spent a lonely night in the unfamiliar house, feeling aimless. How could he ever hope to refashion himself and his marriage if he was to be forever castigated and humiliated for mistakes he had made in the past? Anger rose. He was sick of being given no chance to apologise, sick of being forgiven yet not forgiven, of being played for a fool by the queen and the men she now kept around her. She would *rely* on any man, certainly – even arch-heretics like the bastard Moray and the ugly Bothwell – as long as they were not her husband. She would share her power with no one who had a right to it by law or custom, only those she could make her vassals. In the morning he left Jedburgh and returned to Stirling without saying goodbye.

When he arrived he set about writing to the kings of France and Spain and to the Holy Father in Rome. It was time to assert himself as a king and a man, to remind the world that he existed and would influence his country's future with whatever means he had at his disposal. His wife, he informed them portentously, was dubious in the faith. She had cast in her lot with heretical men, and who knew what it would mean for Scotland.

To Darnley it ultimately meant that his country would become a satellite state of England even if it retained nominal independence. A small country turned Protestant by rebellion would always be at the mercy of a larger country turned Protestant by reformist monarchs; Scotland had even followed England in breaking from Rome, like the tail of a dog which had turned on its former master. All talk of amity was no more than Scottish clientage, English overlordship by dint of size. He would not have it for his son. He found that imagining his son as a strong, powerful, Catholic King of Scots was an easy means of warming a heart that for too long had been frigid and lonely. The boy would be everything he had hoped to be – even if he had to ruin his embittered wife and flee abroad for him to achieve it. He bent over his quill, pouring as much venom as possible into his words.

27

As the christening of Prince James drew near ugly rumours began to reach Darnley at Stirling. When on her sickbed the queen, it was said, had written to Elizabeth entrusting to her sister-monarch the care of her son should she die. Not only was he thus excluded from the raising of his only child, but he might well be raised a heretic at the behest of the English queen, who would behave as though the boy was a fatherless foundling.

The rumours were confirmed by December. His twenty-first birthday came and went unnoticed by anyone but his father. If his mother wrote him a felicitous letter it did not reach him. The English queen only allowed condemnatory letters out of the Tower. In many ways he felt as though he was back in his sickroom at Stirling: he even occupied the same suite. He might as well have been infectious. For once he could see no way out.

James' christening was scheduled for the second week and it was then that he did receive a visitor. It was George Buchanan, the veteran scholar who had schooled him in Scotland's history in his first zealous weeks as king. His job, he told Darnley, was to prepare the baptismal masques. Yet, though he broke it kindly, Buchanan acknowledged that Darnley was not to be acknowledged by Queen Elizabeth's proxy. He was, in fact, to turn up in his gold suit and be ignored by all. That, Darnley thought as he showed Buchanan out, settled matters. If he was to be treated as nothing, he wouldn't be present at all. Touchingly, the old man hugged him again before leaving, thanking him without explanation for showing the world that kings were flesh-and-blood men. As usual, the scholar left muttering: this time it was something about Hermaphroditus, a figure Darnley couldn't place.

Darnley spent the day of his son's christening trying to peer at events through a window of his room. No one looked up to see the drawn face of the king pressed against the glass. He could hear laughter and music ringing out increasingly loudly as the day and night wore on. From the Great Hall the sound of cheering and toasting seemed to go on for hours. People were enjoying themselves. Night fell early and swiftly and the windows of his apartments were occasionally illuminated by fireworks.

The clothes he was to have worn lay untouched in his bedchamber: another glittering golden suit that would never see use.

***

On Christmas Eve snow began to fall, silently drifting down like specks of dust, cushioning the world. Darnley was in his rooms, warming himself by the fire when a knock came. Will admitted a royal herald, young, ruddy and full of self-importance.

'What news, sir?' asked Darnley. He was not expecting much. Mary only allowed news to drift to him if it was inconsequential or likely to upset him. On Christmas Eve it would surely be the former.

'Your Grace, the queen wishes you to know that she has this day formally pardoned your kinsman the Earl of Morton, along with sundry others for their role in the late affrights touching the death of her former secretary.'

He jerked up, his eyes wide. 'She has done what?'

'The queen has this day formally pardoned-'

'I heard you. Get out of here.' The herald bowed without much sincerity and left him.

It couln't be. She despised those men more than she

despised him. What was happening? Morton and his false friend and amoral Uncle George had even, in their exile, been heard to claim that they considered that they were in a blood feud with the so-called King of Scots and would slit his throat themselves. These were desperate men and they would not stop until he was dead.

He badly wanted a drink. The familiar feeling of drunken release, of bottled confidence and self-assurance, of lapsing into a stupor in which nothing and no one mattered was inviting. But that desire – that instinctive impulse to seek comfort in drink – frightened him too. Instead he called Will in and ordered him to pack. He would not sit around Stirling like a lamb tied to the stake. He would go to loyal Glasgow where where men would carry news to him as their king. His father would know what to do – Lennox understood these men more than he ever would. As always, once he had made the decision he was eager for it to be underway. He would be riding in the snow. But he was by now used to that.

They rode southwest that night. Almost as soon as they were on the road, however, he had to rein in. A sudden nausea gripped him; he thought he was going to fall from his horse. He leant forward, burying his face in a mane specked with flakes of snow. Heat was tearing through his face and the feel of the bracing cold helped. Presently it passed and he felt normal. Then another wave hit him.

'We goin' back, your Grace?' asked Will, not fully resigned to a freezing ride. Things had been going badly for too long, for his tastes. Too many frightening brutes had been crossed, and a master's disgrace redounded on his servants. He would never find a bride or a real home in Scotland. Even his tubby little pantry maid had cast her bonnet at someone else, apparently offended that, on her birthday, he had given her a dress made for a much slighter lady with the hope that she would soon fit into it. He had already decided to give notice after the festive period and return to Yorkshire. He would stay only as long as the appearance of loyalty compelled him.

'No. We ride on. I'll puke when I must.'

They continued, making the journey to Glasgow in fits and starts, stopping repeatedly so Darnley could vomit up thin streams of bile. By the time they reached the Castle of Glasgow his groin was on fire from the ride and he felt like he was radiating heat. Will had to help him inside. His face was red, not from the cold but from some strange ague. His father, nursing a fever himself, had his retainers half-drag him to bed.

In the morning every muscle in his body was in agony. When he moved he felt like there was broken glass under his skin, the shards jabbing through the flesh. Grinding his teeth against the pain, he sat up and twisted around to where he could see himself in a mirror. He could not believe the sight at first; he thought his vision was failing or that the light of the thin, wintry sun coming into the room was somehow wrong. His face was a hideous shade of bluish purple, like a rotting corpse. He turned away, moaning.

When his father came to see how he was he fled the room in horror as soon as he laid eyes on him. Physicians were called – Glasgow's finest, Lennox assured him. Two of them arrived, officious-looking men in the dark cloaks of their trade. They spoke in low tones to one another, shaking their heads and muttering darkly.

'Poison,' was their verdict. 'The king has been poisoned.'

***

Darnley fell in and out of consciousness on Christmas Day. Throughout the rest of the festive period he had no perception of time as he was rubbed with acidic-smelling ointments and left in shuttered, stifling rooms to sweat out the illness: but still he clung on. His hair did not. Great strands of gold were scattered across his bedclothes every day.

In January he began to recover. His doctors told him that whatever mysterious poison he had ingested – and he knew of no poison that had these terrible effects – it was being purged from his system, his humours rebalancing. But his face remained livid with blisters which reminded him horribly of the outbreak of measles he had suffered at Stirling. Further, from his armpits and thighs poured endless, stinking sweat.

Mary's physician arrived to assess him. Unlike Darnley's own doctors he decided that the king was suffering from smallpox. He was terrified – this was the illness which carried people off every year, and often left those who survived it with hideous, scorched-meat skin.

He feared the pox but it put his mind at rest. He hadn't been poisoned – an idea he had been loath to accept. Whatever strange malady was ravaging his body it was not inflicted by man and it would soon pass if yet more sweating was encouraged and hot ointments applied. It was a different illness from that suspected by the Glasgow doctors, to be sure – but the same remedy would be efficacious. Hot on the heels of the physician came a messenger. He had come to fear such men.

'What news?' he asked without enthusiasm. He had put a taffeta mask over his face which made him sound muffled. He had discovered that his breath had taken on a sulphurous, pestilent reek, like the slit-open carcass of a hunted animal. The mask, which covered his lower face, assured that at least he was the only one that had to suffer the noxious fumes. And the damn thing was meant to protect him from unhealthy, harmful airs. He knew it made him look ghoulish and cursed that his options were to appear a ghastly spectre or a deformed monster.

'The queen wishes to know if her presence might lend you

comfort. If it be so, she will come.'

'If she come it shall be to my comfort and she shall be welcome,' he said. 'And she can stay as long as it pleases her. Convey that to her, sir.' After a bow the man turned to go, and Darnley suddenly remembered his reception when he had visited her on her sickbed. 'But I also would she knows,' he called, 'that I only wish that I was the Earl of Bothwell, for then I'm sure she would be here whether wanted or not.' The herald nodded hesitantly. But his wife came.

She arrived in Glasgow in the company of armed men, commandeering the old Lennox castle of Crookston. By the time she visited his little chamber, alleviated only by rich bed hangings, He had given a great deal of thought to what he ought to say to her.

She entered his room alone and looked at him with pity. He wore his unsettling mask. It did not cover the patches of bald scalp where tufts of hair had been lost. He wasted little time in small talk. They were beyond that now.

Convalescing had given him time to think. He had reflected on his strange marriage. He had considered his love of Scotland, and the disillusion he had felt on realising that his belief in its sovereignty and future were not shared by the men who wielded power. But mostly he thought about his wife. Had he ever loved her? He decided that he had: if not when he first courted her, at least when he had been willing to execute a man he had been led to believe was cuckolding him. What else but love could drive a man to do that? She was perplexing – infuriating, even – but he must love her. Only love could explain why he had let her raise him up and strike him down, treat him like her plaything, and still come back for more.

True they had fought, they had hurt, undermined and used each other – but God had joined them together. Still, no marriage could long survive without love, or with the unforgiving demon of the past clinging to the backs of husband or wife, weighing them down and whispering things best forgotten in their ear. He would think of some way to make her love him, to make her forget the past and embrace their future.

She might continue to reject him – she might reject his anointment as king – but who could blame her? That cunning, insecure English vixen had played them off against one other, first showing him great favour then transferring that favour and recognition to his wife. The shadow of England's throne, occupied only by an ageing virgin, had come between them so completely it had obscured their lives together at Scotland's helm.

At any rate, he was decided: his wife would not find the spoiled, sullen, dissolute youth of his enemies' imaginations, but a mature and reflective man. She would find a man whom she might welcome as a real king when she saw how contrite he was.

'Ah, my Mary,' he said, enjoying her name. 'Look at us. How have we fallen so low?' She made no response. She only stood before him, clad in pale blue. Her neck was as long and pale as ever, her skin as fresh, her eyes as enchanting and her lips as full and red. 'As I have lain here these weeks I have thought on many things. I have thought on your cruelty –' She opened her mouth to object, her eyes already flashing, and he silenced her with a finger. She would be unable to see his mouth, he knew: only the awkward flexing of white cloth. 'On your cruelty,' he repeated, 'and on my own faults. I have been wrong and I have done wrong. And you have said you forgive me. Yet we have allowed us to be goaded into being rivals rather than lovers. We've brought out the worst in each other.' He paused.

'You have more to say,' she said. It was not a barb. He

nodded.

'I am yet young. I know you have had cause to forgive me, more times than I need recount; but is it not common for a man of my age to fall once, twice, thrice and still repent, and become a better man for the experience?' She only looked at him. But he could see she was listening. 'I do not believe it is too late for us, Mary. Even after everything, I do not – not at our age and with a son so newly brought. I have had bad counsel; you have said so yourself. I have allowed myself to be used and corrupted and I am truly sorry for it. Men such as those you have lately pardoned – Morton, Douglas, even Ruthven – these men knew me to be a young fool, eager to please. They hated me and hate me yet because they do not wish a stranger, a foreigner who loves Scotland, to take it from them their grasp. They are the menace to this nation. They are the real poison in the body politic. They are rogues who will suck the country dry.'

He was finally giving voice to thoughts which he had harboured for months, and now that the floodgate was open he found he could not stop. 'I believe, Mary, that they hated Riccio for the same reason. He was a threat to them, to the Scotland they keep in their own pockets, like misers with their stores of gold. You see, do you not, that these men are the enemies of Scotland – the ones who profit by keeping the nation in thrall?'

He nodded emphasis into his words, willing her to agree. She winced, he noticed, at Riccio's name. 'Ah,' he said, bringing a hand up to his covered mouth. 'I'm sorry to remind you of … of the past.'

'I have no need to be reminded. I have never forgotten. Davy liked you. It was only for my friendship that he relinquished yours. He needed someone who could protect his … his secrets. His only crime was not being as other men. This world was too hard for him, but I understood. Poor Davy. Continuez s'il vous plaît.'

'Thank you, Mary. I've been a jealous fool and allowed these men to prey on that fault. I have thought of you as a goddess – unknowable and awesome – and have gone on to debase myself.'

'I have been aware of your feelings towards me. I have been sorry for them,' she said, not looking displeased with her elevation.

'I've come to realise that it's not always the power we have that corrupts us, but the power we are denied. You see the result before you. I promise you that I desire nothing more than for us to put the past behind us, and to let our minds meet, not run from each other. Otherwise I would be content never to rise from this bed.'

He settled back. His mind went back over the speech, wondering if he had forgotten anything.

'I am sorry you are so unwell,' she said. 'I have heard fresh bruits you intend to leave the country. Your father has been heard declaring that he has a ship in readiness. Are such rumours well founded?'

Had she been listening to him? He had thought his speech impressive. It had certainly been honest. 'I will go nowhere without cause, though I cannot speak for my father. But I thank you for your sympathy. How do you find our pardoned lords? Do they behave? I have heard that they would happily see me dead, which grieves me. I find it uncreditable that my wife would have men around her that would do her husband ill.'

'I assure you you are quite safe. It is my intention to finally bring tranquillity to this troubled realm,' she sighed. 'To that end I would have you reconciled to your former conspirators. I will have no feuds and factions in this kingdom. Those are the old ways, and I *will* stamp them out. I have even brought a horse-litter that will convey you comfortably to Edinburgh. I have removed the prince there. There are rumours you planned to take custody of him by secret means. You would like to be near our little man free of suspicion, would you not?' She raised a bent forefinger to her mouth preparing to chew on it.

'You know I would. Such rumours are false.'

'Good.' Her hand fell to her side. 'Then matters are concluded,' she said. 'You will return with me to Craigmillar.' His eyes narrowed. Craigmillar was an old citadel not far from Holyrood. It had a dark reputation; men who hated him had been rumoured there according to his father. 'It has baths that will do a better job of purging your sickness than anything that can be given you here.' There was a sudden soft thump against the door, as though something had slid against it, and she turned sharply. 'What on earth? Who is there?' But there was no answer and the door remained closed.

'A servant, I imagine. One of your ladies?'

'They are without,' she said, still looking at the door.

'No matter. We're undisturbed. I will come,' he said, and she turned back to him with a tight smile, 'if you agree to put the past behind us. We can make things anew, and be as husband and wife once more, to bed and board together without secrets.'

'Would I have come into your father's lands and lodged in his castle were I not willing to take you as my husband?' His stomach fluttered. He reached out and took her hand weakly. It was chilly but yielding. 'I will not pretend it shall be easy. But for the sake of our son and the tranquillity of our realm, I realise that we must try. A house – a royal house particulièrement – that is divided against itself cannot stand, and it is want of unity that has brought us to this place. You see, you are not the only one who has been forced to think of late, nor to have realised that the past can be a cruel tyrant whom we cannot let govern the future. Alors, we must move forward as grown people, putting aside childish things.' There was composure in her voice and a noticeably resigned set to her chin.

'You cannot know how much that pleases me. Perhaps this is why God has spared me: so that we might have a second chance to do His work. One thing only – and I am sorry for it – I do not like the idea of Craigmillar. Think of it as the indulgent mind of a sick man,' he smiled, 'but I have no good feeling about it. I will return with you and happily, but I will lodge elsewhere. Somewhere private, somewhere I will not be regarded by any man.' He shrugged sheepishly. 'Who would wish to look upon this?'

'Very well. We will find you somewhere small and private. On the south side of the town. Yes, there the air is better. It will be a more potent restorative. There are empty houses at Kirk o' Field. The Hamilton place is vacant. You might-'

'Hang the Hamiltons. I should not sleep safely in any home of theirs. They ... they discomfit me. I am sorry to be trouble.' Here he was seeing shadows when he had promised himself to see only light.

'There is no trouble; it is the prerogative of the patient. I will look into the other residences. Rooms shall be found befitting your degree. Until then, adieu.' She gave him one of her old, coquettish smiles, detached her hand from his and left the room, looking both ways as she did.

Darnley settled back on his thick sheets and blankets, content to doze, when his father slid in. Evidently it had been him hovering outside the room like an old busybody, eavesdropping and eager to say his piece. If she had seen him as she left she had ignored him.

'Son,' he said, 'you must not go with her. Something is

amiss.'

He groaned. 'Oh father,' he said. 'It is no more time for these games. My wife has requested my presence and like any good husband I do not mean to deprive her. Nor do I wish to be clear across the country from my boy.'

'Ach, soft notions; you're your mother's son alright. I tell you, this sudden change is no good omen and I don't trust it. Or her,' he said, turning to the door and sniffing deeply. 'There is no heart within her. Besides, how do you ever expect to gain the respect of the people and the Crown Matrimonial if you're seen to obey the commands of your woman, chasing after her as a dog? Our family stands now ready for redemption, for the sins and misdeeds of the past to be blotted out by a glorious future. How do you expect to command the liberty of your mother and own dear brother without strength? How –'

'Father, please' he said, raising a hand to quiet him. 'I love and honour you as a son should. As ever I have. But I cannot unburden your conscience. Whatever it is disquiets and haunts you is yours alone, not for me to undo. I have atonement enough of my own to occupy me. I shall no longer be fed with ideas about strength and glory, or tortuous visions of mother and Charlie's suffering.'

'The boy's unharmed,' barked Lennox, grasping on to the image. 'He's leading as cosseted a life as ever he did with us. And your mother! The lady has the strength of ten men. She would happily board a century in the Earl of Hell's jakes if it assured your success and our family's honour. All we have done we have done for you, boy, for you!'

'But where has your advice got me? Here, in this place, unhappy and stinking. Now I shall follow my own star. I will hear no more of you.'

His father looked shocked, his mouth working as he tried to

summon up fresh words of reproach, or anger, or hurt. 'Well, go your way,' he rasped. 'And Hell mend you if you have judged your wife ill.' A drop of blood fell from his nose, and he looked down, dumbfounded, at the red splash. Staunching the sudden flow, he fled the room.

28

Metropolitan Scotland was buzzing with rumours about the mystifying royal couple and their strange, unpredictable marriage. In taverns and alehouses, in marketplaces and in the servant quarters of castles and townhouses, people speculated with glee about whether the queen would divorce the king. Such a thing had never been thought possible: an anointed queen divorcing her husband after less than two years of marriage, and when an heir had just been born. Oh no, she would never be so foolish as to damage the status of her young son, said some. She will have a new husband before the year is out, said others. What else can we expect from Papists, and a Papist woman especially? was the opinion of those educated at the school of Knox.

The Scots were equally divided on the nature of their king. To some he was a proud young foreigner come from England to rule them like an ignorant conqueror. To others he was young King Harry of Scottish stock, who eschewed pretension and came amongst his people, drinking their health and generous of his royal presence. To still others he was a harbinger of a return to the Catholic fold, which was to be welcomed or feared depending on the believer. The prospects for his marriage likewise differed according to the image of the king favoured by Scots as they indulged in increasingly lively discussion about the country's future over ale and over laundry.

It was the end of January before he felt ready to be moved and it was then that they took a leisurely journey from the west of Scotland, northeast along the highway, through Stirlingshire and on to the capital. The going was slow with Darnley carried gently in his litter; it took several short winter days. His facial inflammation had died down, the blisters scabbed over – but he decided to keep wearing his unsightly mask, fearing that the encrusted flesh beneath was more unsightly still. It was with mixed feelings that he left Glasgow: hope, sadness at the loss of a safe and friendly atmosphere, and a wearied acceptance. A flock of ravens wheeled above the royal cortege. It was a good omen. Birds were free, the sky their kingdom.

He had chosen as the residence for his full recovery the old Provost's lodging: a small building on the south side of a quadrangle which was, as Mary had suggested, on the city's southern edge. It backed right onto the city walls, on the border between civilisation and untamed nature. As he was drawn towards it, his bones weary from lying in in his litter long hours at a stretch, his heart sank. The building was ugly, angular and dark. It looked like a tall shard of the countryside's ashen, volcanic rock had pierced Edinburgh's wall and was doing a poor job of masquerading as a townhouse. He cursed his rash decision, which had alighted on any house other than one owned by his father's enemies.

'Your Grace,' he called up to his wife. 'This house doesn't please me. It's far too small.'

'Oh, Harry. The house is well-furnished. I gave the orders myself. It well befits such a king as you,' she replied from atop her horse.

'Very well, sweetheart. If you think it will serve our turn.' He smiled up at her. He was determined that he would not make trouble or give her cause to think him contrary.

The house seemed bigger on the inside and Mary had been right – it had been decorated with all finery. Darnley had been designated the main bedchamber upstairs – a room that had been fitted out with a bed bordered with black velvet hangings. She apologised for the dour black and for the stale smell which came from the old hangings. She had already ordered her mother's great bed brought from Holyroodhouse. He was pleased – black velvet in a sickroom presaged death. But otherwise the room filled was already filled with furniture – obviously expensive – as well as games and a bath where he could take his treatments. It was like a playroom. She had her own bedroom directly below his. It was, he joked, a novelty to have their old roles reversed.

In this pleasant atmosphere calm and happiness prevailed. His new bed arrived and was set up, decked in violet and blue. Mary slept downstairs, but spent her days playing games and reading with him. He could almost forget that the rest of the world existed and imagine that they were once again a courting couple. They lived chastely, as he was still a convalescent, but in some ways it felt fitting. They were only just getting to know one another. When she laughed his heart soared – he had thought he would never hear her laugh again. His mind was liberated and turned to the future. There would be more children, brothers and sisters for James. A full royal household could take shape, presided over by doting parents. He could see a trio of boys with a shared love of sports and learning, at least one of them a poet. Girls would join them – each as pretty as their mother – studying, singing and sewing whilst their brothers were at the hunt: little princesses reared to beguile the princes of Europe, the youngest her father's pet. A family awaiting chronicles.

He wrote to inform his father that peace was returning to his life along with good health. Mary read the letter over his shoulder, her silken bosom whispering against his back, and kissed him when she had finished. Most importantly they talked. He shared with her his disillusion with Scotland and was happy to report that it had passed. More than that, he had decided to redouble his efforts to secure the future of the state.

He told her about the young thief who had assailed him outside Peebles, whose pitiful dagger he now kept amongst his things, and she had been suitably horrified and saddened. She listened intently to his stories about the history that had led to Scotland's division – caused by those who sought to make it a mendicant nation constantly seeking approval of the English queen – and how that might be remedied. The ire of some of their treacherous nobility would doubtless be stirred by any move on their sovereigns' part that threatened their Anglophile policy. The reaction to their marriage itself had revealed the nature of those who feared upsetting their beloved English queen. But together he and she could flaunt Scotland's place as proud nation in those faces. He grew more and more enthused as he convinced himself of the importance of his theories.

They shared the gossip that had been flying up and down the country about the plotting and scheming which those around them would inveigle them to join in the pursuit of their own goals. Those who wished to take advantage of their separation would be confounded by the sharing of intelligence between husband and wife. Together nothing could touch them. They talked a great deal about James and what a strong, athletic ruler he would become. He will, said Darnley, have the example of his father to look to. The youthful errors and follies of Scotland's Prince Hal and his subsequent redemption would become a lesson for all Christian princes.

Recognising that the king had been restored to favour, some of the men who had shunned him began to pay court. He had the largest room in the house fixed up as a Presence Chamber, the walls covered in tapestries, and received homages from Moray, who spoke kindly and asked after his health; from Bothwell, whom people said had grown haughty and arrogant, but was charm personified; from Huntly and Atholl, who bowed deeply; and even from Lethington, of whom he had made no secret of his distrust. Only his old drinking companion Robert sounded a note of discord.

'Harry, I don't like this,' he said on entering Darnley's audience room and casting furtive glances around and behind him. 'There's something unnatural in the air. The Earl of Bothwell and the Earl of Morton have been seen together. There are whispers abroad in the town; something jangles and jars. Don't trust them, and don't reside in this house. It just doesn't smell right.'

Darnley shook his head in wonderment. 'Robert, your nose is too close to your arse.'

'It's not right, none of this,' said Robert, gesturing around the room, his childish face open and eager.

'Then leave off,' said Darnley, tired already of the threat of plots and hearsay. 'The old days are past. I'm leaving them where they belong and leaving behind all who belong to them.'

His friend stalked off, muttering under his breath.

During Darnley's entire life in Scotland things had never been so peaceful. Robert was jumping at shadows, seeing chariots in the clouds, probably unused to a country in which the queen had successfully brokered peace and fostered reconciliation. She laughed when he told her. She had faith in her policies. The days of a violent, divided Scotland were, she assured him, at an end. Besides, although she had formally pardoned Morton, she had denied him the right to come near Court and excluded from the general pardon George Douglas, who had sworn to be revenged on his turncoat kinsman. She was making sure, she said, that friendship was won slowly and that those who had expressed a desire to renew hostilities would not tolerated.

A few days into his stay Mary's physician decided that he

would soon be ready to return to public life. Darnley was almost disappointed. He had always hated medical confinement, considering it no better than imprisonment, but he had had no violent rages at being cooped up this time. He was too grateful: to his wife, to God, to the men who had visited him and were willing to turn the page.

His last day at the old Provost's lodging was a Sunday – the last before Lent – and he began it by hearing Mass. He passed the day playing games and daydreaming. Mary was attending a wedding feast at Holyrood, but she had promised to return to him in the evening. She arrived flushed with merriment.

'You look as though you have ridden to Hell and back,' he said.

'And do I not feel it,' she said, drawing a hand across her forehead. 'I have not danced so merrily nor with such vigour for a long time. Oh, I love seeing people happy.'

'Don't spoil your pumps. I shall want a dance when I am able.'

'Which shall be soon?'

'I think it. The physician says on the morrow. I feel well – healthy.'

'I am glad.'

'And look,' he said, pulling off the taffeta mask with a flourish. He had been wearing it needlessly for some days, but he wanted to pull off a coup and surprise her. His face was unblemished and shining.

'Oh Harry, you really are cured!'

'I sure am.' She laughed and hugged him, ruffling the hair he had carefully arranged to cover the patchiness. 'Be careful,' he said, pulling down her hand, self-consciousness in his voice.

'You are silly. My Lords of Bothwell, Argyll and Huntly await an audience. And the Savoyard ambassador wishes to see the king before leaving Scotland. Shall we?'

'Why not,' he said, giving her his old smile.

The evening passed in gossip and laughter. Dreary Lethington was apparently losing interest in managing the state – he had absented himself from Court, having just married the queen's pretty young Mary Fleming. Exhaustion taking its toll was Bothwell's saucy guess – and he should know, he laughed, having married himself. Darnley wondered what the fox might be overseeing from safety now. Poor Moray's wife had miscarried; he too had had to leave Edinburgh to be by her side. There was melancholy shaking of heads at this news. He refused any strong liquor and drank only diluted ale and hippocras; the phrase, 'shall we have a drink this evening' had been irreversibly eradicated from his vocabulary. Eventually the Earl of Bothwell, draped in black and silver velvet that shone like scales, struck a hand to his forehead.

'Your Grace, we have lost all sense of time, so pleasant has the evening been. You have faithfully promised the bride and groom that you would return to the palace to watch their masque. It is being given in your honour.'

'Damn,' she said. 'I had forgotten about that. Je suis désolée.'

'Be not sorry, sweetheart. It troubles me not at all. A promise is a promise. But you will return tonight?'

'Without doubt.'

'That may not be wise, your Grace,' said Bothwell, raising a fist to his mouth and coughing.

'Why not?' she asked in irritation, 'the masque will not last long past midnight.'

'Indeed not, but you are riding to Seton in the morning. Your train leaves Holyroodhouse at dawn. It would be quicker you were with us.'

'Ah, I had forgotten this. I suppose that makes sense. Harry, do you object? It cannot be helped.'

'I do not mind at all,' he lied. He was disappointed that he was to be left alone again.

'I shall not be away long. When I return you will be out of this place. Here,' she slipped a ring from her finger, 'is my pledge. You shall be free by my return.' Her smile was dazzling.

When she had left Darnley called for his servants. 'Make ready our horses,' he said. 'I wish us to surprise the queen by being ready to ride with her to Seton in the morning.' He skipped up to his bedchamber, stretching his long limbs. He could not wait to see the look on her face in the morning.

***

He dreamt of the cemetery. This time the narrow, cobbled path glowed white in the moonlight. The sky, usually a dark purple, was black. Somewhere beyond his vision a dog was whimpering. He was aware that he was dreaming – he was expecting the tumble of bodies from their bent and awkward positions. But they did not fall. Instead, he was able to follow the path to its conclusion. This was a sunken, circular courtyard. It was very small. Perched on a pedestal in the centre, seated with his legs bent up under his chin and his head face down between his knees, was his own body. He yelped and drew back. His body, frozen in the stiffness of death, fell to the side. The courtyard was so small that his corpse smacked into its fellows arranged around the perimeter. The sound of crashing bodies was so loud, it was so discordant, it was so terrible, it was so –

– real. The noises were real. Outside. He sat up, his back like a poker. People were outside. He jumped up on the bed, feeling tendrils of fear, like the leaves of the spidery plants which grew between the cobblestones in his haunting, nightmare cemetery. He yanked open blue bed-curtains dyed black by darkness, ran to the blank, white window through which the noises were drifting and gently opened it a crack. A blade of frigid air cut into the room. He gritted his teeth against it and peered through the gap into the darkness below. This part of the room jutted over the town wall and overlooked the house's eastern garden. There was movement down there – black shapes moving against a dark background. As his eyes grew accustomed to the gloom, those shapes resolved themselves into men. Men were flooding into the house. Panic gripped him; his mind raced: *what to do, what to do, what to do?* The door, downstairs, outside, away, to freedom, to safety.

'Will,' he hissed. 'Will Taylor!' His valet, no more than an indistinct dark shape in the light of a nub of candle that had been left burning, was sitting up, rubbing sleep from his eyes.

'Your Grace? What are you for?'

'There are men downstairs, Will. Something is afoot.'

'Christ! We got to get out of 'ere,' was his reply. Will had a nose for danger. Already, he was rolling onto the floor and scrabbling for the scrap of candle.

'How?'

'Through t'other window, there's the west garden. There's a gate to't orchards outside the wall. I've been there before. It'll freeze our bollocks off at this time, but.'

'That is a straight drop, Will.'

'Better than stayin' 'ere, i'n't it?' Darnley thought for a second and then nodded. He pulled sheets from his bed.

'Take the other end of these, tie them to the bedstead, we shall fashion a rope.' Will did as he was told. They were both moving jerkily in the tiny glow of the candle. Men could be filling the house as they worked. They could be setting fires, hoping to burn their king to death. Why had he not listened to Robert? Why had he not listened to Mary, who had warned him that there were men in Scotland for whom regicide was not a crime against God?

When the rope was secured Darnley ran to the window. 'Stay quiet, make no sound,' he whispered to Will. He opened the tall window carefully. Icy air assaulted the room, tearing the air from his lungs and extinguishing the little candle flame. He was still wearing only his nightshirt. The blast caught some embers in the fireplace and they tried vainly to recapture life. 'I'll fetch your sable robe, your Grace. I'll toss it after you. Mind 'ow you go.'

'Bless you, Will. Follow me down.'

He braced himself against the cold and threw down the sheet, which had been wound into a makeshift rope. He took a firm grip and stepped onto the windowsill. Nonsensically, a voice in his head began to sing, 'windows in winter; why is it always windows in winter'. His feet were bare. He pressed them against the icy side of the house as he lowered himself down. The cold sailed up his nightshirt and around his body, stabbing him everywhere with needle-sharp points. He could not stop shivering. He thought he would lose his grip, his hands were so numb. His sable robe railed over his head, disappearing into the void, and he dropped the last few feet onto hard, frozen ground that bit into the soles of his feet like sharp teeth.

He stepped back and looked up to see Will standing in the window. What was he waiting for, the fool? Four black sticks appeared, and a chair flew down from above in a thundering clatter. Darnley put his hands to his head. Will then came sliding down the rope, a dagger clenched between his teeth. Still he managed to whimper. The rope lost its grip on the bedpost above and came racing through the window after him.

'The chair,' whispered Darnley harshly, 'why did you throw a chair?'

'I'm afraid of 'eights, your Grace,' he said, taking the dagger from his mouth and handing it to him. Absently, he realised it was the young thief's weapon that he had kept amongst his things as a memento. 'I'm not afraid of nobody, but I'm feared of 'eights. Thought I'd lessen the fall and climb down only a little onto t' chair.' Darnley's anger flared and faded. The boy was as terrified as he was himself. He was shaking with it.

'Will, for fu-' began Darnley, catching himself. 'We shall have them on top of us if their ears are sharp.'

Will seemed rooted to the spot at the prospect. Darnley gave him a hard shove to get him moving. Like ghosts, the two figures in their flowing white robes dashed through trees whose branches writhed in the moonlight, making for the gate that would lead them out of the garden and to safety.

Before they could make it, dark shapes moving silently on slippered feet detached themselves from a cluster of bushes. Behind Darnley Will was pushed to the ground, his scream swiftly becoming the gurgling groans of a dying boy. Darnley made to turn, to see who had got him, to shout at them to reveal themselves and leave Will alone. But suddenly someone had him too; someone short and stocky rolled into him from behind like a cannonball, sending him to his knees and then onto his stomach. The ancient dagger flew from his fingers, skittering away across the cold ground. He was pinned down, winded. His arms were flailing wildly, his legs kicking, and he was being rolled over.

The smell of musk washed over him. It was the smell of a forest floor after a hard rain, like dead leaves and stale water and corruption. He looked into the face of Archibald Douglas, that surly creature of the Earl of Morton.

'For the sake of merciful *Christ*, cousin, have pity,' Darnley gasped up at his attacker, hoping to keep the man talking long enough for help to arrive or some avenue of escape to open.

'You were warned, big man. Cousin Morton bids you adieu,' snarled Douglas, before spitting a thin gob of phlegm in Darnley's face. In revulsion he clamped his mouth shut. Seizing the opportunity Douglas produced some thick, wadded material from his belt and pressed it hard over his mouth and nose.

He struggled violently, but Douglas was now sitting on his chest. His right arm was rendered immobile by Douglas's knee; with his left he tried to hit him, but he could get no force behind the wild, faltering blows. Douglas ignored them and pressed his weight down harder, crushing his chest. His lungs were contracting, flaming – he wondered dimly if he had been stabbed in them. Thrashing his head from side to side, he tried to bite down on the rough material that was blocking the flow of air, his jaw aching from the effort. He kicked and kicked but hit nothing. It was no use. He was overpowered by the unyielding weight of Douglas, of his unforgiving enemies and family.

Presently he ceased the struggle. His throat was burning with it. He looked up and could see the deep blue-grey sky, blocked only by the implacable silhouette of his relative. Little lights began to pop before his eyes, like candle flames bursting in and out of life. He could still see their outlines after they were swallowed up by darkness. Then a remarkable thing happened. The heavens blazed forth and there was a roar of thunder. The world turned a brilliant orange and the stars were snatched from the sky.

Author's Note

Henry, Lord Darnley has the distinction of being one of the most hated figures in Scottish, and English, history. Yet he is a figure about whom much is assumed and surprisingly little known. Casual readers might recall him being played as a bisexual, violent drunk by Timothy Dalton in Mary Queen of Scots (1971) or a capering dandy by Douglas Walton in Mary of Scotland (1936). In terms of popular history, he was, to Antonia Fraser, a shiny red apple with a rotten core, and to John Guy a foolish drunkard to be marshalled by a far more intelligent queen. His only biographer, Caroline Bingham, notes that Darnley has not so much been ignored by historians as he has been cast as a villain in the innumerable biographies of his famous wife.

Certainly, in Darnley's own lifetime, he had plenty of detractors. In the copious dispatches of the English ambassador, Thomas Randolph, he was 'proud, disdainful, and ambitious', amongst many other colourful insults. But the scandal-loving Randolph had his own diplomatic axe to grind; the young Darnley had thwarted his hare-brained mission to bring about the marriage of Mary and Leicester. During his time at the English court, Darnley was reputed also to be a 'great cock chick', with both John Guy and Roderick Graham making the case that a pun was intended on his homosexuality. However, the historical record reveals no contemporary claims of homosexuality, and the use of the word as slang for 'penis' did not emerge until the following century. Rather, a 'cock' in the 1560s was a strutting fellow, with 'chick' mocking the pretensions of youth. This reading is, I think, safer than attributing too much to a man who had no rumoured lovers, male or female, beyond an unnamed 'Douglas girl'. The claims of an affair with Riccio seem to have been embroidered later out of the fact that the pair might have shared a bed – a common thing for all sexes in the period.

On the credit side, we have the accounts of foreign ambassadors. To Castelnau de Mauvissière, it was 'not possible to see a more beautiful prince ... and he is accomplished in all courtly exercises'. Flattery aside, there remains the fact that his murder seemed to mark the beginning of the end of his wife's once-popular reign. Had he been the hated tyrant of his enemies' imaginations, it would hardly seem likely that his disposal would have been met with anything other than muted joy.

The evidence we have of Darnley's behaviour and person throughout his life is contrary and hopelessly weighted in favour of his political enemies (which came to include his wife). His death, before the first parliament at which he would be twenty-one, was a political assassination. Post-death, he was, as Black Ormiston recalled – admittedly when facing the gallows – a 'young fool and proud tyrant'. But to Sir James Melville, though, Darnley was to be remembered as a young man who had lacked good counsel, and in George Buchanan's highly dubious account of events, he was the innocent victim of a monstrous and murderous wife. Unsurprisingly, the Earl and Countess of Lennox were full of sorrow and fury at the loss of their 'innocent lamb'.

In seeking to research Darnley, the late Jenny Wormald cautioned me that I would need several gallons of whitewash to make him palatable. When discussing Darnley with Julian Goodare of the University of Edinburgh, Dr Goodare, however, made the compelling point that the historical Darnley was only in his teens at the time of his marriage, and probably deserved to be cut some slack. I found that of the verifiable behaviours Darnley exhibited in life, they ranged from the admirable to the monstrous. The latter, his involvement in the murder of David Riccio, does, it must be admitted, leave an indelible stain. To play Devil's advocate, though, political murder was nothing new in Scotland or abroad in this period. Darnley's sponsoring of a death, whilst ugly, pales in comparison to the actions of the other crowned heads of his age. And, it might be recalled, he is said to have repented (we hear of no such regret on the parts of Henry VIII, Mary Tudor, or even his son James). In fact, he likely stirred more ire for disavowing his conspirators than signing away a man's life.

What struck me about Darnley was his youth, and his proximity to the English throne. In his *The Rough Wooings of Mary Queen of Scots* (Tuckwell Press, 2000), Marcus Merriman comments on more than one occasion that, during the 1560s, there was a strong likelihood of Darnley one day being crowned Henry IX of England. He was, as the novel depicts, 'first prince of the blood' to Elizabeth, and it was in this role that he carried the sword of state at Dudley's investiture as the Earl of Leicester. As seen in the novel, the queen really did turn the occasion into a chance to flirt with Leicester and turn attention to Darnley – but never has anyone considered how Darnley might have felt at being brushed off as 'beardless and lady-faced'.

A number of books were invaluable in writing Darnley's story. Foremost was Caroline Bingham's *Darnley* (Phoenix Giant, 1995). Although Ms Bingham is hostile to her subject, and I disagree with some of her conclusions (for example, I find it unlikely Darnley hoped for Mary to miscarry and die herself during the Riccio assassination, given that she was his only route to power and authority), her book is the only serious attempt to chart this dynastically-important Tudor nobleman's life. In addition, it was from Bingham that I discovered how intently Darnley sought to have his mother freed from captivity: even Ms Bingham allows that this is probably one of the best indicators of gentle feeling on his part. Though a Yorkshireman, Darnley appears to have had a very Scottish affinity with family ties.

In trying to piece together Darnley's story, I had a veritable treasure trove of books on Mary Stuart to pick from. The best of these are Antonia Fraser's majestic *Mary Queen of Scots* (W&N, 2015), which has the distinction of being one of those books I can look for a reference in and find myself reading to the end every time. I would also recommend John Guy's *My Heart is My Own* (Harper Perennial, 2004); Gordon Donaldson's *Mary Queen of Scots* (Hachette, 1974) and *All the Queen's Men* (Harper Collins, 1983); and Alison Weir's extraordinarily rich *Mary Queen of Scots and the Murder of Lord Darnley* (Vintage, 2008). The latter makes a fantastic case for the identity of Darnley's murderers. For a somewhat older perspective, but one that has the bonus of being the only one to provide a sympathetic view of Darnley, I enjoyed Marjorie Bowen's *Mary Queen of Scots: Daughter of Debate* (John Lane, 1943).

The characters in this story are drawn from the historical record, right down to the dog given Darnley by Sir James Melville (although its real name is unrecorded, and I have invented its demise). The Duke of Hamilton's *Maria R: Mary Queen of Scots, the Crucial Years* (Mainstream, 1991) provides excellent biographical sketches of all the main players. The Earl of Moray deserves his own book, but interested readers can find a comprehensive account of his political career in Claire L. Webb's unpublished PhD thesis, 'The "Gude Regent"? A Diplomatic Perspective upon the Earl of Moray, Mary Queen of Scots and the Scottish Regency,

1567 – 1570' (St Andrews, 2008). My favourite biography of Elizabeth remains Anne Somerset's *Elizabeth I* (Knopf Doubleday, 2010), although the shorter *The Virgin Queen* (Taurus, 1990) by Christopher Hibbert is also excellent. *The Memoirs of Sir James Melville of Halhill* (Folio Society, 1969) is highly recommended (for information on custom as well as events), Alison Weir's *The Lost Tudor Princess* (Jonathan Cape, 2015) is an excellent account of Margaret Lennox, and for those interested in the Earl of Leicester, see *Robert Dudley, Earl of Leicester* (Littlehampton, 1980), by Alan Kendall.

In closing, I must thank Alison Thorne, my former PhD supervisor, who nurtured an enduring love of this period and its culture, people, and literature. I also want to thank everyone who has read this far, showing as it does a willingness to read all about a man who is mostly known for being at best a fool, and at worst a murderer. I have tried not to whitewash Darnley, but rather show him warts and all: a naïve, petted child thrust into the politically-charged arena of Elizabeth's court and then the suspicious and divided court of Queen Mary. Throughout, I have tried to be fair, whilst illustrating how unusual – and sixteenth-century-mind-boggling – it was for a man to be proclaimed king but denied power. Mary had admirably modern views on the rights and privileges of a queen regnant over a male consort, but they were not shared by the men around her (or her husband). As for the age-old question that remains at the end of this story – did Mary collude in Darnley's death … what do you think? Let me know on Twitter @ScrutinEye.

Printed in Great Britain
by Amazon